# My Seduction

# PRAISE FOR
# CONNIE BROCKWAY

"Romance with strength, wit, and intelligence. Connie Brockway delivers!"

> —*New York Times* bestselling author Tami Hoag

"Connie Brockway is truly an innovative, wonderful writer whose work belongs on every reader's shelf."

> —*Romantic Times*

"If it's smart, sexy and impossible to put down, it's a book by Connie Brockway."

> —*New York Times* bestselling author Christina Dodd

"Connie Brockway's work brims with warmth, wit, sensuality, and intelligence."

> —*New York Times* bestselling author Amanda Quick

"If you're looking for passion, tenderness, wit, and warmth, you need look no further. Connie Brockway is simply the best!"

> —*New York Times* bestselling author Teresa Medeiros

## BRIDAL FAVORS

"A scrumptious literary treat . . . wonderfully engaging characters, superbly crafted plot, and prose rich in wit and humor."

## McCLAIREN'S ISLE: THE PASSIONATE ONE

"An undercurrent of danger ripples through this exquisite romance, set in the 1700s, and Brockway's lush, lyrical writing style is a perfect match for her vivid characters, beautifully atmospheric settings, and sensuous love scenes."

## ALL THROUGH THE NIGHT

"Intricately plotted, with highly inventive lead characters, Brockway's latest is an intense and complicated romance. . . . There is excitement, chemistry, obsession, and best of all, a tortured romance."

BOOKS BY CONNIE BROCKWAY

*Once upon a Pillow*
(with Christina Dodd)

Published by Pocket Books

# CONNIE BROCKWAY

## My Seduction

POCKET BOOKS
New York   London   Toronto   Sydney

This book is a work of fiction. Names, characters, places and incidents are products of the author's imagination or are used fictitiously. Any resemblance to actual events or locales or persons, living or dead, is entirely coincidental.

 POCKET BOOKS, a division of Simon & Schuster, Inc.
1230 Avenue of the Americas
New York, NY 10020

ISBN: 0-7394-4224-4

Designed by Christine Weathersbee
Cover illustration by Alan Ayers
Handlettering by Ron Zinn

Manufactured in the United States of America

# PROLOGUE

*York, 1801*

CHARLOTTE ELIZABETH NASH, reading in the window alcove, shrank back against the wall when she heard people entering the cavernous, sparsely furnished drawing room. She did not want company. She was sick of people, the whisperers and sympathizers who couldn't ever quite keep their eyes from straying to the empty places on the walls where pictures had once hung.

She dropped her book into her lap and pulled the curtain partially covering the niche farther closed. But male voices, rare in what had become an all female household since Kate had "let go" the butler, piqued her interest.

At sixteen and not yet having made her bow, she knew that making her presence known would only invite dismissal. Charlotte did not want to be dismissed. She was as saddened as anyone by their father's death and equally affected by the ramifications, but she had the resilience of youth—and its attendant callousness—and over the long months of mourning had grown a little . . . well, *bored*. Besides, visitors might distract Kate from her constant litany about economy and Helena from donning her mask of forced optimism. And a little male attention might even bring a pink of pleasure to their mother's wan cheeks.

Charlotte inserted a finger between curtain and wall and peeked out. Her mother had taken possession of the lone settee left in the room and was reading a sheet of paper. Charlotte's two older sisters sat flanking her: Helena, pale as winter sunlight, and Katherine, heated and dark as a moonless summer night. They sat with their hands clasped lightly in their laps, their postures straight, their polite gazes numbed to the presence of the trio of young men standing before them.

Charlotte could not see them clearly, but she didn't dare risk pulling the curtain farther open. Instead, she dropped noiselessly to the immaculate floorboards and lifted the curtain hem. Ah. Better.

From this unseen vantage she studied the young men as they introduced themselves: they were decidedly not of the Nashes' class. Of what class they were remained to be seen.

She couldn't say exactly why she had come to this conclusion. True, their clothing, though scrupulously clean, was shabby—cuffs frayed at the edges and fabric pulling across shoulders and backs—but since the war with France had begun, many people had been forced to eschew fashion as money grew tighter. Nor was it their bearing that revealed them as something other than gentlemen in reduced circumstances. Indeed, they comported themselves in the most correct and circumspect fashion.

No, it was something subtler. More elemental. It seemed as if something untamed had come in through the front door, disturbing the air in the quiet York town house, something dangerous.

She scooted closer as the man in front introduced himself as Andrew Ross, in a deep voice touched with a Highland burr. Medium height, brown-haired and tanned, with a loose-knit physique, he smiled easily and looked genial. Except . . . when one studied him closer, one noted the wicked scar that traversed his lean cheek and the flint that belied the warm color of his brown eyes.

Beside him stood easily the most handsome man Charlotte had ever seen. Ramsey Munro, he'd said. Tall, slender, and pale, with black glossy curls falling over his white brow and deep blue eyes glittering between a thick bank of lashes, his features were both sardonic and aristocratic. Charlotte could imagine *him* in the ton, his grace masking a subtle but undeniable predatory aspect. Like the panther she had seen at the menagerie last summer.

The last young man—Christian MacNeill—hung back, his broad-shouldered figure tense. Raggedly chopped, overlong red-gold hair framed a lean, hungry face made remarkable by pale green, watchful eyes. He looked the roughest of the trio, with deep-set eyes, a wide, sensual mouth, and a hard, angular jaw.

Charlotte cocked her head. He reminded her of someone . . . Ah, yes. She remembered now.

Late one night several years ago, when she had been in the kitchen soothing a troubled stomach with a glass of brandied milk, she had heard a whistle outside. The upstairs maid, Annie, had come running in to fling open the back door. A man emerged from the darkness, everything about him troubling and exciting, and scooped Annie up in his arms, wheeling her about until he noticed Charlotte. He stopped wheeling, but he didn't put Annie down. Annie had left with him that night, her eyes wide with fear and pleasure. She had never returned.

This Christian MacNeill reminded Charlotte of that other man, that "born-to-be-hung blackguard" who'd stolen Annie away.

Not that Annie would be here now, even if she hadn't run off, Charlotte reminded herself. Except for Cook and a pair of overworked maids, all of the other servants had been let go.

"I don't know what they want," her mother suddenly murmured in the bewildered voice that had become hers the day she had learned she was a widow. She looked askance at Helena, who touched her shoulder consolingly. Wordlessly, Kate took possession of the paper and began to read.

"We don't *want* anything, Mrs. Nash," Mr. Ross said. "We have come to present your family an oath.

Whether you see fit to avail yourselves of it is your decision. But whether or no you do, the oath stands for as long as any of us lives."

Charlotte's eyes widened in fascination. *An oath?* She knew the young men had, in some way, been associated with her father, and assumed they'd been members of his staff come to pay their respects.

"What sort of oath?" Helena asked.

"A pledge of service," Kate said, still reading the letter.

Charlotte regarded her middle sister with grudging admiration. Throughout the past year Kate, not Helena, had emerged as the family's bastion of strength, despite having more reason than any of them to be devastated.

Married at nineteen to a dashing lieutenant, Michael Blackburn, Kate had no sooner settled into her Plymouth home than her husband had died while en route to India. She'd returned to York a widow less than a year after she'd become a bride. Six months later, word came that their father had been killed in France, where he'd been secretly meeting with the deposed heads of Louis XVI's government—at least those few with heads still attached.

The family had still been reeling from the shock when the solicitors arrived and informed them that the annuity they had lived upon had died with Lord Nash. Almost at once, tradesmen began scratching at the back doors, the servants began looking for more secure positions, and the new owners of the entailed town house commenced sending letters that her mother never opened. *No one did.*

Except Kate. She took upon herself the unimaginable task of selling their personal belongings, writing references for the servants, and settling unpaid bills. *Kate.* Kate who liked dancing more than reading, hated sums and loved gossip, who the matrons had tattled upon as being "flighty" and "capricious." Even now, Charlotte was amazed. She barely recognized her carefree, party-loving sister in the composed young woman calmly refolding the letter their mother had handed her.

"Thank you for your offer, gentlemen," Kate said now. "But we do not stand in need of your aid. Nor do we expect to."

Charlotte felt her mouth sag. They most certainly *were* in need. Dire need! But then, their needs began and ended with money, and clearly these three young men were no better off than they were. Mayhap less. Though that would have been hard to imagine.

She wasn't supposed to know about the family's financial straits. Her sisters maintained a facade of confident calm, but soft-footed as she was, Charlotte had heard enough through closed doors and in the late hours of the night to understand perfectly well how very desperate their situation had become.

"I see." Mr. Ross kept his gaze courteously fixed on the three women seated before him, and Ramsey Munro remained impassive, but Christian MacNeill's frosted gaze prowled about the room, pausing at the faded rectangles on the striped silk wall-covering, the dents in the Persian rug that revealed the absence of heavy furniture, and the lack of ornamentation on the single, lonely sideboard.

He knows, Charlotte thought. Yet what can he do in the face of Kate's refusal?

"We have no desire to burden you further, Mrs. Blackburn. But before we leave"—Mr. Ross gestured vaguely at his companions—"would you do us the great kindness of accepting something from us?"

He held up a canvas bag Charlotte had not previously noted. A small knob of wood protruded from the twine-wrapped top.

"What is it?" Helena asked.

"A rose, Miss Nash," Mr. Ross answered. "Should you ever find you stand in any need for which we might prove of service, you have only to send one of the flowers to the abbot at St. Bride's in Scotland. He will know how to contact us, and as soon as humanly possible we will come to you."

A small, confused smile touched Helena's lips. "Why a—"

"A rose?" a female voice asked incredulously from the doorway. Their cousin Grace swept into the chill drawing room, all golden ringlets and dewy skin, untying a velvet pelisse from about her shoulders.

"Hello, my dears!" She bent down to place a perfunctory kiss on her aunt's cheek before straightening and regarding the young men with a faint touch of surprised superiority.

"Grace, these are the young men whom your uncle . . . who . . ." Charlotte's mother floundered, uncertain how to proceed. Helena saved her.

"These are the young men whom Father was able to aid in rescuing before his demise: Mr. Ross, Mr. Munro, and Mr. MacNeill. Gentlemen, our cousin, Grace Deals-Cotton."

Rescued? *These* were the young men her father died saving? Charlotte lifted the curtain higher, fascinated.

The young men bowed and murmured appropriate greetings and Grace smiled her catlike, three-pointed smile, her large eyes narrowed assessingly.

"I see," she said. "And you've brought a . . . rose? How very sentimental." Grace turned to her aunt. "Did Uncle Roderick like roses? I never realized. But then, I've only been with you a year." She smiled again. "This time."

"I am sure Lord Nash would have appreciated the roses very much," Charlotte's mother said with rote politeness. "As we shall when the plant blooms . . . later this year."

Her hesitation betrayed the thought unspoken but held by them all that they would not be here long enough to see the rose bloom. No one, of course, revealed this to their guests. They were proud, the Nashes were.

"But surely you can't mean to try and stay . . . Oh. You mean you will take a cutting when you relocate," Grace said. She took a seat on the far end of the sofa, picking up the embroidery hoop she'd abandoned last evening.

"You are moving household?" Ramsey Munro asked sharply.

"Yes," Helena said, darting an uneasy glance at Kate. "Eventually. The memories . . ." She trailed off vaguely, her hand rising and falling to her side.

Kate shot a daggered look at Grace, who returned her look with one of confused hurt. Charlotte let the hem drop a little, a touch irritated with Kate. Of course Grace hadn't purposely revealed their need to move from the fashionable town house but Kate would never believe that. The animosity between the two was long-standing—perhaps because they were, or at one time had been, so much alike. Once Kate had been just as fey and artless as Grace. She ought to remember that rather than always finding fault with their vivacious cousin.

"As are you, Grace," Helena said, diverting everyone's attention. "Relocating, that is."

"Ah, yes!" Grace said, lowering her eyes prettily as she commenced embroidering. "But I, poor creature, am to be relegated to the wilderness, while you all shall at least be able to avail yourself of society." She smiled at Mr. Ross. "Five months hence, I am marrying Charles Murdoch. His brother is the marquis of Parnell. I daresay you won't be known—"

She caught the faux pas before she had completed it. "You probably would not know him. His castle"—there was no disguising the satisfaction with which she said the word, and why shouldn't she feel satisfaction? A castle was, after all, a castle—"his *castle* is on the north coast of Scotland. We shall live there when we are not in London."

"London, not Edinburgh?" Ramsay Munro asked smoothly. "I own, I am surprised. The Scots are inordinately proud of Edinburgh."

Something about the manner in which he spoke to Grace told Charlotte that Ramsay Munro was not overwhelmed by her cousin's charms, making him, in Charlotte's admittedly limited experience, unique among young men.

"Edinburgh?" Grace repeated. The silk-strung needle flashed seemingly without volition as she pondered his words. Grace was a marvelous embroiderer, another similarity between her and Kate. "I suppose. In truth, I haven't given it much thought. The wedding has, I own, rather consumed my attention."

"My felicitations on your upcoming nuptials," Mr. Ross said. He turned to the other women. "Now, perhaps I might impose upon you for one last kindness?"

"Of course," Helena answered before Kate could demur.

"If we might see the rose planted?"

"Oh." Helena blinked in surprise. "Oh, of course. Kate, where do you think we might plant—"

"No, darling, you must say. You and mother. You are the gardeners, not I."

Their mother looked up from whatever reverie she'd been lost in, and for a moment the smile that animated her face made her look almost herself again.

"The garden? Of, course." She rose unsteadily to

her feet, and Helena gave her the support of her arm. "We shall do so at once. You must come too, Grace. You have an artistic eye."

"I am happy to be of service, Aunt Elizabeth." Grace set down the embroidery hoop.

Their mother, leaning on Helena, preceded the others out of the door and into the soft morning light. Charlotte, on the verge of slipping out from under the curtain and making her escape, froze as she realized that Kate had not gone with the others and that the green-eyed man, Christian MacNeill, had stopped beside the threshold of the door.

"After you, ma'am." His deep voice was smooth and polite.

"No, thank you, sir. I am certain my opinion will not see your rose more congenially situated. But please, you go ahead."

"I am just as certain three of us are not needed to plant that root," Mr. MacNeill returned wryly. "Do you mind if I wait with you?"

"Of course not." A dubious-sounding consent. "Would you like some . . . punch?"

Charlotte almost laughed at the picture her imagination conjured of Christian MacNeill drinking punch from a dainty cup. His large hands would simply swallow a delicate crystal glass. But then she frowned as she remembered they no longer owned a punch bowl. Kate had apparently forgotten it had been sold last week. Oh dear. Kate would be mortified if she had to serve punch in teacups—

"Thank you, no."

Charlotte sighed in relief. At least Kate was saved *that* embarrassment.

Christian MacNeill waited while Kate settled herself on the sofa's edge, looking as if she might bolt at any moment. What had gotten into her self-possessed sister? She is nervous, Charlotte realized in amazement. She could not remember when Kate had been discombobulated by anyone! Before Michael began his courtship, Kate had led a dozen young men a merry chase. No one, no matter how sophisticated or urbane, had dinted her laughing self-possession.

Charlotte scrunched forward, peering intently at the rough, gilt-haired Highlander. He'd come back into the room and stood over Kate, watching her. She'd turned her face to look out the window, and he looked amused. But still . . . hungry.

"I hope I am not discomforting you, Mrs. Blackburn," he said. His voice was a rough-smooth rumble. Like water over river rock.

"Not at all."

*Liar,* Charlotte thought.

"I am afraid I am a bit distracted. Forgive me." Kate arranged her hands in her lap in the same way she had in the schoolroom years earlier when she had been practicing her conversational skills with the governess. She cleared her throat. Minutes ticked by and the tall Scot remained almost preternaturally still, not a trace of unease in his expression or a hint of discomposure in his bearing. Kate, on the other hand, looked as if she might fly out of her skin in spite of the rigid self-control that kept her statue-still. Finally, she could take it no longer.

"If I have the correct understanding of the situation, you were imprisoned. I am sorry for your ordeal."

The words were polite and proper. His nod accepting her sympathy was the same.

"If I might ask, during the course of what battle were you captured?" she continued somberly.

"I wasn't in a battle," he said calmly.

"Oh." Kate frowned. "I assumed—but then, how did you and your friends come to be in France during this time of war, Mr. MacNeill?" Real interest had replaced Kate's conversational tone.

"I have wondered the same myself, more times than I can tell you," he said. "It was because of the roses, I suppose."

Kate's smooth brow furrowed slightly, and she plucked at her fingers. She looked very young, Charlotte thought. Her skin looked pale against her dark hair, and her throat slender and vulnerable as it arched forward. And despite knowing that she was a bastion of strength, and a formidable one at that, Charlotte thought she looked very . . . slight. Fragile.

With the breathless sense of stepping through a door into an unknown and dark room, Charlotte wondered if all that had happened to Kate had been . . . well . . . quite as fair as she and Helena and even their mother might have made it.

"How did roses lead to your imprisonment?" she

asked, her dark eyes darting up to meet Christian MacNeill's.

Mr. MacNeill clasped his hands behind his back. He looked down at Kate, his expression enigmatic. A shiver coursed through Charlotte. He was so much larger than she'd realized, his gauntness giving an impression of lightness that his proximity to Kate now belied. He was a terribly hard-looking young man.

"It's an uncomfortable tale, Mrs. Blackburn."

"Tell me."

Her sister's stark words startled Charlotte. Their governess would *not* have approved. One did not make personal demands of an acquaintance, let alone a stranger. He did not seem to take offense. Indeed, something in his hard face relaxed.

"All of us had some knowledge of gardens," he said. "One of our duties was tending the roses where we were raised."

"I'm sorry." Her voice was ripe with sympathy.

He laughed shortly. "Don't waste your pity. It was *not* a workhouse. Workhouses, in my memory, do not have rose gardens. No, this was a sort of orphanage, I suppose. It doesn't matter."

Kate waited.

"But because of the roses, and some other skills we had developed, my companions and I were approached by a gentleman who asked us to journey to France and, among other things, bring a lady an extremely rare yellow rose. In doing so we hoped to gain entrée to her world and thereby"—he shrugged—"change the world."

"A lady who could change the world?" Kate said incredulously, and once more Charlotte felt a prick of embarrassment. No matter what a visitor said, one must never openly doubt his veracity.

"Her name was Marie-Rose, but her husband calls her Josephine."

Charlotte's mouth formed a soundless O! and she dug her knuckles into her mouth, barely suppressing her gasp. This man knew Napoleon Bonaparte's wife?

Kate, too, could not conceal her amazement. "You have met Josephine?"

Christian MacNeill's smile held no pleasure. "Once, and briefly, ma'am. Shortly after we arrived, our plans were discovered—No." His face hardened into an expression from which Charlotte recoiled. "Our plans were not discovered; they were revealed. By a traitor. Someone who knew of our mission. We were taken prisoner and would have been executed had your father not intervened. One of our number *was* executed."

"I'm sorry." Kate said. "I'm sorry my father's sacrifice didn't come in time to save your friend." She looked up. "I mean, if one insists on being a martyr, one might as well have some good come of it—Dear God! I am so sorry! I don't know why I said that. Please, I am . . . forgive me. I truly did not mean to offend you. It's just that . . . often"—her voice dropped to a harsh whisper—"my father's death feels like a betrayal."

Charlotte edged back into her alcove, stunned by her sister's confession. She'd had no idea Kate felt that way. She peered back into the room. The passion that had darkened Mr. MacNeill's face evaporated as he looked down at Kate, sitting with her head bowed above her lap.

Abruptly, he bent down on his knee, bringing his eyes level with Kate's. "I swear, ma'am, had it been in our power to keep your father from making such a sacrifice, we would have done so," he said softly. "We understood the risks of what we sought to do, and we would never have knowingly volunteered another to pay the penalty of our actions. It was not our choice to make, however. No one asked us."

Charlotte drew back farther, scowling. This was not a proper conversation between people who did not know one another! People did not ask one another pointed questions. People did not reveal the intimate details of their lives to one another on the basis of half an hour's knowledge. People did not speak *passionately* to strangers! Why, people didn't speak passionately to those they knew well! It was . . . bad form.

Charlotte was shocked, a little offended, and a great deal unsettled. She had been right to think of these young men as feral. They had come into her home and broken down the rules by which she and her family lived.

Sure enough, Kate's next words confirmed Charlotte's supposition.

"How *did* my father die, Mr. MacNeill? *What happened?* No one will tell us." The whispered words seemed to emerge from deep within Kate, desperate and aching.

A muscle leapt at the corner of Christian McNeill's jaw, a hard angular jaw recently scraped smooth. His skin was darkly tanned, not the pale, well-padded flesh of a gentleman. Little lines fanned out at the corners of his green eyes, making him look wicked. Should Charlotte do something?

With feline grace, he uncoiled from where he'd knelt and folded his hands behind his back. He moved restlessly about the room, finally stopping, half turned from Kate, fixing his gaze on the empty wall ahead.

"Lord Nash shouldn't have been there. It was a mistake. Our names chanced to be mentioned by some drunken officer who shouldn't have even known of our existence. Once your father heard we were being held and the duration of our imprisonment, he insisted on trading himself in exchange for our freedom."

"We were told my father died in a rescue attempt," Kate said.

"One does not *rescue* a man from a French dungeon, Mrs. Blackburn. One makes deals, promises money, or if one does not have the ready, one makes trades. Your father offered himself in our stead. Since he was a far greater prize than three filthy lads, the French colonel holding us seized the opportunity presented, doubtless thinking to make a name for himself. He proposed that during negotiations your father enter the castle where we were held.

"Lord Nash agreed, but only on the condition that we were first released," he continued. "The French colonel was furious, but your father refused to be coerced. Lord Nash waited at the bridge until we . . . walked out. Then he crossed over."

With that hesitation, MacNeill betrayed himself. However the prisoners had returned, clearly they had not simply "walked out." He looked down into Kate's upturned face. "He was supposed to return in a few days, a week at most, as soon as a ransom was arranged. He was supposed to have had diplomatic immunity.

"A few hours later, the gates opened again and a rid-erless horse emerged, a box strapped to the saddle." His eyelids closed briefly, as though he were trying to erase some image from his eyes. "In it was a note saying that your father was dead and that henceforth all British spies would be treated similarly. He died in our place. Your father was not a spy, Mrs. Blackburn."

She raised her head. "But you *were* spies. You and the others."

"We knew the risks," he answered obliquely. "We were prepared to pay the penalty. I did not foresee another doing so in my place, though. I have to live with that. That's why we are here."

"I see." Her gaze fixed unhappily on some place only she could see. "And are you still . . . spies?"

"I am, as you see me. A man without occupation or home or family."

"Hardly in a position to offer aid to another," Kate said, but mildly.

A little smile turned his hard mouth. "Without much, but still in possession of some talents. And determination." The smile faded. "That I own in abundance, ma'am."

"I see."

"Do you?" he asked, suddenly fierce. "*Can* you understand?"

"Yes. Of course," Kate answered, but she sounded distracted. "You were going to be heroes. Young men aspire to be heroes, do they not? It is perfectly understandable. Only my father beat you to it, didn't he?

"He had no right, you know." Kate's voice deepened, became husky with emotion. "He *never* had the right to put himself in such danger. Not knowing, as he must have *always* known, that his death would see us—"

*Impoverished.* Charlotte silently provided the word Kate choked off. But it hung there, as clearly as if she'd shouted it. Kate never shouted anymore. She never did anything untoward or unseemly or rash or passionate, yet this young man had peeled back all her social defenses, exposing her, revealing all her hurt and doubts and anger to Charlotte.

She hated it. It frightened her, and the world was already a frightening place; enough things had changed. She couldn't lose the idea of Kate she had held so long.

"I cannot promise to make use of your offer, Mr.

MacNeill, however nobly meant." Kate took a deep breath. "I have had enough heroes in my life," she whispered. "I am done with them. You must find someone else to benefit from your gesture."

"You misunderstand if you think our offer noble or gallant."

"I *do* understand, though. I understand that you feel the need to repay us. You don't. Your debt is to my father."

He shook his head, and the light caught in his shining hair and carved shadows in the hard planes of his face. "You ask me to shoulder an impossible burden, Mrs. Blackburn, one which we cannot be relieved of unless we *do* something. *I* do something.

"I *have* to believe that someday I might be able to repay some of the debt I owe your family, just as I *have* to believe that someday I will discover who betrayed us. As you can see, Mrs. Blackburn, I haven't much in this world left to me but . . . honor. I must repay my debts and avenge my losses. So I will wait. For however long it takes."

Without another word, he strode from the room.

# ONE

⬦⬦⬦

# UPON BEING ABANDONED
# BY ONE'S SERVANTS

*The southern edge of
the Scottish Highlands, 1803*

*Mrs. Blackburn,*
*This jurnie is mad and I am not one as to give no*
*filthy hiwayman a chans at killin us even if you pays*
*me double my wages which I do not think like to*
*happen. I no you won't give me a refrence neether*
*but don't care because what good is a refrence to a*
*dead woman? Good luck to you, you been a fair*
*mistress and I will say a prayer for yore soul.*
                                          *Sue McCray*

WELL NOW, THOUGHT KATE, just when she'd thought life
couldn't hold any more surprises, here was another;
she'd no idea Sue McCray could write. At least after a
fashion, Kate thought, eyeing the word *jurnie*.

The laugh escaped before she could stop it. At the sound, the din from the next room faded, and the men who made it stared across the half-wall separating the White Rose's public area from the "private room" where Kate sat. She edged closer to the miserly fire she'd bullied the innkeeper into setting.

Crunching up the note, she dropped it into the embers, amazed her maid's desertion had taken her by surprise. Her situation had been farcical for so long now that one would think she'd have grown accustomed to such things.

First, a pickpocket in Edinburgh had relieved her of her purse. Then, not thirty miles out of the city, their carriage had broken down, and she and Sue McCray had spent a cold night huddled under too few blankets while the driver, Dougal, fixed it. After which Dougal had demanded pay additional to that owed his company by the marquis of Parnell, who'd employed him from afar. Added to which, a winter storm had then come upon them so precipitately one might reasonably suspect the elements of being in cahoots with the blackguard.

Not yet done making her its goat, Fate had finally led her here, to the guilefully misnamed White Rose, where the number of evil-looking—and far more evil-smelling—refugees from the storm swelled its cramped quarters. Now, to ice the cake, her lady's maid—who had not only worked cheap but had been relatively good in spite of being half-soused most days—had decamped. What more could possibly happen?

Kate's bemused eyes strayed to the men in the other room. Alcohol-clouded gazes slunk toward her. *Ah, yes. That.*

She pulled her cloak tighter about her shoulders, weighing her options. By now her gossiping host would have spread the word that her maid had left and she was alone except for Dougal's dubious protection. She probably shouldn't stay out here, but one of the "gentlemen" in the next room might see her withdrawal to her room as an invitation. Men, in her recently acquired experience, were always seeing invitations where none existed. Especially from impoverished widows. On the other hand, staying here "on display," as it were, might be construed as even more of an invitation. And she still hadn't eaten since . . . why, early this morning.

She flipped a mental coin and chose to stay despite the anxiety sitting like stones in her stomach. At least here the men would be forced to take one another into account. Despite the sloppy sounds of masculine bonhomie, they were not friends. They were forced together by weather, not inclination.

Only the cluster of four men sitting around a low table seemed like cohorts. Through the haze of wood smoke, she couldn't make them out clearly, but they were all big, rough-looking fellows with thick shoulders and bullish necks, beefy hands cupping tin mugs the innkeeper kept filled with strong ale. The rest of the travelers had straggled in alone or in pairs, finding shelter before darkness added its misery to the ice storm that was shaking the windows and howling at the door.

She darted a sidelong glance toward where the latest arrival sat. Unlike the majority in the room who were lowland Scots, he was a Highlander.

He'd come in with his great, worn plaid billowing out from his shoulders like the wings of some giant bird of prey, his face obscured beneath the wide brim of a battered hat. Wordlessly, he'd retreated to a dark corner and an empty seat. Flinging the raggedy-looking plaid back, he'd tipped his chair against the wall and stretched out long legs wrapped to the calves in scarred leather boots. Beneath the plaid he wore a dark green jacket figured with black braids and silver buttons.

He drew worn leather gloves from his hands and, digging into a pocket, retrieved a clay pipe and pouch. He'd been sitting there ever since, the pipe clenched between his teeth, his chin sunk into his collar, the only part of his face visible the glint of dark gold stubble on his jaw. Pale eyes flickered in the erratic light from the bowl of embers. He made no effort to join in the growing camaraderie of his fellows, just as he made no effort to disguise the direction of his gaze.

He was watching her.

Kate disliked it. In fact, it was primarily his gaze that kept her here, tired and aching after a long day on bad roads in a worse-sprung carriage. He alarmed her.

She darted another quick glance at him. The smoke from his pipe drifted up and was absorbed in the shadows beneath his hat's brim. The bowl had grown fallow. Darkness obliterated his eyes.

She looked hastily away, struck anew by how far she'd become removed from the sheltered young woman she'd once been. There had been a time when the notion that his path and hers could converge would have struck her as ludicrous. But three years had taught her that her sort, the genteel poor, was constantly "converging" with undesirable types.

And not always to her detriment.

For instance, she'd learned that a drunken maid without references could fix hair quite acceptably and that an accommodating schedule might entice such a maid into overlooking being paid irregularly. Though, Kate thought with a small smile, apparently travel to "hethen parts" constituted an unforgivable rift in the employer-employee relationship.

She must commit that to memory: Never force a hazardous journey on an unpaid maid.

Perhaps she ought to write an instructional book? A pamphlet. Something along the lines of *A Necessary Guide for the Well-bred Gentlewoman Anticipating a Life Spent in Reduced Circumstances*. Certainly the merchant class devoured instructional books on how to emulate the aristocracy. Why not a book dedicated to maintaining a dignified poverty? If that wasn't an oxymoron.

Her lips twitched with amusement, and she recalled

how once she'd thought she'd never smile again.
Thank God, she'd been wrong. Still, she reminded
herself, this was no time for levity. Her sense of
humor may have saved her from the despair that had
so quickly taken her mother's life, but it could also
cause problems. Such as the time she had convinced
the butcher that as the Jaspers' houseguest was a strict
vegetarian, they wouldn't need the roast he'd
trimmed up for their Sunday dinner, and she would
take it off his hands. At a reduced cost, of course. Mrs.
Jasper never had spoken to her after that.

A loud bang announced the arrival of another
refugee from the storm. A red-faced youngster stumbled through the doorway, pushed by a curtain of
sleet, his hands clamped under his armpits, his face
raw and frost-rimed.

"Shut the door, you fool!" bellowed one of the men
at the table, pushing to his feet.

The lad didn't appear to hear. He'd doubled over at
the waist as soon as he'd crossed the threshold and
was blowing desperately into his cupped hands, wincing as he did so. His fingertips looked white and glas-
sine. The poor lad could lose those fingers—

"I said, *shut the bleedin' door!*" The big brute
grabbed the boy by the shoulders and shoved him
against the wall. The boy's outstretched hands struck
the wood and he screamed. Kate's heart thundered in
sympathetic response.

"Out with you, boy! No one wants to hear yer
blubberin'!" As the man grabbed the lad's collar,

preparing to pitch him back through the open door, Kate recognized the man. It was Dougal, her driver. *Her* driver.

The room had fallen silent. A few faces twisted derisively, one of Dougal's compatriots sneered in amusement, but most of them simply looked on uncomprehendingly.

With a sick sense of inevitability, Kate realized she had stood up. She was shaking as thoroughly as the boy, yet incapable of retreat. Because, along with that completely fallacious sense of her own worth she'd once had, she'd also had an equally overblown sense of responsibility. And *that* damned characteristic she never had been able to make tractable. She did not *want* to speak. She wanted to shut her eyes and turn away like some of the others. But . . . but Dougal worked for her. He was *her* responsibility.

Her heart was racing now and she was afraid. Nearly paralyzed with the fear of what would happen if she interfered. *Nearly* paralyzed.

Her feet dragged her over the threshold into the public room. Dougal gave the howling boy another shake. "Maybe I'll let you in when you can remember how to close a—"

"Let him go," Kate heard a calm voice say. Thank God, it was not hers.

Dougal looked about to see who dared interfere with him. It was the tall man in the ancient plaid.

"And," the Highlander continued mildly, "close the damn door, will you?"

"Who the bloody hell are you to be giving me orders?" Dougal demanded, the cringing boy dangling from one ham-fisted hand.

The front legs of the chair settled gently on the floor, and with an eerie, silky grace the ragged figure rose, his face still obscured by his hat. "A fellow who's gettin' cold—and," the man reminded Dougal, "you still haven't let the lad go or closed the door." Something dangerous slipped beneath his tranquil tone.

"Go to hell!" Dougal said. "I'll shut the door after I throw out this—"

The lad was plucked as neatly as a ripe pear from a low-hanging branch, one moment cowering in Dougal's clasp, the next being pushed toward a pair of young men, crofters by the look of them, who had been watching in silent but obvious distress. Then, just as smoothly as he'd appropriated the boy, the Highlander reached past Dougal and slammed the door shut.

"There. Sooner begun, sooner done, as my old mater would have said." The man cocked his head and continued ruefully. "Well, *if* I'd had a mater, I'm sure she would have said some such thing."

A few of the other men in the room chuckled nervously, but Dougal was not to be cajoled. His face had turned beet red.

"I don't like meddlers, mister. And that's what you are. Ain't he?" Dougal turned to his companions. They nodded, regarding the boy's deliverer narrowly. Worse than snatching Dougal's prey from him, they'd been deprived of their night's entertainment.

The Highlander didn't appear overly concerned. But Kate was. The fear that had begun slowly loosening its clamp around her chest began constricting again.

"I suspect you're right," the tall man allowed. "A failing more than one has tried to beat out of me."

"Yeah? Well, we'll just see if this time we can make the lesson stick, eh, lads?" Dougal promised.

The men growled their assent. At the same time, the two young men who had been given custody of Dougal's intended victim stepped forward.

"See now," the stockier one addressed Dougal. "We don't much like the odds of what you're proposing—"

"Back away, friend," the Highlander cut in. "I appreciate your gesture, but what with four such braw warriors planning me demise, I don't have time to spare fretting over your welfare."

The two young crofters exchanged startled glances.

"Sit down, lads, and I'll stand you a pint." The Highlander turned toward the innkeeper, stripping off his faded green jacket, and Dougal, like a jackal that sees an exposed piece of flesh, charged.

"Watch out!" Kate cried, but the Highlander had already ducked beneath Dougal's two-fisted blow, pivoting, his fist exploding up into Dougal's thick gut. With an *Uff!* Dougal doubled up and fell to the floor.

Dougal's friends launched themselves forward as the other men in the tavern surged to their feet to better see the unfolding spectacle. One of Dougal's cohorts grabbed a heavy metal platter and began swinging its edge forward like a hatchet. The tall Scot jerked back, his hat falling off, freeing a tangle of overlong red-gold hair.

Kate had an impression of a sharp jaw and a lean face streaked with the grime of hard travel, and then he was backing away, Dougal's largest companion following his retreat. The other two flanked him, herding him toward the wall, and ... and the ring of spectators closed in front of her, leaving her outside, Dougal still gasping at her feet.

The crowd erupted in shouts. Hats waved, arms windmilled in the air. Some of the watchers winced at what they saw, others bellowed louder. She could see little; a flurry of fists, a dark red-gold head, a blurred glimpse of taut, sweat-streaked faces. Curses and invectives rose from the mill along with the thud of fist on flesh.

Someone let out a warning cry, and abruptly the circle of men split open in front of her. She saw two of Dougal's drinking companions, one lying in an insensate heap, the other trying to drag himself to his knees. And then, suddenly, there he was, directly in front of her.

He'd shed his tartan, and his linen shirt had been yanked from the waist of his trousers, one sleeve torn across the shoulder, exposing a glimpse of a broad, muscled back. His hair clung in dark, damp strands to his neck as he fought Dougal's most fearsome-looking cohort. He was winning, slapping away the man's swings as if they were inconsequential.

He fought like some sort of diabolical machine, methodical, his movements concentrated, invested with a terrible, economical beauty. He parried each of the other man's punches precisely, taking advantage of the smallest opening with immediate and savage dispatch. Finally, an upward blow caught his opponent beneath the jaw, lifting him from his feet and sending him careening across the floor and sliding to a stop at Kate's feet.

The Highlander followed, the attitude of his shoulders, the look in his face, frightening her. The man at her feet flopped over on his belly and began crawling away. The Scot leaned down and grabbed the fallen man's collar. His teeth, startlingly white in his dark face, flashed in a grin.

With a grunt, he heaved the big-bellied brute to his feet. "You wouldn't be thinking of deprivin' me of your company so soon, would you, me friend? Well, if go you must, so be it. But first I'll be takin' that dagger from you, the one you nicked me with, since I've no mind to feel it in me back."

He had forgotten about Dougal.

So had she.

Dougal roared a challenge and launched himself up from the ground straight for the Highlander, heedless of Kate standing between them. The Scot let go of the man he held, sweeping his foot beneath his heels and felling him like an oak. With lightning reflexes, he dropped to a knee, reached out, grabbed Kate's wrist, and jerked her out of Dougal's path, pitching her into the wall of spectators. The young crofters caught her before she fell.

She scrambled around just in time to see Dougal raise his dirk and plunge it downward. Still braced on one knee, the Highlander grabbed Dougal's wrist, arresting it in midflight. His shoulders bunched and strained. His throat corded in his effort to keep the blade from its lethal descent.

Dougal ground his teeth together, spittle forming at the corners of his mouth as slowly, laboriously, the Highlander rose to his feet against all sixteen stone of the massive body Dougal brought to bear.

The crowd hushed.

"Leave off now and save yerself a fair bit of pain," the Highlander advised grimly.

"Go to hell, you bastard!"

"Ah, grand! I admit I would have been sorely disappointed if you'd chosen otherwise."

With a sudden twist, the Highlander pivoted, jerking Dougal's arm straight out. At the same time, he dropped his shoulder beneath Dougal's elbow and wrenched down. The muffled crunch of breaking bone filled the room.

Kate's stomach roiled at the sound. Dougal's face drained of color. His blade dropped from nerveless fingers and clattered to the floor. He opened his mouth and howled.

With a look of disgust, the Highlander pushed the

gibbering Dougal toward his friends. He spied the innkeeper. "You best get a splint on his arm, or he'll no be driving a team agin."

His words penetrated Kate's frightened thoughts. She stared, no longer seeing the Scotsman, but only hearing his prophetic words, suddenly comprehending what had happened: she no longer had a driver.

Leaden feet carried her to the innkeeper's side. With numb fingers she reached into her pocket and withdrew a few of the precious coins she'd sewn into her cloak's hem. "Find someone to set his arm," she said woodenly and turned to leave, uncertain of her destination.

Unless she could hire another driver, she would have to take the mail coach back to York. What with the increasing number of highwaymen, thieves, and brigands on the roads, and the early onset of what promised to be a fierce winter, few private agencies risked sending their cattle—or their men—to northern Scotland. She'd been surprised that the marquis had found a company willing to do so this late in the year. If she went back to York, there would be no second chance to make it to Clyth this winter.

She *had* to make it to Clyth. It seemed to her she'd been given one final chance to regain what they'd lost. And now that was being lost, too.

Her head swam, and for the first time in her life she felt faint. Too little food, too little hope. She swayed. Closed her eyes. Reached out for something to hold on to. Failed to find anything.

On the other hand, it might be a relief to give in, to finally just stop trying . . .

Strong arms gripped her elbows, steadying her. He smelled of leather and sweat and an odd metallic tang. She opened her eyes.

His back was to the hearth, and the light from behind created a nimbus of fire about his red-gold hair. She could see little of his features except for the stubble of his beard glinting along the edge of a hard jaw.

"Who are you?" she asked.

"Me?" the rich voice purred, "Why, I'd be yer guardian angel, love."

The sense that something momentous was about to happen crawled up Kate's spine. She stumbled back, and to keep her from falling, the Highlander shifted, pulling her lightly against his side. The movement brought him around so that the light fell fully on his face. For the first time that evening she got a good, clear look at him: ruthless, icy green eyes, the lips of a rake, and the jaw of a Celtic warrior.

She crumpled in a dead faint into Christian MacNeill's arms.

# TWO

⌖

# OVERNIGHTING
# AT TAVERNS, INNS,
# HOSTELRIES, AND
# OTHER LOW PLACES

KATE FLOATED BETWEEN consciousness and dream. A warm, masculine scent penetrated the darkness, rising from the dense surface against which she lay. She felt safe, utterly relaxed . . . slightly . . . blowsy. *Blowsy?*

She came more fully awake, her eyes opening upon a hard jaw and a strong, masculine throat. The gilt-haired Highlander looked down with eyes like chalcedony: pale green, silvery, and unreadable.

"Do you remember me, Mrs. Blackburn?" he asked. "Kit MacNeill?"

"Christian."

The corner of his generous mouth twitched into a brief smile. "More Kit than Christian, I'm afraid. So, you do remember."

*Oh, yes.* She remembered. She remembered sitting shivering in a room stripped of every ornamentation, staring into the wounded, fierce gray-green eyes of a young man who prowled the room like a wild beast, a man so outside her sphere of experience that she'd felt able to reveal to him things she hadn't even told her own family—bitter things, angry things—because she'd been certain that their worlds, having collided for one brief hour, would never again overlap. She should have known better.

"Yes, I remember." Heat piled into her cheeks and throat. "How—why are you here?"

A dark-winged brow split by a deep scar rose sardonically. "You don't believe in guardian angels?"

"No." If there were such things, hers had been so derelict in his duties he'd probably been drummed from the ranks years ago. She shifted, and he jounced her in his arms, settling her more comfortably and forcibly reminding her that she was being carried by a man who was for all purposes a stranger to her. "Please. I can stand."

Without comment, he set her down and she swayed, light-headed. He reached out, but she drew back. "I'm fine."

His well-shaped mouth flattened into an enigmatic smile. The young man who'd brought her family the glorious golden roses had been fierce, but there had been something about him that had touched a kindred spark in her. In some odd manner, she'd felt she'd known that Christian MacNeill. She did not feel that way about this hard, lean "Kit" MacNeill. What *was* he doing here?

"Which room is yours?"

She indicated the nearest door, and he pushed it open, stepping aside so she could enter. She turned, and the light spilling out of her doorway revealed what the shadowed corridor had concealed: blood clotted the gilt hair at his temple. Wounds from a tavern brawl. Her gaze slipped to his hands. The knuckles were raw and bleeding, broken on another man. She shivered at this evidence of brute violence.

"You've been hurt."

"It doubtless looks worse than it is. 'Tis often the way of head wounds."

She hesitated. Perhaps it was his familiarity with wounds, perhaps another vestige of her sense of duty; for whatever reason, she held the door open. "At least avail yourself of the washbasin. It's better than the horse trough."

"And that is my only option?" he asked with a wry smile.

"I took the last room, and unless one has since been vacated, yes, it is," she answered coolly, refusing to be baited. She gestured toward the chipped china bowl. "Please."

He snorted and then, with the air of one indulging another's incomprehensible whim, came in, shutting the door behind him. He went to the bowl and bent over it, splashing water on his face, leaving her to study him.

It was no wonder she hadn't recognized him at first. The gaunt lines of his face had fleshed out, developing hard angles and planes. More marks had been added to the scar on his brow that she had noted earlier. Three years ago he'd already had too many scars.

He was bigger than she remembered, too. Broader. His back flexed as he scrubbed his face, stretching the torn linen shirt, revealing glimpses of heavy muscles bunching and shifting. Everything about him was masculine. Too masculine.

Why had he shut the door? He should have left it open. A gentleman would have found another woman to act as chaperone—God! What was she thinking? A tavern girl was hardly an adequate doyenne. And he was hardly a gentleman—despite his educated accent. And that accent hadn't been so refined in the tavern room. What was going on?

She shouldn't have invited him in. Perhaps he'd think she'd some other reason than simple human kindness for doing so. She had no idea what sort of man he was, what he did, or what he had done.

Roars from the tavern room below shook the thin floorboards further, bearing in upon her the potential danger she was in. If she was to cry out, no one would hear her. She glanced furtively at the closed door and edged nearer it.

"Do you have a towel?" He straightened, and she started, but handed him a cloth before darting nervously back. He regarded her a moment before turning his back to her.

"I assume you are acting like a scared rabbit because you are afraid of me. I am not going to rape you, Mrs. Blackburn," he said, toweling off his face, as if accusations of rape were a daily and tiresome occurrence.

Her cheeks burned, and she felt sheepish.

He turned back to the basin and the mirror hanging above it, leaning forward and studying the cut on his temple. She relaxed a bit as he ignored her and wrung out the cloth, wiping the blood from his hands.

Even his eyes had changed, she noted, watching him in the mirror. Once they had been doors leading to a savaged interior; now they gave nothing away, not even a glimpse of the man they served. The only thing familiar about them was their beauty—long eyes, frosted green between thick gold-tipped lashes. He pitched the stained towel aside. Fresh blood oozed from the cut at his temple.

"You're still bleeding," she murmured.

He touched the wound and looked at his blood-tipped fingers in annoyance. He stood uncertainly. There were no other towels in sight. She hesitated a moment, then impulsively reached under the bed for her deceased cousin's luggage, an ornately tooled leather trunk with brass fittings.

As well as Grace Murdoch's belongings, it contained the sum total of Kate's own wardrobe: three of her mother's best gowns, made up so that when she arrived at Castle Parnell, she wouldn't look like the beggar she was. Carefully, she lifted the tissue-wrapped dresses onto the bed. At the bottom, she'd carefully folded her undergarments.

Once they'd been a new bride's treasure, made from the sheerest batiste, embroidered in silk, and edged in Brussels lace. The finest had worn out long ago, the lace having been stripped to adorn Charlotte's school dresses. What were left were thin from washings and repaired more times than Kate could remember. There were bandages in the hospitals with more thread in them.

"What are you doing?" MacNeill asked.

"You can't go about bleeding like that." She ripped an ancient chemise at its seam. "It isn't decent. Sit down."

He tilted his head, regarding her with surprise, but came to her side and sat down on the room's only chair. She moved behind him, tearing her chemise into thin strips. Then, making a thick pad, she pressed it over the cut on his temple. "Hold this."

He clamped his hand over hers. Like the rest of him, it was large and rough and scarred but with unexpected notes of elegance, the fingers slender and long, his wrists broad but lean. Hastily, she slipped her hand free from under his and began wrapping his head.

His breath checked at her touch.

"Am I hurting you?" she asked.

"No." He probably had other wounds hidden beneath the thick, disheveled red-gold hair. With gentle fingers, she explored his scalp, moving closer. He stayed very still, his hands upon his knees, his gaze fixed straight ahead.

Standing over him, she glanced down and through

the rent in his shirt glimpsed the heavy plane of his chest, glinting with dark hairs. A man's body. She'd forgotten the contours a masculine form—

"It's low you've fallen, darlin'," he said.

She jumped guiltily, but he only said, "I doubt you would have bandaged my head three years ago."

"Oh?"

"You were very much a fashionable young lady. Perfect. Clean." His voice dropped to a musing whisper. "The cleanest thing I had ever seen."

She straightened, stung by his implication. "If I am less than immaculate now it is because I have been traveling," she said.

He laughed, a sound of amusement that utterly disconcerted her. She searched his words for some underlying meaning. Was he trying to gauge whether her reduced circumstances led to reduced morals? More than one man had made that mistake and had been given an ear-blistering lecture in reply; for all that they'd been low, lousy creatures, they had still been ruled by some social considerations. Kit MacNeill didn't look as if he was ruled by anything. He certainly didn't look as if he'd be deterred by a tongue-lashing.

She cleared her throat. "You're quite correct, three years ago I would have sent you to the kitchen and had the housekeeper attend you. I may no longer have a housekeeper or a kitchen, but I have not fallen so low that I do not understand the concept of obligation and gratitude, particularly on behalf of one less fortunate than myself. I hope I always shall."

Another flash of amusement lightened his harsh visage. "I stand corrected, then. You would have, of course, acted properly. How fortunate for me that you have not abandoned your manners. "

"You say that as if there was something fundamentally suspect about proper behavior, Mr. MacNeill," she replied haughtily, tearing off another strip of batiste with her teeth. "From what I have seen of the world, behaving in a manner prescribed by polite society is an agreeable alternative to acting on base impulses and violent tendencies."

She did not look at him as she said it. She did not need to. Her meaning was quite clear.

Her temerity amazed her. She should have clung to her earlier fear. Her unquestioning belief in her invulnerability was yet another vestige of a way of life long ago ended. And another entry for her book: *As one of the genteel poor, a lady need be constantly mindful that she is no longer a part of society where a lady's safety, if not welfare, was once guaranteed.*

"I do not mean to sound ungrateful," she added nervously.

"Not at all," he replied. "I am indebted to you for your tutelage."

She didn't want his thanks. She wanted him gone. He disturbed her. He frightened her. But long ago, riding lessons had taught her that one must never allow a dangerous animal to sense one's fear.

"The bleeding should stop now," she said. "Thank you for what you did for that boy." She stepped aside, clearly indicating that he should leave. He didn't. "And now, allow me to bid you good-bye."

Still, he didn't move. "I fear my actions have left you stranded."

"You were entirely courageous." She wadded up the cloth scraps, facing him with a smile she hoped looked calm and dismissive. "Any inconvenience must be weighed against the greater good."

"I didn't risk much," he said.

"I disagree. Dougal had a knife. I saw it. You were most heroic." This time she took a step toward the door and placed her hand on the latch, preparing to open it.

"And you, if I recall, have no use for heroes," he murmured.

At her silence, he shrugged, effectively dismissing both Dougal's knife and the potential outcome as equally unimportant. *Why* was he still sitting there?

"At the very least I owe you coach fare to"—his brow lifted inquiringly—"York?"

"No."

"Surely 'proper behavior' doesn't prevent you from accepting money from me?"

"I'm not going to York. I am headed in the opposite direction."

She meant it. True, she had no money, but certainly Grace's brother-in-law, the marquis, would pay whatever price a driver demanded. He'd already sent one coach for her. And she *was* making this journey on his behalf. Well, somewhat on his behalf. *Ostensibly* on his behalf—

MacNeill's gaze raked her from top to bottom, missing nothing from the telltale rust of her gown's thrice-turned seams to the worn leather of her oft-resoled boots. "And having no driver, you believe you can make other arrangements?"

"Yes. I am certain of it."

"I am afraid you are going to be disappointed," he said. "This is not a coaching inn, Mrs. Blackburn. It's a haunt for thieves and highwaymen."

"You sound as if you are well acquainted with it," she clipped out.

"And a hundred just like it," he replied agreeably.

She didn't care how many dens of iniquity he'd frequented. He did not know her situation. He did not know what was risked and what stood to be gained. He did not understand that she might, if she managed everything perfectly, win back her life. As well as her sisters'.

"Your welfare is at risk," he said. "I cannot, in good conscience, leave you, especially as it is my actions that have marooned you."

"It is none of your concern." She carefully iced each syllable with all the hauteur at her command.

Satisfaction licked his slow smile. "But, my dear Mrs. Blackburn, moments ago you lectured me on how important proper behavior was in separating civilized man from the likes of, oh, say, heathen Scotsmen. You can't permit yourself *proper* behavior and deny me the same."

She flushed. He'd maneuvered her most adroitly. "You are wasting your time trying to convince me to turn back. I am going north, to Clyth and from there to Castle Parnell. That is, unless you intend to physically remove me from here, Mr. MacNeill," she threw out recklessly.

His smile became gentle, as if she'd said something profoundly quaint. "My dear woman, look at me."

With lethal grace, he uncoiled from the chair and spread his long arms out at his sides. Muscle rippled beneath tanned flesh. Blood stained his damp shirt. Sweat still shimmered at the base of his throat. Everything about him was uncivilized and torn and *dangerous*. "Do you doubt for a moment that I'm capable of doing just that?"

"I think," she said in a small voice, "that because of that debt you once insisted you owed my family, you would not like to cause me any distress."

He tensed as if struck. A sharp smiled cleaved his face. "A palpable hit, ma'am. I commend you. But now you've put me in the difficult position of either importuning you or allowing you to endanger yourself."

"This has nothing to do with you. Forget we met if it troubles your conscience."

"I am cursed with an excellent memory. I told you once being in debt was a burden. I pay my debts, ma'am, that I might be beholden to no one," he said. "So, tell me, my dark little instructress, what does polite society dictate I do?"

She wrenched open the door. "Without question you must not importune a lady—no matter what pricks of conscience you endure. Now, I would like to retire. Again, thank you for championing that boy. Again, good-bye."

He followed her with suspect obedience. But at her side, he reached beyond her and shoved the door shut, bracing it closed with his palm flat on the panel. The muscles of his exposed biceps bunched beside her cheek, but she refused to back away. "Where will you find another driver?"

"I shall inquire of the innkeeper," she answered in exasperation. "He's bound to know of someone willing to drive me."

"You'll have to flash a handful of gold to get anyone to head north at this time of year." He studied her carefully. "You don't *have* a handful of gold, do you?"

There was no use denying it. "No."

"So. This driver that you haven't met is supposed to take you to northern Scotland on the basis of what? Your pretty face?"

"You needn't sneer," she said. "I shall assure him that the marquis of Parnell will compensate him upon our arrival."

"And you think that will prove enough to persuade this unnamed gallant?"

"I don't see why it shouldn't."

"It *won't*, because these people have been promised things all their lives, Mrs. Blackburn. Lower rents by absent landlords, laws to protect what little they have by politicians, a higher day's wage by estate managers, and justice by the courts. None of those promises have been kept.

"We Scots are wary of promises, Mrs. Blackburn. Even from such a comely lass as yourself. Or maybe especially from such a comely lass."

"But I am not lying!"

"It doesn't matter. No one here knows you. Except me."

For some reason, his self-assured claim drove the breath from her lungs. "You don't know me. You know *nothing* about me." She ducked beneath his arm, but he caught her wrist, swinging her around to face him.

He jerked her closer, and she pulled back frantically. No one had ever laid hands on her in such a way before, a way that expressed violence in check and effortlessly demonstrated a complete physical control. Helplessness bloomed within her, full and terrifying, closing her throat and pulsing in her temples.

"*Listen to me,*" he said, oblivious to her distress. "Even if you found some man who would accept your terms, have you thought about what sort he must be? What happens two days out, alone on the road? Your last driver was vouched for by an agency, and look at his sterling character. Any man you find willing to drive you won't come with a recommendation."

She finally yanked free, or rather, he let her go so quickly that she fell back, her shoulders banging against the wall. He followed her in swiftly, looming over her, cutting her off from the rest of the room.

"Say you were to just disappear." His beautiful eyes rested on her like some sated predator still capable of being roused for a bit of sport. Her heart leapt in her chest. "Who'll find you? Who'll even look for you?"

He leaned over her, bracing a brawny forearm on the wall above her head, his body caging her in. She twisted, pressing her cheek hard against the wall. His fingertips dangled near her temple. If she moved, he'd touch her. Panic swirled in her blood like some potent drug. His gaze slipped languidly over her face, falling to ponder on her lips. She shut her eyes, trembling. "Who'll know where to ask or who to ask it of?"

He could do whatever he wanted to her right here, right now, and no one would interfere. But that was his point: If she was vulnerable here, how much greater were her risks on the open road? She understood. She agreed. It still didn't matter.

For years, she'd searched for a way out of their present circumstance. This was the first meager opening she'd found. Fear and risk, no matter how great, weren't enough to make her turn back. Not now.

She opened her eyes. "I *have* to go."

"Why?" She'd thought he was done with his instruction, but apparently the lesson was not yet over, for he continued watching her mouth, as though the manner in which she formed words fascinated him.

"Do you remember my cousin Grace?"

"Aye?"

"She married the marquis of Parnell's younger brother, Charles. They lived in his family's castle near Clyth." The words tumbled out in a rush. "A few months ago Grace wrote that she and Charles were relocating to London." She hazarded a glance at MacNeill's lean face.

"She sent a trunk filled with personal items, things of little monetary value, which she asked me to keep until their arrival." She gestured to the open trunk. A brass telescope, several books, and a flat traveling writing case filled the top layer. "Shortly afterward, we learned that Grace and Charles had died in a boating accident.

"The marquis is grief-stricken and has written asking that, for sentimental reasons, I return their effects. I promised that I would bring them myself."

"Why, Mrs. Blackburn, you are a veritable font of tender feelings," MacNeill said wryly. He brushed away a strand of hair that caught at the corner of her mouth. "But I am sure his lordship can struggle through one winter without his brother's bric-a-brac."

He was forcing confessions she did not want to make. She looked away. "The marquis and I . . . we met some years ago. I believe he remembers me kindly," she said, abdicating pride to necessity. "I hope that in his sorrow, and by way of his onetime . . . regard, I can encourage him to become my family's benefactor. We are Grace's last living relations."

MacNeill laughed. "The poor relation? It doesn't suit you, Mrs. Blackburn."

"Starvation suits me even less!" Her head snapped around. How dare he judge her? Many lived on the sufferance of family members luckier than themselves. She and her sisters wouldn't be the first.

He held her gaze a short moment before his mouth twisted, wordlessly conceding her the point. "The spring will serve as good a time as any for your mission."

"I will not have the wherewithal to make this journey come spring."

"I have the ready." Abruptly, he pushed himself away from the wall, his hand dropping to his side, no longer interested in toying with her. She'd been dismissed. To his mind, the matter had been dealt with. He would send her back to York and give her a purse with enough coin to hire a coach come spring and then ride off, having finally satisfied his debt to her family. Only spring would be too late. She needed the marquis's help *now*.

"And have you the ready to support us through the winter? To pay the tuition at Charlotte's school? To buy her dresses?" She had too much pride to let him know that dresses were hardly the most pressing of their problems. Her gaze trailed tellingly over his ragged hair, torn shirt, and scuffed boots.

He returned her regard with hard, sardonic eyes. "Had I realized that the situation was so dire—"

"Mr. MacNeill," she said, "I would not be here, in this place tonight, if I did not consider my situation 'dire.' Few opportunities have come our way these past years. I cannot afford to delay in acting on any that do.

"By spring the marquis's sorrow will have subsided, practicality will have returned, and my heroic efforts to return his brother's things to him will no longer seem so impressive. Or worthy of reward."

"You *are* a calculating creature. Tell me, is that, too, a characteristic of the . . . *better* classes?"

"I am whatever circumstances demand," she said. How could he understand? He had health and strength and no obligations—except this one that he was desperate to fulfill. "Right now circumstances demand action. I *must* trust to the innkeeper's judgment and find a driver. I have no choice."

"Yes, you do," he said. "I will take you."

"No!" The word erupted from her lips.

His lips twisted. "What's wrong, Mrs. Blackburn? Don't you trust me?"

"No."

He laughed without bitterness. "Wise, but unnecessary. I won't hurt you. Having little, I value what little I own: my word and my honor and my independence. The first I can keep because I have the skills and strength to do so, the second, because I have the will to do so, and the third, because I am tied to no man or woman *except* those to whom I am indebted. And among that *very* small number, your family is preeminent."

She searched his harsh countenance, her thoughts awhirl. She wasn't a fool. He was possibly her only real chance of getting to Castle Parnell. She had no desire to brave the road with some stranger, especially under the conditions MacNeill had so succinctly out-lined. But he frightened her. Instinctively, she knew he could cause her great harm, and she trusted those instincts. "No."

His hand tightened into a fist. She shrank back involuntarily, thinking of the anger she'd seen him unleash upon Dougal and his cohorts. With a low curse, MacNeill stepped away from her.

"Maybe you are right," he said harshly. "God knows. You may be right."

Then, as she watched in amazement, he dropped to one knee and lowered his head, crossing his forearm over his chest, his fist clenched above his heart. The guttering candlelight glinted in his dark red-gold hair.

"Katherine Blackburn, I vow to serve you. I pledge my arm and my sword, my breath and my blood to that service." His voice vibrated with intensity. "Whatever you ask, I will do; whatever you require, I will provide. By God's will alone, and no man's, I do faithfully pledge."

He raised his face to hers. "Pretty words, are they not? And ones I'd die before I betrayed."

His last words were so low, Kate wasn't certain she had heard right. But he was speaking again, his pale eyes glittering. "This is my country. I know these mountains and these rivers. I know where to find shelter and where there is none. I can tell the wind's caprice from her savagery, and I know paths that will lead us to your destination without taking us into harm's way.

"I told you once that I would wait for however long it was necessary to discharge my vow. I have waited a long time. Faithfully. You can free me of the burden of my obligation *and* travel safely to Clyth. *Let me do this.*"

She flushed, amazed by the fervor in his voice. Three years ago he had surprised candor from her. Now, she heard an echo of that candor in his voice. This was madness, but surely the alternative—to trust her care to a complete stranger—was madder still.

"Yes."

"I'll get my things." He rose with liquid grace, his attitude once again cool. His passionate pledge might never have been uttered. "We leave at first light."

# THREE

⬚⬚⬚⬚

# ACKNOWLEDGING ONE'S
# NEW CIRCUMSTANCES

She was afraid of him. In spite of her bravado, she hadn't been able to hide the flinch of apprehension, the start of anxiety whenever he'd moved.

Kit MacNeill strode across the dark yard, heedless of the sting of the icy rain or the wind whipping his hair. He had done what he'd been asked. After nearly two years in India, three weeks ago he'd stepped ashore at Bristol and promptly contacted the London solicitor to whom the abbot would relay any messages. He hadn't expected any news. He'd been frankly amazed when the rose had arrived at his boardinghouse, shriveled and small but still golden.

The message that came with it asked him to safeguard Kate Blackburn's trip to northern Scotland, relating the route she was to take and warning him that she would bitterly resent interference, so much so that the sender—had it been Charlotte? The signature was blurred—had begged him to let Kate believe that their meeting was happenstance. He had, of course, done as instructed. He had no choice. He had made a vow.

But that hadn't kept him from resenting this interference in his life and the time wasted squiring a young beauty to her next potential husband's home. He had a purpose in returning to England after so many years, and now that purpose was being delayed.

He'd spent three years trying to forget that he'd once had "brothers," a surrogate family whom he had loved and trusted and to whom he'd been fiercely loyal. He'd spent the same three years trying to forget the past. He hadn't. He couldn't. There would be only one way he could move forward, by finding the man—possibly one of those self-same brothers—who'd betrayed him to an almost certain death in a French prison. But now . . . His pale gaze swung toward the dark inn. First there was Kate Blackburn.

So, she was frightened of him. Good. A frightened woman was more likely to do as she was bid. And that would expedite this little sojourn. He always did what best served his purpose.

Then why did he keep seeing her image, pale and stricken, as she'd watched the brawl? So what? She'd glimpsed a world where when people were hit, they bled. His world. Imagine her terror if she'd known some of the things he'd seen—or even done—in the last three years. A soldier's life was not pretty.

True, she wasn't *all* shock and fear. She had

courage. His lips curved in an unwilling smile as he recalled her attempt to cow him. She'd glared down that straight little nose of hers like some haughty goddess condemned to a mortal frame, still acting as if she lived in York's most fashionable and exclusive neighborhood and could, with a withering glance, send her inferiors on their way.

Well, in York, inferior he might be. But not here.

But neither was she. True, she'd come down a fair step, yet it hadn't appreciably eroded her self-assurance, as if she had been born better than the rest of the world and nothing could erase her knowledge of that fact. Damn, but looking at her one could believe that her poise, the hauteur still flashing in her eyes, even the tilt of her chin, was indeed something that needed to be bred into a person. Her superiority was as much a part of her as the devil was part of him. Or so the monks had claimed. Which meant, quite simply, that no one could stand further from him than Kate Blackburn.

Too bad that knowledge didn't keep his body from tensing under the lash of desire.

He slipped into the dark stables and found the stall housing his gelding, Doran. Hauling his ruined shirt over his head, he pulled off the wad of wool he'd pressed over the nick Dougal's companion had opened in his side. He tossed it aside. She hadn't seen that, thank God, or he might still be up in her room enduring an even more intimate touch.

He opened his leather satchel and withdrew one of his two remaining shirts, donned it, and settled down, his back to the stall door. From here he could see her lighted window. He would not sleep, because he had sworn to protect her, and nothing would keep him from fulfilling that pledge.

A dark shape crossed the lighted pane in her room. Kate.

He disdained the acceleration of his pulse, but he did not deny it; he'd had enough hairshirts to last a lifetime. Instead, he allowed her image to bloom unhindered in his mind's eye, to study in reverie what he hadn't permitted himself in actuality.

Time had pared away her dewy youth, revealing the strong yet delicate bones of a narrow face that angled more than curved. Mauve smudges rode beneath eyes as fine and dark as onyx. Only her mouth, plush and wounded, vulnerable and ripe, remained completely familiar. And why not? He'd mused on those soft, sweet lips through many a night and in many a terrible place.

He moved silently to the stable door, lifting his face to the icy rain, cooling the heated progress of his thoughts.

"I never seen a man so braw," a feminine voice purred.

Kit looked over his shoulder at the girl standing in the far doorway. He'd scented her before he'd seen her, all earth and musk and want.

"They're all talking aboot it. Aboot how ye caught up that dark lady and took her up the stairs to her room. They thought ye and her were"—she paused, grinning lasciviously—"keeping the night alive."

"They were wrong."

"I know." She sidled closer and wet her lips with her tongue. "I dinna ken yer plaid. Where is it from?"

"Nowhere."

She smiled pertly. "Where do you come from then? Somewhere far away, I'll warrant."

"What do you want, lass?" But he already knew: a few hours of forgetfulness or a coin to purchase liquor or just a night of excitement with a savage-looking Scot to alleviate boredom. The camp followers and even some of the officers' wives had wanted the same thing. At night, in the dark, lines separating gentleman and commoner, peer and pauper, blurred. Want was want.

The girl had laughed at his question but didn't answer it. "I seen yer kind now and agin, come down from the mountains. Half tame they be. Like you." Her gaze slid appreciatively up his frame. "Mostly they go south and that's the end of them. But sometimes, I seen 'em heading back to the mountains after the world's hurt them some and pleasured them some. Then what happens to them, I'd like to know? Not fit fer this world anymore, but neither fit for the one they run from."

"What, indeed?" he murmured.

"Ye speak a good sight better than any of them that I ever heard, I'll grant, but even educated-sounding ye can't hide what you are."

"And what is that?"

"A Highlander," she said, as if surprised he needed to ask. "An uncivilized"—she sashayed closer—"home-less"—she wet her lips again—"two-fisted blackguard."

She rose on her tiptoes and swept her tongue up his throat to the cleft in his chin. "And that is just the sort of man I've a yen fer."

When he did not react, her smile thinned. "Yer not in here wanting *her?*" she asked disbelievingly, jerking her head toward the tavern. "Yer wastin' yer time. She's above ye. Yer howlin' at the moon.

"*I'm* yer sort. I know how to please a man like you in ways a lady like that couldn't even think up."

He barely heard her; his gaze kept straying to Kate's window. "Oh?"

She settled her arms about his neck and nipped his shoulder. He closed his eyes, and at once saw a fall of shimmering dark hair, irises as black as a tarn at midnight, and a soft, full mouth. His eyes snapped open. He'd lost his bleeding mind.

"Go back to the tavern." He unclasped the girl's arms, and she glared up at him.

"Yer a fool, turning down what's offered free. Why?" she demanded,

He answered with a twisted smile, "It would appear I'm not done howling yet."

*St. Bride's Abbey,*
*Scottish Highlands, 1789*

*"He's no devil." The lad with the clever face and blue eyes snickered at the boys ringing Kit. The boy who'd tried to steal Kit's biscuit lay in a sniveling ball at Kit's feet.*

*"He's the devil's spawn then, Dougie," one of the other*

boys—Kit was too new to know any of their names yet—declared. "Or a wolf cub. I heard the brothers talking aboot him. They said he were born bad."

Kit's unlooked-for, and as yet unappreciated, champion scoffed. "They see wickedness everywhere. They be a bunch of priests," he finished with unimpeachable logic.

"I say he looks wicked with them green eyes," another young male opined from within the crowd. "Unnatural."

How many times in Kit's ten short years had he heard that? He balled his hands into fists, waiting for the blows that always seemed to follow those words.

"And you look stupid, Angus." A tall, black-haired boy, a year or so older than Kit, pushed his way to the front of the crowd. Kit had never seen so bonny a lad, yet there was nothing feminine about him. "But I guess there's nothing unnatural aboot that seeing how you are stupid."

Douglas smiled at the newcomer with obvious relief. "Ye have a fair way with words, Ramsey Munro."

Kit stood, waiting. Like he always had. Like he had when his mum had disappeared for days on end in town after town, like when the tavern lasses played with him like some amusing lapdog, like when the men his mum went off with cuffed him across the face and told him to wait in the alley, or the stable, or somewhere where they wouldn't have to look at him.

"What's this about?" the black-haired lad asked. Though clearly Scottish, he spoke in smooth, unfamiliar accents.

"John decided the new lad here had had enough supper and so took his biscuit," Douglas explained. "Only the lad here didn't agree. Now some of the others are thinking it *the devil's work that someone half John's weight and size should beat him so handily."*

*"Yer a swine, John," Ramsey Munro said amiably, nudging the lad with the worn toe of his shoe. John sat up, wiping the snot from beneath his nose. "And a glutton. Did ye not ken the abbot's lecture on the Seven Deadly Sins?*

*"As for this lad here giving John a thrashing," Ramsey continued, "it was only a matter of time before someone figured out that John is only half threat, the other half being bluster."*

*"He's too damn still except fer his eyes, and they be hot as hellfire and cold as North Sea ice. T'aint natural the way he looks at a body," a new voice said.*

*Most of the time his mum didn't like looking at him either, but every now and then she'd grab his jaw in her long fingers and stare into his face until tears came to her eyes. Then she'd push him away and disappear. Last time she hadn't come back.*

*Instead, a large, wide-girthed monk called Fidelis had appeared one morning, and after paying a coin to the hag who'd rented his mum a bed, he'd loaded Kit into a cart and driven him away. A week later, here he was, deep in the Scottish Highlands, at some place called St. Brides with another dozen or so lads, most of them no nearer God than Kit himself. But at least they looked nearer God.*

*He would have run off, except St. Brides sat as clean in the middle of nowhere as a place could be. Besides, he liked the mountains and the scent of pine trees, the clarity of the air, and the colors of the sky. And he certainly liked the fresh bread he got every morning and the biscuits and cheese that came each afternoon.*

*Kit looked down at John, knowing he hadn't hurt the boy near as bad as he was like to be hurt by John's friends. That was the way of things. But now, it looked like there might not be a fight after all, because of this Douglas—who even then Kit recognized as having that aura of authority that made leaders—and the black-haired Ramsey Munro.*

*But . . . why?*

*"Get up, John. Yer pride's more hurt than anything else." Douglas reached his hand down to John and with a sullen glance at Kit, the bigger boy allowed himself to be hauled to his feet.*

*"And don't go glowering at our boy." Douglas looked around at Kit. "What's yer name, lad?"*

*"Christian. MacNeill."*

*"MacNeill, is it? Hear that, lads? And he's wearing a plaid," he said, looking Kit over. "It is a plaid, in't it? Hard to tell beneath so much filth."*

*"It's a plaid," Kit said gruffly. His mother had given it to him a few years ago upon retrieving it from a priest in Glasgow. She hadn't told him anything about it, except that it was his and his alone and better than nothing to keep out the cold.*

*"Aha! This isn't just some Highland brat, boys," Douglas declared to the group enthusiastically. "I remember I seen this plaid afore. Belongs to an ancient secret clan. Christian MacNeill could be one of their princes!"*

*Ramsey leaned toward Kit and spoke in a low voice as Douglas worked the crowd into a better mood. "Best mind*

*John from here out, Christian—"* He stopped. *"Couldn't be a more unlikely name for you, lad. You must go by another."*

*"I been called Kit."*

*"Devil's kit?"* Ramsey's winged brow lifted, but with such obvious irony that Kit didn't hold back his answering grin.

*"Sometimes,"* he admitted.

*"You! New boy!"* A deep baritone shouted from the arched entry to the cloisters. Brother Fidelis, fourteen stones of benevolent kidnapper, came charging down the pea gravel path, his brown robes flapping about his stout ankles. The boys surrounding them fled at his approach, but he ignored their flight.

*"I saw it all! I saw you strike one of the other boys. That is wicked! I will not stand for that sort of wickedness here. Do you understand?"* Brother Fidelis pointed one dirt encrusted finger under Kit's nose.

*"It weren't his fault,"* Douglas said.

*" 'Wasn't,' not 'weren't,' "* Brother Fidelis corrected.

*"John was trying to filch his biscuit,"* Ramsey piped in.

Fidelis sniffed suspiciously, eyeing Kit sharply. *"Striking one's brother is a sin."*

*"He ain't my brother,"* Kit proclaimed flatly. He had no family. And now that his mum had decamped, he was on his own. And best that way, it was, too.

*" 'Isn't,' and we are all brothers here. All of us. It is how we survive. Without one's brother, one is alone. Do you want to be alone for all eternity?"*

Kit shrugged, Douglas shook his head emphatically, and Ramsey's long eyes narrowed slightly. Fidelis sighed. *"No, you don't. But you'll learn. As for fighting, if you are indeed wicked, I can do nothing for you. Wickedness is a matter for the Lord to attend. However, boys with too much time on their hands I can do something about. Come with me." He chugged forth, confident his orders would be obeyed.*

*Wicked he might be, but a coward Kit was not, and so he followed behind the monk, noting a few seconds later that both Ramsey Munro and Douglas Stewart had fallen into step beside him.*

*"What are you doing?" he whispered.*

*"Going with you," Douglas answered calmly.*

*"I have never seen Brother Fidelis punish anyone. I'm curious," Ramsey added.*

*The monk led them on a circuitous route through the decrepit abbey, some of the ancient buildings so dilapidated that the walls were caving in under the weight of their years. He ducked around the priory and headed for a high stone wall overgrown with vines, stopping before an arched wooden door and withdrawing a heavy key from an inside pocket. He fixed it in the lock and pushed the door open on a groan, turning to the trio. If he was surprised that Kit had been joined by Ramsey and Douglas, he didn't show it, but as his little raisin dark eyes peered over their heads, his mouth pursed.*

*"Another soul ripe for a fall!" he murmured, pointing to an old apple tree nearby. "You! Andrew Ross, you may as well come, too!"*

*"Huh?" A young male voice asked from somewhere overhead.*

*Kit looked up. For a minute he didn't see anyone. Then*

*a slight rustle drew his gaze higher still, into the uppermost branches of the old tree. A pair of brown legs dangled from the leaves.*

*"Get down from there, Dand!" Brother Fidelis said with more volume than ire. A second later a wiry, dusty-haired boy slipped to the ground, his warm brown eyes wide with innocence.*

*"Come here!"*

*With a cringe, the boy dragged his feet toward them.*

*"Andrew Ross," Ramsey whispered to Kit. "Now, there's someone who'll be glad you're here."*

*"Why's that?"*

*"Because everyone's called him the devil's kit." Ramsey flashed his knowing smile. "Until now."*

*"I didn't do anything!" the tanned boy said, holding his hands out at his sides to give proof to his claim.*

*"You will," Brother Fidelis snorted. "Follow along with the rest." The monk pushed through the door. "Now, stay on the path and do not touch anything." With a wave of his hand, he ushered the boys in, closing the door behind him.*

*At once, an overpowering scent assailed Kit with a perfume so heavy and exotic, it made his head swim. He stared about, dazed by a fragrance part clove and part ambrosial sweetness, both as thick as cream and slight as mist. He turned slowly around and found the source.*

*Roses. Everywhere, roses. Roses climbed crumbled brick and mossy stone. Roses dangled from half-tumbled archways. Roses cascaded off the top of broken walls and spread in thick mats across ill-marked paths. They burst in fountains of color, and they nestled in small, furtive clusters.*

They blazed and they flickered, soft and bold, brash and delicate.

Scarlet and crimson, blush and cherry. Roses, pure white and shell pink, thick ivory and fresh cream. But most startling of all, most spectacular, close by where they stood, amidst an exuberance of mint green leaves with finely serrated edges, bloomed a pure yellow rose. It glowed in the bright light of day, seeming to catch some of the sun's own brilliance in its joyous, vibrant color.

"It's wonderful," Kit murmured, bending closer to the saffron blossom. "As yellow as an egg yolk. I never seen a rose such a color."

"No one has."

Kit looked up. Fidelis was looking down at him with something akin to approval.

"Well, not many, anyway," Fidelis elaborated. "No more than a handful in England and Scotland combined. Most rose fanciers would swear that there are no yellow roses."

"Where did it come from?" Ramsey asked, unable to take his eyes from the beautiful thing.

"The story goes that a crusader brought it back from the Holy Land and gave it as a gift to the abbey for their care of his family during the Black Death. In return, we—" He abruptly broke off. "It's been here ever since."

"And the rest of the roses?" Douglas asked.

"Collected over the years. Hunted and brought back from all four corners of the world. Once St. Brides was known for its roses," he said proudly. "But after the Forty-five, when the king had the Roman Church expelled from Scotland, roses didn't seem to matter anymore. We here at St. Brides didn't *leave. We were so far out, you see, away from everyone. No one took note of us this far up. This place"—he swept his hand out—"while not exactly abandoned, has been ignored."*

*"Pretty." The boy Andrew bent over and sniffed. "Like to get a headache in here though, smelling so strong as it does."*

*Brother Fidelis's conciliatory mood disappeared, and he regarded Andrew dryly. "I forget what a heathen little jackanapes you are, Andrew Ross. But thank you for reminding me that you are not here to learn the history of the garden. You are here to work."*

*"Us, too?" Ramsey asked in alarm.*

*"Oh, yes. You, Ramsey Munro, have just as much devil in you as Christian here. You just keep him dressed up in company clothes."*

*Kit hadn't any idea what that meant, but he liked the notion that someone else was wicked.*

*"And me?" Douglas asked, his face reflecting his grievance.*

*"You always take the leadership role, Mr. Stewart. I see no reason for you to forfeit it now." He turned to Andrew Ross. "And as for you . . ." He shook his head without bothering to finish.*

*Kit didn't see what all the fuss was about. He'd picked oakum, swept stables, and hauled water for eight hours at a time. How hard could work in a garden be compared to that?*

*"For how long?" Ramsey asked.*

*"Until the weeds are gone," Brother Fidelis said. "And maybe a few of the walls are repaired."*

*Kit felt his grin broaden. Pick weeds? Pull lovely soft, green weeds from the ground? Move a few stones? He almost laughed out loud.*

*Six hours later Kit's back ached, his thighs throbbed from squatting down, his arms were covered with welts from the millions of hairlike barbs that covered the rose stems, and his hands itched from the sting of the nettles he'd pulled. His face was burned red, and his knees under his patched breeches were scraped raw. He didn't complain, though. And he didn't quit. And neither did the others.*

*Two hours later they finished. With groans and oaths, they made their way beneath the shade of one of the stone arches that decorated the garden. As one, they sank wearily to the ground.*

*"I should have let them beat the bloody hell out of you," Douglas said without any real rancor.*

*"I should have walked right by," Ramsey agreed.*

*"But you didn't, did you?" Kit said. "Bloody fools."*

*"What about me?!" Andrew Ross exclaimed indignantly. "Minding me own concerns, I was."*

*"Like stealing apples."*

*Andrew shrugged. "Sinful concerns, I'll grant you," he admitted unrepentantly, "but me own."*

*They grinned at each other in sudden idiotic empathy and they were still grinning when Brother Fidelis arrived a few minutes later.*

*"So, you're all done, are you?" he asked mildly.*

*"Aye, Brother Fidelis. Not a weed in the place. Nothin' but roses." Douglas scrambled to his feet.*

*"For today."*

*"Eh?"*

*"For today, Douglas. Today there are no weeds, but a rose garden, like one's soul, must be tended vigilantly, hourly.*

*Weeds, like sins, spring up overnight. Come back tomorrow. All of you."*

*"But what if there aren't any weeds?" Ramsey burst out, momentarily losing the insouciance Kit was beginning to realize characterized this boy.*

*"Well then, there are paths to re-create, walls to rebuild, a well to dredge, arches to repair. Oh, we'll find something," Brother Fidelis assured them. "Now, I'll let you out."*

*As he held the door open, Andrew gave Kit a look that said they might as well accept their fate. But Kit didn't want to accept his fate, especially since he wasn't at all certain of what it was, or had become, since he'd come here, wherever "here" was.*

*"Why are we here? All us boys?" he whispered urgently to Douglas.*

*"Don't you know? We're here because of what the knight of the Yellow Rose asked in return for his patronage," he whispered and trotted on ahead. "We're to become knights."*

# FOUR

⊠⊠⊠

# THE DIRE CONSEQUENCES
# OF IMPULSIVE BEHAVIOR

BETWEEN THE NOISE FROM the tavern below and the howling of the storm without, Kate slept fitfully. She dreamed about her husband, Michael, but his eyes kept turning green and a Scottish burr invested his speech. She awoke before dawn, anxious and guilt-ridden.

She had met, married, and been widowed all within two years, her father having introduced her to Lt. Michael Blackburn. In hindsight, it was small wonder her father had pressed Michael's suit for him. Like her father, Michael was dashing and courageous and entirely dedicated. And, also like him, the son of an impoverished, if genteel, family.

She had not regretted her marriage. She did regret, however, that she'd wed a hero, the sort of man who acted without stopping to consider the fates of those he left behind.

How she did resent heroes.

She stumbled from bed, the disloyal, half-conscious

thought chasing her from sleep, and set about dressing in the same cotton gown she'd been traveling in for three days. Then she packed her few belongings back into Grace's trunk, took a deep breath, and went downstairs.

Below, men lay strewn about the room like bodies on a field after a great battle. They huddled on the floor and lined the walls. Some tilted upright against one another, while a few lucky souls had commandeered benches as pallets. The stench of stale beer and wet wood ash clogged her nostrils, and the sound of snores was punctuated by other, less pleasant noises. A serving girl hurried in from a side door, her blouse askew and her arms full of kindling.

"Mrs. Blackburn," a deep voice called.

Kate looked around. Kit MacNeill stood framed in the open door, behind him leaden clouds churning above the dim horizon. The wind rippled the edge of his plaid, affording a few glimpses of a forest green jacket. The flat light delineated scars on his lean, burnished countenance. How many men bore the scars he'd given them? How many hadn't lived to see their handiwork? She shuddered. She had made a mistake. She could not go with this man. He was—

"Are your things ready?"

She stuttered into speech. "I have rethought my plans."

He waited.

"I shall stay here," she announced. "The agency that owns the carriage will send someone to replace

Dougal, or at the very least, reacquire their carriage. I shall convince the new driver to take me to Clyth rather than back to York."

"Dougal and the carriage are gone," Kit said. "He and one of his friends took it last night."

"Really?" Relief swept through her.

Fate had delivered her from Kit MacNeill.

"Then I shall *have* to wait here until another carriage comes."

"I have another carriage," he said. "The innkeeper had an old phaeton in the back of the stables."

Fate dumped her back in Kit MacNeill's lap.

"Oh." A phaeton? The small two-person carriage had no proper back compartment for passengers, only a bench that the driver shared with his fellow traveler. Neither was it enclosed, having only a partially retractable hood. Yet it may well be the only chance she had of getting to Castle Parnell. "I . . . My things are ready."

"I'll get them." His cape swung out from his broad shoulders as he mounted the stairs and disappeared. He returned a few minutes later, handling the heavy chest as if it were inconsequential. He stopped at the bottom of the steps. "I'll settle with the innkeeper—easy! Do not take me to task over something so trifling. Repay me when we arrive at your marquis's castle."

She flushed. "He is not 'my marquis.' "

His expression accused her of being disingenuous, but he only said, "The horse is hitched and the carriage is waiting. At your leisure, ma'am." He swept his hand out in a mocking invitation, and she preceded him into the stable yard.

At the sight of the phaeton, her heart sank. It stood in a churned yard of ice and mud, old and terribly dilapidated. Two rough wooden planks nailed together replaced what should have been the upholstered bench. A cracked and faded hood half shielded the interior, condensed fog dripping from its tattered edge. Only the young roan gelding standing in the traces looked capable.

"Where did you find a horse?" she asked.

"India. Two years ago. He's mine."

"India," she repeated in surprise.

"Aye." He deposited the trunk onto the shelf on the back of the carriage next to a saddle and came round the side. He held out his hand. She hesitated. He waited, his bare hand palm up, moisture beading on his broad shoulders and the cool fog drifting behind him.

Hesitantly, she placed her gloved hand in his. Heat vibrated through her, charged with awareness. She tried to withdraw her hand, but he gave it a little jerk.

"I'd rather your scorn than your flinches, Mrs. Blackburn."

His words brought the heat rushing to her cheeks and her chin snapping up.

"Aye. Like that."

She snatched her hand free and climbed unaided onto the rough plank. He grinned and left her, heading back into the tavern.

"Ma'am?" The tavern girl she had noted earlier

appeared at the side of the carriage holding up a squat wicker basket and a crockery jug. "He asked me to bring ye some food." There was no need asking who "he" was. "There's just a bit of bread and cheese and a jar of ale," she said apologetically. "The men what come in last night ate every bit of what we had."

"Thank you," Kate said, accepting the goods and stowing it under the seat. She found a coin in her pocket and handed it to her. The girl snatched it up and started off but then hesitated.

"I know precious little of what goes on in the world beyond." She nodded to the southern hills. "But men be the same everywhere, I reckon. I seen how you watched the Scot. Yer afraid of him."

Kate did not reply. She *was* afraid of him.

"The *rest* of the world, now," the girl continued, "they might have cause to worrit some if he's a mind to do a bit of destruction. But not you."

Before Kate could reply, she hurried away, passing Kit as he emerged from the inn. Wordlessly, he secured his satchel atop the trunk and then vaulted lightly into the seat beside her. He tossed her a thick wool blanket.

"You'll want to wrap this about your legs," he said. "We're heading out onto the moors, and the wind is fierce there. 'Twill be cold. Bitterly cold."

"Then why are we going that way?" she asked.

"There were men in that tavern who were watching you with an interest that didn't stop at your pretty face," he said, untying the reins. "I'll wager they watched Dougal haul your trunk up the stairs to your room, too."

She understood. "I should think we would want to put a great deal of distance between ourselves and them, then. Wouldn't that be best done on well-traveled highways?"

That brokered a short laugh. "There are no 'well-traveled highways' in the north of Scotland, Mrs. Blackburn."

"Still, it seems to me the best course would be to stay on the *most* traveled roads."

"You're not in England now. You'll have to trust me." He clucked, and the carriage started forward. "We're going by way of the moors, Mrs. Blackburn, because the Highlands are filled with murderers, thieves, and brigands these days. But not fools. And only a fool would go out onto a Highland moor come November."

Most of the Nashes' social acquaintances had been frankly, if not vocally, surprised that the three orphans had been able to carry on as long as they had after their mother's death. If pushed, they would have ascribed that success to Kate's frugality and caution. They would have been wrong.

Kate had quickly learned the necessity of what she privately called "circumspect boldness"—not only the willingness to seize opportunities as they presented themselves but, more importantly, the ability to facilitate those opportunities. If at times she had skirted the conventions of her former life or occasionally deviated from what she might consider "nice" behavior, she had done so to good effect. But this, traveling alone in the company of a very rough, very hard, and very dangerous-looking man, went beyond what even she would have imagined herself capable of doing. And the notion that she might not survive this error in judgment was occurring to her with increasing regularity as the minutes ticked by and MacNeill, his cold eyes narrowed against the horizon and his jaw limned with the red-gold stubble of a two-day-old beard, drove on in complete silence.

She looked around, gaining no comfort from her bleak surroundings. She had never been in a place so . . . empty. Yesterday she had traveled cocooned within the snug confines of a closed carriage, only rarely drawing back the heavy curtain to view the scenery. But the phaeton afforded no distinct separation between passenger and environs, and she found the immediacy of her surroundings breathtaking. And unsettling. Like her proximity to the taciturn MacNeill.

Near noon, MacNeill pulled the phaeton into a small copse of aspen growing by the side of the track and leapt to the ground. Kate followed on legs grown numb from hours on the hard seat and, after attending to certain necessities, returned to find MacNeill already back on the seat, stolidly chewing the bread the tavern girl had supplied. Wordlessly, he held out his hand to help her back into the carriage. When she obliged, he unceremoniously hauled her up, handed her a napkin with a portion of bread in it, and commanded her to eat. He didn't wait before snapping the traces and setting out again.

They traveled into mountains that thrust through the earth's crust like Atlas's shoulders, hunched and muscular, cloaked by thin blankets of pine. Gorse and fern, dark gold and russet, crowded the roadside, shivering in a brisk breeze. The vastness, the immense emptiness, surpassed anything in Kate's experience. It seemed to her the wind was the sound of the mountain breathing, that the road, having no proper beginning would never arrive at an end, that they would be marooned here forever, caught on a Sisyphean journey.

She had spent her life in comfortable claustrophobia, the sound of horse and harness, the muttering of street vendors and the shouts of laborers filling her ears, a potage of coal smoke and factory fumes, fresh starch and beeswax filling her nostrils. Her eye was attuned to the textures and colors of city life, the regularity of cobblestone and iron rail, the geometry of urban architecture and streets. Here there was no such imposed symmetry. The road dipped and coiled, the mountains bunched and thrust, the sky churned and bloomed.

Kate looked over at MacNeill. His profile looked carved from the same rock as the mountains. His jaw jutted in a bold block, and his deeply carved nostrils flared. Only the gilt-tipped fringe of eyelashes and the glint of red-gold in the hair that brushed his cape's collar held any warmth. He looked every bit a part of this hard, obdurate landscape. Just as tough, just as unyielding, and just as isolated and aloof.

He hadn't said a word since luncheon, and Kate told herself she ought to be happy for his complete indifference. Rather than worrying about what was now too late to remedy, she should be fanning the spark of satisfaction she'd felt upon leaving the White Rose.

Despite all odds, she was going to make it to Castle Parnell. She was going to petition the marquis for aid. The chance of her and her sisters returning to some semblance of their former lives, the chance that had so long eluded them, was finally within reach. Not only would she and Helena and Charlotte survive, but they might actually win freedom from this fear-laden state called poverty. The idea of sitting in a warm, comfortable room sipping well-sugared coffee without having to wonder how they would pay for it brought a smile to her lips.

"You have the look of a cream-sotted tabby, Mrs. Blackburn."

MacNeill's deep burr startled Kate from her reverie. She hadn't thought he'd been paying a speck of attention to her. The realization that he had not only remarked on her expression but had been evidently watching her alarmed her. What thoughts and considerations moved behind MacNeill's enigmatic visage?

"I was thinking of coffee," she said, with forced brightness.

"You must be right fond of coffee then," he said.

As Kate wasn't certain how to take that, she ignored it. Maybe he couldn't help intimidating people. He just looked threatening, the physical embodiment of menace. And she had learned that the best way to eliminate a menace was to make its agent your ally.

MacNeill, her ally? She swallowed, though objectively she knew the idea had merit.

Besides, there was good material for her book to be plumbed here. How often did one get to interview a ruffian? Possibly someone with bona fide connections to the dark underbelly of society? He might prove a veritable font of information on how one might circumnavigate the dangers of the lower economic orders. The opportunity was too good to pass up.

"Ahem."

His gaze remained locked on the road ahead.

"So." She clapped her hands together in the manner of one embarking on a pleasurable conversational voyage. "What have you been doing for the last three years?"

His head turned slowly in her direction. "I beg your pardon?"

"How have you been occupying your time?" *Done anything criminal?* "Where have you been living?" *In a rookery?*

He hesitated, as though trying to gauge the dangers of answering, and oddly, that comforted her. How could she pose any danger to such as him? "In India."

"Ah, yes. Where the gelding came from."

"Aye."

"Were you a spy there, too?"

His gaze snapped, startled, to hers. "No!"

"You needn't look so off-put. When you came to

York, you quite clearly intimated that you had been spying in France when you were caught and imprisoned."

"Not caught," he corrected flatly. "Turned in."

A long moment of silence followed.

"Did you spend the entire three years in India?" Kate finally asked. Her father had told them stories about the deprivations and hardships soldiers faced in India: heat and dust and sickness. "It must have been terribly hard. How did you endure it?"

Her sympathy was lost on MacNeill. He looked, in fact, amused. "My choices were somewhat limited, Mrs. Blackburn. A Rifleman goes where he's sent."

So he was a soldier in the new Rifleman's regiment. Chosen Men, she believed the soldiers who served in that unit were called. Surely he was not an officer. How could he be? A Scottish orphan without name or money would not have the wherewithal to buy a commission.

But if he was only a simple soldier, what was he doing here? A soldier enlisted for life unless wounded. He didn't look injured. He looked in the prime of health.

"What about the others? Did they enlist, too?"

"Others?" His brief glance was quizzical.

"The two young men who came to York with you. Mr. Ross and Mr. Munro. Are they soldiers too?"

The flint returned to his green eyes. "No."

"Where are they?"

"Last I heard Munro is in London, teaching boys to prick each other for sport. Dand . . . I do not know where Mr. Ross is. I'll find out, though." Darkness invested his voice.

"And when you find him?"

"We'll have a conversation," he said. "Talk over old times."

The words themselves were innocuous, but the way he said them made Kate shiver. So much for her momentary ease. Too much about MacNeill made Kate afraid. She hated being afraid. She reacted badly to it. She reacted badly now.

"Do you do that on purpose?" she blurted out.

He frowned without looking at her, his eyes on the road. "Do what?"

"Intimidate people? Because if you do, I think it exceptionally bad form."

His brows flew up. "Bad form?"

"Yes. *Very* bad form. I should think it beneath you to intimidate helpless widows into a state of abject terror."

"Abject terror?"

"Yes! It can hardly be worth your effort. I am far too easy a mark to waste such a talent on, but if it makes you feel somehow superior, then fine, I admit, I am entirely in awe of you."

"In awe?"

"Would you *kindly* stop repeating me?" she asked, her tone edging toward shrillness. "It's most disconcerting!"

"Disconcert—" His expression relaxed, and one corner of his mouth curved up into a grin that scored a dimple deep into his lean cheek. "Forgive me. It's just that I've never had a lady confess to holding me in awe. It's beyond flattering."

She gasped just as the carriage jolted over a rut in the road, pitching her against MacNeill. His arm shot out, his hand clamping down on her hip, big and broad and entirely male, sealing her tightly to his side. Even through the layers of petticoat, gown and cloak, she could feel his heat. "Careful, Mrs. Blackburn. A man can handle only so much . . . 'awe.' "

"Oh!" She jerked back, scooting as far from him as possible. The blackguard!

He laughed. "Ach, lass. Beg pardon. I'm a mannerless brute who never could resist tweaking a few tail feathers—especially when they are being swished right beneath my nose," he said with unexpected charm.

It wasn't the words that disarmed her. It was his smile. For the first time, she saw a hint of boyishness in his countenance and realized that he was, for all his hardness and his history, still a very young man. He seemed so capable and so . . . used.

She must remember not to let a person's manner cloud her perceptions.

Abruptly, she reached beneath the plank seat and from her reticule withdrew a stub of a pencil and sheet of foolscap she kept folded within. Hastily, she jotted down her insights. He watched her without commenting until she finished and tucked the paper back.

"Difficult to write a letter in a carriage," he said in a neutral voice. "I suppose you must miss the company of your mother and sisters." He hesitated, as though making conversation was unnatural and uncomfortable for him.

"My mother died of a fever a few months after you saw us in York."

His brows flashed together. "I didn't know. I am sorry."

Kate nodded, caught off guard by the surge of loss that swept through her, and with it, the familiar sense of panic. There were only her and her sisters now. Her mother had fought her illness valiantly, but in the end it had proved too strong. Her last words to Kate had been "I am sorry."

Weren't they all? Had her father, too, been sorry as he faced his executioner? Had Michael died regretting he'd volunteered for his assignment? She slammed the door shut on the hurtful thought.

"And your sisters?"

She considered telling him a lie that would leave her with some dignity, but then remembered all too vividly her confessions of the preceding night. From their first meeting, MacNeill had known the baldest truths about her. What matter if he knew the extent to which her family's fortunes had fallen?

"Helena has become the companion to an elderly neighbor." She did not elaborate by telling him what a despicable old cat that neighbor was or the manner in which she bullied Helena. Kate herself wouldn't have been able to stand one hour of the old harridan's tyranny, but Helena, cool and poised as an ice sculpture, endured all with utter aplomb and a calm, if sardonic, smile.

"You had a younger sister, too," MacNeill prompted.

"Yes. Charlotte." Kate smiled, thinking about the beautiful, if willful, baby of the family. At least Charlotte had landed on her feet. "She is at school. Come spring she has been invited to spend the season with her good friend Margaret Welton, the Baron and Baroness Welton's only daughter."

"You are impressed."

"I am relieved," Kate said stiffly, reacting more to the disdain in his tone than his words. "She might make a decent match yet."

"She might make a decent match, yet here you are, sitting in an open carriage with a most indecent companion. It hardly seems fair, does it?" His voice grew musing. "How you must resent this."

She did not reply, flustered by him: his size; the leathery masculine scent of him; the breadth of his shoulders; the rough stubble on his chin and cheeks; the easy competence of his hands on the reins. She was entirely too aware of him.

A group of sheep lifted their heads from the steep flanks of a mountainside and watched their passage. She seized on the distraction they offered. "I was beginning to think there was nothing alive out here."

"Those are cheviots," MacNeill said. "Four-legged Highlanders, some call them."

"Why?" Kate asked, startled.

He shrugged. "They're the lairds' newest tenants. Their only tenants. The people have been moved out to make way for them."

"*All* of the people?" Kate asked disbelievingly.

"Most. You ken the White Rose?" The Scottish burr had thickened in his voice. "Time was it was the center of a wee town. Until Lord Ross moved it."

"Moved an entire village? Where?"

MacNeill's eyes stayed fast on the road ahead. "The shore. Some to collect kelp, others to try their hand at fishing. But the Ross men are no fishermen. So they left. Sailed west. To Canada, often as not."

"But . . . why would anyone do such a thing?"

"Well, lass"—his voice dripped irony—"see those great fat sheep staring down at you? Acre for acre they make far less troublesome tenants than a few old men running cattle. They produce more profit, too. And that's the whole and sum of it," he said. "It's happening all over the Highlands. Soon there'll be no Scots in Scotland."

"It isn't right to take everything away from a people."

"Not everything," MacNeill said, with a twisted smile. "You can take a man's land and his horse, ye can outlaw his plaid and his pipes, but you can't steal away the nature of a man, and it's the nature of the Scot to be proud and to be loyal.

"That's why the Highland regiments fight so hard for your king, Mrs. Blackburn. We took an oath, and we'll stay faithful to that oath past death." His gaze became dark and shuttered. "And damned be those who aren't."

He fell silent after that and would say no more.

⬔⬔⬔⬔

# OVERNIGHTING IN LOWER PLACES THAN INNS, TAVERNS, AND HOSTELRIES

DUSK CAME, AND THE TEMPERATURE PLUNGED. Kate had no clothes appropriate for traveling in an open carriage, and her boots had been created in another life for a fashionable young wife to saunter along grassy garden paths, not over frost-rimed rock. She shut her eyes and willed herself into a light sleep, escaping the icy grip of dusk as best she could.

"Here we are."

She came awake at once, lifting her head and peering about from under the hood. "Where? I don't see anything," she said, looking about for the lights that marked a village.

He pulled the horse to a halt and sprang lightly to the ground. In the gloaming, his features were obscured. He came round the side and without hesitation picked her up before she could react, set her down, and turned back to the carriage.

As her eyesight adjusted, she saw that they were standing among a cluster of crude stone shanties, their tiny windows gaping into black interiors and their doors ajar. The buildings had been abandoned.

"What is this place?" she asked.

MacNeill, busy unharnessing his gelding, shrugged. "Never had a name that I heard." He motioned toward the nearest building. "That'll do as good as any. Go in there."

"In there?" She had expected to be overnighting at an inn or a stable, or at the very least, at some farm where they could purchase the use of a bed. It had never occurred to her that she would be alone at night in the middle of nowhere with Kit MacNeill. "Isn't there a tavern or something nearby where we could stay?"

"Not for miles."

"That's all right. I don't mind if it takes a bit longer. It's a lovely night . . ."

His hands stilled on the harness and he turned his head, looking at her over his shoulder. She smiled tentatively.

"There's no moon, and when I say miles, I mean miles, not a matter of another hour or two. The road is rough and going to get rougher before we crawl up onto the moors and I'll not risk Doran's footing to assuage your delicate sensibilities." His tone brooked no argument. "So, Mrs. Blackburn, I suggest you pick your accommodation."

"I see. Well, if it's a matter of safeguarding your horse's health, of course, we must stay," she said with forced brightness and headed into the nearest hovel.

And it was a hovel.

The door was half off the hinges and tilted tipsily on the frame. A tattered rag curtain covered a tiny opening, and the dirt floor within was sloped toward a low flat stone hearth beneath a rude chimney. Other than a bit of broken crockery, it was empty.

What was she supposed to do? There was no furniture. She hovered indecisively near the door, miserable, cold, and frightened.

"Step aside." She jumped at the sound of his voice so close behind her, but he affected not to notice, edging past with an armful of kindling. He dumped the wood on the hearth and reached into his jacket, pulling out a tinder box which he used to light a fire. He stood up. "I'll get your trunk."

"Thank you."

He disappeared, returning within a few minutes with her luggage and the basket from the White Rose. He sat down on the edge of the hearth and fed the fire a few sticks of wood before rummaging into the basket and taking out the jug of ale.

*Dear God, please do not let him get drunk. I don't know what I'll do if he gets drunk.* She edged closer to the door, preparing to bolt. But to where?

He uncorked the jug with his teeth and spat the top onto the hearth, tipping the crock back against his forearm and lifting the opening to his lips. Then he tipped his head back and poured the beer down his throat for, what seemed to Kate, a great long while. Finally he lowered the jug, wiped his mouth against his sleeve, and held it out to her. "Here. It'll warm you better than water, not as much as brandy."

She didn't want the raw ale, but the alternative, to leave it all for him, seemed unwise. Hesitantly, she accepted the jug. His eyes glittered in the dancing firelight. "Do you have a drinking utensil of any type?"

He regarded her flatly. "Aye. It's called a mouth. I suggest you use it."

"I see."

He broke off a chunk of bread, watching her as she tried to emulate his movements, but the jug was heavy, and though she tried, as he had, to brace its weight against the back of her forearm, it slipped as she hefted it, spilling ale down her bodice. "Damn!"

His brow flew up at her language. She didn't care. She was now wet and sticky as well as cold. The road that had seemed endless to her today promised to be eternal tomorrow, she hadn't a proper bed to sleep in, and she was alone with a tall, rough-looking Highlander who, for all she knew, had committed untold atrocities against any number of women. And worse, she was here of her own volition. She was frankly afraid, and Kate Blackburn, ever since she'd been a child, met her fear with anger. Now was no exception.

"*Damn*, I say! How the am I to drink out of this . . . thing?" she demanded. "Why the devil don't you own a cup, or is that somehow contrary to your Highlander's code of self-abnegation? Not everything has to be a trial, you know. A few utensils wouldn't unman you! Or *un-Scot* you, should you be unable to differentiate between the two!"

He unfolded with quick, lethal grace and in a single stride stood before her, looking down into her upturned face. His eyes sparked with hot-cold lights. His smile was not pleasant. Still, somehow she kept her chin up, her gaze challenging his.

"Well now, lass. I can only assure you of my manliness, unless you'd prefer a demonstration?" he purred. She flushed. His gaze slid to her mouth. It took all her restraint not to bite her lips to keep them from trembling. "As to a drinking utensil . . . You can drink from my mouth, if you'd like. Because that's the only other vessel here. And I *promise* I won't find it a trial."

She gasped. Her gaze plummeted from his and scorching heat swept up her throat and covered her face.

"No?" he asked. Abruptly the lambent sensual quality disappeared from his expression. "Then get some sleep, Mrs. Blackburn," he said flatly. "Tomorrow we have some real driving to do, and I don't trust the weather to hold." He turned back toward the hearth, pausing to look at her over his shoulder. "And do not bait a man unless you're willing to pay the price of the sport."

*Yes. She would remember that. To her grave.*

With trembling fingers, she unlatched the trunk, looking for something to don that would provide added warmth. There was nothing. The dresses she'd had remade from her mother's once fashionable gowns were made of silk and muslin, as sheer and delicate as moth wings. She took a deep breath. She supposed he meant for her to sleep on the ground.

"Mrs. Blackburn."

She looked around. MacNeill stood over his plaid, neatly folded at his feet into some semblance of a bedsheet.

"You can sleep here. I am going to see to Doran and find some more wood. If you're wise, you'll eat and go to sleep."

He didn't wait for her answer, but before he stepped out into the night he said, "You have nothing to fear from me, lass." Then added so softly she might have imagined it, "The moon doesn't fear the wolf's howls. Hell. She doesn't even know he's howling."

"Time to rise, Mrs. Blackburn."

Kate rolled over and with great effort kept from moaning. She peeked out of one eye. It was still dark. "We should wait until it's lighter," she muttered. "Your horse's welfare and all . . ."

"It's lighter outside, and there's a storm bearing down on us from the north. I don't want to be on the moors when it overtakes us. We'll start now."

She didn't protest. Late last night she had promised

herself not to give in to any more low impulses. She *was* a lady. She may have momentarily forgotten that, but she wouldn't again. She got up stiffly, noting that the embers had already been doused and her trunk already removed.

He'd let her sleep as long as possible.

"Here," he said, handing her a short cylindrical object. "It's a sort of mountain tea. Drink up, and we'll eat on the road."

She accepted it in surprise, gratefully cupping the warm metal between her cool palms. "But where did you find a vessel?"

"It's the cap off the telescope in your trunk. I saw it when I shut the lid." He'd actually given credence to her snappish demands? She stared at him, mystified by such unexpected gallantry.

"I wasn't going through your things, if that's what you're thinking," he said wryly. "As a Scot, I'd consider it unmanly."

"Of course not." She flushed and was amazed by the smile that flickered across his face. She drank the bitter, hot liquid, uncertain whether he was teasing or not.

She followed him outside, tucking the empty brass cap in her pocket and climbing into the carriage without waiting for his aid. She would prove to him that she wasn't a complete fribble of femininity.

If he was impressed, he didn't show it. He made some adjustments to Doran's harness and sprang into the seat beside her, picking up the reins and snapping them sharply across the gelding's rump.

They did not eat either soon or later. Within a few miles of the abandoned village they forded a fast-moving stream. The carriage's rear wheel caught on a rock hidden in the bottom, and the entire vehicle rose against the current, tilting sharply and threatening to spill them into the icy water. MacNeill grabbed her around the waist and pitched them both toward the rising side, shouting at Doran, who strained forward against the current and finally pulled the carriage clear.

They dropped with a splash that sent their basket of food tumbling into the water, upending as it spun into the current. Only the fact that MacNeill's saddle and her trunk had been strapped to the back had saved them from a similar fate. Not that that proved much comfort hours later as Kate sat huddled on the hard plank seat, her raw chin burrowed in the folds of the cape, her arms wrapped tightly beneath, her stomach growling insistently.

Near noon, they crested a low hill that marked the entrance to the high, desolate landscape of the moors. The wind howled down upon them like a beast that had been lying in wait. The phaeton shook and rocked with every blast of wind, snatching the breath from Kate's lungs. Icy fingers stabbed through her cloak, and the air frosted in her nostril. She clenched her teeth together to keep them from chattering.

She could not remember ever being so cold.

She squinted through the buffeting winds. Dull mustard-colored gorse and dank green bracken shifted and whirled, undulating across the endless horizon. A thin, ox-blood colored line of clouds separated the earth from a gunmetal gray sky. The storm that had assailed them two nights ago had regrouped for another attack.

The thought of being out here when it broke sent Kate's spirits plummeting. She didn't say anything to MacNeill, though. What was there to say? There was nothing to do but drive until they reached the other side of this emptiness. Complaints would be useless, or worse, received with scorn. *He* seemed impervious to the cold, as if the elements had long ago ceased to affect him.

She needed only to endure. And at that, she'd had nearly three years of practice.

# SIX

## ⬦⬦⬦

# FASHION OR HEALTH?
# A CHOICE IMPOSED BY
# ECONOMIC NECESSITY

KATE SLUMPED AGAINST KIT and didn't jerk away. That alone told him something was wrong. The girl—for all her widowhood implied, there was something heart-achingly young about her—was nothing if not proper.

He pulled Doran to a halt, and she drooped forward and would have pitched to the floor if he hadn't caught her. He pulled her onto his lap, looking down at her face. Her eyelids were as white as alabaster, tinged with blue, and her lips were colorless. She'd fainted.

"Mrs. Blackburn!"

He shook her gently, and her eyelids fluttered open. "Have we made it across? Is it over?"

"Not yet." Damn. They still had hours to go before making it out of the moors. He scanned the horizon, looking for a familiar landmark. A thin, freezing rain had begun to fall, driven sideways by a blasting wind. The tattered hood was no protection. He was her only protection. He gathered her nearer, looking about. There had to be something that would offer shelter: A croft, even an outcropping of stone, *any* place—

He saw it then, some distance away, like a ghost ship adrift in an uncharted sea of mist. His heart thundered in recognition. He hadn't realized they were so close to the castle.

He snapped the reins over Doran's back, pulling the carriage around and heading south. It looked to be about a mile away.

A mile, give or take a lifetime.


*"Whose is it, do you think?"* Dand asked, his dark eyes narrowed thoughtfully on the hulking ruin.

*"Was,"* Ramsey said, shrugging in disdain. *"Whose ever it was, it belongs to the moor now."*

*"I heard Father Abbot say it belonged to one of the lairds that fought in the Forty-five,"* Douglas said. *"A great warrior chief."*

*"A greater fool if he fought against the throne at Culloden Moor,"* Ramsey said.

*"All great warriors are fools,"* Dand answered.

The Castle. Kit had never heard it referred to by any other name. None of them had. Its ragged outline rose starkly against the sky like an artist's rendition of a witch's tower. Most castles sat atop rocky plateaus or cliffs; some squatted in thick forest or at the branching of a river. For whatever reason, hubris or folly, the builder of this castle had decided to make the moors the castle's guardian.

Kit pulled Doran to a halt before the huge gap that had once held massive doors, conscious only of Kate's light, chill body in his arm and the need to warm her. He lifted her carefully and climbed the stairs into the castle. He carried her down the long empty corridor, heedless of the wind muttering in the exposed rafters, his boot heels muffled by the rotting leaves of more than fifty autumns that carpeted the cracked and heaving floor.

"Where are we?" Kate murmured. Her eyes were still closed, but a frown marked twin lines between her brows.

"Rest."

At the end of the hall, he descended a short flight of stairs, emerging into a subterranean kitchen where, high in an exterior corner, a smoke hole allowed in the afternoon's pallid light. The chimneys in the other rooms had long since been clogged with debris. This would be the only place a fire could burn safely.

He knelt and eased Kate down, spread his plaid on the floor, and shifted her atop it before tucking the wool blanket about her. He straightened. "I'll build a fire."

Her eyes flickered open. "Thank you."

She would probably have thanked the devil for opening the gates of hell for her. *Aristocrats. Such bloody good manners.* Except for last night when fear had unleashed an unexpected and impressive temper from her.

He searched the room for something with which to make a fire and gathered up what bits he could find.

"What is this place?" he heard Kate ask.

"An old rubble pile. Once was a castle."

"How did you know it was here?"

"I came here when I was a boy. We used to sneak out of the dormitory and spend the night and be back by matins."

"Matins? You were at a *monastery?*"

"An abbey. St. Bride's."

"You trained to be a *monk?*" Even weak as her voice was, he could hear her amazement.

"No."

"Oh." She suddenly pushed herself up on her elbows. "If you could come here as a boy, this abbey must be nearby then," she said.

He struck a spark into a pile of shavings. "Two hours as the crow flies, but Doran is no crow. It would take us five hours or more following the roads, and the storm has come in full now. We can't go until the weather breaks."

"Oh."

He blew on the little ember, and the kindling burst into flame. Quickly, he fed the fire until he had a proper blaze going, then he returned to where Kate lay. Her eyes had fallen shut while he'd tended the fire, and thinking she'd fallen asleep, he reached down to take the damp cloak from around her.

As soon as he touched her, her eyes snapped open and she bolted upright, scuttling backward on her heels as her hands clutched the cloak.

"I assure you, I am not going to ravage you." He sat back on his heels. "Not only is it unmanly, and thus un-Scotslike, it's too bloody cold."

That won an unwilling smile from her.

She wouldn't have looked so comforted had she known it for the lie it was. She had no idea how appealing she looked, lying on his pooled plaid, her hair a witchy tumble about her face, her eyes dark and apprehensive. He was the worst sort of dog, panting after a woman who could barely hold her head up. But he did.

"Your cloak is wet," he said gruffly, holding out his hand. "Take it off, and I'll hang it near the fire."

Her gaze fixed on his face, she untied the laces at her throat. The cape slipped from her shoulder. When he saw her dress, he swore under his breath. She had on the same thin cotton gown she'd worn yesterday. No wonder she was freezing.

Without waiting for her permission he pulled off his jacket and wrapped it around her. She didn't protest, and that sent unfamiliar ripples of alarm racing through him. How could he have failed to notice she wasn't dressed for such a journey as they'd undertaken?

Easily. He'd assumed she would be well insulated because she was traveling in Scotland in November. He hadn't considered that, never having traveled in Scotland in November, she would not know what was required. But being a lady, she had dressed to travel in the style in which a lady travels.

"Why would anyone risk her health for fashion's sake, when—"

"I hate to contradict you, MacNeill!" Kate interrupted with a faint but triumphant smile. "But my gown isn't a fashionable choice; It's my *only* choice."

"Don't smile at me," he said roughly. "Do you not understand? I may have *killed* you with my ignorance!"

Her eyes rounded in surprise and then softened, dealing a far more telling blow to him than her scorn or accusation ever could have done. "Well, if this is the afterlife, MacNeill, there's a priest in York who has a fair bit of explaining to do. Don't look like that. I just need to warm up a bit and—" She broke off, coloring so that Kit knew she had been about to request something to eat. There was nothing. Not yet.

He straightened. "I'm going to see to Doran and then have a look about. There used to be rabbits aplenty on the moors." He didn't tell her that the rabbits, being far more sensible than their two-legged counterparts, burrowed deep during storms. But he would do everything in his power to find some food.

"Oh."

"You'll be fine here."

"I know."

"The hearth is deep enough that no sparks will fly out, and I'll be back before the embers die. You rest."

"Of course.

If he stayed longer, he wouldn't leave, and she

needed food, fresh water at the least. He looked down at her. She'd shut her eyes and was already mostly asleep. She would be fine here. No one came to the castle. No one ever had.

He found Doran where he'd left him, fidgeting nervously in his traces as the wind buffeted the carriage from side to side. He unhitched and hobbled him, leading him to the ruined side of the castle where a creek overflowed its banks, and let him go.

Then, after loading and priming his rifle, he headed out into the storm.

Kate slept in fits and starts, awakening with her limbs shaking so hard her teeth chattered. She couldn't seem to get warm, no matter how close she snuggled to the fire, even though its heat pricked her cheeks and scorched her knuckles as she gripped the blanket to her chin. It seemed forever before she heard MacNeill's voice.

"Kate. Drink this." He slipped his arm beneath her shoulders and lifted her, patiently trickling the water into her mouth. He was wet. Not damp but soaked through. And cold. So cold. The water wicked into her dress, setting her to violent trembling.

"I'm so cold," she mumbled plaintively.

He eased her to the ground, and she curled on her side, trying to stop the quaking, watching him through slit eyes. He stood up, dropped the sodden cape to the ground, and with a quick, easy movement stripped his shirt over his head. Backlit against the guttering light, his lean body gleamed strong and sleekly muscled, broad and flat-bellied. The firelight prowled over his broad shoulders and curled around his throat but could not reach his features, leaving them in dusky shadow.

He knelt and gathered her against his naked chest. Already the heat of his blood had reached his skin, and now it sank into her, delicious and warm and life-giving. She should be mortified. She should be trying to free herself. Instead, she burrowed as close as she could physically get, wrapping her arms around his flanks and pushing her cheek into the dense muscle of his chest. She relaxed, absorbing his heat, accepting his body as her bed.

And slept.

Kit sank down with his back against the wall, his leg stretched out before him, Kate on his lap. Hesitantly, he stroked the hair back from her face. It curled around his fingers, silky and soft as kitten's fur, black as oiled satin. He tipped his head back and stared unseeingly at the ceiling.

She slept on, perfectly relaxed, exquisitely vulnerable, sublimely undone. Deep within him, hunger awoke and prowled. Her soft contours melted against him, conforming to his hard angles like warm wax while, with a sigh of lush abandonment, she nestled her head beneath his chin. Her hand strayed up his chest, her fingers lax. Her breath sluiced across his skin, as gentle as the childhood dreams he'd never had, as sweet as summers he couldn't remember.

He looked down. Her lips parted, her lashes trembled against the crest of her cheekbone as she dreamed. She was elegant and refined, even in sleep. What would the likes of him do with a creature like this? A creature whose main interest lay in finding someone to put her and her sisters back in paisley shawls?

Even three years ago he'd realized that the brief exchange they'd shared had been an accident. He shouldn't have remained in the drawing room; he should have gone with the others. She shouldn't have stayed with him. She had spoken to him as an equal, and he wasn't. In any other place, at any other time, it wouldn't have happened.

He'd left the Nashes' York townhouse and headed for the docks, intent on getting drunk. He'd managed that, right enough, and woken to discover he'd been conscripted into the army and was aboard a transport ship heading for India. Now, if there was one thing a foot soldier in His Majesty's army has, it is time to think.

He'd thought about two things, the first being Kate. There was no harm in it. The harm came in not knowing a fancy from reality. His burned skin and blistered lungs were real; the open sores that covered his feet beneath the ill-fitting boots were real; the salty rivulets that pasted his uniform to his back were real; the blood of the men who died was real. Aye. He knew reality, well enough. Kate Blackburn was a harmless diversion from it.

So he didn't begrudge himself the pleasure of

thinking of her; the midnight color of her eyes and the shimmer of the sun in her sable hair, her white skin and narrow-boned wrists and soft, plush mouth. She was just a place to flee when reality got a bit overpowering, was all. He never thought to see her again. He'd read the pride in her easily enough during those short minutes in the drawing room. She'd never send a yellow rose to St. Bride's.

But there were times when the death and cries of the wounded, the memories of battle, were so vivid that he could not conjure her image. Then he thought of betrayal. Then he thought of the man who had murdered Douglas Stewart as surely as if he'd dropped the guillotine blade himself.

While Kit pondered the identity of the traitor, the army marched. The war with France spilled over into wars with Indian potentates and Russians and Spaniards. Before he was finished, Kit had seen dozens of skirmishes and battles. It really only needed a matter of time and a bit of luck before his "talents" were noted. What with officers falling in battle like wheat before the scythe, his skills were rewarded on bloodsoaked ground with a battlefield commission. Not once, but thrice.

He was, he realized, a good commander. His men trusted him, depended on his judgment. But each time he was promoted, each time more men's lives were entrusted to him, the betrayal in the past loomed greater and greater. How could he trust his judgment when it had been so blinding, so disastrously defective? It became an obsession with him. He had to discover the identity of his betrayer and confront him, and in doing so discover and confront his own failings. He had requested and been granted a leave from the army.

But Fate mocks intention.

Kate stirred suddenly, and he stilled when she lifted her head and peered drowsily around, rubbing the silk crown of her head against his jaw, still more asleep than awake. He stopped breathing altogether until her head dropped heavily to his chest once more, her lips against the base of his throat.

And he thanked God that he knew what was real and what wasn't.

# SEVEN

※※※※

# UPON AWAKING
# IN UNFAMILIAR
# SURROUNDINGS

"So PRETTY, KIT. I ALMOST ENVY YOU." The voice was no more than a murmur. Something cool and dry caressed the side of Kate's neck, fluttered across her collarbone, and drifted lower . . . She shifted, rolling away from the familiarity, groggy with fever and exhaustion.

"But why envy you when I can take whatever I want of yours?" His breathing was light, too, excited. "Including your life."

The phantom fingers hooked beneath the edge of her bodice, pulling it lower. She flinched against the unwelcome intimacy, struggling to wake. The phantom hand caressed her breast languidly. Something moved close to her face.

"Tell Kit to enjoy the roses." A mouth touched hers—She gasped, bolting upright.

In the corner of the black room something shifted,

a darker blot dissolving into the corner. A sound like a soft laugh—or was it the wind in the smoke hole?—trembled across the air.

She struggled to her feet, light-headed and disoriented. She shivered, looking about. There were still a few embers in the hearth. They hadn't been there when she'd woken. Unless someone had been standing between her and the fire.

Fear jerked her into full wakefulness. She turned, stumbling over MacNeill's regimental jacket. *Where was MacNeill?*

She spied a short flight of stairs and staggered up them on wobbly legs. "MacNeill!" she croaked. Her throat rasped painfully, and the effort made her dizzy. "MacNeill!"

No answer. She started down a long, dim corridor, a shaft of moonlight piercing its length. She limped forward, passing room after empty room. All dark. All silent. Like tombs awaiting their tenants.

Finally, she emerged into a huge entry filled with dim gray light. She looked up. Three stories overhead a huge gaping wound in the roof revealed a dark, bruised sky. Clouds drifted across the face of a half-gone moon, and a cold, bitter wind spiraled down from above, stirring the leaves at her feet and tossing her hair about her face.

"MacNeill!" The wind caught her feeble cry and carried it away.

No one answered.

Her worst fear taunted her with pricks of panic: He'd left her. Abandoned her.

*Not again. Please.* She blinked back tears, refusing to cry even though her thoughts kept unraveling like mist in the wind and her legs felt like jelly, and the cold was sucking the last bit of heat from her and . . . and she saw a faint flicker of light.

He *hadn't* left her.

With a sob, she hobbled toward the lighted room, dizzy and disoriented, her heart pattering like a snared rabbit's. MacNeill stood inside, his back to her, the burning brand he held lashing the room's dark walls.

"MacNeill—" Her greeting died in her throat as she took in the scene. A massive oak table lay on its side, its surface scarred with deep cuts, as if an ax had been taken to it. What might have once been benches or chairs lay in splinters. Glass shards covered the floor like a jeweled carpet, and dinted pewter trays and cups lay twisted at the base of scarred and notched plaster walls.

"What happened in here?" she asked.

"It looks," MacNeill said calmly, "as though someone was unhappy." He raised the brand he carried and illuminated the walls higher up.

Kate recoiled. Three feet above them a dagger pinned the carcass of a rat to the wall. Twined around the desiccated creature's neck was a quartet of flowers, dried and shriveled, but still identifiable as roses. Small yellow roses. She put a hand behind her, groping for the wall.

MacNeill lowered his torch and the gruesome little

corpse disappeared. His gaze swept over the room, noting, discarding, missing nothing, searching.

"Who did that?" she whispered "Was it him?"

He turned his head, regarding her intently. "Who?"

"There was a man in the kitchen when I woke. He said . . . your name and then he said he could take anything of yours he wanted, including your life. Then—"

He swung around. "Then what?"

"He touched me."

"The hell he did!" He strode toward her, a suddenly furious and formidable looking Celtic warrior. He grasped her upper arms, staring down into her face. "Are you hurt? Did he violate you?"

For a second she didn't take his meaning. Of course she'd been violated. Then she understood. Her face burned. "No. No. He just touched me . . ." Her hand fluttered to her loosened bodice.

MacNeill growled savagely, releasing her and looking about.

"And said to tell you to enjoy the roses."

"What?"

"He said, 'Tell Kit to enjoy the roses.' "

Once more he swore. He reached out, gripping her shoulder and spinning her around, setting her world tilting.

"How dare you!" she protested, batting feebly at his arm, but his grip was like steel and he heeded her objections not at all. "You can't—"

"I can."

She set her heels, in her exhaustion and fear stumbling, and would have fallen to her knees but he was already sweeping her up against his broad chest, carrying her easily as he left the room and moved into the corridor, still managing to hold the torch.

"You must tell me," she said. "You promised. You swore! What is going on?"

"Then by all means, be it as you wish, ma'am." His laugh was bitter and short. "You saw the rat with the flower necklet?"

"Yes." She searched through the haze clouding her thoughts for— "They're the same roses you brought us in York."

"Yes. The person who skewered that rat did not do so by way of a love token," Kit went on grimly. "I don't know who he is or what he wants, but I will warrant well I do not want you here when I find out."

He stopped in the center of the hall, his eyes fiery and intent. Conflict marked his hard face. "Damnation," he muttered. "Damn it to a bloody hell."

"He knows," he finally said. "He knows I can't take the time to look for him. He's taunting me. There are a thousand places for him to hide and I don't have the time. Not with you here. Not with you so weak and . . . *Bloody, bloody hell!*"

Frightened by the violence of his words and in his face, Kate shrank in his embrace and at once the fire in his eyes died away, the coolness returned to his expression. "It is time for us to leave. But first—hold this."

He handed her the torch, and she took it. He strode to the far end of the narrow passage, her body rigid in his arms. He shouldered open a heavy oak door and peered down a steep flight of stairs into blackness.

"Beg pardon," he said and with a slight grimace against her anticipated outrage, took the torch from her and tossed her over his shoulder, freeing his hands. She didn't disappoint.

"You can't— Ah!" Holding the burning brand aloft, he started downstairs, each of her remonstrations checked by the jolt of his step on a tread.

The cellar hadn't changed. Cobwebs still hung in thick sheets from the low, damp stone arches, and the sound of scurrying things still echoed eerily in the darkness. The smell of mold and dampness still thickened the chill air.

He set Kate's feet on the ground, then leaned her against the wall, handing her back the torch. "Hold this and wait here."

She took the torch without a word, blinking rapidly as though trying to focus her gaze. She was ill—whether from lack of food, cold, sleeplessness, he could not say. He only knew he had to get her to St. Bride's as soon as humanly possible. Nothing else mattered. Not even *him*, damn his soul, though the need to find him, to punish him for touching her, raged within Kit like a living thing.

He turned back into the moldering cellar and, at the far wall, stopped and ran his hands across the pitted surface until he felt the raised edge of a masonry block. With a grunt, he pulled it free and thrust his hand into the revealed crevasse. From deep within, he withdrew a leather-wrapped parcel. He unwrapped it, exposing a long, heavy-looking blade.

*"What are you doing, Kit?"*

*"Setting stores, Dand. You can't be too sure when you'll need a weapon."*

*Dand laughed. "But here? Why? Ye fear the cattle might take up arms agin ye someday?"*

"What is it?" Kate's weak voice recalled him to the present.

"A claymore," he said, lifting the cumbersome-looking thing as though it were its lighter cousin and eyeing its blunted edge with the eye of a connoisseur.

*"Why do you insist on using that bludgeon, Kit, when you could use something with a bit of finesse?" Ramsey asked.*

*"Because a bludgeon gets yer point across a sight better than a hint."*

He lifted a leather scabbard from the same roll and strapped it on his back between his shoulder blades. With a hiss of steel, he slid the heavy blade into its sheath. "Now we leave."

The intensity in his voice marshaled Kate's scattered thoughts. She nodded, and this time when he scooped her up, she clung to him. Back in the kitchen, he gathered their belongings and took her outside. He left her next to an exterior wall, telling her to wait while he caught and harnessed Doran.

A faint thinning of darkness marked the eastern horizon. She stayed where he bade her, unpleasantly woozy, and felt the castle behind her, its oppressive weight and terrible patience. Uneasily, she turned and looked up and so for the first time saw the castle from without, its massive dimensions, the shorn roofline exposing the charred half walls of second-story rooms, the entire facade pockmarked with shadowed recesses and black, empty windows. High above, marsh grasses had seeded themselves amid the crumbling crenulations. The coarse stalks shifted in the wind, pale in the gloaming, like the spectral arms of little children beckoning to her to climb up to them, and behind that a dark figure—

"KATE!"

Startled, she wheeled. Too late, she heard the ominous rumble from above and then he was sweeping her up, driving her hard against the castle, his arms above their heads, pinning her to the wall as the sky rained rock down on them. She clung to him, her face pressed against the base of his throat, and felt his big body jar as pieces struck him. Not a shard touched her.

As abruptly as it had started, it ended. He pushed her away, holding her at arm's length. "Are you hurt?"

"No."

He released his breath, his eyes rising to the treacherous roofline above.

"Did you see something? Someone?"

"I don't know. I thought . . ." She shook her head. "I don't know."

He dipped down and caught her behind the knees, taking her to the carriage and depositing her as the gelding pawed the ground. He climbed in after her.

"Where are we going?" she asked.

"To where it all began," he said. "To St. Bride's."

# EIGHT

⬦⬦⬦⬦

# FORGETTING THE PAST: A USEFUL THOUGH OFTEN FUTILE ENDEAVOR

KIT TOUCHED THE WHIP lightly to Doran's flanks, and the gelding extended his trot. He could feel the enmity following their flight. But no one could see them with the carriage hood raised. Even more important, they were not targets, though without conceit, he knew himself to be the only one capable of making such a shot.

"Are we safe?" Kate asked breathlessly.

"Aye."

"But what if he follows? What if he's waiting ahead of us?"

"Look around, Mrs. Blackburn. There's no place to hide for miles. Besides, if he'd wanted to kill us, he could have done so while we slept."

"Oh," she murmured faintly, tipping slowly against him. He looked down at her and was once more struck by the pallor of her face and the dark smudges beneath her eyes and cheekbones.

"My God," he said. "You look terrible."

She struggled upright. Her chin trembled, then firmed into the imperious angle that was becoming so familiar. "*You,*" she declared, "are a boor."

"I only meant that—"

"I know exactly what you meant," she said. "Earlier you told me I am dirty—"

"What?" He reached out, disliking the way she was canting forward, and grasped her arm, but she yanked free of his grip. "I never—"

"Yes, you did. You *implied* it! At that inn! And now you tell me I look terrible. Are there any other overly familiar comments you'd like to make?"

"Jesus! You look ill, and I don't have a bleeding clue what you mean about implying you're dirty, but in point of fact, you are dirty."

God help him, she sniffled.

He stared at her in horror. He had never been this close to a crying woman. Her breath broke on a full-fledged sob.

"I'm dirty, too!" he said frantically. "We've been traveling. You've been sleeping on the floor. You look . . . you look . . ." God, he couldn't believe he was driving through a freezing moor, in possible danger, trying to frame a compliment! And that she was making him do so! What the hell had happened to him? "I cannot believe this."

"What?" she sniffed.

"That you are offended that a man you can have no possible interest in might not find you attractive. Is there anything but vanity to you well-bred ladies? Well, for whatever it's worth, *I do find you attractive. But you still look like hell.*"

Her face crumpled "I *feel* like hell!" She promptly buried her face in her hands.

"Kate."

"No!" She gave herself a little shake and dashed the tears from her cheeks with the backs of her hands. "I promised myself I would act like a lady. I would endure with equanimity whatever this trip entailed. *Or* who-ever. So I will. But"—she fixed him with a dark glare— "I want some answers. Who was that man?"

He did not want to have this conversation.

"You *have* to tell me. He . . . took liberties."

"Don't you think I am fully aware of that?" he grated out. "That I do not feel that outrage in my very bones? I assure you, madam, I do. I also assure you, he will pay dearly for that insult."

"Your indignation isn't any balm. I want the truth. I deserve to know."

Her gaze scoured his face, seeking answers. Fear stamped her features, but she did not give in to it. "MacNeill."

His gaze had returned to the road. His hands on

the reins had tightened, the worn leather gloves stretching taut across the knuckles.

"There were four of us," he began.

"The men who came with you to York and the one who died in prison?" she prompted.

"Yes."

"How did you know one another?"

"We were orphans, collected like bits of wool from Highland thornbushes, gathered from the cities and the villages and brought to St. Bride's, the last of the Catholic clans."

"Who collected you?"

MacNeill shrugged. "The abbot. His monks."

"And how did they find you? How did they know where you were? Why you in particular?"

"God, you are full of questions." When he saw that she was not to be deterred, he sighed. "A letter, a rumor, a bit of gossip from an old drover, or the whispered word of a clandestine follower would be enough to send them harrying off to find us."

"To what end?"

"I'm not certain. I can only guess." He frowned. "When we were boys, they let us believe we were destined to be knights of the old order. We believed them. We even made up a vow of fidelity." He smiled bitterly. "Later, even after we realized we wouldn't be given any silver chargers, we still kept faith to that vow. Only the pledge of fidelity we made wasn't to St. Bride's, it was to one another."

"That's the vow you pledged me," she said with slow-dawning certainty.

"Yes."

"But what has this to do with that ruined castle or the man hiding inside?"

"Someone broke that vow. And I believe it might be the man you saw."

"I don't understand."

His brow furrowed in frustration and annoyance. "We weren't being groomed to be knights, we were being groomed to be . . . warriors, I suppose. Our actions directed by and sanctioned by the church."

"Like the Knights Templar?"

"Nothing so formalized. We were tools to be used in times of great upheaval and danger. Such as occurred in France during '93. That September, in Paris alone, four hundred priests and over a thousand Catholic nobility were massacred.

"Some priests fled to England, one to St. Bride's. Brother Toussaint. He had been a great soldier before seeking holy orders. He taught us his skills.

"Then, one day, a man came to the abbey. A Frenchman. I don't know his real name—he called himself Duchesne, and he had obviously known Brother Toussaint in Paris. I suspect now that he was of French royal blood. At that time the royalists and the church had similar interests, that being to return the French monarchy to the throne and thus the Catholic Church to France.

"He had a plan. We were to go to France, posing as

adventurers who traveled the world looking for unknown species of plants and animals, but most particularly roses. And as rose hunters we were to have come to present Josephine Bonaparte our discoveries."

"Roses?" She must have sounded incredulous, for a touch of wry amusement crossed his face.

"Napoleon Bonaparte's wife has accumulated the largest collection of roses in the world at her home, Malmaison. She is obsessed with roses, and Napoleon, as a fond husband, indulges her.

"Her gardens are legendary, and she has sent envoys across the world to find her new varieties. Diplomats, sycophants, ambassadors from any number of countries and principalities, are constantly arriving at her door with their offerings. You can well imagine what a fertile ground for intelligence gathering such a place must be. Certainly the possibilities have not been lost on the king's advisers—or the Holy See's."

Kate waited. He had lost himself in the story, no longer simply providing her with information, but putting a perspective on his past.

"There was a man in her employ willing to relay information about Napoleon's associates, his schedule, even his correspondence. We were to meet with him. But before we could—indeed, before we even knew his name—we were caught, accused of spying, and imprisoned."

"And you believe that one of your companions, or this French priest, revealed your intentions?"

"Yes."

"Why?"

"Because the day they led Douglas to the guillotine, the warden told us that he knew everything: all the contacts we had made, the priests we met with, the name of the French ship captain who brought us across, even the tavern owner in whose place we sheltered. And all those people were dead. Betrayed. He took especial delight in telling us we had not only been betrayed, but we had been betrayed from within."

"How can you be sure he was telling you the truth?" Kate asked. "He may have been trying to torture you with suspicion. Trick you into revealing more information."

MacNeill shook his head. "There was no more information. He knew everything. Including the oath, which was known to only five men: Douglas, Ram, Dand, myself, and Brother Toussaint, in whom we confided."

"It makes no sense. All of you were in that dungeon. All of you suffered."

"Did we?" Kit's gaze met hers. "We were taken away separately when we were interrogated. It's common practice to separate a man from his fellows, especially when you hope to get information from him. Yes, we all suffered. But did we all suffer to the same extent?"

"But why betray you?" Kate asked, shaking her head. "No one was released. No one gained anything."

"Because the price for his betrayal was to trade his

life for ours. He was supposed to have been the sole survivor, don't you see? The sole wealthy survivor, I presume." A nasty smile played over Kit's mouth. "Whoever betrayed us could not live with the thought of his treachery being revealed, even to those he'd betrayed. His ego, his guilt, was too overwhelming. His rewards were to have come *after* our deaths.

"Douglas was only the first. The rest of us would have followed shortly, but your father arrived and ruined the plan."

"But why kill Douglas and not the rest of you at once?"

"I can only think the warden wanted to make sure of his informant. Wanted him to see what would happen if he thought to betray France as well as his companions."

"You came to my family as a group. If you thought that one of the survivors was the traitor, why did you travel with them? Why didn't you confront the others?"

"I did!" he grated out. "*We* did. But two of us are blameless. Perhaps all of us. Perhaps Brother Toussaint was at that French prison and revealed the information, though I cannot imagine how . . ." He shook his head. "Suffice to say, accusations were made, and every accusation was met with a denial. Ram and Dand both accused me. I accused both in turn."

"How terrible."

He ignored her sympathy. "After we made our vow

to your family, we, who had been closer than brothers, could not stand to look at one another. We separated, expecting never to meet again. Only . . ."

"Only . . . ?"

"Only I could not leave it there. For three years it has preyed on me. How can I trust myself if I cannot trust my past? How can I trust my judgment, my emotions, and the loyalties upon which I founded my entire life when it might be a lie? I *have* to know."

He looked away from her. "And now I have added impetus."

"Then . . . why didn't you stay?" she asked, confused. The answers to his questions had seemingly been within his grasp, and he had opted to leave them behind. "Why didn't you look for whoever was in the castle?"

"Because I promised I would see you safely to your destination. And you are ill, and I can't take any chance with your health by delaying a minute longer than necessary." He flicked the reins across Doran's rump as though reminded of the need for haste.

"There. I have answered your questions. Your right to know has been appeased." He sounded unfriendly. His gaze stayed away from her. "Now rest. We'll be at St. Bride's by nightfall."

# NINE

✖✖✖✖

# MAKING NEW FRIENDS

"WHAT IS THAT?" Kate whispered without lifting her head from Kit's shoulder. She'd awoken a few minutes ago to find herself looking up into a pair of small dark eyes, fleshy pink cheeks, and a mouth rounded in an *O* of silent amazement.

"Not *what*," Kit replied easily. "Who. That is Brother Fidelis."

The round, brown-robed man inspecting her near-sightedly edged a little closer. "Merciful heaven, Christian, what is it?"

"Not *what*," Kit repeated with what sounded suspiciously like amusement, "who. This is Mrs. Katherine Blackburn."

"A woman!" several male voices gasped as though they had been awaiting confirmation of a terrible suspicion.

Kate roused herself from her comfortable position nestled against Kit and looked beyond Brother Fidelis to a small group of similarly clad men milling about a short distance away, their faces variously inquisitive and anxious but all, to some degree, shocked.

She supposed she could understand why. Here she was, dressed in Kit's oversize shirt and wrapped in his plaid, sprawled in the most abandoned manner against him. She struggled to right herself and—oh! Without any forewarning, the world spun in big circles and pitched her facefirst back into Kit's arms.

She'd forgotten how lightheaded she'd been—still was. Though she seemed to be thinking more clearly, and she didn't feel as cold anymore. Indeed, she felt quite relaxed, and for the first time since she had begun the journey, she realized she wasn't afraid. She had ceased to be afraid sometime during the story she had forced MacNeill to relate. She had begun to understand the tenor of the man sworn to protect her. Kit MacNeill was not some terrible, cold machine of destruction. In many ways, he was . . . not unlike her.

The realization was startling. Confusing. In fact, disturbing.

Just when she was finally beginning to feel comfortable. She released a deep sigh.

"What is she saying?"

"What have you done?"

"Oh, Christian, you haven't—"

"The poor creature—"

"I haven't *done* anything!" Kit said forcefully. "But thank you for the touching demonstration of confidence in my morals." He swept her neatly into his lap. The movement tipped her world into lazy revolutions. She squeezed her eyes shut and willed it to a standstill. The world did not obey.

"Now, Christian, we never thought *that*."

"Oh, not *that*. Just *that*," Kit said sarcastically, gathering her closer as he swung his legs over the side of the carriage.

"Would one of you mind the horse's head?" Kit leapt to the ground, jolting her. Pinpricks of light sprinkled across her closed lids.

"Oh!"

"Christian, what are you doing with that woman?" A new voice, ripe with authority and filled with suspicion, broke through the masculine garble.

"Holding her." Kit didn't sound overly impressed. "And I intend to keep doing so."

For a scant second, Kate considered opening her eyes and explaining the situation to the men surrounding them, but she didn't really feel up to making explanations, and she really didn't want the world to spin into another orbit, and it was rather nice having someone else cope with matters. Altogether, she was much more comfortable this way. So she kept her eyes closed and her body lax and wondered why she hadn't ever before recognized the advantages of pretending to faint?

"I see that," the authoritative voice said. "What I meant is, why have you brought this woman here? We are a monastic order, Christian. Women are not allowed."

"This one is," Kit replied and began to move forward. "She's unwell."

"What is wrong with her?" Brother Fidelis asked, compassion replacing his earlier suspicion.

"Mostly she's half frozen, but from the feel of her, I'd say a bit starved, too." He accented his point by jouncing her lightly in his arms. Her world reeled. "Where should I take her?"

"Christian." MacNeill stopped. Kate could feel tension tighten his arms and chest.

"Father Abbot." The respectful address coming from MacNeill sounded grudging, "I have not brought this young lady here to rob her or compromise her. Nor have I, in spite of the entertainment it would doubtless provide, brought her here that she might peel off her clothes and run amuck through the cloisters.

"I have brought her here because I had no other choice. Just as you, as a good Christian and a Benedictine priest, have no choice but to take her in. After all, *Shepherd*"—his deep voice dripped honeyed sarcasm—"she is one very lost, very cold little lamb."

She counted five steady heartbeats in the hush following Kit's challenge, for even in her present state she recognized it as that.

Then the abbot said, "Sarcasm does not become a man of your education and—"

"—and breeding?" The question was lightly asked, but something beneath the surface rang hard.

"I was going to say *merit*, Christian," the abbot answered calmly. "As for this young lady, she may stay until she is well enough to travel. And she *will* be well enough to travel very, very soon. I depend on it,

Brother Martin," he finished sternly, and somewhere someone grumbled.

"You may take her to the . . ."—the abbot hesitated—"to the greenhouse. There's a small shed in the back. I believe there is also a cot.

"After you have seen this young woman settled, you will do me the favor of coming to my quarters, Christian." It was not a request.

"You may depend on it, sir." It was not a concession.

Without waiting for further instruction, Kit strode away from the cluster of whispering monks. They'd gone only a few yards before he murmured, "You can open your eyes now; the brown horde is well behind us, and if I know them, and I do, they won't scratch up enough courage to come calling until after dinner."

"How did you know I was awake?" Kate asked, looking up into his face. It was a very hard, grim countenance, carved from a life of hardship and severity. But there was humor, too, in the gaze he turned on her.

"In spite of the convincing manner in which you're lolling against my chest?"

Her head snapped up at that.

She released an unhappy little sigh. Now, propriety demanded she extricate herself forthwith from his embrace. Though she felt remarkably comfortable with matters just as they were. Still, a lady did what a lady must. "I can walk."

"Maybe," he agreed. "But you wouldn't want to spoil our performance at this stage. The good brothers already have a most biased view of womanhood. Not that they fault your gender as individuals, mind you. *That* would be unchristian.

"They do, however, hold grave misgivings about females in general. They consider them weak and perfidious—but only in an entirely enchanting and morally corrupting sort of way. And only for those poor, misguided sots who fall under their spell.

"I would not be in the least surprised to discover that even now my immortal and all-too-susceptible soul is being edified by dozens of prayers."

"Ah!"

"Now then, save those gasps of outrage, Mrs. Blackburn. After all, you *were* pretending to have fainted, and that does rather lend credibility to the good brothers' assumptions."

"You are suggesting that I am perfidious?" she asked, wide-eyed with innocence.

He smiled. "Just so. And if you were to suddenly leap from my arms and begin marching merrily along, it would only confirm their suspicion that women are not to be trusted."

"Maybe they aren't," Kate said. "Maybe you are in dire threat of being corrupted by my weak and perfidious nature. I should never forgive myself for putting such an innocent as you at such risk. I *insist* you put me down."

He broke into a rich laugh. "Kate Blackburn, who would have suspected you capable of such brazen cheek?"

His laughter disarmed her. For a moment, his green eyes had looked warm with merriment.

"I don't know what you mean," she said, wishing he would laugh again.

"What I meant is, young widows of impeccable lineage with an eye to reentering society shouldn't bedevil commoners." His expression altered subtly, his gaze becoming both lambent and predatory. "It could be dangerous. You never know what they might do."

He lifted her higher in his arms, drawing her closer to his mouth. She shrank back, though part of her wanted to meet his bold taunting in kind, stay where she was, see what he would do. Fear returned, but it was not fear of Kit MacNeill. It was fear of herself, of what she might be capable of with the slightest encouragement. Thank God she was a coward.

"Do you?" he whispered, staring down into her eyes.

"No," she breathed, and looked away, forcing herself to take in her surroundings.

To Kate's uneducated eye, St. Bride's did not seem much of an abbey, just a tiny village built in a rectangle and surrounded by walls. A low stone building formed one side of the rectangle, its roof covering an open front passage that gave on to a dozen or so doorways. Adjoining this, at the corner, rose a two-story edifice with a steeply pitched roof. The chapel, she supposed. Aligned along the remaining two walls were a series of structures of various sizes and ages, none being distinguished by any particular architectural style and all having obviously been built as need dictated and available material allowed.

In fact, the only thing distinguishing the place at all was its setting. For above and surrounding the monastery on all sides were glorious snowcapped mountains. To the east, sunlight streamed down the mountain's white flanks, warming the small settlement nestled at its feet and allowing, even in November, a few patches of green to hold against the browning of winter. The cold wind that had been their constant companion over the last two days had completely vanished, and the air felt subtle and soft. They must be in a deep valley that created a sort of false climate.

"It's . . . it's not so cold here, is it?" she murmured.

"No. It never is," Kit answered, barely pausing before a stout door in a stone wall. He turned and backed his way through.

They emerged into a rose garden tended as well as any in all England. A pea-gravel path encircled a marble-mantled well, its circumference interrupted at regular intervals by bare arbors. Flanking either side of the door through which they'd come were terraced beds newly ticked beneath thick layers of leaves, awaiting winter's assault, while the entire back portion of the garden, she was amazed to see, had been covered over by glass, forming what she was certain must be the most isolated, if not northernmost, greenhouse in all of Great Britain.

Kit carried her straight toward this structure and nudged open the greenhouse door with his knee. Kate's breath caught. While outside, the brown-gray mantle of winter had been donned, within the greenhouse the last vestiges of summer's regalia had yet to be doffed. Climbing roses coursed up the greenhouse's fretwork, forming a ceiling where still a few roses, red and carmine and shell pink, hung. But they were the last survivors of this year's bounty, old sentinel blooms pushed past their natural life span. Even the tiny rush of air caused by the opening of the door had sent a swirl of brown-rimmed petals drifting down from above.

Kit moved through the magnificent blooms without pausing, coming shortly to a small shed with a divided door. Inside was a small rope cot covered with some blankets and several shelves supporting trowels and implements and pots containing grafts in varying states of growth.

Without fanfare, Kit deposited her on the cot and straightened, reaching for an earthenware jug by his feet. He sniffed it and then poured the contents into a stoneware mug and offered it to her. "Here. Drink."

She accepted the mug gratefully, gulping great mouthfuls of the clear cool water, not caring when it dribbled down her chin. She was parched. She finished and handed him the mug, self-consciously dabbing her wet chin and mouth against her sleeve. She looked out the top half of the doorway which Kit had left open into the green tangle of roses.

"This is . . . fantastical."

Kit's gaze followed hers. "We built it," he murmured, as if recalling something he'd forgotten.

"Who?"

"Me and Ramsey and Dand . . . and Douglas." He looked down at her. "This is where I was raised. Where I learned to speak, read, write. And where we were trained."

"But not to be priests," she recalled.

He laughed at that. "No. Not even Father Tarkin could reconcile the idea of priests as assassins."

"Assassins?" He'd shocked her yet again.

He shrugged. "What do you call someone you've trained to be used as a weapon? What did you think we were ultimately to do at Malmaison?"

Before she could reply, he was gone.

*Assassin.*

It was none of her concern. Not the terrible word he'd applied to himself, nor the haunted expression in his eyes, nor the bitter amusement with which he watched her turn from him.

Thank God he'd said that, she told herself fiercely. Here she'd been thinking him a tame lamb, when at every step of their journey she had had abundant proof that he was every inch a wolf. She wouldn't forget again. The past few days' stress and lack of sleep and hunger had conspired to turn her unwilling dependency on MacNeill into something— No! *Nothing* had been turned into *less* than nothing.

Christian MacNeill would soon be gone from her life. She didn't have to think about his past or his future. Nor should she. She had her own history and future to concern her.

A tap on the side of the shed caught her attention. She looked around and saw a pair of monks crouched over either end of Grace's trunk, panting from the exertion of carrying it here. She had completely forgotten Grace's trunk. Indeed, she had nearly forgotten why she was on this journey in the first place and what the hoped-for end of that journey would be. She would do well to remind herself.

The monks took one look at her, dropped the trunk at the door, and fled. Still weak, she fell back against the pillow. She would recuperate and then she would continue on to Castle Parnell, and this odd side trip would become an anecdote with which to regale the marquis at some not-too-distant-future dinner.

She wondered if Kit had eaten . . .

"Mrs. Blackburn?" The massive Brother Fidelis appeared in the open door, accompanied by a wizened white-haired antique whom Kate suspected headed the infirmary, since he brought with him various ill-smelling tinctures. With apologetic smiles and mutters from the round monk and unapologetic gibes from the ancient one, they saw her dosed and scurried off.

As soon as they left, a nervous little fellow arrived, pressed a plate of steaming beef stew in her hands, and backed out of the room, where a thickset monk waited. Ravenous, she forced herself to eat the delicious fare slowly. By the time she finished, she felt a world better and determined to ask any other visitors where Kit had gone. Before long, another twosome arrived to take the cleaned plate, but they beat a hasty retreat before she could question them.

It took Kate a while to figure out what was going on, but when she did, she broke into a wide grin: They were being sent in pairs so that they might protect one another. From her! How empowering! It might even warrant its own section in her book: *Terrorizing Celibate Men*. She couldn't help giggling.

When Brother Martin and Brother Fidelis reappeared, this time to check her pulse and gauge her pallor, she swung her legs over the side of the cot, and the two monks back-pedaled from her as though she might at any moment sprout another head.

"You just lie back and rest, young lady!" the ancient Brother Martin squeaked, scooting behind Brother Fidelis who attempted to look formidable. Unfortunately, his worried expression negated any threat his size suggested.

"I feel much better," she said, though in truth her joints felt knit together with jelly and her throat was raw. "I would like to see Mr. MacNeill."

"He'll come when he comes," Brother Martin announced forcefully from behind Brother Fidelis. Brother Fidelis offered a sickly smile.

"Then I shall have to find him."

"You can't! You aren't allowed. It's against the rules."

"I'm not a monk, so your rules do not apply to me."

"The rules apply to everyone! Besides, he's busy getting ready to leave."

"What?" Kate's light mood evaporated. He was abandoning her?

"Just for a few days," Brother Fidelis said soothingly. "Until you're better and can travel. He has some, er, pressing concerns he needs to look into."

"What pressing concerns?" Kate asked.

"As to that, I couldn't say, Mrs. Blackburn. But I do know that he asked the abbot for us to tend you whilst he's gone."

"He did?" she asked, oddly touched, which was ridiculous; what else was he going to do but ask the abbot? He couldn't very well dump her on their doorstep and ride off as if she was a foundling. Well, actually he could.

"Aye. He did," sputtered the disembodied voice from behind Fidelis's bulk. "He's gone daft. That's what the world's done to him."

Kate had had enough of the crabbed old monk's malicious pronouncements. "I refuse to hold a conversation with someone I cannot see," she muttered, skirting Brother Fidelis.

At once, Brother Martin popped out on the opposite side of him, his knobby hands planted on his scrawny hips. "*This* is why we eschew the company of women, Brother Fidelis," he announced darkly. "Five minutes in one's company, and I recall all too clearly how obdurate and intractable, willful and contrary, they are. Don't you?"

"Not really."

"What?" Brother Martin turned a look upon his fellow monk that clearly questioned his loyalty.

"I entered the holy orders when my mother died. I was ten." Brother Fidelis's round face took on a beatific expression. "I was most fond of my mum. She had hair as dark as this young lady's. I forgot how pretty it was."

Kate smiled triumphantly at the old misogynist, who without another word snatched his robes up and stalked from the shed, leaving Brother Fidelis alone with her. At his companion's retreat, Brother Fidelis's courage faltered. He began to sidle toward the door.

"Don't go," she said.

"I don't think Father Abbot would approve."

"Then you stand outside the shed, and I'll stay in here. What harm is there in that?"

He didn't look much comforted. She tried another tack. "The greenhouse is a marvel, isn't it?"

He stopped, his face filled with pride.

"Mr. MacNeill said he and his friends built it."

"That they did. When they were but lads. Either put their hands to God's use or the devil will put them to his, I used to tell the abbot."

"Very wise." She sat down on the cot again and regarded him attentively. "But the structure. So unusual. Someone must have given much thought to its construction. Surely that wasn't the work of mere boys. Would the architect be you?"

He turned pink with pleasure. "Well . . ."

"Ah!" She nodded. "I thought as much. Tell me, however did you come up with the design?"

He lowered his eyes modestly. And came in.

⟨⟨⟨⟨⟩⟩⟩⟩

# IDENTIFYING AND CONCENTRATING ON ATTAINABLE GOALS

*St. Bride's, 1797*

"*ARE THEY DEDICATED?*" *the Frenchman asked, eyeing them carefully.*

"*Yes.*" *Father Abbot's gaze touched Kit and moved on to Douglas, then Dand and Ramsey. "But they serve God. Not France.*"

"*In serving France, they will be serving God.*"

"*They were meant for this!*" *The voice of the exiled French priest Toussaint rang with frustration. "In all of England we could search for a hundred years and never find young men better equipped to do what these can.*"

"*And what is that?*" *Douglas had moved forward.*

*The newly arrived French gentleman regarded him coolly, yet he answered. "Go to France and aid in the restoration of the monarchy.*"

*"And the Holy Church," the abbot reminded his visitor.*

*"And if we do not succeed?" Dand asked.*

*"You must succeed," the man said. "The time is ripe. After having the audacity to have the Holy Father removed from Rome, the Directoire falters. The people are finally sickening of their sacrilege, such as when they desecrated the cathedral of Notre Dame, renaming it the Temple of Reason and installing a whore as their priestess."* *He crossed himself. "It would take little to put the so-called government into turmoil, and then? We take back France!"*

Kit strode across the yard, the vivid memory of his last visit to these quarters ambushing him. How eager they'd been, with their youthful ardor, their dreams of glory, their piety and hubris.

As he walked, he was well aware of the many eyes marking his passage and the alarm in them. Let them be afraid. He didn't give a damn about their apprehension. *Or hers.* He closed his mind to the image of her face, stark with confusion and fear, when he'd said the word *assassin.* Well, she wouldn't have to suffer his company for a few days at least. As he wouldn't have to suffer hers.

She knew too much about him, had come too close. There was danger there, a siren call to intimacy that he could not afford to heed. Nor did he want to. She'd become an abrasion, rubbing him raw, revealing all the hunger and desires he'd thought dead but instead had only gone dormant.

Want. Desire. Need. They didn't coexist easily within the man he'd become. So, he would purge himself of them. And that would be easier done away from her. Away from her scent and voice and dark eyes and supple body—

He jerked open the door to the abbot's house and let it slam behind him, moving past the young acolyte standing guard and heading for the library. The door stood open. Inside, the abbot sat behind his huge desk, waiting for him, his hands folded atop a stack of papers.

He looked exactly as Kit remembered him: the same thick thatch of white hair, the same beaked nose above the thin severe mouth, the deep-set eyes regarding the world with unruffled calm. It offended Kit that while he had changed so drastically, not only in body but in spirit, this man should seem so untouched by the world into which he'd sent Kit and his companions.

"Christian." The abbot held out his hand to be kissed. Kit regarded it coolly. The abbot withdrew it.

"I have prayed you would return, Christian." The same voice, imbued with quiet dignity and power.

"I didn't have any alternative."

"I know. Nonetheless, you are here, and I am glad." There was not a hint of fear or reproach or disingenuousness in his manner or expression.

"Why?"

The abbot did not answer the question, as if Kit must already know and was being deliberately obtuse. "You are troubled. I would ease you."

"Would you?" Kit smiled thinly. "Good. Tell me who betrayed us to the French."

The abbot sighed softly. "I do not know."

Kit's hands slammed against the surface of the desk, making the papers on it jump. The abbot didn't flinch.

"There were only five men who could have betrayed us." Kit leaned across the wide desk. "Ramsey Munro, Andrew Ross, Douglas Stewart, Brother Toussaint, and myself. Douglas is dead. That leaves four."

"What would you have me say, Christian? If anyone *had* confessed, I could not tell you."

"I want the name of the man who betrayed us, who is responsible for Douglas's murder. And I will have it. By God, I will."

"I hope you are taking an oath and not making one?"

With a strangled sound of frustration, Kit pushed off the desk, wheeling around. "Then tell me this: Who among us would you judge capable of this sort of betrayal?"

"I cannot conceive any of you capable of such treachery. Not Ramsey, not Andrew," the abbot said quietly. "Not you."

Exasperated, Christian raked the red-gold hair back from his face. "What of Toussaint, then? I have not seen him. That alone surely indicates a guilty—"

"Brother Toussaint left the monastery five years ago and returned to France. He went to minister secretly, at great risk to himself."

"Did he?" Kit's voice dripped doubt. "And what have you heard from him since?"

"It is feared that he was found out and executed," he answered obliquely.

Kit's eyes narrowed. "But you are not certain."

"No," the abbot reluctantly admitted. He rose to his feet. "Can you not let this go? You have a young woman—"

"She is *not* mine," Christian said. "She is an obligation. I honor my commitments, and she is one of them. When I have finished with her, I will find Douglas's murderer."

"Yes," the abbot agreed. "And when you find him, what will you do then, Christian?"

A wolfish smile flashed on the young man's sundarkened face. "*Not* turn the other cheek. That I can assure you."

" 'Vengeance is mine, sayeth the Lord.' "

"And I am an instrument of the Lord. Isn't that what you taught me?"

"There is darkness in you, Christian, that never was there before."

"I was never branded before, Father Abbot," he replied coldly. "Not every fire refines the spirit. Sometimes it simply burns."

*A smoking oil torch fitted into a sconce beside the door flickered maniacally, spitting light across the dark walls. In the center of the room, a shallow brazier smoked and flamed, and before this stood the warden, his hands clasped behind his back, rocking slightly on the balls of his feet.*

*"I have a gift for you." With a smile, he hefted a long iron rod from the fire. The end, twisted into the shape of a stylized rose, glowed orange in the dark room.*

"I refuse to believe that."

"Believe what you want. I did once. I believed in us."

"You would have done better to have believed in God's plan."

"I thought we *were* God's plan!" The words came from his soul, anguished and heated. Then the expression of anguish faded, leaving only a cold, hard-eyed young man. "That's not why I came."

"Why then, Christian?"

"I found a garland of roses. Yellow roses."

"Where?" the abbot asked, startled.

"In the old castle ruins across the moor. They were laced around a dead rat's throat."

The creases alongside the abbot's nose deepened as he stared unseeingly at the paper under his hand. "What do you make of it?"

"I don't know," Kit answered. He did not know what the abbot's game was, but until he did, he would not be handing him any free information. "I want to go back. Have a closer look. But"—his gaze fell—"I cannot take her."

A pause. "What are you doing with this young woman, Christian?"

"I am her guard." He shrugged elaborately. "Driver, if you will. I am seeing her safely to Castle Parnell."

The abbot's gaze sharpened. "Castle Parnell is in Clyth, is it not? Clyth is a dangerous place these days, filled with many troubled souls. The marquis and his family have been visited by tragedy recently."

"How would you know that?" Kit asked, considering

the straight-backed old man speculatively. The abbot had always seemed to know more than his place as the simple leader of a cloistered order might suggest. Even when Kit had been a boy here, the abbot's reach had been subtle but long-ranging. "And what have troubled souls to do with the marquis's recent bereavement? The deaths of his brother and sister-in-law were accidents."

"So I have heard."

"You don't believe it?"

"I have no reason not to," the abbot answered mildly. "I only know that where poverty and desperation are living cheek by jowl with wealth and privilege, there is fertile ground for mischief."

Kit did not know whether to give credence to the abbot's suspicions. "I would like to leave Mrs. Blackburn here. With you. I want to see if I can pick up the trail of whoever left that rat. Barring that, I'll ask about the countryside if anyone might have seen a stranger traveling through these parts."

"I fear you're hunting a ghost, Christian."

"I'm not hunting. Not yet. Not until I have delivered Mrs. Blackburn safely. Until then, I am simply studying the field. When I do hunt, I'll not come back empty-handed, I promise that." He held the abbot's considering gaze. "Will you keep her?"

The abbot nodded. "All right, Christian. We will tend your Mrs. Blackburn until you return. But return before the Sabbath."

"Three days," Christian promised. "And she's not mine."

\*   \*   \*

The abbot stared thoughtfully at his folded hands, listening to Christian's boot heels clicking on the corridor floor. The young man had grown more dangerous and vastly more threatening. The promise of violence made at his birth had been kept; the young wolf hadn't been tamed after all.

The abbot's thoughts rolled back twenty years. Early in his priesthood, he'd made it his mission to find the flower of Catholic Scotland, the last blooms of the old blood, the Highland blood. He'd scoured the country, sending out emissaries to seek those lost sons, having no other thought than to salvage them from the cesspits and stews of the cities. He'd only found four in the end.

Not that that mattered. Once he had discovered the metal of which his young charges were made, another idea had replaced his original intent. He would train them, hone them, and create modern-day knights, present-day crusaders. They wanted only a purpose, one which in time the French Terror had provided.

The abbot shook his head at such vanity, such amazing conceit. He had paid a dire penalty for his pride. But Christian and the others had paid even more dearly. They'd been so close. More like brothers than even . . . well, even the brothers of this order. Indeed, their friendship had been the single most important factor in their young lives. And that friendship had been destroyed by someone.

What would such a thing do to a sensitive young man like Andrew Ross, who hid his feelings behind devil-may-care japes? Or Ramsey, who'd adopted his urbane veneer from a half-remembered past that he dared not explore? Or Christian, who had never belonged to anyone or anything until these young men had claimed him?

The abbot rubbed his hand across his eyes, recalling Christian's expression. He'd looked jaded, disillusioned, battered and lethal. So lethal, in fact, that for a moment, staring into Christian's eyes, the abbot had felt his own mortality. The idea brokered no terror, just a deep frustration that those people who relied upon his information and knowledge would be stranded without his aid, and his penance would be forfeit.

But Christian hadn't laid a hand on him. There was something in that, he supposed. Just as there was something in his care of Mrs. Blackburn. He'd seen the possessiveness in his posture, the manner in which he'd looked at her, held her.

But now . . . he had other matters to attend to.

With a sigh, he uncovered the letter that had arrived earlier that day. He recognized the hand; its owner wrote periodically if infrequently, and always had something interesting to impart.

That was, after all, Dand Ross's job as a spy in Napoleon's France.

# ELEVEN

# INTIMACY WITH ONE'S DRIVER: A SITUATION TO BE AVOIDED AT ALL COSTS

ONE OF THE MONKS had dragged a small, stone bench to the outside of the shed, and this is where Kit found Kate, her face lifted to a heaven scoured clean, the sun melting into the mountaintops. A few stars sparkled on the smooth twilight surface.

"We might see Andromeda tonight," Kate said softly. She looked far better than she had upon their arrival just a few hours before. Warmth had given her cheeks back their color, and her eyes were clear and dark.

He'd come to tell her he was leaving her to the care of the monks, but now that he stood before her, he found himself reluctant to do so. She was so damned pretty, even pale and fragile looking, much like starlight. And just as unreachable.

Something had changed in their relationship, a shift in her manner toward him; there was an accessibility to her that he craved to take advantage of even though he knew that to do so would be the sheerest folly. But he could not walk away. "Andromeda?"

"The constellation," she said with a shade of pride. "Named for Andromeda, the daughter of Cepheus, the king of a seafaring people, and his beautiful queen, Cassiopeia."

"Tell me more," he suggested, half expecting her to turn him down. He was a scarred commoner and a soldier. She was a lady. She might have tolerated his company when she'd had no alternative, but surely she'd cut herself off from him now. Kindly, of course. She would rebuff him with exemplary good manners.

"If you sit down."

There was only one place to sit, and that was beside her. "I would rather stand."

"And I would rather not get a crick in my neck. You're very tall, you know. And you do rather loom when you are trying to drive home a particular point you wish to make, which you do often. At least to me."

He looked down at her, startled and was amazed to see that she was smiling. Teasingly. It completely undermined every intention he had of leaving quickly.

"That is, unless you feel in *need* of the advantage afforded by your loftier position?"

He sat. "My position is, as you well know, in every

way inferior to your own," he said gruffly. "Now tell me about Cassiopeia."

"Well," she began, "Cassiopeia boasted that her beauty was greater than their neighbor's, a lady sea goddess. Now, not only did this statement prove deplorably bad manners, but it showed an appalling lack of judgment, because Greek goddesses are not renowned for their charity. They are, however, right proficient with vengeance."

She grinned impishly, and he saw the young woman that circumstance kept hidden too often. It might have been better had she remained that way. This young, bright-eyed Kate was too captivating, too vivacious by half.

"Are they?"

"Oh, yes." She nodded solemnly. "We mortals are pitiful amateurs when it comes to vengeance, Mr. MacNeill."

He did not bother arguing. He had his own notions about vengeance and his proficiency with it.

"The offended goddess demanded that her papa, who happened to be Poseidon, penalize the mortal queen for her vanity," Kate continued. "Being a fond parent, Poseidon agreed, forcing King Cepheus to make a terrible choice: He must sacrifice either his daughter or his country to a horrific sea monster."

"Unpleasant alternatives," Kit prompted, for Kate had stopped speaking, her teasing smile fading. "Which did he choose?"

"He chose to be a hero to his people." She spoke

in a determinedly light voice. "He had his daughter Andromeda chained to a rock in the midst of the sea to await her fate, not only abandoning her but leaving her without any weapons with which to defend herself."

She was no longer speaking of a mythological princess, he realized. She was speaking of herself, her sisters, and her father.

"What happened?"

"Perseus," she said with forced airiness. "He was speeding along high above the earth on his winged sandals when he spied this poor, miserable girl latched to a half-submerged boulder. He flew down, demanded the particulars of her situation, and adjudged correctly that to act might prove extremely lucrative to an enterprising young hero."

"A born politician," Kit said with a smile, and for a second Kate's brittleness melted.

"Indeed!" she agreed. "Then, as quick as the bronze on brass, Perseus slew the evil monster, rescued the girl, and accepted part of Cepheus's kingdom as a reward. And everyone lived happily ever after.

"Much later, when all the principals of the story were dead, the gods decided it made a pretty enough story for a celestial tapestry, and so"—her voice softened—"there she is." One slender finger pointed out a cluster of stars. "The Chained Maiden."

"Did she ever forgive her father?" he asked.

Her face remained lifted to the bright night sky. "Forgive him for what? He did what a king does.

Though I don't doubt Andromeda found that an easier sentiment to embrace once she was off her rock and safely ensconced in her rich, handsome husband's palace." Her tone warned him not to press further, and he allowed her the evasion.

"Are there any others maidens up there?"

She released a small breath. "Not yet. But soon we might see the queen, Cassiopeia herself."

"How do you come to know these things? I cannot imagine that astronomy is requisite in a young lady's education. But then, I would hardly know what a young lady ought to learn." Who was he reminding? Her or himself?

"It doesn't matter what she learns," Kate murmured. "Nothing can negate her vulnerability or her dependence. Except wealth."

*Ah, yes. The lifeblood of the aristocracy, without which nothing works, nothing matters, and nothing is worthwhile.*

She looked over her shoulder at him, and her dark hair caught the fire of the setting sun. Her lips, ever a lure and an enticement, glistened—she had been sipping water or wine—and he remembered his suggestion—his threat—that she might drink from his mouth. His belly muscles tightened with lust, and she did not know. She was completely unaware of the devastation she was wreaking on his body.

"But we were speaking of the stars, weren't we?" She smiled, clearly resolving not to let anything mar the conversation. Though why she should take such pains with him, he could not imagine.

"My father was an ardent astronomer. One of my earliest memories is of sitting on his lap late at night, looking through his telescope. If the nursemaid caught us, she'd tell my mother, and then there was the devil to pay!" She laughed, and his pulse quickened in response. He wanted to feel her melt against him again, lithe and indolent with sleep—or pleasure.

He struggled to marshal his rampant thoughts. "Did your sisters find it as enthralling as you?"

"No." A remnant of childish scorn touched her voice, and she must have heard it, for she wrinkled her nose in self-deprecation. "Charlotte was just a tiny baby. Sometimes Helena would appear, but she always fell asleep within a few minutes and had to be carried back to bed.

"But sometimes Grace stayed up to see the night sky." Her expression grew melancholy. "She was always so inquisitive and so very precocious. She used to insist she was going to buy the stars and make them into a necklace."

Her fingertip moved slowly across the sky, pointing out a wide swath of concentrated stars. "The Greeks called it the 'Road of the Gods.' He taught me that."

*Her father.* Kit hesitated, pulled by an impulse he barely understood. He knew less about the relationships between parent and child than he did about the far side of the moon. But he'd seen her anguish, her sense of betrayal. God help him, compassion filled him. He didn't want to feel anything for her, not compassion, not tenderness, not empathy or understanding. He would accept the lust that rode him because lust was safe. Distancing.

"He didn't mean to leave you and your sisters, Kate. He didn't expect to die."

She stiffened, but her eyes remained fixed on the sky. "He didn't *have* to die. He had a choice. You said so yourself." Her dark gaze fell to his. "Offering himself like that was . . . *irresponsible*! He owed it to us to safeguard our futures by safeguarding his life! What I would dearly love to know is, why did he chose to *die* for you rather than *live* for us?"

He did not take offense. He understood perfectly, to a degree he doubted any other man could. She had lost those things she held most dear through what she thought of as betrayal. Aye, *that* he understood.

Abruptly, her eyes widened with mortification. "Oh! I am so sorry. I didn't mean it that way. It's just that I thought he loved us—"

He ignored her apology. "He did. But he had to do what he"—he searched for the right words—"what he had to do."

"I wish I could believe that." She looked down at her hands twisting in her lap. "I know it is wrong to feel this way. It doesn't matter, though, does it? Right or wrong. When a person feels something deeply, logic cannot dislodge it."

Dear God, was she a Sybil or a siren?

She looked over at him helplessly. "How can I possibly explain?"

"I understand."

She tilted her head questioningly, her realization that someone else shared a similar burden obvious in her midnight-colored eyes. "Yes," she breathed. "Yes. Of course you do."

Amazingly, he felt mostly sadness rather than the familiar black current of rage that usually swept through him at the thought of his betrayal, his lost comrades.

Kate's eyes shimmered in the shadows. "How do you live with it? The betrayal?"

"I don't," he said, his voice hardening. "I hold on to the belief I'll find the truth and someday be able to confront the man who betrayed us."

"And if he's dead? The man who betrayed you?"

Why her? Why did this empathy, this deep, effortless honesty, have to be with her? "I don't know."

"I do." She said somberly. She leaned toward him. "Let him go. Whoever he is."

"I can't. There's a debt to pay, the debt I owe Douglas."

The earnest plea in her lovely face faded. "Certainly I am in no position to criticize that quality in you."

What did she want from him? A declaration that even if he hadn't promised her family every effort on their behalf, that even if he hadn't pledged an oath to serve her, he would still have done everything in his power to see her safe and cared for and content? That he would fight for her? Steal for her? Give up his life for her?

Abruptly he stood up.

"You're leaving," she said tonelessly.

"Aye."

"A pressing engagement, no doubt."

He wanted to hear her laughter again. But another part of him wanted to hear an entirely different sound, wanted to hear her breathing catch in hunger and surrender. His gaze fixed unwillingly on the soft swell of her lower lip, the sheen of skin disappearing beneath the wool collar of her cape, the thin, blue-veined delicacy of her wrists, and the glow of her eye.

Desire for her exploded within him so thickly that for a second his head swam with the rush of it. He had to get out of here.

"MacNeill?"

There was a well outside the garden walls. The water used to be icy cold. God willing, it still was. "You'll be fine here. They're deluded and naive, but decent men. They'll see you fed and rested."

"How long will you be gone?"

"I'll be back in a few days."

"Will you—" She paused, her brow wrinkled. "Are you going back to that castle? Because I do not think it safe."

He laughed, and the lie came easily. "No. I told you. I will see you safely to your destination before I pursue my own concerns."

She relaxed, and his heart thundered in his chest that she had cared enough to ask, that she had worried over his welfare. It had been years since anyone had cared about his safety. There was a trap there. A snare.

"And after you come back, we will go on to Clyth?"

He should be thanking her for reminding him of where she was going and to whom and why. But he only felt a fire in his gut and a coldness settle over his heart.

"Yes, ma'am." He bowed formally, and before she could flay him with more innocent words, he left.

# TWELVE

※※※

# THE DANGERS
# OF FOLLOWING
# GARDEN PATHS

*My darling Helena,*
*I beg you share the contents of this letter with*
*Charlotte if and when she finds time in the*
*Weltons' hectic social schedule to visit you.*
*You must not worry, dear, that I have only*
*now written because my journey was interrupted*
*by an Unfortunate Climatic Episode which has*
*obliged us to take refuge in an unexpected and*
*utterly charming little Scottish . . .*

KATE BIT THE END of her pen and considered her
word. *Abbey* would only confirm Helena's fears that
she had been irresponsible in allowing Kate to travel
without her. *Tavern* was worse.

"*. . . spa,*" she wrote. And then, "*I hope, dear, that*

*Your Employer does not impose too much on your Good Nature but I fear, knowing both you and her, that such hope is futile."*

She hesitated.

*"You will, of course, burn this letter as soon as you have read it."*

"You are lucky you did not develop an inflammation of the lungs, Mrs. Blackburn."

"Father Abbot!" Kate bolted upright from where she'd been sitting outside the greenhouse and nearly tripped over the end of the brown robe covering her.

The abbot pretended not to notice. "I am interrupting your correspondence. Forgive me."

"No, no," Kate hastily assured him. "I was just finishing a short letter to my sister, Helena. I don't suppose there is anyone to post it?"

"Yes, of course. We are not so far removed from the world as that. A messenger is due this afternoon. I will send it back with him."

"Thank you." She looked around, uncertain what protocol demanded, wondering if she could be seated before the abbot.

He removed the question by gracefully taking a seat on the marble bench nearby and indicated that she might return to her stool. "How are you faring, Mrs. Blackburn?"

"Very well, sir." It had been two days since Kit had left, and she felt entirely herself again. At least, in the physical sense. "I must thank you again for your hospitality. Once I arrive at the marquis of Parnell's home, I will ask that he compensate you for my care—"

"It is completely unnecessary. We are a Benedictine order, Mrs. Blackburn. Serving travelers and indigents is our mission."

"Indigents?" Kate echoed numbly.

The abbot smiled. "I did not mean to imply that you were of the latter category, Mrs. Blackburn. Excuse me for being unclear."

"Not at all," Kate muttered. "It is just that . . . since my parents' deaths, I have been closer to that state than I am comfortable admitting."

"It has been difficult for you," he acknowledged mildly, "what with your maid deserting you and your driver absconding with your carriage."

Kate nodded. Kit must have related her situation to the priest.

"Added to which, you were then forced to rely upon the good offices of a man you must regard as a stranger."

"He has done everything in his power to protect and serve me," she answered a little coolly.

"Ah!" The abbot smiled. "I am glad to hear that."

"Why?" Kate asked suspiciously. "Do you have any reason to suppose he would act otherwise? You do not know him then. He is a most honorable and capable gentleman."

"Of course. How felicitous that you recognize his value."

"Hm." Kate's back, which had unaccountably stiffened in the past moments, relaxed.

"Is there is anything else I might see you provided?"

She hesitated. She meant only to pass the time. "Yes. Tell me about Christian MacNeill."

Kit's pace quickened as he headed toward the rose garden. His trip to the ruined castle and its surroundings had been fruitless. No one had seen any stranger who might have been the man who'd accosted Kate, and Kit had found little sign of his passage other then the tumbled wall where he'd tethered his horse.

He'd returned to St. Bride's earlier in the day and been met at once by the abbot, who had informed him that Kate was well—"blooming," he'd said, launching into an uncharacteristic flight of fancy. Then, at the abbot's insistence, he had taken a bath— and then, and then, well, he hadn't been able to stay away any longer.

She was his responsibility, he told himself. And therefore it was for him to judge whether she suffered any ill effects from their ride across the moors.

"Ah! I see." Kate's voice drifted over the stone-walled garden. Proper little English accent, pretty round vowels and crisp consonants.

"And these are the parts that inform me it is male? Not very spectacular, are they?" Kate sounded a little disappointed.

What the hell was going on?

"They don't need to be spectacular." Was that Brother Martin? Irascible, misogynistic Brother

Martin? "They only need to do the work of procreation and that they do well enough."

Kit pushed open the door to the walled garden and moved silently through the tangle of shrubs crowding the entrance until he spied Kate sitting outside the greenhouse on a marble bench alongside the crabbed old monk. She was studying a rose, carefully severed in half, that had been spread on the white marble surface between them.

He could only see her profile, but her brow was puckered in concentration and her hair, plaited simply into one long sable rope, trailed down her back. Someone had found a novitiate's robe for her to wear over her dress—perhaps as a buttress against her womanly charms. An ineffectual effort. It did nothing but enhance her femininity.

Clearly, the abbot was correct. She was blooming with health. Kit settled his shoulders against the stone, enjoying the sight of her: the carnelian flush on the crest of her cheek, the little bump on the bridge of her nose, the tender nape of her neck, the manner in which the clear morning light shimmered across her dark braid. If he closed his eyes, he could almost imagine the silken feel of it spilling over his palms.

Happily, his two days away had restored him to his sanity. He'd thought about Kate and her appeal for him and had decided it was simply a matter of proximity and the age-old problem of wanting things one couldn't possibly have. He'd simply been howling at the moon again. Well, no more.

"Mr. MacNeill knows all of this, you say?" she asked artlessly.

His eyes opened and fell upon her guileless visage. What was she up to?

"If he doesn't, it isn't for any lack of effort on my part. All those boys were well schooled in horticulture. Give them something to occupy their brains, is what the abbot said."

"And why did they need to have their minds occupied? I would have thought Latin and history and geography would have been enough."

Busy, she'd been. What else had she found out?

"Too sharp by half, the lot of them. Smartest lads I ever seen. Taken individual or as a whole, but truth be told, you had to take them as a whole."

"Oh?"

"They held together tighter than sin does to Satan— God grant us deliverance from his wiles—four smart foundlings." He snorted. "What does one want smarts for? Where did it get any of *them?* Smarts only means you know to a degree exactly how miserable you be. Better to be like Brother John, who only suspects, and dimly at that, what a miserable place the world is."

Kate must have raised one of those delicately arched brows, for when Brother Martin spoke again, he grumbled. "A man is entitled to his opinion."

"Of course." There was no censure in her voice. "But if a man, or a woman, doesn't know the extent of their misery, how can they appreciate the glory of salvation?"

"You, Mrs. Blackburn, would have made a good Jesuit," Brother Martin said darkly.

"I'll take that as a compliment," she answered. "But we were talking about Mr. MacNeill."

"*You* were talking about Mr. MacNeill. Again. *I* was talking about flowers."

"Again."

"Humph." He could hear Brother Martin's gruff amusement. So she'd managed to charm the old woman-hater. And in two days. God alone knew what had befallen the other monks. They were probably all at confession relating all sorts of interesting and sinful musings. God knew, he ought to be there himself for some of the thoughts he'd indulged.

"You are most enlightening on any number of complex subjects."

"You're thinking of Mr. MacNeill agin."

"Am I?"

*Was she?* And why should she be doing that? Kit wondered. But he already knew the answer. She had told him once that she would be whatever the situation demanded. Apparently, she felt this situation demanded she learn something of Kit's past.

It was time to put an end to her delving. He moved out from the shadows, studying his little berobed temptress. Her head was tilted at a nearly flirtatious angle, and her lashes held the light at their very tips, as though dipped in gold. Brother Martin, even from a distance, had the unhappily bemused expression of an utterly captivated man.

What had she learned from the monks? he wondered. That he was a prostitute's by-blow? That he'd been in more fights than any of the other lads? And what did that knowledge reap for her? How would she use it? Because a person does not acquire something she has no intention of using—another lesson the world had been eager to teach him after he'd left St. Bride's.

Yes, it was good that he'd left her for a while. He'd forgotten for a short space what the world could do to you if your life became entangled too much with another's. Better to be alone.

Brother Martin had picked a little twig from the ground and was using it as a pointing stick, but the palsy that had plagued him years before had only grown worse, and his hand trembled. Without calling any undue attention to it, Kate covered the gnarled, liver-spotted old hand with her own, steadying it.

A spurt of jealousy rippled through Kit, and he smiled at the absurdity of it. But the fact remained that she had never touched him. Not of her own volition. Even when she'd bandaged him, duty alone had inspired her.

He wondered what those long, delicate hands would feel like flowing over his skin, his arms, his chest. Were a lady's hands more or less adept at lovemaking? Would soft palms and uncalloused fingertips provide more pleasure than a tavern girl's rougher counterparts? Or did being a lady or a tavern maid have nothing to do with it, and would Kate

Blackburn's touch be eviscerating no matter what she was or where she came from?

But it was impossible to separate it out like that. Because where she came from had fashioned who she was, and *that* was a lady. Far above his common touch.

She stopped suddenly, as if sensing his scrutiny, and lifted her head, doelike, looking about. Slowly she turned her head, and her eyes met his. They gladdened with the smile already curving her lips. He resisted, feeling her draw on him like steel tailings to a magnet.

"MacNeill," she called softly.

"Ma'am."

"You've come back earlier than the abbot said to expect you." She sounded happy. She sounded pleased. Perversely, it angered him, even though he knew it was unfair. What right did she have to welcome him? What right did she have to make him want that welcome?

Sometimes, to rid oneself of madness, madness needs to be indulged. Or so he told himself as he went to her, an idea forming with lightning rapidity. If he could just taste her, he would discover that she tasted like every other woman, that she felt like every other woman. Then he could release himself from wanting to . . . experience her. Then he could get on with the business of revenge.

"There was no reason to keep searching for something that wasn't there, Mrs. Blackburn." *Like you. You aren't really here, are you? You're just marking time.*

"I'm sorry you were disappointed."

"There are compensations for returning," he said steadily, his gaze sharp on her face. *Look at me. Want me. Just a little.*

Her extraordinary eyes widened, as if he'd voiced his thoughts. Good. He didn't want any unsuspecting victim. Let her be put on notice: he intended to have her. Just a little of her. Just a kiss.

"Back, are you, Christian?" Brother Martin said sourly, unhappy to have his tête-à-tête interrupted.

"Yes." He didn't take his eyes off Kate. "I trust you are well, Mrs. Blackburn?"

"Of course she's well," Brother Martin harrumphed. "She's had a tisane of primrose, mallow, and lemon balm three days running. Got rid of her sore throat straight off. Then we fed her. Poor thing was near half starved." His gaze clearly faulted Kit for her condition.

"I can see she is in the best of health."

Her gaze fell before his, and a faint color tinted her cheeks.

He turned his attention to ridding himself of the monk. "You have found a new pupil, Brother Martin?"

The old monk sniffed. "Mrs. Blackburn grew restive waiting for you, and in the spirit of hospitality, I thought it only right to provide her with some company while you went off and did whatever it is you did and left her stranded here. Poor lamb."

Poor lamb, indeed. Kate had lifted her head during Brother Martin's diatribe, her dutifully wounded expression contradicted by bright, merry eyes.

"You needn't justify your presence here, Brother

Martin," Kit said. "One has only to look at Mrs. Blackburn, and any further explanation is quite unnecessary." Her blush deepened charmingly.

Brother Martin had no answer for this. To deny it would hurt his "lamb," and to affirm it would be to admit to an earthly fancy. So instead he scowled and sought another topic.

"Mrs. Blackburn wondered if you remembered any of the things I taught you." He angled his head up, watching Kit with the blithe acrimony of a rival. "Do you?"

"Oh, a thing or two. You're not going to test me?" he asked in mock despair. Failing Brother Martin's quizzes had been a painful business. The old malcontent might look as frail as a glass straw, but he'd wielded a switch with expertise.

"If we were in my garden, I would," Brother Martin said. "But this is Brother Fidelis's. I always said as how he cosseted you boys as much as these prickly pretties here. Never saw the sense of it, wasting all this effort on roses when pennyroyal and feverfew and lady's mantle and good, medicinal plants struggle outside."

"Roses thrive only in rarefied sites," Kit said. His gaze stayed on Kate as he spoke. "Put them out in the real world, and they die."

"Then why go through all the trouble?" she asked.

"At first," he said softly, "because we had no choice. Later, well, you wouldn't want something so bonny to suffer simply for want of a little effort."

He didn't like his own answer, she could see it in

his quick frown. "I suppose Brother Fidelis has taken you on a tour of the garden?"

"No."

"An oversight we must rectify. It's a fascinating place, a rose garden. Troublesome and hard work to maintain."

"But worth the effort."

"Sometimes. For the brief season they bloom. And it is a *very* brief season. The end is always bitter-sweet." He lightened his words with a quick smile, charming and ruthless. Trepidation danced a warning along Kate's flesh.

What was he up to? The man who'd left the abbey was not the one who'd returned. This Kit was hard-eyed and sexual, predatory and focused. On her. He held out his hand, waiting until she placed her own in it to draw her to her feet. "Brother Martin?"

The old man struggled to his feet. "What? You expect me to shamble along in your wake while you spout a bunch of Latin names for ridiculously cosseted flowers? I have more important work to do." He shot a superior, telling look at Kate. "With my herbs." And with a har-rumph of disdain, he plodded off toward the door.

"Shall we?"

She cocked her head. "Thank you, yes. But be forewarned, I expect to be fascinated."

He secured her hand in the crook of his arm. "I shall endeavor not to disappoint."

"You know, Mr. MacNeill," she said after a pause, "you profess to be nothing more than an ill-bred orphan, and yet you sometimes evince manners that would be more suited to a fine drawing room than a garret."

"Stage dressing," he assured her. "Nothing more. Over the years I've picked up a few manners that I dust off now and again. One of my—my earlier companions had a tongue so subtle and smooth he could seduce a song from a cat."

"I don't know whether to believe you or not."

"As you will, ma'am," he said, his manner light and accommodating, his gaze frankly admiring. Almost as if—

A sudden suspicion caused her to stop, and she spoke without thinking. "Are you trying to *seduce* me, Mr. MacNeill?"

He, too, stopped. His lips twitched as if he might laugh, but when he looked down at her, his eyes were utterly sober. "Why, yes, Mrs. Blackburn, I am. Does the prospect alarm you?"

"Yes," she said at once. "It does."

"Ah. Regrettable and I should think unnecessary, though from my position, I'd much rather your alarm be warranted."

"Should I call out for help?" she asked, trying valiantly to sound as sophisticated as he.

He bent a sardonic eye on her. "I believe the word used was *seduce*, not rape. You are in no danger from me. Well, that's not precisely true," he allowed. "But you are only in as much danger as you allow yourself to be."

"I see," she said breathlessly.

"Good. We understand each other, then." He

tucked her hand back in the crook of his arm and would have begun to walk again, but she remained firmly planted. He looked down at her.

"Can I convince you *not* to attempt to seduce me?"

His brows drew together for a few seconds as he considered her request. "No," he finally said. "No. I do not think you can."

"Then my options are . . . ?"

"To continue our walk and let me test my skills. Or not."

Her heart had begun racing the moment he'd stated his intent. Now it galloped in her throat.

His smile grew rueful. "Come, Mrs. Blackburn. My skills, even by my own decidedly prejudiced account, are not so great."

She didn't believe him. He looked entirely capable of seduction. Big, masculine, bold, and healthy. He'd washed his hair recently, she realized. It gleamed like molten bronze, and his tanned, lean countenance had been scraped clean of the stubble it had worn since she'd met him at the White Rose. He looked dangerously appealing, alarmingly enticing, and— She gulped. She wanted to continue on with him. For a little while.

"I really am interested in the roses," she pronounced stiffly.

"Of course you are." His tone was warm with humor, but this time when he moved forward, her hand firmly caught beneath his, she went without resistance.

They moved down the pea-gravel path to the glass house, where he opened the door, waiting for her to enter before following her in. Not many of the roses inside were still blooming, though all of them retained their green foliage. He stopped first beside a small shrubby plant, bristling with thousands of needlelike thorns. "*Rosa gallica*. Judging from its size and habit, this would be the Rose of Lancaster. It is the only rose that finds favor with Brother Martin, as it is also known as the Apothecary Rose."

"And what of its bloom?"

"It blooms profusely. But only once." He pointed to a similarly shaped shrub next to it. "This is *Rosa Mundi*. It is a Gallica, also, but its petals are striped with red."

"I've seen this," Kate said with an air of discovery.

"I dare say you have. They are a very ancient variety." He moved on, passing several more low-growing plants before stopping beside one taller and with more elongated leaves than the others. "Here would be a Damask, brought to Britain from Persia."

She leaned over to search for a bloom and was disappointed to find none. She straightened to find he'd moved close behind her. She could feel his breath stirring the hair at the nape of her neck.

She froze. Her heartbeat grew heavy as a drumbeat in her chest. From back and shoulder, to hip and thigh, she was tingling, alive to his proximity.

"When you sit at your toilette some far-distant morning"—his richly accented burr was a low purr, reaching into her thoughts and caressing her—"and dab some scent here"—he touched the side of her throat and her breath checked, on a gasp or a sigh she couldn't have said—"or here"—his fingertips skated up her throat and stroked the tender skin behind her ear with gossamer lightness—"remember the roses sacrificed by the thousands to distill that fragrance, and grieve a little for their loss."

He shouldn't take such liberties. She shouldn't allow him to. And yet she couldn't seem to move. A sheath of awareness shimmered along her skin's surface. His head dipped, his lips hovered inches above her throat. She trembled, swaying toward him.

"But isn't that the way of it?" he whispered, the movement of his mouth causing his lips to flirt with the nape of her neck. "The world must sacrifice beauty for beauty's sake."

She held her breath, waiting for him to kiss her. He didn't. She felt the teasing imprint of his smile against the curve where neck flowed into shoulder, and then he lifted his head, moved to her side, and secured her hand in his arm. Disappointment flooded through her. He started forward, and she went with him, a little breathless, much confused. He only guided her to a side path and from there to a patch of bushes as tall as she, their foliage silvery green dotted with bright persimmon-colored rose hips.

"*Rosa alba,*" he instructed as if he hadn't touched her, as if she hadn't leaned into his caress, willing him to give more. "Supposedly a Roman introduction. When it flowers, its blooms are, as you might guess, primarily white. This particular one would be *alba semiplena*, historically assumed to be the White Rose of York.

"Come along, I'm saving the best for last," he said, taking her hand and pulling her beneath a small trellis covered in heavy green leaves. On the other side, a smaller path took them down a short, circuitous path where the green foliage grew brighter, glossier. Above them, the glass panes dripped with moisture, as if something breathing dwelt back here. The loamy scent of wet soil gave way to a different fragrance— not the clove spice of the roses she knew but a sweeter, more piercing aroma.

He stopped suddenly, smiling down at her, and lightly clasped her shoulders. Then he spun her around, pulling her sharply back against him and clamp his hands over her eyes. She reached up, disconcerted.

"Wait," he said.

He moved forward into her, herding her with his body as he covered her eyes, forcing her to either walk or endure the intimacy of his thighs against her buttocks. Tension swirled up her throat, and another sort of tension pooled in her belly as the half-remembered pangs of desire taunted her with their slow reawakening.

It wasn't more than a few seconds; it seemed like hours. Even through his shirt, she gauged the exact degree of heat he radiated, felt the impression of each long finger covering her eyes, was cognizant of his lower body brushing against her skirts and, mortifyingly, knew she sought the evidence of his own desire in that contact, and even more humiliatingly, felt the thrill of undeniable feminine triumph when she felt him, hard and aroused, against her.

Finally he stopped. His velvet lips swept against her ear. " 'And I will make thee beds of roses. And a thousand fragrant posies.' "

A scarred young soldier who quoted Christopher Marlowe? She could not make the pieces fit. His hands dropped away, and she opened her eyes and promptly forgot her consternation.

They stood in a small bower of greenery spangled over with sprays of bright golden yellow roses, their heavy heads bobbing in the slight movement of air. She took a step forward, and the lush fragrance she'd noted before swept up and over her. She looked down. She'd stepped on a carpet of glistening petals, crushing their ambrosial silkiness and releasing an otherworldly scent that filled her nostrils.

"What are they?" she breathed. "How can they be blooming now? Is it magic?"

"Of a sort. These are the children of the rose we brought your family."

"Children?"

"The offspring of your rose and a bonny Damask lady, a perpetually blooming rose."

"It never stops blooming?" she asked, reaching up to a spray of flowers. At once a shower of golden petals fluttered down, shimmering in the light. She drew back sharply and looked over her shoulder to find Kit watching her, an unreadable expression on his face.

"Nothing blooms forever."

His simple denial touched Kate with melancholy. Time moved on. Roses died. Worlds changed. Winter always came. She reached out from her side and plucked a single blossom from the branch.

Ah, yes. The magic was fading. Seen close, the satiny petals were lightly rimmed with brown; the dewy center had lost color and was more translucent than gold.

"It's sad, isn't it?"

He understood. He moved toward her. This time she didn't shy away from him like some scared sleek little cat. She stood quietly, pensively regarding the flower. He reached over her head and gave the branch a sharp tug, sending cascades of petals down to veil her dark hair and cloak her shoulders. She looked up at him in surprise.

"Kiss me," he said.

She drew back, and he followed her; when she would have darted past him, he reached out, grabbing hold of the trellis and barring her way.

"You said I would have nothing to be afraid of."

"Are you afraid?"

"I think I am."

"You needn't be," he said, striving for a calm, light tone. He wanted her. He had never wanted anything as much as he wanted to taste her mouth, to bury his hands in her jet hair, and crush her to him. But he wouldn't. "But I cannot help it if you choose to be afraid of nothing."

"You are not nothing."

She'd brokered a twisted smile from him after all. "But I am. Nothing to you. Just an anecdote to recall some day when you are bored."

She blushed furiously, hating that his words so closely echoed her earlier thoughts. But she had never intended *him* to be the anecdote. Never that. She couldn't stand for him to think otherwise.

"And if I kiss you, you will let me go?"

"I'll let you go whether you kiss me or not," he said. "I am simply pressing my suit."

"Really?"

"Really." To prove his point, he dropped the arm barring her way. She looked at him, trying to read his heart in his eyes. But that he kept well guarded, secret even from himself, so how could she hope to divine its intent? And that, finally, is what decided her. He was too dangerous, after all.

"I'm sorry," she murmured, ducking her head and scooting past him.

He grabbed her wrist, spun her around, and pulled her into his arms. She had a glimpse of arctic eyes burning with emotion, of his face set in rough and hungry lines.

"Don't hurt me."

He canted back as if she'd struck him, but then . . .

"Christ!" he muttered thickly and seized her head between his big, scarred soldier's hands. She closed her eyes tightly and waited, unable to control her shaking but perversely wanting this now that the moment was here, now that all choice had been stripped from her.

"Damn it!" He swore again under his breath, harsh, angry, rough words.

"Please."

He kissed her, at first nothing more than a touch of his lips as soft as the petals under their feet. A whisper caress of his mouth, utterly unexpected, utterly undoing her. With exquisite tenderness he siphoned her breath from her, gently, softly, brushing his lips over hers again and again, sweet . . . but sinful, each kiss milking her of her will, stealing her thoughts and burying them in sensation. He paused to tease each corner of her mouth, then with shattering delicacy drew the tip of his tongue down her neck in a slow, melting path and . . . oh, dear God! Deliberately, he licked the pulse fluttering in the hollow at the base of her neck.

Her knees went then. She flung her arms around his neck to keep herself from slipping to the floor.

"Kiss me. Once. One kiss," he muttered urgently, shifting one arm around her waist to support her. With his free hand, he looped her braid around his fist and tugged her head back, making her neck more accessible to him.

"What can it mean to you?" he demanded hoarsely. "Why wouldn't you— Please. Don't make me take. Give."

She wanted nothing else.

Her mouth opened beneath his, hungrily answering the heated demand of his kiss. With a dark sound of want, she gave herself over to his embrace, wrapping her arms more tightly around his neck, her fingers spearing through the cool, silky hair as she returned his kiss. A pleased sound rumbled up in his chest as his mouth slanted across hers, his tongue sweeping deeply into her mouth.

A riptide of want seized her, surging in her, through her, propelling her toward a crescendo, a crest, long suspected, never quite achieved. She felt his hands race down her back to clasp her hips and pull her abruptly into him. Longing became need, coursing out from and into that apex of her thighs. The sudden, potent pleasure vanquished coherent thought, and she became a creature dedicated to fulfilling her body's demand for satisfaction.

It had been so long. Too long.

She pulled his head down, wanting more, more lush tongue mating, and more heated, breath-ending kisses. More of him, big and hard and yearning, straining with desire, a torch to the dry tinder of the years, needs she'd never recognized let alone voiced. She wanted . . . She wanted . . .

"No." His hands clamped onto her shoulders in a painful grip. Roughly, he pushed her away. She stumbled, and if not for his hands gripping her arms, she would have fallen. Uncomprehendingly, she gazed up into his angry, strained face, still too caught in the web of desire to feel any embarrassment yet, or to feel anything other than confusion and frustration.

"What do you mean?" she asked, disoriented by the sudden shift, the rent in the fabric of pleasure.

"I swore you'd find no harm at my hands."

"Is this harm, then?" she asked breathlessly, searching his glittering green eyes. She didn't believe it.

His face tensed with some inner turmoil, and when he spoke it was through clenched teeth. "Yes."

She frowned. Reached out to touch him. He flinched as if her fingertips would burn him. "But—"

"Damnation!" he exploded. "Ten minutes ago you were begging me not to hurt you, and now, Mrs. Blackburn"—he said her name as if, in calling her by her husband's surname, he had erected a physical barrier between them—"now I am endeavoring to do as you bid me."

Each word was bitten off, hard and rife with control, and he held his body as unyielding as his tone. "I won't hurt you. I swear it. But, *the devil take it*"—his voice shook—"it would prove a great deal easier if you would aid rather than hinder that effort!"

"Oh."

*Oh.* His body felt exposed and raw. The simple kiss he'd thought to use as an antidote against her allure had proved lethal, shattering his intentions and nearly bringing him to his knees with desire for her.

He'd been deceiving himself, and he'd known it from the first: Kate wasn't like any other woman. She didn't taste or feel or move under his hands or mouth like any other woman. No other woman in the world, no matter how many he bedded or what exotic bents he pursued, would ever be her. The knowledge was a torment, and he cursed himself for so willingly being a victim of his self-delusions.

He stared at her, and his hands dropped abruptly away, knowing that if he held her an instant longer, he'd drag her back into his arms and— He closed his eyes, fighting primal instinct. If only his senses would stop working. If only he couldn't see the ripe, nearly bruised color of her mouth and hear the breathy catch in her voice. If only he didn't smell the faint astringent tang of her soap mixing with the heady fragrance of the crushed roses. If only he didn't still feel the satiny cool fall of her hair between his fingers. But his senses still worked. He still thirsted.

Kisses only fed the appetite that had been born three years ago in her father's barren drawing room and that he'd nurtured during long marches in the blasted furnace of the Indian desert. Imagination was supposed to have been better than the reality. That's what he had always told himself. But it had been a lie. Her mouth, sweet and rich, her body, supple and warm—nothing in his imagination compared to the last few minutes.

And all she could say was "Oh."

He could either laugh or go mad. So he laughed.

She blinked up at him, the hazy disconnected glow in her dark eyes slowly growing sharper. The languid, questing expression dissolved, replaced by an unreadable, and therefore utterly feminine, one. She stepped back.

She regarded him soberly, and one dark winged brow rose for a second before she turned and headed back down the path. He'd be damned if he knew the question that elegant brow had asked.

But then, he'd probably be damned anyway.

⬛⬛⬛⬛

# THIRTEEN

# THE DIFFERENCES BETWEEN LOW PLACES AND EXTREMELY LOW PLACES

"You're certain you would not like one of us to accompany you?" the abbot asked, studying Kate intently. The good priest had asked her specifically into his offices and just as specificaily had asked Kit to wait outside. The door was thick. They could not be overheard.

"Oh, no," she answered serenely. "I'm sure your monks would do far more good here rather than chaperoning me."

The crystal rosary made a delicate clicking sound in the abbot's hand, his gaze contemplative and remote. "There was a time I would have quite confidently entrusted your welfare to Christian. But I do not know him as I once did."

"I do." She spoke with absolute conviction. Kit hadn't wanted to stop kissing her, and she . . . well, she wasn't ready yet to examine the reasons for her behavior. Suffice to say that she had been quite willing to continue kissing him. Only Kit had stopped it. Because, quite simply, he would not allow injury of any variety, or from any source, to come to her. Including from him.

No, she had no fears that Kit would make another attempt in that vein. Which ought to make her happy. And did. Mostly. When it was not vexing her with half-realized questions and fully formed, and extravagantly improper, speculations.

"I am as safe with Christian MacNeill as I am with Brother Martin." She sounded petulant, even to her own ear.

The abbot smiled. "As you will." He raised his hand; the young monk at the door opened it, and Kit came in at once.

"You've adequately warned her of my myriad short-comings, I presume?"

"I have tried."

"But she wouldn't take your good advice."

"Nor my offer to have someone accompany you."

"Well, that's fortuitous, since I wouldn't allow anyone to come, regardless."

"Christian—"

"No, Father Abbot. She's mine and mine alone until I—"

"Fulfill your duty," Kate interrupted, deciding to put an end to this nonsense. She looked at the abbot. "Believe me, sir. I am in no danger from Mr. MacNeill."

"There is more than one type of danger," the abbot said. "Have you considered that the marquis might find your arrival in the sole company of this man improper?"

"I am convinced I can explain matters to his satisfaction."

Kit grinned at the abbot. "How can he take exception to the lady having a driver?"

"Father Abbot," Kate said, ignoring him and rising, "I thank you again most sincerely for your kindness as well as your hospitality."

She turned to Kit, her expression inscrutable. What had happened to the breathless siren who'd responded so passionately to him yesterday? He knew, damn her. She had disappeared, replaced by this smooth-faced society beauty who had been recalled to her purpose by the mention of the marquis. His jaw tightened.

"Now, unless the abbot has further warnings or instruction?" She looked at the abbot. He shook his head. "I think we can leave, Mr. MacNeill."

Kit bowed with sardonic grace. "As you will, ma'am."

As soon as they left St. Bride's, snow began to fall from a heavy sky, drifting across the road and glistening from the shadows beneath the trees. Kate fell silent, wrapped in the brown robe the monks had

given her. The journey was not going as she'd anticipated.

Not that she was perfectly clear on what she *had*
anticipated, but it wasn't this excruciating silence.
And yes, it had occurred to her that after yesterday
there might be some awkwardness to overcome
before they were quite back on friendly terms.
Friendly? She wasn't certain she could call their relationship that—but certainly . . . communicative. Yet
ever since they'd left the abbey, Kit had acted as if she
was a stranger, someone whose companionship was to
be tolerated, not encouraged.

"Don't be afraid of me." He finally broke the
silence.

"I'm not," she said. Whatever she had anticipated
him saying, it hadn't been that. Even though he had
instigated the kiss, he had also been the one who had
ended it. And that is precisely why she had trusted
him to take her to Clyth.

"I would never force myself on you— Damn," he
burst out. "Why should you believe me? I have already
committed that offense, haven't I?"

"Of course you will not force yourself on me," she
replied calmly. "You are a gentleman."

He laughed at that. "I am no gentleman, ma'am. I
am the bastard son of a Scottish whore." His word
cracked like a whip, stinging her but laying him open.
She saw the wound in his eyes, saw him brace himself
against it.

"I am sorry."

He shook his head in angry exasperation. "I don't want your pity, I want you to see things as they are, not be seduced by the tales of daft old men so long gone from the world that they don't know truth from fancy."

She shook her head. "The abbot isn't daft, and I think he is well aware of what is real and what is not."

"Then I wish he would have taught me that trick of discernment," Kit replied.

"He told me about your heritage."

Kit sighed. "Did he? Let me guess. He told you we were the sons of the last great Scottish chieftains."

She nodded.

"And even though our births might not have been legitimate, we were still the true heirs of the Highlands. Brave, braw warriors of the old blood."

"Yes." That is exactly what the abbot had said.

Kit regarded her with something like pity. "He told us the same when we came to him. But it's just a child's tale, told to make a bitter world a bit more palatable."

No. It wasn't true. And even he did not fully believe that claim, she could see it. The abbot had seemed not only earnest, but utterly calm, with the sort of calm that only complete conviction can convey. "I don't believe that," she said stubbornly.

"I am not a gentleman, Mrs. Blackburn. I am wholly my mother's son. You'd do well to remember that next time you ascribe gentlemanly motives to me."

"Who are you trying to punish?" she asked. "Me, for believing the abbot? Or you, for not?"

For a long moment he drove, his body rigid, his jaw squared.

"Kit," she said tentatively, not liking the dark and empty expression in his eyes. "You mustn't—"

"Mind the road for any travelers. We're getting closer to the coast."

There were no travelers.

Hours passed one into another with him answering her queries with nods. When he did speak—and that was rare enough—he took pains to address her formally, seeking now, quite openly, to put distance between them.

The bracing tang of pine and fir replaced the wet, loamy scent of the vale as they drove up into the blue-green stands of pine. Toward dusk, Kit spied a croft and drove to the door. "Hold Doran while I see to the inside."

He handed her the reins and disappeared inside. He returned in a few minutes and, with only the most cursory touch, aided her descent. She ducked inside and saw that he'd already set a fire below a cutout hole in the ceiling. He hadn't followed her in, and when she turned, she saw that he'd unharnessed Doran and was placing a bridle on him.

"What are you doing?"

"I want to look around," he answered.

"Where?" she asked.

"Up the road a ways. I'm not sure of my bearings anymore. I want to ride about a bit and see if I recognize anything."

It was a palpable lie. How would he have known about the croft if he didn't know the area? Before she could remark on it, he grabbed a handful of mane and vaulted astride Doran's bare back. He looked down at her, and she knew that her heart was in her eyes, her old fear of being abandoned filling them.

With a muttered curse he reached down and cupped her chin roughly in his hand. "Don't look like that," he said harshly. "I promise I will be back. I promise you will come to no harm here while I am gone."

"If I ask you to stay, will you?"

His gaze grew tortured. "I promised I would do as you asked, did I not?"

"Yes. But, would you stay?"

"I would do anything you ask."

"Would you stay?"

A heartbeat passed. "Yes."

She nodded somberly. "Then I won't ask."

He touched his heels to the gelding's side and rode.

Only a few dull embers still glowed on the stone hearth when Kate awoke. She peered groggily into the near-perfect darkness of the windowless croft. A horse nickered outside, and she heard a man speak soothingly to it, his voice low and exhausted. MacNeill.

She hadn't doubted he would return. Not for a minute. Not even when the fire had burned low and the wind had begun its plaintive whisper and darkness had spilled from the sky like a dead bride's veil. He'd been near all along, watching over the croft. She hadn't seen him. She hadn't needed to. She'd just known.

She heard the door creak and opened her eyes a little. For a brief instant, he stood silhouetted against the star-strewn sky. Then the door clicked shut and the room fell into a deep darkness. She heard the crackle of the fire as he fed it more fuel, and a few seconds later golden light bathed her. She rolled her head over onto her arm and studied him through half-opened eyes.

He sat by the fire with his back against the wall, his knees bent, his hand resting on them, the fingers lax. He was watching her, his eyes catching the occasional flare of firelight as the crimson light played fitfully over his face, stark and strong and hard and predatory. Like the ghost of some ancient Celtic king.

Maybe he was, she thought drowsily. So stern and forbidding and beautiful. A living phantom of a glorious, bold past.

"MacNeill?"

"Go back to sleep."

"MacNeill," she insisted groggily. "Do you believe in ghosts?"

She was almost asleep when she heard him answer from a long way off, his voice soft and forsaken. "Yes. Oh, God, yes."

## FOURTEEN

⋈⋈⋈

# CONCERNING THE DOUBTFUL CHARMS OF VILLAGE LIFE

THE NEXT MORNING KATE awoke to find the croft cleared. She hurried outside and found Kit waiting beside the phaeton.

"Good morning," she said. In answer he handed her a hard-cooked egg and a piece of bread from the basket the monks had sent with them. As she reached to take it, the sheet of paper she'd been writing on fell from her pocket and sailed to land at Kit's feet. Hastily, she bent to retrieve it, but Kit was there before her.

He picked up the page and read. " *'The Virtues of Turnips as Kitchen Staple.'* " He looked at her sharply. "What is this?"

"A book I am writing," she sniffed. "I am convinced I may find someone to publish it."

"What is its subject?" His voice was sarcastic. He was in a foul mood.

"I am writing a book on how to come down gracefully in the world."

He stilled. "Is *that* why you have been asking me all those questions?"

"No!"

"You *haven't* been using me for reference?" His gaze shot to the paper and he read, " 'The Ruffian, A Cautionary Description of His Environs and Companions.' "

"Well, perhaps to some degree," she said in a small voice. "But you are deliberately choosing to place the worst possible connotations on what is simply an attempt to provide for myself."

"Aha! I see," he said. "Then pray, excuse me for taking such unwarranted exception. Indeed, if I can be of any further aid in helping you to fathom the workings of the lower class mind, please feel free to avail yourself of my understanding."

She eyed him thoughtfully. "Well, there was one thing I wanted to—"

"I was being *ironical*, ma'am," Kit ground out.

"I understood that," she lied.

He gave a short unamused guffaw and returned to harnessing Doran, his back stiff. When he was done, he silently handed her into the carriage.

So, today was to be a repeat of yesterday's silence, was it? Fine. If he wanted nothing more to do with her, then she had little choice but to bow to his wishes. She had some pride left.

'Twas best, she told herself. Soon she would be away from him, never to see him again. Indeed, Kit was right to distance himself from her. In fact, he showed a great deal more sense than she.

She had other things to consider, important plans quickly coming to fruition. She must keep her eye on the future. By this time tomorrow, she would be at the castle. The thought touched off waves of anxiety. Years ago, the marquis had looked upon her favorably. He'd danced often enough with her to have had it remarked upon and once had even taken her in to dine.

A few of her friends had whispered that he'd been on the cusp of paying her court. But, flattering as such unfounded faith in her appeal had been, Kate had known better. She was country gentry, and he was a marquis. Members of society from such different spheres did not intermarry. But he *had* flirted with her, tamely, circumspectly, so as not to raise false expectations, but sincerely.

She counted on his remembering kindly those short weeks when their circles had overlapped, however briefly. Would he still see something of the vivacious young woman she'd once been? Or would he only see yet another petitioner for his largesse? She reached up to touch her hair.

"There's an inn at Clyth where you can make of yourself what you would before we go on to the castle."

Kate straightened on the hard plank seat, embarrassed that Kit had seen and recognized her vanity.

But a woman without family or income, a woman like her, needed to look well, comport herself better, and adopt an agreeable manner in order to secure herself the charity of such distant connections as she could make herself approach.

"Thank you. That would be most agreeable."

Toward midday the road left the foothills and entered an autumn-hued plain. They passed more crofts, their mossy stone fences crumbled and untended, the abandoned outposts left by a vanishing nation of drovers and farmers. As the day wore on, the briny scent of the sea became pronounced. Seabirds appeared, squalling black-capped terns and white gulls carting and wheeling above a distant silver-edged horizon.

A few miles later they emerged at the tops of sheer white cliffs plunging into the sea. The road pitched abruptly down into a village, small brick houses clinging tenaciously to the cliff side, thin curls of coal smoke drifting above chimneypots like question marks.

At the bottom of the steep road, the houses congregated thickly along a narrow quay. Two ancient piers jutted out from it, casting shadows across a dozen battered, open fishing boats lying on their sides in a bed of shimmering mud. The tide was out, and the scent of fish and kerosene and decaying seaweed hung thick and malodorous in the air.

"Clyth," Kit said, correctly reading her repugnance. "The inn is on the wharf. Perhaps you'd rather continue on to the castle after all?"

"No!" Arrive at the castle in a dress in which she'd

slept? She couldn't. Not when she had a perfectly lovely gown and a hairbrush in her trunk. "Please."

He did not answer, but maneuvered the phaeton down onto the quay. Few people were out. A pair of burly fishermen with weathered faces stared at them with sullen hostility, and a tired-looking woman emerged from a low doorway, clutching a battered pail of coals.

Kit pulled the gelding to a halt before a narrow building sandwiched between two warehouses. A gray board swung from an arm projecting above the doorway, but sea salt and time had obliterated whatever had once been written there. A whey-faced urchin dashed out of the doorway and snatched at Doran's reins.

"Stable's out back," the lad croaked. "I'll rub him down proper and feed him and see him snug and safe fer tuppence, Cap."

Kit flipped a coin to the lad, who snatched it out of the air. Eager to escape the bitter, reeking wind coming off the harbor, Kate did not wait for Kit's help but scrambled down out of the carriage and fled inside. It was better than she expected. A thin layer of dust coated the ceiling beams, but the fire in the hearth burned clean, and the harbor stench faded as soon as the doors closed behind her. The only occupants were a pair of men seated in the gloom at the far side of the room. Upon her entrance, they broke off their conversation and looked up. The older man, a lantern-jawed fellow with thick, hunched shoulders, stood up, wiping his hands on a dirty apron tied about his waist.

His eyes slid slowly over Kate. "Can do fer ye?"

"Are you the innkeeper?"

"Aye."

"How far to Castle Parnell?" Kate asked.

"Under an hour astride, nearer two hours if ye drive."

"I see." She had hoped to be in the castle by night-fall, but it looked as if she would have to be patient and wait until the morrow. She did not examine the reason why she felt more relief than irritation at the delay.

"Is there someone you can send to the castle?" she asked.

The speaker glanced at his companion, an athletic-looking young man with thick black hair and heavy brows, an improbable lace cravat beneath his chin and an even more improbable rapier fastened at his waist. He was a handsome devil, and by the manner in which he let his gaze slip over Kate, he knew it, too. He gave the innkeeper a nod.

"Aye. Can do tha'."

"Then please send him at once. And tell him to inform the castle that Mrs. Katherine Blackburn has arrived in Clyth and will be traveling to the castle at first light."

"Ye'll be Mrs. Blackburn, then?" the innkeeper's companion asked.

"Yes."

"Welcome to Clyth, Mrs. Blackburn," he said. "I'm Callum Lamont."

A sudden burst of cold air stirred the hem of her skirts as the door behind her opened.

"The lady requires a room."

The innkeeper peered beyond Kate to where Kit stood, balancing the heavy trunk easily on his broad shoulder, carrying the crate by its rope ties. He filled the low doorway behind Kate, his height and breadth dwarfing her. Lamont's eyes narrowed sharply, but he did not say a word, instead leaning back into the shadows.

"Three shillings a night," the innkeeper said, shambling behind the bar and motioning for Kit and Kate to follow. "Payable in advance."

Kit placed a crown on the ledger.

"And what of ye, Cap?" the innkeeper asked. "Ye need a room, or—" He smiled unctuously.

"Ye've got it wrong, friend." There was nothing remotely friendly about the way Kit pronounced the word *friend*. "I'm her driver."

The man snorted but decided against pursuing the matter further. "There's only the one room. But I'll let you bed down above the stables for tuppence."

"Done." Kit's chill green eyes flickered toward her. "Is there anything else you need?"

"Yes. I would like a tub with hot water sent up—"

The innkeeper hooted with laughter.

"The lady would like a bath." Kit's tone effectively dampened the innkeeper's hilarity.

With a sullen look, the innkeeper cupped a huge paw around his mouth and bellowed, "Meg!"

A moment later a skinny, harried-looking blond woman appeared. "Wha', Gordie?"

"You and Robbie fetch that copper washtub into the

kitchen and fill it up with hot water. Lady here wants a *bath*." He gave Kate a look that said clearly how daft he thought the notion. "Cannot drag the tub up the stairs. But the kitchen's snug enough. Meg'll tend ye, and Robbie'll watch over the door. Fer another shilling."

"That will be fine," Kate said. She would have bathed in the horse trough if necessary. She only wanted to feel clean again. Meg, her eyes grown round with the wonder of someone bathing in the winter, bobbed a quick curtsey and disappeared.

"Anyt'ing else?" the innkeeper asked, a bit more eager now that he'd seen the color of Kit's gold.

"Do you have anything worth drinking?" Kit asked.

"I've never had no complaints." The innkeeper stooped down and reemerged with a brown glass bottle and two tin cups. Wordlessly, he poured a finger into one cup and shoved it at Kit, who just as silently lifted it to his lips and took a swallow. For a second, his mouth relaxed appreciatively.

"Brandy. French. I can see why you don't have any complaints."

"Found it on the beach, I did."

"Amazing the treasure some people are so careless with." His gaze slipped briefly toward Kate. His face grew grim. He poured out a measure first for her, then himself. He lifted his cup in her direction.

"May you find what you want, Mrs. Blackburn," he said with forced bonhomie.

"And may I find what I *need*, Mr. MacNeill," she replied, holding his gaze.

# FIFTEEN

# REVIVING FLAGGING

# SPIRITS

THE HEAT FROM THE WATER soaked into Kate's tired muscles as the scent of expensive milled soap inveigled her senses. Exhaustion finally allowed her to relax after the strain of the last week.

While Kate soaked, Megan had washed out her petticoat and the chemise, *tch*'ing over the condition of her gown. Now she spread them across the back of a chair before the fire and lifted the steaming kettle from its hook. Carefully, she added more water to the copper tub.

"There, ma'am. That'll be better." The dour-looking woman had slowly unbent as she tended Kate. "Lovely hair ye have. A proper shame 'twas allowed to go wild like, but up here people don't know or care fer what a lady values or a gentleman admires."

"No?" Kate murmured vaguely.

"Tha cap'n cares, clear enough," Meg said slyly.

Kit? Yes. He cared. Unhappily, grimly, and grudgingly. "Why do you call him a captain?"

"What? Oh." Meg brushed at the dress hem. "Believe me, I seen enough uniforms to know one when I see one. Half the young men of Scotland wear regimental rags. That's an officer's jacket he's wearing. As fer why I says cap'n, well, captain is as good as a major when you don't have to prove it.

"Did he come up to join the militia?" she went on. "Cause if he did, I'd warn him not to make it known here in Clyth."

Kate frowned. "What militia?"

"Them that's been staying at Parnell Castle ever since their captain was killed."

"Killed?" Kate repeated.

Meg's little knot of a face closed even tighter. "Aye. His replacement showed up last week, a Captain Watters, and at the marquis's insistence brought the soldiers to the castle." She sneered. "The marquis wouldn't allow what protection he could find to stray far from his own concerns, would he? Besides, no one is fool enough to put militia in Clyth."

"And why is that?" Kate asked, troubled anew.

"Because." Meg's eyes narrowed. She closed them, as though deliberating on something and then spoke in a rush. "Tha last excise man took more'n a day to die."

Kate froze. Fear, abrupt and gut-emptying, flooded her.

Meg cleared her throat, scowling fiercely. "No need for you to look like that." Amazingly, she sounded offended. "*Ye* dinna see him with his blood spilling from his belly," she muttered. "And him so white and scared—" She broke off abruptly, and in rising horror Kate realized: Meg had seen the excise man murdered. She had *been* there.

Revolted, she hunched low in the water. She'd thought she was safe. She wasn't safe. She would never be safe. Not as long as—

"Aye! I was scared!" Meg said shrilly, as if answering an accusation, and Kate suddenly understood that Meg had told her because she was a stranger and because Meg could no longer live with the secret or her guilt. "I'm *still* scared. Too scared to help meself, let alone a stranger. I stood there. I couldn't move! I couldn't breathe." With sudden eagerness she leaned closer, whispering. "But mayhap I can help you. Have a care, ma'am. Be wary of Callum Lamont."

Then, as if she'd alleviated some of her terrible guilt, Meg straightened. "There. As good as I can do."

Kate shivered.

"Ach! Look at ye!" She dashed the back of her hands across her red cheeks. "Yer getting cold. No matter. We're done now." Her tone was determinedly casual. She might never have spoken of murder. "Up with ye now, Mrs. Blackburn."

Kate rose, somehow managing not to flinch when the woman settled a thick towel over her shoulders.

What if Meg told Lamont that she'd confessed to her what she'd seen? What would he do?

"Don't look so worrit, ma'am." Meg wagged her finger playfully, and Kate fought the gorge rising from her belly. How could Meg act as if she hadn't just confessed to witnessing a murder? How could she live with herself for having done nothing to stop it? "Ye'll be fine at the castle. It's only us left here that need fear, and we're used to that.

"Now, yer petticoat and chemise is dry, so you put them on and bundle up in yer cloak and go up to yer room. No one will ken that you've no dress beneath. Seem a shame to put filthy clothes over clean skin."

Kate donned her undergarments, her emotions a riot of conflicting impulses: to condemn, to weep, to flee. To pity.

Would nothing in her life ever be straightforward again? Every turn took her into avenues she had not even known existed, let alone desired to explore. Smugglers and highwaymen, victims and victimizers, she thought, panicked and resentful. Poverty came with an additional penalty: knowledge.

She didn't want to know any more. She needed to get to the castle, to a place where she understood the rules. She wanted nothing to do with such savagery and bestiality. She did not want to know men who killed, or wounded, or hunted one another. Men like Christian MacNeill.

She wanted her sheltered, blissfully ignorant life back.

And the first step to recovering that was to prepare for her arrival at the castle by dressing like a lady. Yes, she thought, her limbs shaking so badly she could barely navigate the sloping kitchen floor. Yes. That is what she would do.

She would wear the lilac batiste. Once she looked like a lady, all this would fade away. She would never again see men brawl in a tavern. She would never speak to another witness to murder. She would never lie sleepless, fearful that she might be accosted during the night. She would never trust her welfare to a stranger.

And Kit MacNeill *was* a stranger. Regardless of what her body told her. She would stop dreaming about his sweet, ravishing kisses and hard, muscular body. She would forget his rare laughter and his brooding eyes. She would not concern herself over wounds she could see and others she only guessed at.

She gathered up her cloak, searching the hem for the last of her coins, and wordlessly placed them in Meg's hand. Then, before the woman could draw her any deeper into her fear-framed life, she fled through the kitchen door.

Only a few men occupied the public room, and Kate lurched up the stairs that led to her room, her urgency to leave growing with each step. She must convince someone to take her to the castle tonight. She could not stand the idea of lying awake through the night, wondering which of the men drinking in the room beneath had knifed open another. She felt ill. Light-headed. Her body trembled.

She pulled the door open and froze.

Grace's trunk lay empty on its side, its blue silk lining ripped, the gold-embroidered stars winking at her from the floor. Smashed and rent, strewn and heaped, the entire contents of the trunk had been upended in the room and rifled through: a ship's barometer, a ruined Chinese puzzle box, Grace's telescope, a smashed porcelain clock, books, their bindings ripped, their pages torn. Her gaze moved dazed among the debris. With a terrible sense of inevitability, she looked down at her feet and saw Charles's leather medicine traveling chest, the drawers yanked out and the vials spilled of their staining contents.

All over her dresses.

Callum Lamont stared ahead of him, fingering his rapier. He was not in the best of moods. He'd been cheated of a grand treasure. True, he'd found some satisfaction in sending both Charles Murdoch and his bitch-wife to their deaths, but that satisfaction had long since disappeared, leaving only impotent anger.

He'd been hasty. He saw that now. But he'd been so very angry. Not only had Charles Murdoch kept secret the message from their "friend" that outlined the route of a richly laden French yawl, but he'd used four of Callum's own men to wreck the damn thing and hide the booty in one of the—Callum looked up at the ceiling and pensively scratched his chin—five? ten thousand? caves or inlets or underwater grottoes that lined the coast. Cheeky bastard.

Charles, Callum thought darkly, had not been a very good associate—not like his "real" partner. Though that devil gave Callum the shivers, what with the way he was always poking holes in his own skin.

Murdoch would have gotten away with his treachery, too, if Callum's partner hadn't warned him. When Callum had found out what Murdoch had done, he'd killed him along with his wife, maintaining just enough presence of mind to set the bodies in Murdoch's yacht and wreck it against the reefs. Then he'd gone in search of his men and the treasure that was rightfully his. So far, so good.

But then, the unthinkable had happened. He'd discovered that Charles Murdoch had killed the men who'd aided him—*Callum's* men—to keep them from either disclosing his treachery or going off with the treasure themselves. At any rate, the men were dead. Blast Murdoch's sly eyes. That had been some months ago, and he'd yet to find the treasure.

Callum drained the last of his whisky. The door banged open, and Callum lifted his head, expecting some of his lads to join him. Instead, the tall "driver" for the dark woman entered. He had the stink of a soldier about him, starting with that jacket and ending with the claymore strapped between his shoulders. And he looked familiar.

Callum cocked his head, considering whether the militia had sent him. Nah. The man was probably just a deserter who'd kept his coat out of sentiment or ire. The militia hadn't stopped one boat from landing, and that, or so he'd been told, rankled Captain Watters, the replacement for the officer who'd been killed.

Callum's dark mood lightened.

The tall man swept the plaid from his shoulders, looking around the room with the natural caution of a man used to danger. His gaze checked on Callum, then moved up the stairs before he crossed the room and commandeered a chair, calling for Brodie to bring him a whisky.

Brodie complied at once, answering the stranger's imperious manner as much as his tone. Both irritated Callum Lamont. He didn't like lads getting above themselves, lest that lad was himself. Callum Lamont was the King of Commoners. Nodding to Brodie to bring him another whisky, he rose and made his way over to the Highlander.

"What regiment did you run off from?"

The stranger slowly raised his gaze. His eyes were pale and dark at the same time, like ice coating basalt, all sparkling clear on the surface and ebon depths beneath. God. Where *had* he seen this bastard before?

"I don't recall being introduced to you."

Callum's brows flew up. "Introduced, is it? My, aren't we grand?" He dragged a nearby chair to the opposite side of the table, swung his leg over it, and sat down. "No," he answered his own question, leaning forward, his hands flat against the table's surface, "we're not grand. We're Highland rubbish, is what we are."

"Are we?" The newcomer met Callum's gaze unin-
terestedly.

"I did not hear your name."

The light, deep eyes flickered up. "I didn't give it."

"Well, you might consider giving it now."

With the speed of a striking serpent, twin dag-
gers suddenly appeared in each of the Highlander's
fists and slammed deep into the table, scoring
Callum's wrists as they pinned his sleeves to the
wood surface. Calmly, the stranger released the hilts
and lifted his cup to his mouth. He took a drink.
"Or I might not."

Callum's lips twitched. "You don't want me for an
enemy, lad."

"I don't want you at all . . . *lad*."

"My men'll be comin' soon. They're not a nice
crew."

" 'Struth?" the Highlander asked with more
amusement than trepidation.

"They're the sort of lads who like a brawl."
Callum's voice dipped suggestively. "Or a good lay."
His gaze moved suggestively toward the stairway.

The Highlander followed his gaze and then looked
back at Callum's sneering visage.

"Unfortunate you can't do both at the same time
now, isn't it? But a man can only be in one place at a
time," he said, confident the stranger would heed his
none-too-subtle threat.

The Highlander's hand shot out, seizing Callum by
the throat. For a second, Callum was too amazed to

react, then he was fighting for his life. Without the least change of expression, the stranger's grip tightened.

Exploding lights skittered across Callum's vision. He heard a rattling sound and through a fog of pain recognized it as himself, trying to breathe.

"Do not ever," he heard the Highlander say quietly, "*ever* threaten Mrs. Blackburn again."

But prudence had never been Callum's strong suit. He couldn't back down from this man. Not in front of Brodie.

"She'll be thanking me when I'm done with her!" he gasped, finally wrenching his arms free. But weakened, he could only claw uselessly at the hand tightening inexorably around his throat.

Above him, eyes as remorseless and cold as the arctic seas gazed down at him. A memory bubbled through the panic gripping him. Green eyes. Guinea gold hair. A filthy, undernourished lad with green eyes and a cold savagery in him that made Callum think he might be useful someday. Might be worth troubling over. Might be worth—

"You gonna kill the man what saved yer hide, Christian MacNeill?" The grip around his throat eased a fraction. The cool eyes flickered with sudden recognition.

"Aye!" Callum croaked in triumph. "*Ye owe me.* Ye can't take me life, ye bastard!"

He could feel his windpipe crushing under the brute force of a grip used to wielding a claymore. His ears thrummed with pressure. Darkness covered him and he heard Christian MacNeill say, "It wasn't much of a life anyway."

And he knew nothing more.

*LeMons Castle dungeon, France May 1799*

*"Watch out!" The Englishman launched himself into Kit's side, knocking him down. Kit rolled and exploded upright, spinning around just in time to see a blade bury itself in the snarling Frenchman's throat as a dagger dropped from the dead man's hand.*

*Kit's heart raced thickly. He knew the dead man, a savage beast who preyed on the young men in the prison and who'd become enamored of Kit's green eyes. Until Kit had disenamored him with his fists.*

*"Thank you," Kit said, turning to his champion.*

*The Englishman nodded, panting, toward the dead man. "He was goin' to kill you."*

*"Thank God you saw what he was about," Douglas said as he and Dand appeared.*

*"Lucky for you I saw what the bastard was up to." The Englishman nodded vigorously "I reckon you owe me proper, in't that right?"*

*"Indeed." Ramsey arrived, taking in the situation at once. "Ask and you shall receive. What's the price of a man's life these days? More to the point, what do you want?"*

*"I know you." He pointed at Ram. "I seen you with a stick, playing at swords, with some of these Frenchie bastards. Look real good doing it. Elegant-like."*

*Ram inclined his head. "You are too kind."*

*"That's what I want. I want you to teach me how to do all that fancy swordwork."*

*"I am in your debt. Not him," Kit said coolly.*

*"So you are, but I ain't seen nothing you have that I want. Yet."*

*"Leave off, Kit." Ram shrugged. "Cut off your arm and pitch it at the poor bugger, you bloody prideful Scottish cur, if you think your honor demands it, but then let me have my bit of fun, will you? It should at least help relieve the tedium between beatings."*

*"All right." Kit allowed grudgingly. "But someday I'll repay him."*

# SIXTEEN

⧓⧓⧓

# TEMPTATIONS, ENTICEMENTS, AND LURES AWAITING THE UNWARY LADY

KIT TIGHTENED HIS HOLD, and Lamont's heels drummed against the floorboards. The innkeeper, witness to God knows how many acts of violence, discreetly disappeared. At the last moment, Kit released his grip and dropped the gasping man like a pox-plagued rat.

With a sound of disgust, Kit stepped over his one-time savior. Kit MacNeill always paid his debts: it was the only reason the bastard still drew breath. But if he ever threatened Kate again—by implication, word, or act—he was dead.

He gazed dispassionately down at the unconscious man, studying his features. He hadn't recognized him. None of them had been shaven; all of them had been encrusted with fleas and sores and filth. But the rapier should have struck a chord. Whoever used a rapier but Ram and his pupil? Kit scowled. Could Ram have sent him up here?

A female's cry of distress abruptly canceled Kit's half-formed thought.

He took the stairs two at a time, pulling the claymore from its scabbard on his back in a smooth, lethal motion. Kate's door stood open, and inside she lay huddled on the floor, her face buried in her hands. Her indigo cape had fallen off one naked shoulder. His heart thundered thickly in his chest. If anyone had touched her—

He shut the door and glided past her, his gaze sweeping the room. There was no place to hide; they were alone. He turned back to her.

"Look at me, lass," he demanded tautly. "Are you injured?"

"No."

*"Did he touch you?"*

"No." She shook her head and her inky tresses streamed out, catching and releasing glints of candlelight. "Why did someone have to do this?"

*Do this . . . ?* He looked around and so for the first time noted the condition of the room. Around them lay pieces of porcelain and glass, splintered wood and torn papers. Someone had destroyed most of the contents of her trunk.

But she hadn't been harmed.

"Are you sure you are not hurt?"

"I didn't even see anyone." She lifted her face. Tears streamed down her pale cheeks.

He relaxed, allowing the readiness to ease back a notch, and slipped the claymore back into its scabbard. Now that he knew she was unhurt, relief flooded him, and with it a dawning awareness of her state. He fervently wished it hadn't. It had been possible to ignore her body when she'd been bundled in her indigo cape and the monk's sturdy wool gown. But her movement had caused the cape to slip off her shoulders, and the thin chemise she wore beneath did nothing to conceal her body. Lace flirted with the top of her bosom, and a white satin ribbon trailed provocatively down the shadowed valley between her breasts. Beneath the thin white material, her areolas gleamed like late buds beneath first snowfall. His mouth went dry with longing.

"Why are you crying then?" He sounded rough and accusatory when, in fact, his accusation was solely for himself. What sort of animal was he to go from fear to lust so quickly?

Her hand fell on the dress piled beside her, her fingers plucking weakly at it. "They're ruined. All ruined."

The gown? he thought incredulously. All her tears were over a bloody *gown*?

"It's just a dress."

"No." She shook her head in violent denial. "No, it's not. It was my way out."

Her way out. She had no idea of the depth of the cut she dealt him with those few words.

"Is it so intolerable, not having wealth?" He could not hide his sneer. "Not having pretty dresses?"

She looked up at him, her eyes brilliant with tears.

"Yes!" she cried. "It is. *Intolerable*. Do you find that superficial?" she demanded. "Well, I am sick unto death of apologizing for not wanting to be poor—as if that desire is somehow cowardly and iniquitous and the endurance of poverty is noble and virtuous.

"There's nothing noble in poverty, MacNeill. Poverty is cold and desperate and anxious—always anxious. It stands by and watches men get sliced open and doesn't dare interfere. Then it chokes you with guilt for surviving."

He frowned, uncertain where her rage came from but knowing without doubt that it was not because of a ruined dress. He reached down to help her up, but she snatched herself back, glaring up at him.

"I want back what I once had. I don't want to be afraid anymore. I don't want to watch a man get killed and do nothing to stop it—" She broke off. "And I *would*. Because I know how afraid she was!"

She? Who had Kate been talking to? "Kate, I am sorry you—"

"No! Do not dare comfort me!"

She'd pressed her hands flat against the floor on either side of her. "I won't graciously accept living the rest of my life like this, as if I had somehow conspired at my state and was paying a penance for some sin."

She pushed herself to her feet, standing toe to toe with him, her dark eyes filled with angry challenge.

Her cape billowed and fell, drifting to the floor. "*He died, not me!*"

Her father? He stood above her, finally understanding.

"I wasn't prepared. I wasn't supposed to be a widow and an orphan." Her voice cracked, anguish abruptly replacing her rage. "And I *know* there are others who have endured far grimmer fates than I, and that I should be grateful things aren't worse. *But I can't*. I'm not. I'm not noble enough to welcome crumbs." Her voice broke. "I'm so *tired* of being afraid, of fearing what challenge the next day will bring. Of fearing that I might not be able to meet it. "

"I understand."

"Do you?" she whispered.

She gazed somberly up at him, and he would surely drown in her eyes, get so lost he would never find his way back. He cupped her face between his palms. He had no right to kiss her. He'd promised her and himself he wouldn't.

He'd lied.


It had been nearly four years since Kate had quickened to a man's touch or she'd arched with instinctive welcome beneath a man's body. Nearly four years since she had wanted and been wanted in return.

It all came rushing back so swiftly that she grew light-headed, sensation igniting long-dormant instincts like lightning to a deadfall. Her knees buckled, and Kit caught her, lowering them both to their knees and looping his arm tightly about her waist, binding her to the hard masculine wall of his chest.

His lips never left hers.

With his free hand he clasped her chin, tipping her face up and holding it as if afraid she would turn away. He needn't have. She kissed him back, her mouth opening to taste him with tongue as well as lips: tangy male, salty and rich.

He pulled back, spreading his hand across the base of her spine just above the flare of her buttocks and slowly pressing her against him, molding her against the hard male ridge. His eyes were no longer light and chill, but dark and reckless.

"I shouldn't do this," he said. But he did not let her go. "I shouldn't have kissed you again. I swore I wouldn't."

"I want you to kiss me," she answered, desire destroying modesty.

"No." He shook his head, stumbling to his feet. Without his support, she sank down atop her ruined gowns.

"Not two days ago I swore that I would not touch you again."

She reached up and placed her palm flat against his belly. A tremor rippled through him. He stared down at her hand, struck still at her touch. When he lifted his head, his eyes were terrible with conflict, damning her, pleading with her. Wanting her.

"I do not remember my husband's embrace." She had to make him understand things she barely understood herself. "I was married for six months, and we enjoyed tenderness and affection, and we made love, but I do not remember it. Except in dreams. And of late, I dream of you."

A strangled sound rose from Kit's throat. "Jesus, Kate."

"You kissed me, and I have been burning ever since. Your kiss burned away everything." She held his gaze. "Everything but you."

He looked stricken, trapped. "I'm sorry. I took that kiss. I shouldn't have."

"I do not accept your apology."

"What else can I do?"

She lowered her eyes, afraid to meet his gaze. "Make love to me," she whispered breathlessly, stunned by her own boldness. "Make me forget. Make something for me to remember."

He raked his hair back from his face with trembling fingers, pacing as he spoke. "You don't mean this. You're scared, and you're feeling vulnerable. You want comfort. Not a lover."

She did not say a word, only tracked him with dark, enigmatic eyes.

"You should have a gentleman lover to kiss your fingertips and write love letters and whisper poetry."

Still, she did not speak.

"I'm not that man, Kate. I'm not a gentleman, Kate, I'm a *soldier*. All I have, all I *am*, is ferocity." The words grated out, vehement and apologetic. "It is all I know."

He moved past her, heading for the door, but she snagged his wrist, stopping him, forcing him to look at her. She pulled at him until he sank again to his knees, conflict playing over his stark features: darkness and light, honor and disgrace, hope and despair.

"I don't believe that." Her fingers curled around the neck of his shirt, the weight of her hand dragging it open over his chest. The dark hairs covering his chest sprang crisply under her knuckles. His body was hard and supple, muscular and sleekly toned.

"God. Please." He closed his eyes, pulling her hand away from him, struggling for words. 'Tisn't my place. That will someday belong to another."

"What other?" she scoffed. "I am an impoverished widow without family connection and past the first blush of youth. My highest aspiration is to live on the charity of a distant connection. There is no *other*, Kit, nor is there like to be."

She pulled free of his clasp and lightly touched his face, the gesture oddly prim, a formal request, a petition and a plea. "There is only you. One night to hold against all the nights to come."

"Is this some diabolical test?" His throat corded with veins. "If it is, how can I possibly succeed?" he demanded, his face stark in the leaping shadows. He grabbed her upper arms with sudden, implacable violence and dragged her up against him. "Listen to me, Kate. Nothing else but harm can come of my taking you here. Now. And *I swore I would cause you no harm.*"

"You also swore you would do anything I ask." Her voice shook with her audacity.

He stared down at her, the light catching in the

jade of his eyes, pearlizing the scar on his chin. His arms trembled, and his body tightened.

"As you will, ma'am," he finally whispered. Then he was lowering her to her back on a pile of ruined satin and lace, silk and velvet. "What's another mark to bear?"

He sat back on his heels and, with an easy fluid movement, unstrapped his claymore and stripped his shirt from his torso. His beauty was entirely masculine, rough and virile. Smooth, fine-grained flesh veiled heavy planes of muscle and bone. He tossed the shirt aside, and the biceps bunched in his arms, the sinew in his forearm flexing. He leaned over her, prowling up her body like a cat over a kill; the muscles in his flat belly jumped into relief.

For a long moment, he held her gaze before turning, deliberately exposing the welts on his back and something else. A thick, raised scar in the rough shape of a rose rode below his right shoulder blade.

"They branded us in France. At LeMons. The warden thought it amusing."

Dear God, the pain he must have endured.

"I wanted you to see this. To drive home what I have been trying to tell you. No man who comes to your bed should be branded, Kate. Or wear scars from a whip. Only a commoner or a criminal would. I am as common as any man on God's earth," he said stonily. "I am unfit for your society, your company, *or* your bed, and that by any, *any* man's, reckoning."

The certainty in his eyes decided her. He expected

her to cringe away. She saw it in his expression, the resignation that lay beneath his calm words.

She wrapped her arms around his neck. "By any man's reckoning, Kit MacNeill, there is nothing common about you." He was warm to the touch, his naked flesh smooth against hers.

His beautiful eyes blazed with sudden triumph. "I will find tenderness. I will give you pleasure, Kate, or I will die in trying."

He grinned then and was suddenly, overwhelmingly, a creature of masculine sexuality. All traces of conflict vanished from his expression. His eyes had gone velvety with intent. In one bold movement, he swept the chemise from her shoulder, baring her breasts.

"Kit—"

Before another word could escape her lips, he covered her mouth.

Desire rode him hard, driving him with brutal spurs. But he would not act. He would not, though her breasts weighed soft in his hands and her nipples puckered, a trap set to annihilate his best intentions. She'd asked for tenderness, and he'd promised to do whatever she asked, and if in keeping that promise he singed himself on the blast furnace of tamped desire, so be it.

He swept her up into his arms and rose, his jaw tightening at the way she shrank, praying for restraint, all the while fully aware he had none. The bed was a step away, and he lowered her to the mattress, looking down at her. Yet not for an instant did he mistake what she wanted for what he wanted to give. That would never be his place. For one night he would be her lover, if not her beloved.

He lowered his head, telling himself to be gentle, to be easy.

She did not react at once to his kiss. He did not need her response. Indeed, her active participation might well have destroyed his self-imposed restraint. He rained light kisses upon her cheeks and eyelids and her temples. His head swam with bliss and lust. He could taste her, not just on his tongue, but in the very air, musky and womanly.

He lowered himself, hissing with pleasure as her soft breasts yielded beneath his chest. And when he felt her clasp his shoulders, her long fingers digging into the muscles and her neck arching back, his body quaked. He plunged his hands into the waves of dark hair, damp and cool in the night air, and feasted on her mouth. Silk, satin, velvet? They were not comparisons he could make. He knew little of silk, less of satin, and naught at all of velvet, but surely nothing on earth could be sleeker than her hair, nothing smoother than her flesh, nothing softer than her lips.

Her mouth opened fully and her tongue met his, playing havoc with his self-control. He rolled, carrying her atop him, her thighs spread across his hips, his arousal thrust into the lee of her legs.

Kate gasped with pleasure at the foreign-familiar sensation. She wanted this. Wanted him inside her. A throbbing had begun where he lodged against her, one that needed him inside her to assuage it.

She grew shameless in her quest. She sprawled over his body, rubbing against him, her invitation clear. She wanted him. She *needed* him. She could not make her need any clearer, and yet he seemed content to play at open-mouthed kisses and slow, languid petting, his hand stroking her idly.

"Please," she panted, frustrated.

"No. Not yet," Kit breathed heavily. The tip of his finger traced a circle around her nipple. She flinched at the delicate touch, overly sensitized and overwhelmed, and felt his erection prod her thigh in response. She rocked against him, and he clasped her hips, pulling her hard against him, stilling her movements, his eyes as dark and violent as his lips were tender and soft.

"Stay," he growled. "I am only human, and if you do that again, then all your hopes for a gentle union will be for naught and all my best intentions destroyed. I am holding on, ma'am. But only just."

Rather than daunting her, his words stimulated her. That he would harness his desire at her request filled her with a sense of power as elemental as it was feminine. But within seconds, her moment of ascendancy evaporated beneath a new onslaught of sensation.

He lifted her by the shoulder and lowered her upper body above his head, hungrily drawing her nipple into his mouth. He suckled her. She gasped, arching more fully, and he squeezed her breast gently between strong fingers, his tongue swirling against the tip of her breast, turning the muscles in her thighs liquid and stealing the breath from her lungs. She nearly swooned, but he caught her, holding her suspended a few inches above him so he could more easily do what he wanted, play and fondle and suckle and nip, and Heaven help her, she could do nothing but revel in his mastery and give herself to his passionate use.

Between her legs, she'd grown wet and sleek with readiness. A rhythm called that her body answered. She moved on him, once again, the feeling between her thighs expanding and contracting at the same time. He tried to stop her, his hand rough in his attempt to hold her still, but she did not care what she risked; anything was worth the price. She rocked against him, each movement settling her more fully on him, the thick ridge beneath her petticoat pulsing with exquisite reaction.

With a low, desperate sound, he caught her up and dumped her flat on her back, his lower body pressing her down into the mattress, stilling her. "Not yet."

"Yes."

"Kiss me." He commanded her, and like a trollop she complied, hungrily pulling his head down. Their kiss was rough, passionate, his nascent beard abrading her tender lips, bruising her mouth. For long minutes she fed the passion he'd incited, wanting him, wanting an end, a release, one brief night to release her from the last four years of her life.

"Kate!" She had found the limits of his self-restraint. Her mons pumped urgently against him. He growled. "Continue this, and I will have you in ways no lady could want."

"What ways?" she asked, shameless and brazen.

His green eyes narrowed between the banks of gilt lashes. "I will have you on your back and I will have you against the wall and I will take you on your knees. I will hear you sob and plead for my touch, and then you will plead again, and I will have you again."

Fearlessly, she gazed up at him, her hair spread like a mantle of night across the pale linen.

"Is that what you want, Kate? Because, by God, I can give you that. It's what I am. But Kate, I would . . . Let me *make love* to you." His voice shook with the force of his emotions, and Kate's eyes darkened with understanding.

He had no idea. But then, until now, neither had she. Amazement filled her, and she reached up, stroking his cheek. He turned his head into the caress, closing his eyes and pressing a hot kiss in the center of her palm.

"I want you as you are, Kit. As *we* are." She stroked him, beginning at one big, scarred shoulder, down the velvety ladder of his ribs, to his hip, and from there burrowed between them, delving beneath the front placket of his trousers and curling her fingers around his erection. He whispered what might have been a curse or a prayer. "This *is* making love, Kit."

The hot flesh moved like a satin sheath over the hard core of him, exciting and wicked and exquisitely male. He sank forward over her, his forehead coming to rest against hers for a short, intense instant. Then he rolled her to her side, the movement pulling him out of her hand.

He wrenched her petticoat up, revealing the dark

curls at the apex of her thighs. His breathing had grown heavy, his lean face stark as he cupped her mound without haste but without delicacy, a gesture of masculine possession. She reacted with a gasp of pleasure, and a smile illuminated his dark, tense features.

He caressed her, and she should have burned with mortification at the familiarity, the certainty with which he fondled and explored her, but she burned for another reason altogether. Her eyelids drifted shut. Her breath grew shallow and quick. Again and again he stroked her, and with each caress her hips rose, pleasure mingling seamlessly with arousal.

She twisted on the sheets, her petticoat rucked up under her waist, her body hot and needy. Helplessly, she opened her eyes and found him watching her.

She did not want to be alone. She held out her arms. "Kit. Please."

"Kate. I am trying—"

"Please!"

With an inarticulate sound, he wrenched the front of his trousers open. She had a glimpse of a stiff and swollen erection rising from a dark thicket, and then he was rolling her beneath him, spreading her thighs with his knees, his head fallen into the vee of her neck. His mouth opened on her throat as he lifted her hips and then, *there!* He drove into her, trying to hold back, trying not to seat himself too deeply with this first thrust, but her hips rose to meet his entry and he took her, filling her.

She cried out, and he cursed, stopping. "I swear I could not—"

"No!" she panted. "No. It is just that . . . You feel . . . so . . ."

"I cannot be . . ." he said helplessly, misunderstanding. "This is my body. It . . . I cannot be less."

"I would not want you to be," she breathed, and at his startled look she half laughed, half sobbed, need rippling through her. He'd begun to withdraw, but now he stopped. She moaned softly.

He was a big man in all ways. She wanted that. She lusted for it. She lifted her hips and clung to his shoulders and squeezed her eyes shut and bucked to meet his next thrust. Another. And another. He plunged deeper now, the cadence taking hold of him, but he never lost his awareness of her.

He knew with each thrust the body receiving him was Kate's, the mouth he plundered was Kate's. He felt the impression of each finger clasping his shoulders, heard each little shivering gasp. He cupped her soft buttocks and rolled over so that she sat straddling him, her knees bent either side of his hips. Her eyes widened, startled by the feeling of him still deep within her.

"This is better," he managed. "I'm too heavy and— Ah!"

She'd lowered herself more fully upon him. Her back arched and her hair fell down her back and trailed across his thighs, silky and fine as kitten fur. He would surely die of pleasure. He cupped her soft, pale breasts, kneading them as she rose and settled, riding him with increasing neediness. Her face grew tense with yearning.

"Use me, Kate," he whispered in a hot, wicked voice. "Use me. I would pleasure you, Kate, I would service you and have you pleasure yourself with me, on me."

The words were a litany of passion and desire, a carnal recitation of want and need, and she heard and heeded, her body tightening, the aching narrowing to a shuddering throb, a point of ever-concentrated passion. She sobbed and he stroked her, she bucked and gasped and . . . and then . . . The world trembled, spiraled, and exploded outward. Pleasure suffused her, liquid and molten, and she cried out with the exquisite culmination.

For a long moment she was suspended there, the world both vortex and vacuum. And when she had finished, she collapsed against Kit's sweat-sheened chest.

But after the last tremors subsided, she heard the thick pounding of his heart, a rhythm at such variance with the tender caress of his hand that she rose once more to her knees. Her hands splayed across his chest, and she dug her nails lightly into his flesh. She looked into his heated gaze.

"I didn't beg," she challenged him.

He laughed, rolled her beneath him, and captured her hands, holding them above her head as he drove deep and smoothly into her.

"Not yet," he agreed.

# SEVENTEEN

❈

# DEALING WITH ERRORS
# IN JUDGMENT

"MRS. BLACKBURN!" MEG CALLED through the chamber door.

"What is it, Meg?" Kate came awake knowing she was alone.

"There's a carriage from the castle standing in the yard come to fetch you."

Kate looked around the room. Kit was gone. Her dresses were gone, too. Only debris littered the floor. The trunk still lay on its side.

Meg tapped on the door. "What should I tell the driver?"

She stood up. She should be assuring Meg of her imminent departure, bounding from the bed to pack what she could salvage of Grace's belongings. But she stayed, wrapping the thin blanket around her, woefully aware that she felt no pleasure in the fact that the marquis had sent his carriage for her.

She was a fool.

"This night is mine," Kit had whispered at one point. They'd both known no future awaited them beyond this chamber's door. He'd left before she'd awakened, and she should be grateful, she told herself.

In the heated darkness she might pretend, but morning brought familiar desperation: she wanted those things she'd once had—security and safety. She wanted to breathe freely, laugh heedlessly, and close her eyes without the next day looming like an enemy. She wanted the life she'd once had back.

Even if he'd asked her to stay with him—which he hadn't—and even if she would have been tempted to say yes—which she wouldn't—what prospects did they have, a penniless soldier and an impoverished widow? Within a year or two, she would be exactly where she stood now, at the threshold of regret, yearning for the past and fearful of the future.

She might be a coward, but she was a sensible coward.

"Ma'am?" Meg called again. "Are you feeling quite yourself?"

How was she to feel herself when she was no longer clear on whom that was? Abruptly, she dropped the blanket. Enough. Nothing had changed. She would put last night from her, stow it away like a maid's tender dreams. Forget it.

If only her body didn't remember what she was trying so hard to forget.

If only Kit MacNeill seemed more like what he was and less like what she wanted him to be.

"I heard someone come in and wrecked yer things,

but I swear I had no to do wid it." Meg called plaintively, alarmed by her continued silence. "Ma'am!"

"Yes! I'll be there at once." Viciously, Kate pinched her cheeks and bit down on her lips. The marquis had sent his carriage. It was an auspicious beginning, one she had to avail herself of. But garbed in what manner? She spied something white wedged between the bed and wall. Her chemise. She snatched it up. It was Kit's shirt.

Her eyes squeezed painfully shut. Her hands fisted in the thin material, his imagined warmth seeping into her palms, the masculine musk subtle and evocative.

"Please, ma'am. Yer frightenin' me. Open the door," Meg implored. "I have the dresses tha cap give me to fix," she called hopefully.

Forcing herself to the door, Kate pulled it open. Meg waited without, Kate's gowns draped over her arm. On her other arm swung a small sewing basket, the cushioned top sprouting pins and needles threaded with silk.

Meg's mouth gaped when she saw the room. "Ach! Look what they done to yer things."

"They aren't mine. They belonged to my cousin Grace and her husband," Kate answered tonelessly. "She sent them to me before she died. I was returning them to the marquis."

"Must have been someone lookin' fer money, and when they dinna find any they took it out on these things. Filthy buggers," Meg said, setting the dresses on the bed.

Meg righted the trunk and pulled the ripped lining

back into place before pinning it there. "A few stitches, and this will be right as rain." She didn't wait for Kate's approval but sank to her knees by the trunk and, with a few neat movements, tacked the lining back into place.

Kate moved among the litter, listlessly collecting a few of the books and stacking them on the bottom of the trunk. *So much ruined. So much lost.*

"There now, ma'am, you needn't look so glum," Meg said, standing up. "Here. Look what I managed, and ye'll feel a sight better." She shook out the blue gown and held it up for Kate's inspection. "There was a nasty bit near the hem, but I used the ribbons to cover it up, see?

"And I cut the stained panel out of the purple one and stitched it back up again. Won't make no difference, seein' how slender you are, ma'am."

Kate accepted the proffered dresses and managed a smile. "I don't have any money," she said. "But I am sure that the marquis—"

Meg flapped a hand dismissively. "The captain already give me payment enough," she said. "I never seen Callum Lamont bested and yer man done that and then some."

"What?" Kate asked. "When?"

"Last night," Meg said. "Just after ye'd gone up from yer bath. I come in here to find Callum danglin' like a rag doll from tha cap's fist, eyes bugged out and tongue lolling and every other man in the room lookin' like the devil hisself had appeared." She gave a short bark of laughter.

"Then all of a sudden he drops Callum and is up the stairs before anyone knew what he was aboot. Not that anyone was like to follow him. Not lookin' like he did."

"My God," she whispered. "Is the man dead?"

Meg shrugged with brutal indifference. "Nah. Heard him moanin' while his lads dragged him oot. Bound to be hurtin' today though," she added with obvious relish.

"*All I am is ferocity.*" Kate's limbs began to tremble. She hadn't believed him. She should have.

How could she have forgotten, especially after witnessing his savagery at the White Rose? The man whose hands had shivered with liquid delicacy over her flesh had only moments before used those same hands to beat a man senseless. God. She pressed the heels of her hands into her eyes.

She needed to get away from here. Find a sanctuary where men were civilized, and women were protected from the world's ugliness, where a man did not come to his lover fresh from the fight.

"I have to go," she whispered urgently.

Meg, misunderstanding, nodded. " 'Course you do. Who'd want to stay here when a castle is waiting?"

Kate began repacking what hadn't been destroyed, focusing intently on the task, refusing to give her thoughts free rein. But her gaze kept straying to the rumpled bed and images of his body, sleek with perspiration, rippling with well-toned muscle— She slammed the lid shut on the trunk. She had to get out of the room. She wheeled about and fled, leaving the rest for Meg.

Below stairs, a coppery-headed young man in smart, clean livery jumped to his feet. "Mrs. Blackburn? I be John, the marquis's driver," he announced proudly, hurrying ahead of her as she raced toward the door.

She paused in her headlong flight, looking about distracted and uncertain. "I must settle with the innkeeper first."

"The marquis had me make all necessary arrangements, ma'am," John said. "If you'd wait in the carriage, I'll see your things are brought down."

"Oh. Of course."

He opened the door for her, bobbing his head respectfully as she exited. Outside an open barouche stood, its sides gleaming like black oil, gold braid holding back the half-collapsed hood. The stable boy stood by the heads of two magnificent matched bays, his face reflecting his awe. When he saw her, he flung open the carriage door and hastily extracted a set of steps from within.

Kate climbed in, forcing her attention on the luxurious appointments. She had never been in so fine a carriage before, not even in York. The marquis was clearly very wealthy. The coach was extremely well maintained, and the horses perfectly groomed. Her visit was bound to be fruitful. She had made some disastrous decisions in the last few days, but coming here was not one of them.

She took a deep breath. Kit was gone. That was the

end of it. There. She took three deep breaths. There. She felt much more herself now. She was going to be fine. She was—

"Mrs. Blackburn."

His smoky voice called from behind her. Her heart jumped into her throat, and for half a moment she remained where she sat, trying to compose herself. She turned.

He was so masculine. So big and tough-looking. So overtly, overpoweringly male.

He sat astride his gelding, the wind whipping the collar of his coat against his lean, bronze cheek. He went bareheaded, as though purposely defying the sun to reveal every scar on his well-weathered face. But he'd shaved, she noted. His jaw would be smooth.

To refer to him as "Mr. MacNeill" seemed disingenuous, "Kit" far too intimate. "Christian. I . . ."

This was impossible. Her skin tingled with sensual memories. The texture of his lips was imprinted on her own. Her breasts carried red abrasions made by his beard, and . . . Her gaze fell to his beautiful, lethal hands. Deep red gouges marked his wrists where his victim had clawed him. She swallowed.

He regarded her with the old, inscrutable expression. She couldn't do this. She was not a woman who took lovers and then met them the next day as if nothing had passed between them. And yet what choice did she have, with the boy standing there, his ears pricked and his expression interested? "Thank you for accompanying me here."

"Next you will be offering me references." He sounded mild enough, but heat flared in his eyes, and she felt an answering flush.

For a moment she thought he would say something else, something disastrously intimate, but he only said, "I'm afraid you're not shy of me yet. I promised to see you safely to the castle, and that's where I will leave you."

*Please. No.* Being with him was like opening a wound. "That isn't necessary."

"I disagree. You've seen the sort who lives here. The roads are filled with the same, and none with the benefit of knowing you've already been robbed. This carriage is too fine. The marquis might as well have sent out an invitation to every highwayman in the district."

She flushed more deeply. "I believe he had my comfort in mind."

"And I have your safety in mine," he clipped out.

"And you always keep your word," she answered heatedly, immediately regretting it.

"You would know, ma'am." His voice dropped low, and she flushed, her gaze dropping as she recalled how last night she had used his fealty to his word to gain his bed. His teeth clenched. "That's not—"

Before he could say more, John emerged from the inn, smiling delightedly. Kate drew back. Kit pulled Doran from the side of the carriage.

"I'll be comin' the distance with you, lad," Kit told the young coachman, winning a surprised look of gratitude. "But I'll be riding ahead a bit to mind the road." He touched his heels to Doran's flanks and sprang ahead up the steep track leading out of the fishing village.

He did not return.

The drive was long and necessarily slow. Toppled mountains fell into the sea, mile after mile of rents and inlets tearing into coastline. Breakers pounded against hidden pockets and subterranean caves, spewing geysers high into the air and veiling the feet of the cliffs in shimmering mist. Kate caught her breath as she looked down over the edge of the road where the sea wall plummeted into the foaming surf.

'Twas small surprise Charles and Grace had died yachting in such a place. The only wonder was that they had trusted themselves to venture out at all.

But too soon even the coast's drama could not keep the previous night's memories at bay. Images crowded her thoughts, and her other senses were quick to ignite them: Kit's mouth on hers, Kit's arms around her, Kit whispering in her ear, urgent and passionate.

Finally, in desperation, she leaned forward. "Have you worked for the marquis long?"

John nodded easily. "Born at the castle, I was. My da was head coachman before me."

"Ah. Then you knew my cousin, Mrs. Murdoch?"

John's smiled faded. "Aye." He shook his head mournfully. "Terrible business, that. But don't you fear, ma'am. The marquis is set on finding those responsible and seeing justice is done."

Kate stared at him in bemusement.

"They'll not go unpunished," he avowed staunchly.

"And why would they ever think they would? Killing the master's own brother and his lady. Mad, they must be."

"Killing them?" Kate echoed in confusion. "But . . . they died in a yachting accident."

John's ears grew bright red. "Oh! I thought ye knew!"

"Knew what? What happened?" Kate asked. "The marquis wrote to us that Grace had drowned in a boating accident. Isn't that true?"

John stared miserably ahead, his shoulders hunched. "That's what we all thought at first. But . . ."

"Tell me, please."

He rubbed a hand through his coppery hair. "There weren't any water in Mr. Charles's lungs, though they pulled him from the sea, and so the marquis knew he hadn't drowned. And once that idea was planted, well, there were marks we thought come from bein' tossed against the rocks, but afterward it seemed like— I'm sorry! Oh, ma'am! Should I pull over?"

"No. I will be fine." She steadied herself with a hand on her stomach. "Why wasn't my family informed of this?"

"I could not say, ma'am," John said glumly. "And I reckon I said enough already."

"Who killed them?"

John's shoulders lifted. "Highwaymen. Smugglers. Everything possible is being done to find out, that you can be sure of, Mrs. Blackburn. Smugglers been in Clyth long as I can remember, but they crossed the line this time, and I 'spect they know it and that's why they went to such pains to make it look like an accident."

"But why kill my cousin and her husband at all?" Kate asked. "Why not just rob them and leave them be?"

"Mr. Charles weren't one to take being robbed lightly. And if he saw the men's faces . . ." He trailed off. "But nothing will save them now, the blackguards, because when the marquis realized murder had been done, he sent to Edinburgh and straight off the militia come to put things right. And now they have their own reason to catch the culprits.

"Fact is, Mrs. Blackburn," John said confidingly, "their captain was killed soon after they arrived, and some say that the smugglers are responsible for that, too." He nodded. "Don't worry. His replacement arrived last week, and a finer, fitter officer and gentleman you never hoped to see. *Now* there'll be justice for Charles Murdoch and your cousin, ma'am!" he finished triumphantly. "You just wait and see."

Parnell was small as castles went, built in a standard, square pattern around a diminutive interior courtyard that Kate glimpsed as they rode past the wide, nonfunctional gate. Happily situated in a rock embrasure above the sea, it had thus been spared the wear most fortress castles incurred, and the stone, though several hundred years old, sparkled as if newly quarried, the many windows gleaming with golden light in the slanting rays of the morning sun.

It was wonderful, Kate thought with a touch of desperate longing, pristine and well-kept and orderly and very much protected. The carriage ground to a halt, and John leapt down, hurrying to hand her out. The door to the castle opened, and there stood the eighth marquis of Parnell, James Murdoch.

She remembered him as a nice-looking youngster, but he had grown into an elegant man with dark blond hair that complemented his large, hazel eyes. He stood just above middling height and had a trim, athletic build that his exquisitely tailored clothes accented. His cravat would make snow weep with jealousy. He was, in a word, perfect.

"Mrs. Blackburn! Even in sad circumstances it is a pleasure to see you again!" He bowed at the waist, and she returned a small curtsey.

"Thank you, milord."

"No. Please. Your cousin was my sister. I insist on the familial rights. You must call me Parnell."

"As you will, sir."

"Allow me to welcome you to my home," he said without making any attempt to hide his pride. Kate liked him for that. She'd had too much of enigmatic men. His open pleasure was refreshing. He stood aside, and Kate moved past him into a wide, light-filled great hall, the black-and-white-checkered flag-stone gleaming ebony and sparkling white. A cluster of maids were assiduously at work bleaching the mar-ble staircase that flowed in a gentle spiral up to a mid-story landing marked by a series of tall, slender windows.

"How lovely."

"I am delighted you approve."

"Milord." A footman spoke from beside them.

"Yes?"

"Captain Watters's compliments, sir. He asks if you would meet him this afternoon at your convenience."

Watters, Kate recalled, was the murdered Captain Greene's replacement. Her tentative pleasure dissolved.

"Inform the captain that I am previously engaged," the marquis said, "but that after dinner I shall be happy to meet him in the library."

"Yes, sir." The footman bowed

The marquis turned to her, and his expression grew concerned. "I am a poor host. You are tired. I will have your maid shown the rooms as soon as she comes in, and then—"

"I have no maid." Her eyes dropped in embarrassment. Now he would know the quality—or lack thereof—of his sister-in-law's relatives. "She decamped."

"How frightful for you," the marquis exclaimed sympathetically. "Then we shall have Peggy perform the necessary duties while you are with us. She was your cousin's maid."

"Thank you."

The door opened, and John appeared, laboring under a crate. Behind him, carrying a traveling trunk as easily as if it were a leather satchel, came MacNeill. His gaze was flat, his manner aloof.

"Your driver, Mrs. Blackburn?" the marquis asked, studying Kit with open and friendly interest. "He looks able to handle himself in any difficulty. I shall commend the carriage company."

"No, sir," she said, feeling her color rise. "He is . . . That is to say—"

"I owed a debt to her father, sir, that Mrs. Blackburn kindly allowed me to repay by seeing her safely on her journey," Kit said smoothly. His cape had swung back, revealing his dark green regimental jacket.

"Ah. You are a military man," the marquis said. "That explains it. I've heard innumerable stories about the loyalty Highlanders have for their commanders. Holdover from the old clan system, I suppose?"

MacNeill didn't bother to correct the marquis's misconception. Why should he? He would be gone soon. He could care less what the marquis thought of him. "That's right, sir."

"Very good . . . er . . ."

"MacNeill, sir. Kit MacNeill."

"Mr. MacNeill," the marquis said, smiling. "Thank you for delivering Mrs. Blackburn safely. I am most beholden to you."

MacNeill's gray-green gaze touched her with deliberate carelessness. "I was happy to be of service."

Kate's chin snapped up. How dare he make his indifference so obvious? Did he fear that their night together would turn her into a romantic ninny? That she would throw over everything that she had hoped and worked to achieve at the mere thought of his touch? His mouth? His whispered words? That she would make a scene by insisting that he offer for her hand?

He needn't fear. She was not some silly schoolroom miss, her head stuffed with sugar-spun mawkishness.

"You'll stay with us a few days while your mount recovers, won't you?" the marquis asked with complete sincerity, a quality MacNeill likely wouldn't be able to identify, not being acquainted with it in his own makeup. "Of course you will. I'll have a room made up at once—No, no! No sense in protesting. I insist. Least I can do."

Before Kit could answer, the marquis raised his hand. "Here, John! Bring Mr. MacNeill's mount down to the stables. John's a magician with horses, aren't you, John? Of course you are."

"Really, sir. That is not necessary," Kit said. At least he had the grace to look uncomfortable.

"Of course it is," the marquis assured him. "Can't have Mrs. Blackburn's protector bedding down with the militia like some commoner." He eyed MacNeill's tattered and worn plaid surreptitiously.

"Peggy!" A small, no-nonsense looking woman bustled forward. "Take Mr. MacNeill up to the tower room and see that he is taken care of, and you might give his coat a brush-down, eh?" He gave MacNeill's jacket a telling look. "We sup in three hours."

With a short word of thanks and a slight bow in her direction, MacNeill followed Peggy up the staircase, and God help her, Kate could not control the deep sense of relief filling her.

The marquis held out his hand.

"Now, my dear Mrs. Blackburn, there is much to tell you."

# EIGHTEEN

⬚⬚⬚⬚

# CONTRIVING TO
# EXTEND ONE'S STAY
# IN CONVIVIAL
# SURROUNDINGS

THE WARMTH OF THE MARQUIS'S greeting bolstered
Kate's flagging spirits, and the kindness in his expression dispelled any lingering discomfort occasioned by
MacNeill's sardonic manner. Her gaze unwillingly
lifted toward the top of the stairs where Kit had
disappeared.

He'd had no difficulty handing her care over to
another man. Why should he? He had important
things to do, people to kill. She should be pleased he'd
been so circumspect. There hadn't been the merest
hint that they had anything but a civil association. She
must remember that he acted in her best interests and
be properly appreciative of it rather than feeling petulant and unhappy and—

She forced a bright smile to her lips and prepared to give her full attention to the marquis.

"I suspect you would like to see your rooms," he said. "But if I might first impose upon you for a few minutes of your time, I would be greatly obliged."

"Of course," Kate said. He waited while the footman took her cloak and bonnet and then hastily stripped her gloves off before he could see the patches on them.

"If you please?" He offered her his arm.

The ability to gauge the exact degree of pressure that signaled friendship without forwardness came back to her at once, as if she had shed the last three years as easily as she'd shed her gloves. It was all familiar: the soft murmur of polite conversation; the susurration a hemline makes while sweeping across a thick, rich carpet; the angle at which one carried one's head to denote interest. All the little things that made life gracious and endurable. She made a mental note to include a section on keeping one's social skills honed in her book.

Yes, she thought with determined conviction, this is where I belong.

It was an impressive home. The grim stone walls she had envisioned did not exist. White-painted walls acted as a foil for exquisite paintings and a charming collection of etchings. She'd expected to see lurking suits of armor, but Castle Parnell held no reminders of its owners' heraldic past. The rooms were comfortably furnished, light and airy, the plastered ceilings bordered with carved moldings.

Three of the castle's four wings, James informed her, were still used by the family, while the fourth, which had been abandoned by the preceding generation, now housed a company of militia—though the presence of military within the castle walls was exceptional.

Parnell's ancestors had, the marquis explained, remained aloof as much as possible from the political fervor that infected many Highland families. That was not to say they did not back the obvious choice when it was politic to do so, but given the opportunity, they generally stayed out of the affairs of kings and generals. They had been rewarded for that prudence by being allowed to keep their ancestral home where many of their neighbors had been forced to forfeit—if not land, titles.

"Do you like it?" the marquis asked shortly. He sounded unexpectedly anxious.

"Oh, yes," she answered. "It is quite wonderful."

"I am delighted it meets your approval."

She darted him a curious glance.

"We are as fortunate in our neighbors, too," he said.

Her brows rose. "I own I am surprised Clyth offers much in the way of polite society."

"Not Clyth." A steely expression replaced his former good-humored one. "I am referring to the neighboring estates. There are two within ten miles. You would never have imagined we are so well populated, would you? And further inland we count fully eight additional families of great merit within a single day's journey. So, you see, we are never short of company."

She regarded him in puzzlement. "How delightful."

"Yes. Exactly," he said, opening a door and stepping aside. "This is my library. Won't you be seated?"

He indicated a silk-covered settee, and after seeing her comfortably settled said, "I confess I have led you here intentionally, Mrs. Blackburn. I wanted to tell you the things I should have written regarding the circumstances of your cousin's death."

"I already know them, sir."

The marquis's brows flew up in surprise.

"I was told my cousin's death was not the result of an accident."

The marquis's expression grew quizzical. "Yes. Just as I wrote to your family in my second letter."

"Second letter?"

"Yes. I wrote as soon as I realized that the . . . deaths could not have been the result of an accident." He regarded her in sober puzzlement. "Did you not receive it?"

"No." She frowned, searching her memory. It was not unheard of for mail to be lost, especially if the maid hadn't paid the postage when the courier arrived. . . . Still, it was odd.

"My dear!" the marquis exclaimed. "My poor Mrs. Blackburn. You did not know?"

"No. I learned of it only after my arrival."

"I am appalled that you should come to my home to be greeted by such news, and now I find myself in the onerous position of having to compound your shock even more."

Kate's head snapped up.

The marquis caught his hands behind his back and paced across the room. "It was wrong of me not to relate the entire truth at once. The fact that you did not receive my second missive in no way exonerates me, but perhaps after you hear my story, you will not think too poorly of me for my decision."

Kate bade him continue.

He took a deep breath. "Charles and Grace had grown restless here in the north of Scotland."

This Kate could well believe. In the few letters Grace had written, she had not bothered to hide her distaste for country living. She had set her eye on London and its many delights.

"Charles repeatedly asked me to purchase a town house in London for their use, but I refused." His color grew bright. "I do not wish to offend you by being too intimate, but I want you to understand the circumstances of this terrible crime."

"Please, go on."

"When he died, my father had been for many years incapable of giving the estate the attention it needed. When I inherited, I borrowed heavily in order to turn the land into a profitable enterprise and return the castle to its former splendor. Gradually, my efforts have been rewarded. Not, however, to the extent necessary to set Charles and Grace up in London in the manner in which they'd envisioned themselves.

"And so I told them. It became a yearly ritual between us—he would ask, I would refuse—but one which I was pleased to think that Charles handled without resentment." His face grew glum. "I was wrong. Charles had not, in fact, ever reconciled himself to my decision. Instead, he had entered into associations by which he hoped to grow wealthy."

"*Had* grown wealthy, if the evidence of Grace's sending her belongings to you is any testimony. At least wealthy enough to relocate to London and stylishly, too."

"I'm not sure I understand."

The marquis sat down beside her. "Charles threw his lot in with a gang of thieves, smugglers, and wreckers." He gestured out of the window toward the coast. "You see how we are situated. Charles allowed these blackguards to use my coastline for smuggling and, God help his soul, to wreck those poor ships that sought safe harbor during storms."

"Dear Lord," Kate whispered. "But what happened?"

The marquis's face reflected a bitterness Kate guessed was foreign to his nature. "What must happen when one involves oneself with brutes and savages? There was a falling-out. The result was murder."

"But I was told that they had been killed by mistake!" Kate exclaimed. "That highwaymen had robbed and then killed them to keep Charles from identifying them."

"That is what I *want* people to think," the marquis said somberly. "That is why I did not write the entire truth of the matter to you. I feared you would involve the British authorities, and they would uncover my brother's involvement with the smugglers."

He clasped her hand imploringly. "I have four sisters. Two of them live nearby, but the others live in society in London. The scandal would ruin them, and I, perhaps wrongly, can see no good come of their paying for their brother's greed."

"No," Kate answered at once. "No, of course not!"

"You speak without hesitation because you have a kind heart, Mrs. Blackburn," the marquis said. "But I would not count myself an honorable man if I did not point out that your cousin Grace was murdered because of my brother's weakness. I would not presume to accuse her of complicity. My intent was never to keep from you the facts as I know them, but rather to wait until we had met before presenting them to you and then allowing you to make a decision as to what course should be taken. Therefore, you must consider whether you think it best to allow me to seek justice without involving the reputations of my family or make a clean breast of the situation to the British authorities."

Though Kate had little doubt of Grace's "complicity," she held her tongue, asking instead, "What course of action will you follow, milord?"

He smiled grimly, releasing her hand. "The militia is already here, Mrs. Blackburn. They shall rout these bas—blackguards from their caves and holes. I will find whoever killed my brother and your cousin, and I *will* have justice."

He quelled his anger with an obvious effort. "Forgive me for burdening you with this so soon after your arrival, but I am a simple man, Mrs. Blackburn. I felt it best to have my say at once and hear your answer."

He would be guided by her decision. The magnitude of what he proposed swept over her. She owed it to the marquis to consider the ramifications carefully. "Do you plan on hunting down the criminals yourself, milord?"

"Good God, no." He sounded surprised. "I would only make a muck of it. Captain Watters has already made great headway in identifying the villains."

"What will happen then?"

"Once we are certain the guilty have been apprehended, I shall hand them over to the authorities for wrecking ships and smuggling. The word 'murder' will never be mentioned."

In other words, there would be no trial for murder, but there would be for wrecking, for which the penalty was the same. Justice would still be served without innocent parties suffering. "I will be guided by what you think best," she replied softly.

"Thank you, ma'am," he breathed, "on my behalf as well as my sisters'. I am in your debt."

"Please. You make me self-conscious."

"I would not embarrass you for the world. And I will have you know that I do not intend your visit to us should be all grim and dour. I am accounted by most an amiable fellow. I would like you to know me."

"I would like that, too," she murmured.

He held out his hand, and she took it. "Then let us continue our walk, shall we?"

Kate approved of the castle. Clearly it was more home than showpiece, and the marquis had made every effort to bring comfort as well as sophistication to these wild parts. She had been exploring a niche in the library when she heard the decisive click of boot heels. Kate looked around as a gentleman in an officer's uniform entered the room. He wore his hair long, clubbed and powdered in an old-fashioned manner, and held his hat under his arm. His hands were encased in white officer's gloves.

Though not as handsome as the marquis or owning Kit MacNeill's rough masculinity, he had a great deal of presence and intensity. His deep-set eyes gazed with an unusual directness above high, angular cheekbones. He looked both intelligent and confident, a credit to his immaculate uniform.

"Milord," he said, approaching the marquis and inclining his head respectfully.

"Captain Watters," the marquis replied in surprise. "I sent word that I would meet with you this evening. Did you not receive it?"

"I did, sir. But I have some information I felt certain you would want to hear at once."

The marquis frowned. "I am currently occupied."

"I understand that, sir. I have been told that the young woman has arrived, and with her a rough-looking fellow in a regimental jacket." He awaited confirmation.

"Yes. Mrs. Blackburn."

"And there *is* a gentleman with her?" Captain Watters prompted.

"Yes, Captain. Though what concern this is of yours I am at a loss to divine."

"It may prove of the greatest concern, sir. I dislike the sudden appearance of strangers. Particularly at this time. We know for a fact that the smugglers have a confidant working with them who remains outside the immediate area. Someone who alerts them—"

"Captain Watters!" The marquis, red-faced with embarrassment, motioned toward Kate. "My guest."

The officer looked around and saw her tucked away in the window embrasure. "Oh!" he exclaimed. "I am so sorry. Please accept my apologies," he said, bowing to Kate.

"No harm done. I can't fault you for zeal, now, can I?" The marquis smiled with a touch of exasperation. "Come, Watters, let me introduce you."

The captain's face lit with unfeigned pleasure.

"Mrs. Blackburn, may I present Captain Watters? Captain Watters, Mrs. Blackburn."

He snapped forward at the waist, bowing deeply.

"How do you do, sir?" Kate murmured, slightly disconcerted by the captain's open admiration. His smile transformed his austere features, making him extremely attractive and warming his eyes with a wealth of feeling. She found herself smiling uncertainly back. Indeed, at that moment she felt she knew him.

"Excellent well, ma'am. Now," he answered with

such good humor she could take no offense. The marquis did not look quite so pleased.

"Very well, Watters. Now what is it you were all in a lather to relate?"

Watters made an effort to attend the marquis, but his appreciative gaze kept straying to Kate. "It can wait, sir. Had I known you were entertaining Mrs. Blackburn I would never have presumed."

"You are suspicious that Mr. MacNeill is involved in the criminal activities hereabouts," Kate said.

"Mr. MacNeill, ma'am?" Captain Watters asked.

"The young man who escorted me here."

"Not I, ma'am," he said staunchly and without the least credibility.

"That was not the impression I received. If I am wrong, I apologize, but if not, I can disabuse you of any such absurd notion. Mr. MacNeill is well known to me"—a little lie and a great truth—"and I can attest that he is not involved with the smugglers."

The captain inclined his head graciously. "That is quite good enough for me, ma'am."

"And me," avowed the marquis.

The captain did not make any further comment, but he did not cease regarding Kate until finally, flustered and unused to such attention, she said, "You are disconcerting me, Captain. Pray, what do you find so fascinating?"

He did not equivocate. "Your visage, ma'am, while fully feminine and lovely, puts me in mind of another. You are not by chance related to a Yorkish family by the name of Nash?"

"Why, yes. My maiden name is Nash, and my father was Colonel Roderick Nash."

"I thought as much!" the captain declared. Deep emotion colored his voice. "I did not know your father personally, nor did I serve in his regiment, but when I was in France I met him there once." His tone grew somber. "His death was a great loss, ma'am."

"Thank you."

"You'll join us for dinner this evening, Watters?" the marquis asked. "Mr. MacNeill will be joining us, and he too is a military man."

"Is he?"

"Perhaps you have some acquaintances in common."

"Doubtless, sir, and at any other time I would gladly accept your invitation, but alas, duty calls. There is a situation farther up the coast that may well be worth my time looking into."

"Very well. When you return, then."

The captain turned to Kate. "I shall look forward to it. By your leave, sir? Ma'am?"

Kate inclined her head, and the captain, after executing another bow, left her once more with the marquis. It was as well. The captain was the sort of man who had such force of personality and presence that other men, regardless of titular superiority, faded before him. Even as estimable a man as the marquis.

Though she doubted Kit MacNeill would be diminished.

She tried to smooth the frown the thought of Kit brought, but the marquis noted it and despite her protests—halfhearted though they were—insisted they end the tour, as she was clearly fatigued. He returned her to Peggy, waiting dutifully in the Great Hall. The maid led her up the long staircase and down a brightly lit corridor to a large, airy room furnished in yellow and white, the walls covered in a peacock blue material. It was, as had been all the rooms Kate had seen, furnished in impeccable taste.

"Here we are, ma'am." Peggy bustled ahead of Kate, clicking her tongue as she plumped the pillows on the chair beside the fireplace. Her broad, comfortable face broke into a grin. "And here is your trunk."

"It's not mine. It belonged to Grace," Kate said.

A cloud passed over her cheerful face. "I'm sorry your visit here is under such sad circumstances."

Kate inclined her head, accepting the maid's sympathy even as she realized that no one had yet voiced any personal grief over Grace's demise. Even Grace's maid did not evince any real sense of loss.

Kate had hoped that Grace had found happiness in her adulthood, but everything suggested that the restless, discontented child she had been had become a woman of similar temperament. The thought led Kate to consider whether she herself had become the sort of young woman she had once hoped to be. Certainly, she would never have thought herself capable of taking a lover outside the sanction of marriage. Yet, disturbingly, it was not this that made her feel that she had compromised herself.

It was . . . being here.

She veered away from the odd, distressing thought.

"Is something wrong, Mrs. Blackburn?" Peggy straightened from unpacking Kate's few dresses.

"No." She forced a smile to her lips.

The maid scowled down at the gowns she held. "John said as how Mrs. Murdoch's things had been ruined, but he didn't mention yer own dresses had been destroyed, too."

"Excuse me?"

Peggy nodded sagely. "They ruined most yer wardrobe, clear as day it is, and you, being the lady you are, didn't want to say." She clucked her tongue. "Poor lambkin, arriving with naught but a pair of old-fashioned gowns to wear. Not to worrit, dear. Mrs. Murdoch was always sending to Inverness for a seamstress to come and make her new frocks. Why, there must be a dozen in her wardrobe she never even had on. You can wear those."

"Oh! I couldn't—"

"Why ever not?" Peggy exclaimed, eyeing her. "You're a bit thinner but close enough in height, and they're only collecting dust now."

"The marquis might not approve of another wearing Mrs. Murdoch's things."

Peggy was having none of it. "He'd only be too pleased someone had found good use for them."

"Well, then, another member of the family might find it painful to see Mrs. Murdoch's things worn by another."

From the manner in which Peggy's eyes darted

away, Kate surmised she was correct. Thank God, at least one person missed Grace.

"Who?" she asked.

Peggy didn't equivocate. "Miss Mertice Benny, Lord Parnell's ward. She pines after Mrs. Murdoch something dreadful. They were very close, both being pretty and both being young." Peggy sighed. "She'll heal though, given time."

"I would not want to add to her affliction."

"And you won't," Peggy replied staunchly, and Kate realized that she had gained an ally in the household. "I'll make certain you only wear dresses Mrs. Murdoch never did."

Kate was not certain she wanted to dress in her dead cousin's things, but she was too tired to argue, and she no longer possessed that air of command that assured her wishes would be carried out without question. She nodded, and Peggy hurried away, eager to carry out her mission.

Kate did not even bother to clean her face before testing the deep, downy mattress. She lay down, and at once the well-remembered luxury entrapped her. It had been such a long time since she had rested her cheek against linens so smooth they felt like satin. She closed her eyes, and the sun poured over her like a warm blanket.

The past was done, both the years that stretched behind her and last night's few hours. It was time to look ahead.

The marquis could not have been more attentive

or considerate, and the dashing Captain Watters reminded her of what it had been like to be admired and not pitied as a woman who'd fallen in the world's estimation. Everything she wanted lay in the palm of her hand. All she had to do was make a fist.

A tear slipped from beneath her lid and trickled down her cheek.

# NINETEEN

※※※

# APPRECIATING THE
# ART OF A DISCREET
# WITHDRAWAL

KIT SAT IN A COPPER TUB of quickly cooling water
wearing a thunderous expression. The damn maid
had taken his jacket and filched his shirt and breeches,
promising to "clean them up a bit," and there was
naught he could do but sit here like a damn fish until
she returned.

A couple of brawny lads had hauled the tub up,
though he had not asked for one, and then another set
of giggling maids had come—how many servants did
a fellow need anyway?—carrying kettle upon kettle of
steaming water. When he had demanded to know
what they expected him to do, the youngest, a tiny
chit no older than his last haircut, had smirked,
looked pointedly at him, and said, "Wash, I 'spect,
sir," before bobbing and fleeing with her gaggle of
cackling cronies.

Tempted beyond resistance, he had washed. It was a luxury and a pleasure, and he did not deny it for a moment. He had spent too many years in conditions so vile and filthy that there had been many times he had felt he would never be clean again. Except in her arms . . .

Abruptly, he stood up, and water sloshed onto the floor. He looked around and snatched the towel left for his use, swiping angrily at his body. He was losing what little grip on sanity he maintained. He felt like a man who had set out on a journey with a clear map in hand, only to discover that the road was not straight and that another presented itself, one that hadn't been charted.

He draped the towel about his hips and stalked across the room, bracing his hand on the windowsill as he stared outside. Where was she? With the marquis, no doubt, and that's as should be, regardless of what one night had done to him. *Damnation!* He knew better then this. Hadn't he had the harshest of all lessons drilled into him? He would *not* trust this fallible organ called his heart. He'd done so before with . . . soul-destroying results.

Abruptly, he hammered his fist against the wall above the window, welcoming the drill of pain.

Someone rapped at the door, and Kit swung toward it, eager for any distraction. A footman entered, carrying a neatly folded pile of clothing. "His lordship's compliments, sir, and he begs that you would accept his sincerest apologies, but it seems that the laundress was neglectful while cleaning your shirt and breeches, and they have been scorched beyond repair."

"What?" Kit asked stupidly. He only owned two shirts, and he had no substitute for his breeches.

"His lordship begs you accept these in their place. He realizes that they may not fit properly, but Peggy is a dab hand with a needle and should be able to make any necessary adjustments."

"Bloody hell."

"Yes, sir. I shall send Peggy at once. May I tell Lord Parnell that you will be ready to dine at eight, sir?"

If this was what having servants was like, Kit was glad he had never been plagued with them. Giggling maids, controlling footmen, and now this seamstress who would like as not draw as much blood with her needle as a desert warrior. "Fine."

"Would you like me to help you dress, sir?" the man asked.

"Not in the least."

"I shall send Peggy directly then, sir." He deposited the pile of clothing on the foot of the bed, bowed, and departed, leaving Kit moodily regarding his borrowed finery.

A snowy neckcloth lay neatly folded atop a fine lawn shirt nearly as white. Beneath these were stockings, garters, a dark waistcoat, and a short wool jacket with silver buttons. Smallclothes had been folded discreetly near the bottom, beneath a pair of buff-colored breeches. He tossed the jacket aside, finding his own near the bottom of the pile.

Thank God, the fool laundress hadn't attempted to boil his regimental jacket. He held it up. She had managed to scrub out some stains and repair a few tears in the fabric. The deep green cloth had faded beneath the hot eastern sun, but where she had turned out the seams, the exposed cloth was vivid against the old, like slashes of Scotland's spring.

Grudgingly he pulled on the smallclothes and the breeches. They were too small in the thigh and constricting at the knee. He'd never liked knee breeches, preferring trews. But they had not been included in the pile. He looked over at the clock. It was half past seven.

The dress was too low-cut, the fabric too sheer, and the pale rose color inappropriate for one supposedly in mourning. But Peggy assured her that the bodice was no lower than any lady might wear at dinner and that the mourning period for Charles and Grace had not only been properly observed but that it was definitely time that His Lordship and the rest of the family got on with the business of living.

So, reminding herself to add a chapter on borrowed finery to her instructional tome and feeling decidedly naked, Kate left the bedchamber and followed the footman to the dining room, trying to quell the racing of her heart. Kit had been invited to dine, too. She took a deep breath, hoping not to appear affected, or worse, anxious.

Inside, the dining room blazed with candlelight

across a sumptuous table spread with crystal and silver, porcelain and gold. The marquis, standing beside a small, birdlike old gentleman, came toward her at once.

Kit, she noted, had yet to arrive.

"Mrs. Blackburn!" the marquis greeted her. "I hope Peggy meets with your approval? If she did not, I own I cannot for the life of me see where she might have failed you."

"Thank you, milord."

He turned and motioned his companion to his side. "Allow me to present you to my uncle. Uncle, Mrs. Blackburn. Mrs. Blackburn, Mr. Kerwin Murdoch, my father's youngest brother."

"How do you do, sir?" Kate murmured, curtseying.

"How'd do," the gentleman nodded. His bright blue eyes peered at her from beneath shelves of bushy white brows, and he cocked his head, magnifying his resemblance to some inquisitive, possibly malevolent bird. "English, ain't you? Grace's kin? Must be English, then."

"Yes, sir." Kate said, a little amused. "I am English."

"Pity," the old gentleman said, cocking his head to the other side. "One would think there were no likely Scotswomen within the area, what with the way my family keeps importing English chits." He peered condemningly at his nephew.

"Uncle."

The old man's rancor abruptly vanished. "I am a relic. Can't help it. No harm meant, eh, young lady?"

"I must have missed something, sir, for I cannot recall anything said to which I could possibly take exception."

He gave a bark of delighted laughter. "English always were good at words. Even Grace, when she'd a mind to bother, could wrap enough words around a threat to make it seem a treat."

"Enough, Uncle," the marquis said in fond exasperation as an elderly woman arrived on the arm of a petite girl.

Kate studied the pair with interest. The old woman had thickly powdered and rouged skin in the style of the French court two decades earlier. Her highly piled hair was obviously a wig. The young girl beside her could be no more than seventeen. Fluffy ice-blond curls lay artfully around a heart-shaped face. Her mouth was red, small, and full-lipped, her eyes tip-tilted and faintly Slavic.

"Aunt Mathilde, this is Mrs. Blackburn, Grace's cousin," the marquis said loudly. "My father's sister, Lady Mathilde."

"Yes, yes, Jamie. This morning you told us she was to arrive." The old lady smiled at Kate. Cataracts clouded her eyes but did not veil the flash of annoyance in their milky depths.

"And this is my ward, Miss Mertice Benny, whom we call Merry."

The young girl perfunctorily murmured her pleasure at making Kate's acquaintance, and for a second Kate could not help but wonder if the pet name had been given in irony, for she could not think of a creature less "merry" than this girl, with her wintry coloring and chill expression. The girl's superior gaze abruptly widened as it fell on Kate's dress with shocked recognition.

"What a lovely gown, Mrs. Blackburn," she said stiffly.

"Thank you." Kate floundered. "As is yours."

"Good heavens, don't tell me we have admitted yet another female into the fold to discourse on the furbelows and gewgaws of feminine self-decoration?" Mr. Murdoch snorted.

"What did you say, Kerwin?" Lady Mathilde said.

"I said, my dear," Mr. Murdoch bellowed, "that you are in rare good looks this evening."

His sister gave him a flat look of exasperation. "I doubt that, Murdoch. And may I advise you, yet again, that you needn't roar. A simple shout will suffice."

She turned to Kate. "Would you be so kind as to escort me to the sofa, m'dear? The side closest the hearth? I feel the cold more keenly each winter, I am afraid."

"But of course," Kate said gladly, offering her arm. Merry's gaze would prick her to bleeding if it grew any sharper.

"I am a trifle hard of hearing, I am afraid, thus my family's insistence on bellowing. Unnecessary if one speaks clearly and distinctly. You have a lovely voice, my dear. Not like Merry here"—she looked back at Merry and Mr. Murdoch, trailing a short ways behind—"who has lately affected a lisp."

"I haven't!" Merry denied hotly.

Lady Mathilde ignored her. "Grace had a lisp, and

Grace"—she leaned confidingly toward Kate—"had much influence over young Merry. She misses her fiercely. Ah! Here we are. Thank you, m'dear."

The old lady took a seat as her brother waddled over to poke at the fire, and the marquis came to stand beside Kate.

"I thought we were to have a real Scotsman dining with us this evening," Mr. Murdoch suddenly declared, as if he'd just realized he'd been promised a sweet and none had appeared.

"I expect you'll have to make do with me, sir." A deep, familiar voice spoke from the hall, and Kate spun around.

Kit MacNeill's great kilt swung freely with his long stride, the muscles in his legs flexing as he came across the room. He wore his plaid draped in the Highland manner across the chest and shoulder of his regimental jacket, the silver buttons freshly polished and gleaming. A brilliant white neck cloth accentuated the darkness of his lean, freshly shaved jaw. His hair gleamed, curling up where it brushed the collar of his shirt. Kate's cheeks warmed with appreciation, and she looked away to find Merry smiling at her in a knowing manner.

"Mr. MacNeill!" the marquis greeted him. "Come, let me present you to my family."

Kit stood easily while the marquis introduced him to members of his household, and Kate felt an utterly unwarranted pride in him. Certainly no one in the household could be measured against him. Not even the marquis. Nor should he, she reminded herself. Kit was a soldier; the marquis was a gentleman.

The introductions complete, the marquis's uncle returned to Lady Mathilde, and the marquis excused himself to give some last-minute instructions to the butler, leaving Kate with Kit and Merry.

"Mrs. Blackburn, I am pleased to see you looking so well." Kit bent over her hand and brushed his lips across her gloved knuckles. Her heart raced. He thought himself graceless and rough, but in truth he was steel to the others' gilt, beautiful, lethal steel.

He lifted his head. His eyes held hers a space too long.

"But of course no introductions are necessary here." Merry smirked. "You must know Mrs. Blackburn rather well, after how many days on the road?"

Heat washed through Kate. Expressionlessly Kit looked down at the girl. "Your point, miss?"

His flat query disconcerted Merry. Kit and she were supposed to have been mortified into dumb silence, Kate realized. His forthrightness had jammed her guns.

"Point?" she stammered. "Oh, I have none, I am sure. Only . . . Mrs. Blackburn was married to an officer of the regiment, wasn't she? Perhaps that is why she is so comfortable with soldiers."

Kit did not speak, but his green-gray eyes narrowed thoughtfully on the chit. She was beyond rude. With relief, Kate saw the marquis returning to join them.

"It's too bad Watters couldn't join us, poor blighter," the marquis said, oblivious to anything being amiss.

"Who is Watters?" Kit asked.

"The man sent to replace the militia's commander, Captain Greene. The fellow had the poor taste to get himself killed," Merry said, with a great deal of blasé sophistication, "making his attempt to rid the area of crime not particularly successful."

"Captain Watters seemed very confident he will succeed," Kate said.

"You met him?" Merry looked surprised.

"Yes. Earlier today. A most capable-seeming man."

The young girl tilted her head sideways, regarding Kit with the air of the practiced coquette, her mannerisms vaguely familiar and oddly disconcerting. "Not nearly as capable-looking as others."

She batted her lashes in a thoroughly vulgar manner.

"You don't think he will be victorious, Miss?" Kit asked.

"I am sure he will make an admirable *attempt*," she drawled. "But I prefer to put my faith in men who do not understand the concept of 'attempt' but only 'success.' Are you such a man, Mr. MacNeill?"

Kate bit down hard on the inside of her cheeks.

"No, Miss Benny," Kit said gravely. "I am all too familiar with failure."

"Are you? La! And here you look positively menacing. How disappointing. I thought we'd found a champion. Is that not disappointing, Mrs. Blackburn?"

"On the contrary, I am not disappointed in any manner in Christian MacNeill," she said quietly.

The girl snickered, and Kit, rather than accepting

the accolade with a smile, looked away, his expression unreadable. Feeling a subtle rebuff, Kate's own gaze faltered. The marquis's gaze moved from Kit's aloof mien to Kate's pink one.

"Is Merry waxing poetic about the smugglers again?" Mr. Murdoch appeared at Kate's side, saving the moment from growing even tenser. "As a child, she was quite smitten with the idea of a smuggler king."

"I am not smitten any longer, I assure you." Merry snapped, the coquette suddenly replaced by a petulant child. "But that does not mean that I do not understand what every man, woman, and child in Clyth already knows: that smugglers are a law unto themselves, fearing no one and nothing."

"By heavens, Merry, you sound as if you admire them," the marquis reproved her. "Pray recall they are responsible for the deaths of family members."

The young girl's face crumpled, her sophisticated facade proving nothing more than a veneer. "*Forget?* How could I forget?" she asked with such deep-felt anguish that Kate forgot her earlier dislike. "I will never forget."

How hard it must be to lose your only confidante, Kate thought. In fact, in hindsight she realized that the girl had been enacting a very passable impersonation of Grace: hard, flippant, and worldly.

The marquis, too, seemed to realize the depth of Merry's pain, for his anger vanished. "There, now. I know you didn't mean anything. And do not worry, Watters will see the scoundrels caught."

"Of course he will," Mr. Murdoch agreed, patting her arm.

Rather than appearing comforted, Merry gave a short bark of bitter laughter. "Yes. Of course he will. Excuse me. I think Lady Mathilde beckoned."

"She has not been herself since Grace's death," the marquis explained, watching her go. "As the only child in the castle she has been overindulged, and I confess I have let her run wild."

"Often as not to Clyth," Mr. Murdoch agreed, nodding portentously.

"Uncle?"

"She rides toward Clyth some nights. Saw her last night, riding out in the moonlight. Rides like Diana, that girl."

"Why ever didn't you say anything before this?" the marquis asked.

Kate looked at Kit. If he felt any of her embarrassment, he showed none. Uncomfortable, she began to edge away but the marquis stopped her. "Please. I am sorry. We are none of us ourselves."

"Understandably so," she murmured.

"You are kind."

She lowered her eyes. She was nothing of the sort. She was simply trying to make these people like her well enough that they would agree to aid her and her sisters. She would have embraced the devil if it would buy her peace and security.

She blushed at the realization, and she felt Kit stiffen beside her. What must he think of her? He who had never bartered one whit of pride for tangibles?

Mr. Murdoch cleared his throat, his eyebrows wiggling like antennae as he searched for a way to fill the awkward silence. He looked at Kit, and his face cleared.

"I see there is more than one captain at the castle," he said. "That's the Ninety-fifth Rifleman's jacket you're wearing, ain't it? A captain's. I didn't realize the Rifles had been demobbed."

"They haven't, sir," Kit replied. "I asked for a leave."

"Of course you have," the marquis said staunchly. "You've done your duty. Earned a bit of peace, I would imagine. Can always go back, I suppose?"

"Aye," Kit answered. "There's always a dearth of officers nowadays. But first I have some personal matters to attend to, some old debts that need to be paid." He smiled, making it seem that these debts were simple, homely things. But she knew better. He was going to hunt the man from the castle. A man who had tacitly threatened to kill him. The realization of the danger he would be deliberately putting himself in hit Kate with the force of a blow.

"Is something wrong, Mrs. Blackburn?" the marquis asked solicitously.

"When will you be leaving?" she asked, ignoring the marquis's solicitous query. Indeed, she was barely aware of the marquis anymore. Everything faded around them, the people, the room—she didn't know where she was, nor did she care. While they'd been traveling, she'd forgotten that Kit's nemesis was nearby. It had been easy to forget the future that awaited him, just as she'd conveniently forgotten her own.

"When are you going?" she insisted. "I thought you were staying a few days?"

But if she had forgotten where they were, Kit had not. He smiled at the others. "Mrs. Blackburn fears she will be marooned here without a driver," he explained readily, "and thus forced to impose upon your hospitality should the roads close. Mrs. Blackburn is—forgive me for the familiarity, ma'am—most proud."

The marquis, whose brows had been drawing together in uneasy consternation, relaxed. "Ah!" he breathed. "You mustn't think that your company could ever be an imposition, Mrs. Blackburn. I may close the roads myself just to avail myself of your charming company."

Kit smiled easily at the marquis, a gentleman approving another gentleman's chivalry. He had bought her a few minutes to recover her aplomb, but a few minutes would not be enough. Dread pooled in her stomach. She could not look at him. She touched her fingertips to her temples. "I . . . I beg you excuse me."

"What is wrong?" the marquis asked in concern.

"Oh, pray do not be alarmed. I am sometimes visited by sudden headaches."

"But what can we do for you?" he asked. Kit watched her expressionlessly.

"Nothing, I fear. A rest in a dim room, and I shall be put to rights in a few hours. If you would please excuse me from dinner?"

"But of course. Merry," he called to his ward, "help Mrs. Blackburn to her room."

"No. I will only feel worse if I disrupt your dinner. Please."

"If that is your desire," the marquis said doubtfully, motioning for the footman.

"It is," she said, and bidding the rest of the room's occupants good evening, she followed the silent footman to her room.

It would have been tolerable except for that damn pink dress. The neckline accentuated the slender column of her neck, revealed the delicate lines of her collarbones, and displayed all too clearly her creamy bosom. If only he hadn't known that a scant one inch below the edge was the mark his mouth had made on its snowy surface. But he did. Just as he knew the mark was fading away as surely as the time they had left together. Thank God. This was hell; hell complete with pleasant company, a superb chef, and the best wine he had ever drunk, but hell nonetheless.

It was a relief when Kate left, when he didn't have to pretend not to notice every nuance playing over her expressive, piquant, and darkly beautiful face. When he didn't have to pretend that his heart wasn't thundering in his throat for fear that she would betray their intimacy and ruin her chances with the marquis. When he wouldn't have to pretend he didn't want her to do just that, wholly, with every greedy, selfish fiber of his being. He missed her as soon as the door shut behind her.

He forced himself to attend the others after her retreat, determined not to let any of his acts or gestures or omissions or anything untoward in his behavior give him away. The older man argued the merit of Napoleon's regime with his nephew while the old lady added her opinions, occasionally calling on Kit to repeat some point. The marquis left the table once to go and see how Kate fared, and Kit had had to restrain himself from claiming that right, staring moodily into his wineglass. He did not think he could endure too much more of the marquis's bonhomie or Kate's responding blushes or his own tortured longing.

He still had a purpose. He clung tightly to that now, as though it offered a lifeline. He was finally free to pursue the goal he'd set for himself years ago. He'd start in Clyth, with Callum Lamont. If that proved fruitless, he would head for London and Ramsey Munro.

And afterward? He would rejoin the army. His men would need him. There was a war being fought and every week that passed he became more aware that his place in it, his part in it, was being filled by another officer, one who may not have his skills or his experience. Besides, he might yet be sent to India and there he might have a chance of scorching Kate's memory from his soul or, he gave an inner shrug, save the empire in trying.

Dinner ended, and the marquis asked him to join him in the next room. Kit accepted, of course; those things you must bear, you did, and if a peer of the realm wanted to amuse himself by playing at commoner, Kit would be his man. For Kate's sake. The marquis ushered him into an anteroom as the others adjourned to play cards.

"Do you gamble, Captain MacNeill?"

"Never, sir."

"No?" the marquis looked surprised. "Thought you soldiers were all inveterate gamblers."

"Only with our lives, sir. Never had anything else I could afford to lose."

The marquis's gaze sharpened. "I strongly suspect, Captain MacNeill, that you are a good deal more than you allow."

"I am just a soldier, sir. Before that, I was nothing."

"Are you? Were you?" The marquis moved to a sideboard and busied himself with a decanter and crystal glasses. "May I pour you a drink?"

Kit wondered what this was all about. "Thank you."

The marquis poured an inch of brandy into two glasses and brought one to Kit. He tipped his glass in his direction, toasting him. Kit returned the salute, and in silence they drank.

"Shall we be seated, MacNeill? Ah. Good." The marquis crossed one leg over the other. His boots gleamed black as a cormorant's feather. "This debt you owe Mrs. Blackburn, might I ask the circumstances of it?"

Ah, so that was the way of it. "It is a matter of long standing, sir."

"A personal matter?"

"Her father saved my life, and in doing so, lost his

own. I vowed I would do whatever I could to aid his family."

The marquis straightened, his booted foot dropping with a thud on the floor. He leaned forward in his chair, regarding him in astonishment. "Why . . . you are one of those boys Colonel Nash saved! Grace told us all about it. Amazing. You were held captive for how long?"

"Twenty-one months."

"My God," the marquis whispered. "And this promise is by way of repaying the Nashes for their loss?"

"Yes."

"Well, then," the marquis murmured. "I can only thank you again for escorting Mrs. Blackburn to me."

The wording was possessive, and Kit understood all too well that he was to comprehend just exactly that. He hated the marquis at that moment for his subtlety and even his kindness. But above all, he wanted to challenge him for her.

But he didn't reply. He didn't flinch. He'd taught himself to absorb the strike of the flail without a whimper. But the flail had never hurt like this.

He would leave tonight.

Kit found John in the process of picking Doran's hooves. The young coachman looked up and greeted him. "Fine animal."

"Aye." He wasn't in the mood to talk.

"Irish?"

"Aye."

John set Doran's foot down and wiped his hands on his leather apron. "Didn't mean to pry, sir."

"Sorry, lad." It was not John's fault that the evening had challenged the limits of what he could endure. "I have the devil's own temper. Doran is a cavalry mount. Spent five years in India being patriotic."

"You were in the cavalry, sir?" John asked, moving behind Doran and squatting down again. He eased his hand down the gelding's fetlock and lifted his foot.

"Not me. The horse," Kit said. "I bought him off an officer who'd just sold his commission."

"I see," John said distractedly.

Kit came to an abrupt decision. "What sort of man do you take the marquis to be, John?" he asked. The driver looked up, startled by such plain speaking.

"An honorable one, sir."

"Fair?"

"More than most," John said readily.

"Generous?"

"Well, he's a proper Scotsman, sir, but no tenant of his will ever go wanting because he gambled, and no roofs on his lands will leak so he can wear the latest fashion. And there's no piece of cattle in these stables the match of your Doran," he said slyly, giving the gelding a friendly pat. "How much did he cost, if you don't mind me asking?"

"A bloody fortune," Kit answered shortly. "But what sort of man is the marquis to those who offer him or his injury?"

"Not one to trifle with, sir."

"How so?"

"Well, he called in the militia to deal with those that murdered Mr. and Mrs. Murdoch, didn't he? And he's sworn to see them brought to justice and so he will. I never heard his lordship make a vow he didn't keep."

Kit's hand, buried in Doran's mane, checked. "They were murdered?"

The coachman rammed his hand against his forehead. "Bloody hell, I thought she would have told you."

"Mrs. Blackburn?"

"Yes. I told her myself, and right surprised I was to find myself being the first to do so."

He disliked this. "Why wouldn't the marquis write and inform Mrs. Blackburn that her cousin had been murdered?"

"I thought he had," John admitted. "He wrote her several times. I know because I give 'em to the courier myself. Right surprised I was when I heard she was coming here, and I had the feeling that the marquis was surprised, too. But he's a marquis, and I'm a coachman, and I'm not one to question my betters." He looked at Kit as if trying to gauge whether he fell into that category. "Sir.

" 'Tweren't a secret about the murders," he continued. "I'm thinking that the courier got drunk in some public house and lost the letter the marquis sent." The young coachman was probably right. "That would explain why Mrs. Blackburn came all this way, wouldn't it?" John went on. "She might have thought twice about journeying so far if she knew a murderer was at liberty up here."

"Yes. She might, mightn't she?" Kit agreed cautiously. "I am surprised the marquis sent a carriage for her. *He* must have considered such a trip ill advised."

John shrugged. "Who knows with women? Maybe she made the suggestion and he didn't want to hurt her feelings by saying no."

Which may be exactly what had happened.

"Things being as they are, all's well that ends well. Mrs. Blackburn is here safe and sound, and his lordship is set the militia on the villains' trail."

Which was good, Kit thought, and just what a decent man would do, and proved how far from decency he himself stood; if it had been his kin who had been murdered, he wouldn't have bothered sending for aid, he would have hunted the bastards down himself and doubtless brought ruin on any number of innocent people in the process.

The marquis was not like him. That could only be good for Kate. It wouldn't be long before Parnell offered for her, no matter what she thought. He'd only had to spend a few minutes in the marquis's company to realize that, despite Kate's apparent blindness to it, the marquis of Parnell was, and probably always had been, a little in love with her. Time could only make his attachment deeper. More passionate.

Kit wanted to beat him bloody.

Every instinct drove him to claim Kate Blackburn for his own. But he wouldn't. He would find something better within himself. She wanted stability and security and wealth. He could provide none of those things.

How in the name of all that was sane could he have let last night happen? Because for one brief night he wanted her to be his. And a brief night was all he would ever have. She'd been a temporary wayfarer in his world; she did not belong there, and Kit could not gainsay the evidence of his eyes: the marquis was wealthy, well respected, and mindful of his responsibilities, and he cared for Kate.

She would do well here. It was everything she wanted. And he had to get away.

"I'll be back, ready to leave in a few hours," he told John.

The coachman looked up mournfully. "You can come back in an hour, or two hours or ten, but if you have a care for this animal you'll not be riding him out this day or the next."

Kit checked. "What do you mean?"

"There was a stone wedged between his sole and his frog, sir. Wee thing it were, and I dug it out, but there's a bruise there, and I wouldn't advise riding him for a day or two."

"Hell and damnation!" The young driver cringed. Kit cursed again, before emitting an evil laugh. "Well, why not? Why bloody not?"

"Sir?"

"A day, you say?"

"At least. Two would be better. I wouldn't risk laming him."

"Nor would I."

He left the stables, heading back to the castle, cursing the fate that held Kate Blackburn just out of his reach, but not out of his sight.

As once it had held Douglas Stewart.

*LeMons Castle, July 1799*

*The guard entered the stinking dungeon and waited a moment for his eyes to adjust to the lack of light. Then he looked around until he spied Dand, sitting listlessly with his back against the wall. "Where are the rest of your friends?"*

*Kit straightened. Across the room he saw Ram, his shoulder jammed against the wall as insouciantly as if he were in a London gentlemen's club, as Douglas threaded his way through the crowd, toward the front.*

*Kit moved more slowly, in no way eager for the next few minutes. They were bound to be painful. Ram, too, hung back. A half-dozen more guards had entered the dungeon. Kit disliked the sudden show of strength.*

*"Yesterday our guillotine malfunctioned!" the head guard cried dramatically. "But"—he held up his hand as if to soothe fretful complaints, though no one had made a sound—"after many hours of labor we think she is now fixed. Of course, we will not know until—well." He smiled deprecatingly. "You understand, eh?"*

*A low, panicked mutter ran through the mob.*

*"So." He rubbed his hands together. "We need a volunteer. A . . . Scottish volunteer. In fact, we insist. And if one does not volunteer, we will take all."*

*Dand froze where he sat. Ram jerked straight, and Kit began pushing his way through the crowd toward Douglas, who was still moving toward the door.*

*"Who would like to volunteer to aid us with our little problem?"*

*"I'll go." Douglas's voice reverberated down Kit's spine like death's own toll.*

*"Ah! Very good—"*

*"No!" Dand launched himself forward, but the guards were ready, knocking him to the ground while another pair took hold of Douglas and shoved him out the cell door. Kit burst through the mob at the same time as Ram, just as the cell doors swung shut.*

*Kit raced to the tiny window set high in the wall and jumped, pulling himself up by the bars and staring out at ground level. Through the milling throng of bloodthirsty spectators' legs and feet it was impossible to see him.*

*"Douglas!"*

*Then he spied them, across the yard, the executioner leading Douglas up the scaffolding to where the guillotine squatted, the crowd jeering and shouting. They were wrapping a black scarf around his eyes, and now they shoved him to his knees. The sun glinted off something bright and—*

*"No!"*

# TWENTY

꧁꧂

# MAKING ONESELF
# AGREEABLE TO THOSE
# WHO ARE IN A POSITION
# TO OFFER AID

MORNING CAME, AND WITH IT Kate discovered that the fictional headache she had pleaded had become a fact. She shrugged into her dress without much thought to her appearance, her thoughts on Kit MacNeill. He was leaving. Maybe even today.

The door to her room suddenly opened, and Merry Benny swept into the room. "I came to see if you need anything."

"No," Kate said. "Everything is quite in order. Thank you."

The girl's gaze fell on the stack of dresses Peggy had brought, and she rushed across the room. "Those are Grace's!" she declared. "I should have them."

"Yes. Of course." Kate had to remind herself of her

former sympathy for the girl. "Since my clothes were ruined, the marquis offered their use to me during my stay. You will have them as soon as I am gone."

"Oh. Of course. I . . ." At least, the girl had the grace to look embarrassed. "I didn't mean to sound so greedy. It's just that I have so little left of Grace that I begrudge anyone else having her things."

She eyed the dress Kate had donned. It was white-and-lilac striped batiste with small puffed sleeves and a delicately embroidered band of deep purple satin tied beneath her breasts. "Grace embroidered the sash herself," she said. "She was so talented with a needle. She could take the most common-looking item and in a few hours make it exquisite."

"You were very close to my cousin."

"I considered her my best friend," she answered softly.

"You must miss her greatly."

"Yes." She looked around. "Is this the trunk Grace sent you?"

"Indeed, it is."

"Would you mind if I looked inside? There are a few things of hers that were missing from her room. I assume she sent them along to you. I would like them. They are nothing of value except to me."

"Of course," Kate answered.

Merry did not need further encouragement. She lifted the trunk's lid and began emptying it, carefully looking over each item before dropping it to the floor.

What with the careful examination of each thing, it took a long time, but gradually a pile of Grace's belongings rose at Merry's feet.

Kate had retreated to the window seat to watch, unwilling to intrude on the girl's grief but not wanting to quit the room. Finally the trunk was empty. Merry peered into it with a dissatisfied air.

"Is that all?" she asked. "There are still some things missing."

Kate nodded in agreement. "A good deal, I am afraid. The same thieves that ruined my dresses ransacked Grace's belongings. There were some books that the thieves defaced and which I gave to the marquis to see if he might repair. The embroidery box is here, but the hoops are broken. Several snuffboxes, a clock, and all of the medicine vials were shattered."

The girl shook her head petulantly. "No. None of those things matter. Perhaps a pastel painting or Grace's diary?"

"There was no diary. And those"—Kate gestured to the folio of now scattered watercolors—"are the only artistic pieces."

"A jewelry box?"

"I'm sorry."

The girl glared at her, as though suspecting her of keeping something back. "I know you are very poor. Grace told me as much."

Kate, in the process of rising, froze.

"I wouldn't blame you if you kept something for yourself. As Grace's only blood relation, you deserve it. But I can assure you that whatever it is means a great deal more to me, and I would be more than willing to see you adequately compensated for it."

"There is nothing."

At the chill in Kate's voice, Merry stretched out her hand imploringly. "I have offended you."

"You sound surprised," Kate said icily. "Perhaps you are accustomed to being accused of theft. I am not."

The girl turned brilliant red. "Of course I'm not. Please." Her lips trembled. "I miss her so very much." There could be no doubting her sincerity. "She is gone, and I have been left behind."

Nothing the girl could have said could have done more to secure Kate's sympathy. She knew what it felt like to feel abandoned and angry.

"I understand," she said, coming to her with her hand outstretched.

"No!" Merry said, backing away. "You can't possibly understand, so don't say you do!"

Kate did not take offense. Since her arrival, the girl's mood had vacillated wildly: one minute seemingly lost and vulnerable, the next, bitter and combative. Very much like Kate herself had been the year of her husband and father's deaths.

The girl wiped at her cheeks. "If only I could read her last words. See if she spared me any thoughts at all."

"Are you certain that would comfort you?" Kate asked carefully.

"I suppose it might only make it worse," the girl

whispered, her hands twisting at her waist. "But I would like to know she was happy before she died. *That* would be a comfort."

Undeniably, a bond existed between them. Both had lost loved ones to violent, unnecessary ends. But where Grace had been a victim of crime, Kate's father had volunteered for his death. It shouldn't matter, but it did. Still, she would have liked to know her father's state of mind before he died. Had he been looking for some means of testing himself, or had his death truly been a matter of circumstances, as Kit seemed convinced it was?

She wished her father had written something so that his family might have comforted themselves with the knowledge that in the days before his death, he had thought of them with pleasure and, perhaps, pride. But her father had never been much of a correspondent, so she would never know.

And neither would Merry.

"I am truly sorry, Miss Merry, but Grace sent no additional letter to me. Only the one saying that she and Charles would soon be moving to London and asking if I would store her things in anticipation of their arrival."

"Did you keep the letter?" Merry asked.

Kate shook her head. "No. It was quite short. A matter of a few lines."

The girl wrapped her arms around her waist, staring unseeingly out of the window. Across the courtyard, Captain Watters appeared, his gold epaulets flashing in the morning light. He looked around the courtyard, and seeing Kate and Merry standing at the upper window, smiled and bowed deeply.

"If it comforts you, the marquis has every confidence in Captain Watters," Kate said. "After meeting him I, too, feel he is a man who will not stop until he has achieved his purpose."

Merry colored faintly. "He is an extraordinary man."

The militia captain had evidently made a conquest of the girl.

"And here I thought you only admired the smugglers," Kate said, hoping to tease her out of her sadness. It worked.

Merry gave a derisive scoff. "Mr. Murdoch mistakes me. I don't admire smugglers. They are unspeakably low." She waved her hand airily. "Oh, at one time I might have imagined them an object of romance in my mind."

"Callum Lamont?"

Merry glanced sharply at Kate. "He has a certain coarse appeal," she admitted. "And a certain presence."

Kate tilted her head. "What do you mean?"

"There are leaders, and there are followers. The former are few, the latter many." Her gaze was drawn once more to Captain Watters crossing the courtyard with four men at his heels. "Like the captain there."

"A good man," Kate said approvingly.

Merry looked at her pityingly. "Don't be naive.

Goodness has naught to do with it, Mrs. Blackburn. It is the will of the leader that describes the movement of the led. Most men will follow the strongest leader and live by whatever rules he adopts." She let out a small sigh. "Goodness rarely stands against strength."

"You are concerned Callum Lamont may prove too formidable a foe for Captain Watters."

Merry shrugged.

"Having met both men, I can say with every confidence that Captain Watters could not fail to inspire more men to his purpose than Mr. Lamont to his," Kate said. "So according to your own philosophy, in this instance the good must win as well as the strong."

The girl's gaze fixed on Captain Watters's manly figure with undisguised admiration, and Kate felt relief on the Murdoch family's behalf. Obviously Merry had traded her infatuation with Callum Lamont for a more acceptable idol.

"It's true that one must believe Captain Watters will achieve whatever purpose he undertakes," Merry murmured. She looked around at Kate, slyness stealing into her expression. "Your Captain MacNeill looks like he *might* have been such a man."

"I wouldn't know," Kate replied.

"Wouldn't you?" Was there a trace of disbelief in Merry's voice, or simply scorn? "Well, I daresay I've kept you from your toilette long enough," she said and without any further word, hurried out of the room as Kate stared in bemusement at Grace's belongings still littering her floor.

*   *   *

As soon as she'd cleared the mess, Kate went down to breakfast. She found the marquis already seated. He rose to see her seated, asking after her health and explaining that his family kept later hours. Then he beckoned a footman, and before long a plate heaping with food—kippers and salt herring, eggs and porridge and cakes—was placed before her.

She toyed with her food while the marquis kept her company, regaling her with delightful anecdotes about his family history. She made every effort to attend him, but her eyes kept straying toward the door, anticipating Kit's arrival.

"You must miss your sisters, Mrs. Murdoch."

Kate started. "Oh. My sisters. Yes. Very much." In truth, she hadn't given much thought to her sisters these last few days. She had been entirely caught up in her own affairs. But now, she did.

How Helena would love this castle. She would love the beauty of it, the graciousness. She would find in the library any number of companions to keep her company over the long winter months. Charlotte, on the other hand, would not be so captivated. She would find the isolation burdensome—unless she found a worthy opponent for her acerbic tongue and agile mind.

"I hope someday that they, too, will be able to visit my home. I know how important family is. My own is most dear to me." For a moment, a shadow of melancholy crept over the marquis's handsome face, but he shook it off. "I have spent so many years putting to rights my inheritance, I have neglected my personal life, I am afraid. I think it is time to change that."

Kate did not reply. She was thinking of her sisters and wondering how she could have left them so far from her thoughts.

The marquis cleared his throat, drawing Kate's attention. "I believe it is time that my family came out of mourning," the marquis said, setting down his napkin with the air of a man who has come to a momentous decision.

"Milord?"

"We cannot shut ourselves away in the castle forever. Especially here in the north, where the customs regarding mourning are not so strict and every person's absence from our small society is counted a hardship by their friends and neighbors. Unless"—he looked at her worriedly—"you think we have not yet paid adequate respect to the deceased?"

"I am certain you have," Kate hastened to reassure him.

The marquis smiled with brilliant and undisguised relief. "Good. Well, the thing is, we have been invited to a small gathering at the MacPhersons' two days hence. I had written and declined, but now I think perhaps we ought to go after all. I would not like you to think we are dull."

"Please, milord, I do not need to be entertained."

"Of course not. But"—he leaned forward, charming in his sincerity—"I want you to like us."

"I would have to be of a particularly unpleasant disposition not to do so, sir."

"Well, then," he said, "I want you to like us a great deal. For I hope you will stay with us."

Kate froze. He could not possibly mean what she thought he'd implied.

Seeing her embarrassment, he hurried on. "At least until spring. The trip back would be too uncomfortable to contemplate. You will stay, won't you?" His gaze was warm and direct, without evasion or pretense:

The marquis was courting her. Kate stared.

"I can send for your sisters to join us."

My God! He really *was* courting her! She waited for the ecstatic leap of her heart. It did not come.

"I hope you do not think me precipitous? What with the house party and all." He was decidedly not talking about the party and they both knew it. "Tell me, Mrs. Blackburn," he asked worriedly, "*do* you think it too soon? I have often recalled your delightful company in Brighton, and I am so very glad to become . . . reacquainted."

She didn't know what to think. Certainly she had realized he once felt a certain partiality for her—it was the basis upon which she had shored up the courage to ask him for financial aid. But she never imagined that he felt anything deeper. Now, he waited for her answer.

She would be a fool not to encourage him, but the words she ought to say lodged in her throat. She would force them out. "I will be guided by you in this, milord."

"You will? Of course you will." He smiled, pleased, and leaned back in his chair. "We will visit the MacPhersons. It will only be a small gathering, most suitable for our first appearance in public, just five or six families for the weekend.

"We live far enough apart that we generally stay a bit when we go. Not overlong," he said hurriedly, as if she might be seeing a future as a perennial house-guest. "Four or five days."

"Yes, milord."

He rose from the table. "I shall send word at once that our circumstances have changed, and we would be honored to accept their invitation. Uncle Kerwin adores Mrs. MacPherson. Her family was stripped of their title in '45, and he derives no end of pleasure in calling her countess and she no end of pleasure in hearing it. And Lady Mathilde will be delighted to be let loose on the neighbors once more."

She smiled, feeling like a cheat and a fraud and hating herself for feeling that and hating Kit for causing that feeling.

She would *not* feel this way. It was ridiculous. She was not some silly heroine in a medieval troubadour's song, eternally belonging to one man because she had spent a night in his bed. Other ladies both grander and lower than she had had lovers and married elsewhere and lived happily thereafter. She would be one of them. She would think of Kit MacNeill and she would smile, and if right now she felt closer to tears, she must be nearing her courses because she wasn't such an imbecile!

"Of course."

"And this afternoon, might I entice you into taking a ride? I have a well-behaved lady's mare in the stable. Or we could drive along the cliffs. The views are spectacular. The choice is yours." He held his hands palm up and grinned boyishly, teasingly, charmingly. "What do you want?"

"A drive would be lovely." *What do you want?*

"I shall see to it at once. Shall we say one o'clock?"

"Yes."

He left to finish up some correspondence and free his afternoon, and she stayed behind in the breakfast room, somberly regarding the china plate before her. It was edged in gilt, bracketed by heavy silver knives and forks. A crystal goblet stood at its upper edge. Beneath her feet lay a thick carpet. A footman stood beside the door, stationed there for one purpose, to see to her every comfort. A fire blazed in the hearth, and the room was warm, blessedly warm even here, in the most northern reaches of Scotland in the middle of November.

*What do you want, Kate?*

She closed her eyes and saw her mother's face, dulled with sadness, and Helena's hands, the bones showing through the backs, the nail beds blue with chill, and finally Charlotte, her pretty face animated by her extraordinary relief as she swept out of the bare rented rooms, kissing her sisters' cheeks and whispering, "The entire season, Katherine! Can you imagine the Weltons' generosity? I shall be in London for the *season!*"

But Charlotte wouldn't *have* a season, not unless the marquis provided one. Kate's lips twisted with self-derision. She would not offer her sisters as an excuse for her intentions. Helena and Charlotte were only part of any reason she would accept the marquis if he should offer for her. *Did* she intend to accept him?

*What do you want, Kate?*

She rose from the table, and the footman leapt to open the door for her. She walked out into a large, well-lit hall, moving past generations of painted Murdochs toward the library on a carpet so thick her passing was soundless. She needed to think. *What do you want, Kate?*

The question, she decided, should be what she did *not* want. She did not want to be hungry. She did not want to be cold. She did not want to worry about her future or that of her sisters. She did not want to be afraid. She did not want to be desperate. She did not want to be poor.

There. She had answered the question.

She put her hand on the library handle, her jaw clenched in frustration because while she knew quite clearly what she did not want, she knew just as clearly what she did.

The door opened. Kit MacNeill looked down into her eyes.

And he was standing right before her.

# TWENTY-ONE

※※※

# MAKING RESPONSIBLE CHOICES

HE HADN'T ANY RIGHT to look so good when he looked so disreputable. The stock about his throat was cheap, his linen shirt threadbare, his coat old, and his boots scarred. But his hands . . . Kit had beautiful hands. Not soft and pink, but calloused and rough, his fingers lean and strong and masculine. They were, she noted, scrubbed clean. But where was his regimental jacket?

"Why didn't you tell me you were a captain?" *Where had that come from?*

The corner of his mouth lifted. "The matter never came up in the course of our conversations. Besides, it hardly bore mentioning."

"I thought you were an enlisted man."

"I *was* an enlisted man, and as such found myself in the right places at the right times, or perhaps I should say the wrong places at the wrong times. Either way, I survived and was given battlefield commissions for my luck."

He tilted his head regarding her sardonically. "And if I *was* an enlisted man, why would I be here rather than with my regiment? Surely the daughter of a colonel must have wondered about that?"

She looked away, embarrassed. "I thought you might have deserted."

"Such a kindly estimation of my character."

"You have gone to great pains to tell me your character is flawed and unworthy; you can't suddenly decide that I am being unfair when I take you at you word."

"Touché." He grinned, and she wished, profoundly, that he wouldn't. He was far too handsome, far too approachable, when he smiled like that.

"Besides," she continued gruffly, looking away from him, because looking would become wanting, "I could not conceive that you would sign up after all that had happened to you."

"I was drunk."

No one would ever accuse MacNeill of sugar-coating his history. A twisted smile played about his lips, as though he had read her thoughts. "I play the lead in no heroic tales, Kate, just common and vulgar ones. You mustn't see things that aren't there. But I didn't come to confess my shortcomings. You know those full well."

"Do I?"

"Covetousness." He raised his hand as if to touch her face and hesitated. "Anger. Pride." The backs of his fingertips brushed a tendril of her hair slowly away from her face. "Bigotry against my betters." She stilled, apprehensive lest he take a greater liberty, more apprehensive that he would not.

"Yes. You know in how many ways I've failed."

"You have never failed me," she breathed, her gaze tangling with the silvered frost of his.

His thumb touched the corner of her eye and lightly brushed her lashes. She turned her head, just a small movement, but enough to force a closer contact. She heard his breath check, and then his thumb was feathering a line down over her cheek, along her jaw to the point of her chin. He tilted her head up, looked down into her eyes. "I've come to tell you that I will be leaving soon."

Her heart beat thickly in her throat, flutters of alarm taking flight in her belly. *No.* "When?" *No!* "Not today?"

"There is no reason to stay and every reason to go," he said soberly.

She shook her head. "No. Not today."

He closed his eyes briefly, evidence of some inner struggle flickering briefly across his lean features. "When will you be ready for me to leave?"

She didn't know. Next month? Next week? Never? The idea that she might never see him again, that when he left the castle it would be with the specific goal of searching for a traitor and murderer, set her limbs trembling and her breath staggering in her lungs. But not today. "Maybe . . . in a few days."

He held her gaze. "Tomorrow, Kate. Don't ask more than that. I beg you."

He would do whatever she asked. He'd sworn to it. He would even stay, and for as long as she bid him do so. But she could not tether him to her with a vow. She could not ask him to stay and witness her encourage the marquis with every remembered wile at her disposal. She was bad, yes, but not wicked.

"Tomorrow." Her voice broke, and she shut her eyes, not wanting him to see her in tears.

"Do you know what the first thing I noticed about you three years ago was?" he asked softly. "It was your courage, Kate. I grew up respecting courage above everything except loyalty. When I saw you that first time, you were like a brand, so fierce and so valiant."

She scoffed, sniffing, amused in spite of her sorrow. "That was not courage, Kit. That was fear."

"I did not know your father, Kate, but in the army I learned his reputation. Colonel Roderick Nash was a just officer and a thoughtful tactician. But above all, he did what needed to be done, without hesitation. You're like that, Kate. You have that courage."

"Rubbish!" She was nothing like her father.

Kit caught her chin in his strong fingers, moving closer. "Your mother was already dying, and your older sister hadn't woken to the fate awaiting you, and your younger one was still trying to make sense of it. In one short year, everything you were and everything you expected to have and to be had been stripped away from you. All comfort and security vanished. A lifestyle. A husband. A father. All gone. But you knew what had to be done, and so you did it."

He tilted her face so that the light streaming in from the high windows fell full upon her visage. "What can one call that but courage? Your father would be proud."

He was wrong. Her father would *not* be proud. She *was* a coward. She would not give up wealth and comfort and security. Not for pride. Not for love. She couldn't.

But she could steal one more moment, one more kiss. Boldly, she put her hand on his chest. His heartbeat thundered beneath her palm. She edged closer. Her hem brushed across the tips of his boots.

"Kit." Her fingers curled against his muscular chest.

"Someone might come in," he whispered, his voice dark and hopeless and tender.

"I don't care."

"Yes," he avowed, a tincture of savagery in his pronouncement, "you do. You *should*. You'll be safe here, Kate. Well cared for. You'll live the life you once had."

"Yes."

"You'll be safe." He was still worrying over her safety. "I saw this Captain Watters and his men heading for Clyth this morning. He'll find those responsible for your cousin's death."

He did not know Charles had been involved with the smugglers and that that is what had occasioned his death. He needn't worry over her safety. She wasn't a smuggler, nor had she betrayed anyone.

*But yourself.*

"I am not rich," she said, seeking to reassure him without breaking the marquis's confidence. "I am not going anywhere unescorted. The marquis is well aware of the situation in the region, and I am certain he will take every precaution."

"And whoever was at the castle on the moors was hunting me, not you," he went on, searching her face. "You'll be safer without me, in fact."

"I can't stay, Kate." His tone demanded that she acknowledge the impossibility of his staying, that she understand that he was not abandoning her.

*Everything you want is within your reach, Kate Blackburn. All you have to do is watch Kit MacNeill walk out the door.* "Of course you must go."

He suddenly reached out and cupped the back of her head, pulling her roughly toward him. His breath had gone ragged. She melted eagerly against him, her lips opening.

"God help me," he muttered roughly. "Not without a kiss"

He crushed her mouth beneath his. All the want and frustration and pain of longing filled that kiss, blistering her with desire. She met his passion with equal ardor, wrapping her arms tightly around his neck and pulling him closer, molding her body against his as if by doing so she could somehow become part of him, kissing him back with all the yearning and hopelessness inside her. For one fleeting instant, he held on to her as if he would never let her go.

Then he did.

"I have to leave."

She couldn't let him go without knowing . . . without letting him know . . . without hope . . .

"The marquis has accepted an invitation for us to visit his neighbors tomorrow," she whispered. "When we return . . . he asked me to stay on."

Kit's body tensed, but his eyes remained fixed on hers.

"I . . ." She swallowed. "Can you think of any reason why I should not stay here with him?"

Five heartbeats. That is how long it took, she discovered, to break a heart. Five heartbeats during which hope rushed, welled, suffused her with joy, and—

"No," he said. "No. I cannot."

—died.

## TWENTY-TWO

⬚⬚⬚⬚

# LIVING WITHIN
# ONE'S MEANS

A FOOTMAN SNAPPED TO attention as Kit strode past, and a maid smiled timidly at him. He saw neither.

Kate had asked him as clearly as her station and pride would allow that he make some claim upon her. He lifted the door latch with a shaking hand. She must never know how completely she'd undone him, or how desperately he'd wanted to do so. He was a selfish brute, but not that selfish. He would leave her with the good marquis, where her future, and her sisters' futures, were assured. And in the years ahead, when he thought of her, he would be satisfied with the idea that, for however short a time, a lady had considered sacrificing everything she valued for him. It was a trade he could live with.

He walked outside, where winter had retreated a half step, the air thin but mild and the sky pale, and headed for the stables. It was deserted save for the horses. He found Doran and ran his hand down the gelding's rear leg, lifting his hoof. He could see no discoloration and, gently probing the frog, found no evidence that Doran felt any discomfort. He'd ride tomorrow.

A furtive sound brought Kit's head up in time to see a feminine figure hurrying between the stalls, clutching the handle of a swollen valise. It was Mertice Benny, the marquis's ward. She made it to the end of the aisle, set the valise down, and attempted to open the last stall door. The latch had evidently stuck, and she pulled angrily on the handle.

"Allow me," he said.

She jumped, wheeling around with her hand at her throat. "You startled me!"

"It was most unintentional, I assure you. May I offer my assistance?"

She regarded him suspiciously, and Kit felt a prick of irritation. Her virtue could not be any safer than with him.

"Well?"

She flounced about and gestured irritably toward the stall, indicating, he presumed, that he might have a go at opening it.

Why not? He examined the stall door and found a piece of wood jammed near the hinge. He pried it out with his dagger, and the door swung open, revealing an empty stall. Empty except for a set of luggage stacked inside. New luggage, by the look of it, the leather still shiny and the brass locks bright. Odd place to store new luggage.

Noting his quizzing glance, Merry tilted her head haughtily, daring him to question her. The truth being that he didn't give a bloody damn about her or her luggage, he stood aside while she picked up the valise and dragged it inside.

"I am . . . planning . . . on taking an extended trip," she panted as she rearranged the heavy luggage. "And I see no reason why my room . . . should be littered with baggage . . . when this is a perfectly reasonable place to store them."

"Some perfectly unreasonable thieves?" he suggested blandly.

The girl scowled and gnawed on her lower lip, obviously debating whether to give him the set-down she so richly wanted to or try to wheedle him into doing her bidding—whatever that might be. At least she was a distraction, however short-lived, from Kate.

She tried a coquettish smile. He supposed it might even have been a fairly good one . . . if one cared. "Please don't tell the marquis."

"Tell the marquis what?"

"About the luggage. About my . . . leaving."

*About her eloping.* The pieces fell neatly into place. She was running off with someone, and Kit had a fairly good idea who that might be. Her face was not particularly transparent, but his life had often relied upon reading people, and this girl was as false as a beggar's empty sleeve.

"The Murdochs wouldn't understand. He isn't like them." She fair quivered with ill-contained excitement.

So Merry's admiration for the stalwart Captain Watters had been a red herring; otherwise she wouldn't have used the term "like them." Captain Watters was decidedly "like them." No one would have objected to a match with the captain of a militia unit. No, the little fool was going to elope with Callum Lamont.

"You needn't look like that. I would think you of all people would understand."

He arched a brow, though acknowledging that her prick had struck deep. He was decidedly more of Callum Lamont's ilk than Captain Watter's. Still, he only said, "Understand that you're running off with a thief and a smuggler?" He paused. "That *is* what you're doing, isn't it?"

For a second, she looked surprised then replied hotly, "It's none of your concern. Besides, we're married."

"Married?" She had surprised him, after all.

"Aye," she said haughtily. "This *is* Scotland. It isn't hard to do."

"I don't believe you."

She shrugged. "I don't care. But you need only ask the blacksmith in Selwick."

"You are a fool."

"Oh, come, Captain. The English have been eloping across our borders for years. There is no reason a Scotswoman shouldn't make use of one of our most celebrated customs."

"You think running off is all very romantic and adventurous," he said. "It's not. It's squalid and vulgar. And the road is lonely."

She lifted her chin. "But I won't be alone."

"Not yet." He regarded her pityingly. "But how long do you think he will he stay with you? A month? A year? Until he dies in some drunken brawl or at the end of a rope?"

"No one will catch him. He's too clever by half," she stated, and Kit stared at her in amazement.

By God, she actually believed it. He tried another tack. "Perhaps not. But the romance will only endure as long as your beauty. How long will that last, do you suppose? A hard life without the sort of luxury and cosseting you are accustomed to enjoying tends to leach away a woman's looks."

"Mrs. Blackburn doesn't appear to have suffered unduly," she said slyly.

The attack was unexpected, and Kit regarded her with some respect. The kitten was a cat after all, and she had sharp claws.

"Mrs. Blackburn is exceptional," he said. "She is also wise enough not to let impossible fantasies rule her life. You would do well to emulate her."

"So stiff, Captain MacNeill?" she purred. "Who was it you said was wise not to let fantasies govern Mrs. Blackburn's life? I could have sworn you said her, but I think"—she sidled closer—"I think it's *you* who have decided for her."

He'd satisfied whatever impulse he'd had to warn her. He turned away, but her hand shot out and grabbed his sleeve.

"I'm right, aren't I? You're leaving her."

"She's not mine to leave or not leave," he said with a calm he wished he felt.

Merry laughed. "No more than the sun belongs to the day and the moon to the night. Do you think it isn't obvious? The way you watch her. The way she *doesn't* watch you."

"You're imagining things."

"You great bloody fool," she sneered. "You'd leave her here? For him? Do you know what happens to a person who is discarded like that? Love turns into hate, Captain MacNeill. And hate is a fertile ground. It breeds all sorts of trouble."

"Shut up," Kit said. Her words were like poison, insidious and lethal.

She sidled closer to him. "Do you want her to hate you? Because she will. What? That never occurred to you? You thought she would thank you for leaving her here?" She shook her head. "Never! She will *hate* you, hate herself, and hate the marquis, because she will always remember that *you* made the choice. She will not think of the poverty you think you are sparing her. She will think of pleasure and passion, and every thought will be tainted with hatred because *you left her behind!*"

Her voice was thick with vitriol. "*I'm* not being left behind. Not again."

She wheeled around, her skirts snapping, and stood with her back to him. She took a deep breath and then another, calming herself. When she looked around again, the fight had drained from her. She looked exhausted, her nerves near unraveling. She lived on a razor's edge, fearing her lover and fearing not to go with him even more. "*Are* you going to tell the marquis?" she whispered.

He regarded her in astonishment. "I have no choice. How can I not tell him that his ward is running off with a possible murderer?"

"He's murdered no one," she declared. "I swear to you that he did not kill Charles or Grace. I know for a fact he is innocent of their deaths, because I know who *is* responsible."

"Who?"

She shook her head. "I won't tell until we're well away from here. Then, I swear, I will write, revealing everything. *If you let me go.* Tomorrow, when the others go to the MacPhersons, I intend to stay behind. We'll leave then, and no one will ever see us again."

"I'm sorry."

She ground her teeth in frustration. "I tell you, he did not kill Grace and Charles. Would I elope with someone who'd killed my dearest friend? My *only* friend?!" Her gaze was hot but level. She sincerely believed Lamont to be innocent of the crime. "Besides, we *are* married, and finally, this is none of your affair."

She was clearly convinced Lamont hadn't killed Grace, and she would be in a better position to judge than he. Maybe she was telling the truth, and if she wasn't . . . ? Well, she would be gone and thus less likely to bring scandal down upon the Murdoch family. And thus, upon Kate. And if she had married

Lamont, there was naught he or the marquis or anyone else could do for her.

"All right," he said, knowing he acted against his
better judgment. But then, his judgment of late had
been none too good.

"Another!" Callum Lamont rasped, raising his cup
and rubbing at his throat. He thought his pipes had
been permanently busted and he'd like as not spend
the rest of his days croaking like a bullfrog, and that
wasn't right. Especially since he'd once saved the bastard's life.

He stared moodily into his empty cup. Ungrateful,
that's what it was. Well, he'd teach him some manners, especially since there wasn't anyone around anymore to watch his back. None of that Scottish wolf
pack ran together anymore, it would seem. Not sur-
prising, seeing how their "brotherhood" hadn't with-
stood a bit of treachery.

The thought brought a smile. "I said another!"

Meg slunk over to refill his cup and then, looking
quickly around, slipped a sealed letter onto his lap.
Callum pushed a coin into her hand, her payment for
acting as a courier between him and the castle. She
darted away as if she feared for her virtue, and Callum
felt a ripple of offense.

He had never forced himself on a woman, and he
never would. He didn't need to coerce a woman into
his bed. Women flocked to him like bees to honey—
the mirror explained that easily enough. But it wasn't

just his success with other women that kept him from the Megs of the world, it was his heart.

He'd already given it to a lady, a true lady, one as beautiful as a rose and just as prickly as one, too. Not that he minded a thorn or two, he thought, his memory unfurling over evenings when she had warmed his bed and he had warmed her in all other places. Soon they would be together again.

Callum Lamont, bastard and foul-tempered, murdering demon that he was, loved mean but true. He was as faithful as the tides and just as unfailing. But musing on Merry's charms wasn't getting either of them any nearer their fortune, so with a sigh he tore open the letter's seal and got down to business.

Carefully, he studied the elegant hand. There were only a few words, but they caused him to break into a grin. He crumpled the sheet and tossed it into the fire, and as he watched the flame consume it, he laughed.

Who said work and pleasure never mixed?

# TWENTY-THREE

⬚⬚⬚⬚

# LEARNING TO LIVE

# WITHOUT

KERWIN MURDOCH STOOD BESIDE the luggage filling the hallway while Lady Mathilde kept up a running patter to Kate and the marquis gave last-minute instructions to the butler. Miss Merry would not be going with them. She had told the marquis she would not shorten her mourning period for "dearest Grace" by so much as an hour, and that to force her to do so would be unforgivable.

The marquis, clearly caught unprepared, had been put in a dreadful quandary. He had refused the MacPhersons' initial invitation, only to ask that the invitation be reissued so that he might accept it. Now he must renege.

Lady Mathilde, concerned that her reentry into society was being revoked, pointed out that the girl would do very well alone in the castle guarded by those of Captain Watters's men left behind and their own fifty-odd servants. But it took a letter, arriving via the hand of a militia courier, to persuade the marquis that his ward could remain safely at the castle.

Lady Mathilde, having satisfactorily dealt with the obstacle presented by Merry, muttered to herself as she mentally dissected her wardrobe. "Half a dozen dresses for the day? Should do. But only four for the evening. I hope it suffices. Lord knows what MacPhersons' flues are like this winter. Place could be warm and snug or drafty as a cathedral. One must be prepared for either," she told Kate.

"You'll want a nice riding habit, Mrs. Blackburn. You do ride? No? Pity. Parnell is an avid rider. Still, there is nothing wrong with being decorous rather than robust." She peered closely at Kate. "One can hardly accuse you of the latter." Her elderly mouth pleated with sympathy. "You look unwell, child. Are you feeling up to this trip?"

Kate smiled gratefully at the old woman. No. She was not. She had not seen Kit since yesterday, and every waking moment she felt his absence more keenly.

He was still here, somewhere, but he hadn't dined with them last night, and so dinner had become for her an arduous, drawn-out affair. It hadn't made it any more palatable that each kindness, each pleasantry, drove home to her the magnitude of her insupportable ingratitude. Though the marquis did not know the source of her lassitude, he could not fail to notice it. He had been wonderfully solicitous. And Merry, her campaign to continue her mourning having been successful, not only appeared at the dinner table but then proceeded to captivate everyone with unexpected charm.

All the while Kate kept wondering where Kit was, at what hour he would leave, if he would think of her, and if so, how long she would retain a part of his heart. She had finally conceded that she'd lost a portion of her own that she would never recover. But . . . he hadn't made any claim upon her affections. He'd all but handed her to the marquis.

Thank God one of them had some common sense.

"Mrs. Blackburn?" Lady Mathilde asked worriedly, and Kate realized she'd been talking to her for some time.

"I'm sorry. What were you saying? I am, I confess, extremely tired."

"Ah!" Lady Mathilde waggled her finger beneath Kate's nose. "Fatigue often becomes illness. I should have expected as much. After all, you traveled here in an open coach. To think!" Her eyes grew round with amazement at such a feat.

"I should have cautioned James against this, but . . . well, I am a selfish old woman," she said remorsefully. "And he was so eager to introduce you." She trailed off, a blush staining her papery cheeks.

Kate squirmed under Lady Mathilde's obvious approval, feeling base and guilt-ridden and . . . *No!* She must stop this wrong thinking. But how? And where? Under the MacPhersons' interested gaze?

*No.* She just needed time. Everything had happened so quickly. She had not anticipated becoming

Kit's lover any more than she had anticipated the marquis's interest. Both had happened within hours of one another. Was it any wonder she felt confused, her head spinning, her thoughts a jumble, and her heart brok— her heart sore?

She was a soldier's daughter. When outstripped and outgunned, one fell back and regrouped.

"I fear you are right, Lady Mathilde," she said, coming to a decision. "My travels have dealt more roughly with me than I realized. I would do best remaining here and recovering my full health."

Lady Mathilde nodded sadly, unable to hide her disappointment. "I shall inform the marquis that we will be staying after all."

"Not a bit of it," Kate declared. "It would be unconscionable for you to cry off at such short notice." Kate could not refrain from smiling at the sudden hopefulness in the old lady's face. "I will speak to the marquis."

Twenty minutes later the marquis and the others stood outside, preparing to leave as Kate stood beside them, saying temporary farewells. She had told the marquis that not only was she more tired than she'd originally realized, but that she felt she might actually do some good in staying back and offering what comfort she could to Merry, still cloistered in her rooms.

The marquis, of course, had agreed. He had been about to have the luggage returned to their rooms when Kate had asked him not to abandon his plans on her account. She asked with such gentle gravity that he could be in no doubt that she intended to use the weekend to sort out her thoughts. Being a gentleman, he had made no further protest but only took her hand and reverently kissed the backs of her fingers.

"I doubt any person could be more anxious that convivial hours pass swiftly than I will upon quitting your company, Mrs. Blackburn." It was a truly handsome compliment. He was a truly handsome man. "I would not leave you here, even with the militia and my servants, had I not just received word from Captain Watters that he is within hours of bringing to justice those responsible for our mutual sorrow. He is well away from here."

"I was never afraid," she assured him.

"I know you will be well." He still didn't look happy.

"You are concerning yourself unduly, milord."

He collected himself and stood back. "I look forward to that time when I can introduce you to my friends, Mrs. Blackburn."

"You are kind, sir."

He hesitated, seeming about to say more, and she shifted uneasily, not ready. He smiled wanly, understanding, and turned toward his aunt and uncle. "My dears, if you are ready?"

As they settled in the carriage, a horseman emerged near the top of the drive, a tall, lean man on a big roan gelding, the wind in his cloak and the sun bright in his hair. Kate's lips curved into a smile of welcome and anticipation. Kit had come back after all.

Her heart fluttered in equal parts trepidation and anticipation. She waited, frozen in the open doorway.

Even from this distance, she felt his gaze on her, his regard as sweet as the warmth of the sun on her cheeks. She took a step down the stairs, wondering why he was waiting, and then, abruptly, she understood: he wasn't going to come any closer.

*No.* She stepped off the landing down to the first stairs, pulled by an invisible cord. Below her, John stowed the carriage steps inside as a hundred yards away Kit lifted his hand in farewell.

She was being left behind. But, oddly, looking at the lonely figure raked by a rising wind, it felt more like she was the one doing the abandoning. Then why was he still there, his arm aloft, like one seeking permission to leave?

And what else could she do but grant it?

She raised her hand slowly. He turned his horse. A few seconds later he had vanished beyond the trees. Ten minutes later the carriage left, too.

He'd been given his leave. He was his own man again. And wasn't that better? Wasn't that what he'd wanted from the beginning? To strip himself of every obligation? And, by God, he'd managed that right enough.

Aye. It would be better for Kate, too. She was off to dine on gold plate and drink from crystal goblets. Tonight she would be dressed in silk, and her eyes would sparkle like black diamonds, and her skin would glow beneath the light of a thousand candles. She would smile and grow warm with the exertions of the dance and her cheeks would flush, and the marquis, unable to resist her, would come and tell her she was beautiful. But he would never know how truly beautiful she was because he would never see her eyes still black with passion, her skin damp, her hair wild about her shoulders— Or maybe he would.

Kit spurred Doran into a canter, as though he could outdistance his thoughts, and the big gelding's long legs effortlessly ate up the miles. Nothing kept him here any longer. He had thanked the marquis for his generosity and once more been forced to accept his gratitude for bringing him Kate. He'd stood, listening politely to the marquis's plans to introduce her at some house party and murmuring appropriately over the marquis's concern that Merry was staying back. And he had held his tongue because it was none of his concern, none of it, not Merry, not the marquis, not Kate.

The sound of the surf mingled with the wind rushing in his ears, and still it did not drown out the sound of her voice: "Can you think of any reason why I should not stay?"

A thousand. None of them good enough.

He'd fulfilled his obligation to Colonel Nash's daughter, and he was free to pursue his own inclination, to repay that final debt, to find his betrayer and Douglas's murderer. And then he could . . . What?

Rejoin his regiment, he supposed. He was a soldier, a good tactician and a canny judge of a battlefield. With luck in a few years he might make major.

But why? Toward what end? So that he could live out his life independent, separate in heart and soul from all others. That was, after all, the promise he'd made himself after their betrayal at LeMons.

But he wasn't. He never could be. Not ever again. No matter whether he'd done his duty by her, fulfilled his vow, discharged his obligation, he would always be tied to Kate Nash Blackburn by bonds stronger than oaths and duty and intent and purpose. He loved her. He always would—

"Halt!"

Four men stepped out from behind boulders on either side of the road, two in front and two behind. They had pikes. One held a primed pistol. Kit hauled back on Doran's mouth, grabbing the hilt of the claymore sheathed between his shoulder blades. With a steely hiss it slid halfway from the scabbard before he heard a familiar voice behind him. "Ye never learn, do you, lad?"

Kit turned as Callum Lamont strode up, a musket leveled at his belly. There was murder in his face and an unholy excitement in the faces of his men.

"You'd think after being gulled in France, you'd be a mite more careful who you trust."

There was no hope of running. But that didn't mean he had to cringe.

"For God's sake, Callum," Kit drawled, letting the blade slip back into its sheath. "Speak up, lad. You sound like a half-wrung pullet."

Callum made a chopping motion with his hand, and Kit's head exploded in pain.

And then there was nothing.

# TWENTY-FOUR

⬦⬦⬦

# DEALING WITH PHYSICAL DISCOMFORT

THE THIRD BUCKET of snow thrown in his face revived Kit. He gasped for breath, shivering and retching, the burning in his arms and shoulders obliterating the pain of broken ribs. They'd thrown a rope over a hook suspended from the croft's low ceiling and bound his wrists at each end, and then . . . then Callum had had a bit of fun, but he still didn't have the information he wanted.

He was good at beating a man, Callum was. Better than Kit would have suspected of a buggering, trumped-up sod of a Scottish whoreson. Through the red veil of pain threatening to drown him, Kit tallied the damage: a couple of broken ribs, one eye closed, a tooth knocked out, and two fingers of his right hand aligned into a symmetry God never meant.

"I know you came for the treasure," Callum said, pacing back and forth in front of Kit. "But you won't have it. It's mine. I killed before for that treasure, and I'll kill you now for it. You're only choice is whether you want to die fast or slow. Either way, you'll tell me where it's hid."

"I don't know." He'd already told them a dozen times, and each time won another beating. Soon he wouldn't be answering at all.

"You do." With a savage snarl, Callum jerked Kit up by his shirt collar, splitting the abused material down the back. Behind, one of Callum's men whistled.

"Sweet Jesus. The bastard's been branded," the one called Ben whispered.

"Impressed?" Kit sneered thickly. "Maybe you'd like one. Or maybe you'd rather taste the whip? Callum here always enjoyed the tickler."

"What's he mean?"

"Callum and I are old mates, aren't we, Callum? Saved my life in prison."

"That true?" one of the men asked.

Kit kept talking, because as long as they were listening, Callum's men weren't beating him. "There's something I been meaning to ask you, Callum."

"You're here to answer questions, not ask 'em."

He ignored that. "Who betrayed us, Callum? Me and Ram and Dand and Douglas? Do you know?"

"I knew it!" he crowed, grinning broadly. "I knew you never tumbled to it! Ha! That's rich, that is! Lovely, even."

"Who was it?"

Callum's smiled thinned. He leaned down, bringing his face within inches of Kit's. "Tell me what I want to know, and as soon as I have the treasure, I'll tell you what you want to know."

Kit ground his teeth. "I don't know."

Callum straightened, thwarted. "A right fine piece of work the Frogs done on him, eh, lads? But I'll wager I can do as good."

Kit met his glare through a haze of agony. He'd be damned to hell if he showed a shred of fear to the likes of Callum Lamont. "You're sure you're up to the task, Callum? You sound a bit hoarse. Maybe you're coming down—ah!"

Callum's fist slammed against Kit's jaw, snapping his head back. "We'll see how quick ye are with a quip by nightfall. Get me the reins from your horse, Ben."

"Dinna think you should, Callum?" Ben asked.

"What?"

"It's just that it was hard to wake him last time, and if ye lay on too hard, he'll not be able to tell us where Murdoch and his wife stored the gold."

"Lad has a point," Kit said.

"Shut up."

"Yer sure he knows where it is, Callum?" another asked. "We been at him, and he swears he don't know nothing. And I'm thinkin' maybe he don't."

"Thinkin'?" Callum shouted. He impaled each of his men with a challenging glare. "Well, they say there's a first for everything."

Kit waited, trying to gather what strength he had. He knew men like these, had trained them, led them, and fought beside them. They respected but one thing: strength. Right now Callum had pitted his will against Kit's, and the smuggler understood well enough that to fail to get the information he sought would undermine his power.

Kit would have smiled if his face hadn't hurt so. Callum could beat him until the marrow ran like jelly from his bones—he didn't know where any "treasure" was.

"Why do you think he knows something, Callum? She tell you?"

*She*. Merry.

"Nah. I had it direct from our partner. He's proved oft times enough that he knows what's what and, more important, what's where, hasn't he, now?"

"Aye," a couple agreed.

"I thought he was in France," Ben said.

"Not no more. He didn't want to lose his part of that last wreck any more than we did, lads. King's ransom, it's worth. We been working on it, him at the castle and me here in Clyth."

*At the castle?*

Callum was boasting now, trying to impress his men with his cleverness and his partner's usefulness. "He found out that Murdoch's wife sent her cousin a letter telling where the loot was hid, and that the widow and lover here come to fetch it for themselves."

Someone grabbed a hank of Kit's hair and lifted his head. "That true, Cap? You come here to steal our booty?"

"Yours? You're wreckers." Kit did not keep the sneer from his voice. Wreckers were worse than pirates, who at least met their victims on level ground.

Wreckers waited for storms to bring in ships looking for safety, using lanterns and shore fires to lure them onto reefs where the sea and surf would batter them to bits. Then they collected the ship's cargo from the beaches, murdering any survivors who made it to shore so they couldn't carry tales. "Murderers."

The backhanded blow caught Kit on the temple, snapping his head back. *"Where is my gold?!"*

"If you wanted the letter Grace Murdoch wrote to Mrs. Blackburn, why didn't you just have your bride steal it when she ransacked Mrs. Blackburn's room at the tavern?" he asked scornfully. "Why? Because there isn't a letter. Where is the fair Mrs. Lamont anyway? Outside, waiting in the carriage? I wouldn't have taken her for a squeamish lass."

"Mrs. Lamont?" Callum stared at him.

"Surprised I know?" Kit asked, hoping for a brief respite to gather his wits. "I found her in the stables, hiding her luggage in anticipation of going off with you. It's why she stayed home, isn't it?"

Something was wrong. Callum had stepped back, blinking rapidly, his expression dumbfounded. Shocked. And suddenly Kit understood. *"She set you up."* He laughed. "We've *both* been set up."

"What's he talking about?"

"Shut up."

Sensing Callum's thickening anxiety, a worry that hung over him like the stink on a peat bog, Ben edged forward. "What's he mean?"

"Look outside," Kit ordered. "Is the militia here yet?

Nah. He'd wait a while to be certain you've killed me first. You still have time to escape, Callum. Best take it."

"The militia!"

"Shut up!" Callum bellowed.

"I thought she meant she'd eloped with you, but she meant Captain Watters. *Your partner*," Kit said. "I should know. Nothing in the army is quick, and the replacement for the dead captain arrived *right* quick. Watters killed Captain Greene, didn't he? Then he lay low. Probably in this very croft. That's why he told you to take me here, so he'd know exactly where to send the militia."

"*What* militia?" Panic had entered Ben's voice.

Kit ignored him, musing through it. "He kills Greene, dons the dead man's own tunic and sash, rides to the castle and takes over the militia, marries the girl, collects a fortune, kills the witnesses—and the partners—and rides out. Cocky bastard. But brilliant." He didn't bother hiding his admiration.

Callum closed the distance between them, slamming his fist into Kit's gut. "Shut yer hole!"

Kit gasped, fighting the clouds dimming his vision. "She's leaving with him, Callum," he croaked. "Maybe already left.

"Think about it! She was with the marquis when he received word that Kate Blackburn had arrived in Clyth. She rode to the inn that afternoon and searched her room, looking for whatever it was that told where Grace had hid the treasure.

"She found it. Don't you see? They already *have*

the treasure. They set this up to get rid of everyone who knows that she conspired at Grace's murder, everyone who knows that Captain Watters doesn't exist, everyone who might want a piece of that treasure. That's you, Callum!

"You fool, *they set us up*. She rides off with Watters or whatever the hell his name is and the treasure and you and I and all your men are killed, surrounded by Greene's militia—"

A door banged open, and Callum spun around as Ben raced out of the croft. "Ben!" he shouted. "Get the hell back here! He's trying to save his own neck! It's lies!"

"Easy enough to find out!" Ben shouted back. "You said Merry Benny went to MacPhersons'. I'll just ride to the castle and see."

Before Callum could stop him, he'd vanished.

"Bloody bastard!" Callum exploded. The blow to his gut took Kit out at the knees. The weight of his falling body nearly pulled his arms from their sockets, but he did nothing to regain his feet, feigning unconsciousness. He hung a long, long time.

The other men kept mum. Through the slit of his remaining good eye, Kit watched Callum swear, pace, pour half a skin of wine down his throat, and pace some more. The minutes dragged by, the men sullen and wary, Callum pacing the croft like a caged beast. He muttered to himself as he walked, "She wouldn't dare," "She knows I'd kill her if I found out," "She loves me," and worse, once, a broken sound of panic and fury, "She knows how much I love her!"

Kit's strength faded with each minute. If Ben didn't return soon, he wouldn't be conscious to take advantage of whatever edge the resultant confusion might create. Finally, when the pain had become nearly unbearable, he heard the sound of an approaching horse. Callum swung the door wide and shouted, "I told you it was a pack of lies!"

"She's at the castle!" Ben came breathless into the room. "She's there, and what's more I seen her packing them bags he talked about with me own eyes. She's getting ready to fly, Callum, and if you didn't know about it, I want to know why—"

"Get out of my way!" With a roar of rage, Callum shouldered his way through the group of men at the door and rushed out into the fading afternoon light, the sounds of hoofbeats following.

"Do you think the Cap here was telling the truth about the militia, too?" one man finally asked.

"Do you want to stay and find out?" Ben sneered.

"What about Callum?"

"What about Callum?" Ben shot back. "He's gone to deal with his woman." His voice dropped. "I wouldn't want to be that little bitch for any money on earth. It's terrible and wonderful the things a man in love is capable of doing," he finished solemnly. "He'll kill her sure, and if the widow tries to stop him, he'll kill her, too."

Kit's breath caught. Kate had gone to the MacPhersons. He had seen her leaving himself.

"The widow? She was supposed to be with the marquis. You sure she's there?" someone asked.

"Aye. Saw her standing at a window, staring out to sea. "

*Dear God. Watters had already murdered to keep his involvement a secret. If Kate found him with Merry . . .*

"I don't like none of this no more. I say we clear out, back to Clyth," Ben said.

"What aboot him?"

"We kill him. Slit his throat."

He couldn't die. He had to protect Kate, and no act of man or God, no failure of flesh or spirit, was going to keep him from doing just that. Every muscle within him tensed. He waited, his head lolling, until a pair of boots appeared before him.

The man sighed and grabbed a handful of his hair, yanking Kit's head back. Only Kit's head didn't yank. Using every bit of strength he owned, he drove upright, kneeing the man hard in the groin. His knife clattered to the ground as the pain sent the bastard to his knees and Kit leapt atop his back, flicking the rope binding his wrists free of the hook.

Before anyone had moved, he dropped to the floor and scooped up the fallen dagger. Ben reached for his pistol, and Kit threw the dagger, impaling him in the throat. The other two men scrambled for their swords as Kit launched himself toward the great claymore in the croft's corner.

"His sword hand is all smashed!" someone cried. "He's crippled. Kill him!"

But Kit had learned to fight as well with one hand

as the other. With a roar, Kit pivoted on his knees, swinging the blade in a lethal arc. Not high where they expected it, but low, the steel edge slashing through thigh muscles and sinew, biting bone before swinging on. The men screamed and grabbed at their legs, blood pulsing between their fingers as they collapsed.

They weren't a threat any longer. He faced the man he'd kneed and saw that the bastard had recovered sufficiently to begin crawling toward the door. Kit turned the heavy sword in his hand and brought the hilt crashing down on the back of his head, dropping him flat on his face in the dirt.

Staggering, his vision blurred and his limbs shaking, Kit kicked the weapons out of his way and retrieved the claymore's scabbard. He jerked off his ruined shirt and with his teeth tore a strip from it, binding his broken fingers tightly together. His ribs would have to wait. Then, with a growl of pain, he strapped the leather sheath in place and headed outside. Doran stood tied to a post rail. They'd taken off his saddle but not his bridle.

Grinding his teeth, Kit grabbed a handful of mane and dragged himself astride. He looked behind him. One, probably two, dead, two more grievously hurt. Ben had been right. Terrible and wonderful were the things a man in love was capable of.

He dug his heels into Doran's flanks and rode.

He had more "terrible things" yet to do.

※※※

# TWENTY-FIVE

# THE IMPORTANCE OF MAINTAINING HIGH PERSONAL STANDARDS

THE BRIGHT SKIES ENDED with the afternoon. The weather blew in off the sea, bringing with it snow as hard as beads of glass. They pelted the windows and skittered on the roof. The darkening skies and plunging temperature sent the servants hurrying to complete their duties and retreat to belowstairs.

Kate stood by the library window and watched the surf pounding the shore. Inside, a roaring fire crackled in the hearth, warming the entire room as bright candlelight chased the shadows from even the deepest corners. Everything about Castle Parnell encouraged her to accept the staggering good fortune fate had thrown her way and forget Kit MacNeill. That she could not do so troubled her. She considered herself a practical woman.

What was she supposed to have done? She had no

use for the sort of self-romanticization that left families without resources, and it was entirely impractical to pine after a Scottish soldier. Was she to ignore the lessons that in her twenty-four short years had been driven home with such exquisite emphasis? She had already lost a father and her first husband because they were soldiers.

It would be much wiser to marry the marquis and remain safe from grief and shielded from tragedy. Except . . . except . . . what was more tragic than losing someone you loved? And what difference did it make whether that loss was to death or prudence?

She quit the window with a sound of irritation and took a chair near the fire. But the book she sought to divert herself with provided no haven, and within a quarter of an hour, she gave up. All right, if she would have no peace until she had exhausted herself with thinking the unthinkable, so be it: she could not marry the marquis.

It wasn't right, and not because she'd been Kit's lover. Nothing she had done with Kit had been wrong. It *would* be wrong to lie in the arms of another. She frowned, tucking her legs beneath her.

She understood now those soldiers' wives who never remarried after receiving word that their husbands were missing and presumably dead. When Michael had died, she had had a body to bury, and in preparing that body she had understood in a way no simple words could convey that he would never again speak to her and that his eyes would never again light upon seeing her. Not to have had that ineffable knowledge, to be sentenced to a lifetime of hateful hope, impossibly believing that someday, by some chance, some grace, one's beloved would walk through the doors and everything would be right again, would have been unendurable.

That is what she was feeling now. Kit hadn't asked a thing of her, had not made the slightest claim upon her, and yet he owned her very heart. Until one of them died, she did not think she would ever stop hoping that someday he would come back and tell her all the things his hands and eyes had so eloquently said.

She closed her eyes, trying to sort out this knotted skein. She had lived these three and more years wanting only to feel like herself again. How many times had she expressed that desire? And here she was, in a place so like the one she'd been raised in, among people very similar in type to the ones she'd known as a young lady, and still she didn't feel like Katherine Nash, or even Katherine Blackburn, for that matter.

And that bade the question: Who had she become? Only in Kit MacNeill's company and in Kit MacNeill's arms had she felt certain of who she was. Did the person she was trying so desperately to recoup even exist anymore? And, she thought breathlessly, would she want her back?

*No.*

No. She liked the woman she'd become. She wouldn't want back that gay, charming, inconsequential child who'd lived on buttercakes, the promise of fêtes, and others' approval. She approved of herself. She wanted to be no one else.

*Or with anyone else but Kit MacNeill.*

There. So easy. So final. So stupid and so magnificently brilliant.

When the marquis returned, she would tell him that she appreciated his hospitality but she must leave at once, and by the by, could she impose upon him to finance her and her family to the sum of, say two hundred pounds a year? She was amazed she could laugh at herself. Amazed and delighted.

She wrapped her shawl around her shoulders. Her decision made, she could not bring herself to linger. She must pack. She needed to find Kit, to tell him what she felt, what she wanted, no longer content to trust her fate to his overdeveloped sense of honor. And that meant she had a yellow rose to send. She hurried from the library, heading for the back staircase.

Not surprisingly, the halls were deserted, the servants having finished their chores. She shivered, unable to shake the feeling that she was being studied by malevolent eyes, and hurried along the empty corridors, her relief upon hearing a voice almost palpable.

It sounded like Merry. She followed the voice, feeling remiss in not having already offered the girl a shoulder to cry on if that is, indeed, what she wanted. As much as she empathized with the girl's loss, something about the manner in which she had turned Grace's death into a personal affront, as though Grace had died only to hurt her, repelled Kate. She'd just put her hand on the door when she heard a man's voice, hard and angry.

"—thought I was too stupid to figure it out, didn't you? God, how could you? I *loved* you!"

Kate's hand dropped. It was Callum Lamont, the man Meg said had slit open a young revenuer.

"I swear it was Watters, Callum." Merry's voice, wheedling and tiny. "He made me— Ah!"

The sound of flesh hitting flesh cracked through the closed door, and Kate backed away, appalled. "He didn't do nuthin' but get twisted up with you, the poor bugger! You do that to a man, Merry," Callum said hoarsely. "You twist him up until he doesn't know what he's doing. I never kilt a woman afore Grace Murdoch, didn't think I could, but you talked me into it."

"She deserved to die!" Merry's voice was raw and venomous. Kate's knees began to shake. *Merry had orchestrated Grace's death.*

"She lied to me! She said we would always be together and that we would go to London and live like princesses. Only she—" She broke off on a sob.

She'd killed her best friend because she'd been about to abandon her. The realization horrified Kate.

"She's the one that betrayed you, Callum. Betrayed *us*." Merry had regained mastery of her voice. "I told you how I followed her and Charles that night, how I saw Charles shoot your men, Callum. Shoot them like dogs. When they came back, I confronted Grace and forced her to take me into her confidence and tell me all about the rich French yawl they'd wrecked. I told you all of it. I was honest with you."

"I doubt you've ever been honest to a soul in your life, Merry Benny."

"I was to you." A light, nervous laugh. She thought she had won his trust again.

Kate looked around, hoping to see someone.

"If it wasn't for me, you never would have known about the treasure, Callum."

"How stupid do you think I am, Merry?" Callum sounded wretched, but even Kate could hear his desperate desire to believe her. "I don't see any treasure. Do you? Or have you and Watters already got it?"

"No! I swear it. We didn't—"

Too late she realized her mistake.

"We?" Callum's voice was a low hiss. "What 'we' would that be, Merry?"

"Callum, I beg you—" There was the sound of feet running, a roar of rage, a gasp and a choked-off cry. Kate turned, knowing she must run and find someone, knowing she wouldn't be fast enough. She would be sentencing Merry to death if she left.

"Beg all you like. It'll do you no good. You betrayed me as surely as that bitch Grace betrayed you. Grace sent something to her cousin hidden in her trunk that told where they'd hid the treasure, didn't she? And you knew it right from the start, only you never told me.

"No, you set me searching the coast, and if I stumbled on it, good and fine, it was a chance you were willing to take. But all the time you knew the treasure's location was on its way to her cousin. 'Twas *you*, not the marquis, who wrote and asked Mrs. Blackburn to come quick and bring with her everything Grace Murdoch had sent, no matter how small it might seem. And *you* tore up his other letters, the ones that told the widow that Charles and his wife were murdered, because you didn't want her canceling her trip out of fear. Then you waited.

"Well, now you got what you wanted, and I want what I deserve for doing yer dirty work, and if you live through this day, it'll be a rare miracle. So don't try me any more than I been tried."

"I don't *have* the treasure!" Merry cried frantically. There was a crash and a thump and Kate realized Merry had been hurled against the wall. Kate closed her eyes and willed the stupid, wretched girl to tell him what he wanted to know.

"Sure you do. And if you want to live, you'll tell me where it is."

"I don't know! *Grace lied!*" Merry cried out. "She swore she'd sent a map to her cousin because they'd buried it in a place that was so remote they wouldn't be able to find it without a map. Especially after they'd been gone a year or so."

"A year?"

"Yes, because we were all going to go to London until after the smugglers—"

"Until the smugglers had been rounded up and killed?" Callum snarled.

"Yes! *They* were planning on having you killed and

coming back later, after there would be no one left who knew about Charles's involvement with you. But not me!" She hurried on. "Grace laughed about it when she told me and said her cousin wouldn't know what she had when she saw it. But there wasn't a map or anything like it. I ripped apart everything. I searched every seam, *everything*. Both at the inn and here. But Grace lied to me!"

Her voice was raw, nothing left in it but pure outrage because, Kate suddenly realized, if Merry let go of her outrage at the dead woman, she would be forced to confront the horror of having killed her best friend.

"If you haven't found the gold, why are you planning on running off with Watters while me and my men were at the croft? Aye. I know all about it, Merry."

"I didn't want to go with him! He forced me. He said that there's no sense in staying, we should cut our losses and run. He's forced me from the beginning!" Merry's voice was frantically pitched. "He said he'd tell you about us, and you wouldn't have me anymore and no one else would either. I knew nothing about his setting a trap for you—"

"I didn't say anything about a trap," Callum broke in softly. "I just said we were at the croft."

Merry howled then, a howl of impotent rage, and his answering laugh was cruel and wounded, so terribly wounded, that Kate felt a flicker of pity for him.

"There's nothing in you but lies and deceit. I'm well shut of you. The world will be well shut of you."

"I didn't mean to!" Merry wailed like an angry child, and Kate could not say what she was attempting to revoke: lies, deceit, or the death she had begged this man to cause.

"You're breaking my heart, Merry. Like I'll break yours if you don't tell me where that gold is."

Her voice grew muffled, as if she'd buried her head in her arms. "I don't know."

"Then I'll just kill you now, you slut."

*Dear God.*

"Please!"

"Don't waste your final few breaths, Merry. You don't think I'll do it, do you?" He was working himself into a fury. Kate could hear him pacing, faster and faster. "You used me. You betrayed me. Did you go direct from my bed to his? Did you?"

"No," Merry whimpered.

Kate held her breath. In Merry's very core, some moral rot had taken hold that nothing would ever purge. To intervene would be stupid. Reckless. She had two sisters. She owed it to them to take care of herself. To safeguard their futures by safeguarding her life. And . . . and . . . God, she needed to live to see Kit again.

The pacing stopped. "You murderous, black-hearted, conniving whore."

Merry was unsalvageable. She wasn't worth risking her life over— "Callum, no!"

"*Stop!*"

The door swung open on a scene as terrible as the one

in Kate's imagination. Callum stood over Merry who was cowering at his feet. Her arms were raised to shield herself from his blows, and her lips were swollen and bleeding. A trickle of blood flowed down her brow and dribbled on her gown. Her wide eyes swung toward the open door with the avidity of a hare seeing the snare opening. She shot to her feet and would have dashed forward, but Callum caught her, savagely wrenching her back. She cried out, and Kate jerked forward a step. The well-oiled, exquisitely hung door swung shut behind her.

"Well, if it isn't the handsome widow. Come in, Mrs. Blackburn."

"Let her go."

"Her?" Callum looked down at Merry, trembling in his clasp, as if surprised to find her there. "I'm afraid I can't oblige. She has something of mine, you see, and I'll not be leaving here without it." His voice flattened on the threat. "But you pose a most worrisome problem, Mrs. Blackburn."

"Let her go and ride out now, Mr. Lamont, while you still have a chance." Her voice was cool. Composed. Her insides were turning to jelly. "Captain Watters is due back at any time."

"Oh, I have no doubt of that. In truth, I wouldn't mind having a word with him."

Merry began struggling. Casually, Callum backhanded her with enough force to knock her off her feet, leaving her dangling helplessly in his clasp.

"Stop it!" Kate cried. "You'll kill her."

"Probably. Believe me, Mrs. Blackburn, the world

will be a fairer place without this asp slithering through it."

"You can't kill her."

"Oh, but I can."

He grabbed a handful of Merry's thick pale hair and yanked her upright. She cried out, clawing at his hand as she stumbled to her feet. "She killed your cousin, you know. Or as good as done."

"It doesn't matter. Let her go. *Please.*"

He cocked his head. "Why should you care about her?"

"I don't. It doesn't have anything to do with *her*. This is about me."

He studied her, curious in spite of his anger.

"If I let you kill her without trying to stop you, I am not the person I think myself. I cannot let someone die without trying to prevent it." *Like her father.* Her father hadn't chosen to sacrifice himself; he'd simply done what he had to do. "Can you understand that?"

"Not a word."

"I can't let you kill her."

"And how will you stop me?"

"By offering you something you want more."

"And that would be?" His eyes slipped dubiously down her thin figure, and she found herself seized by the bizarre desire to laugh.

"Not me. The treasure."

All his attention snapped to focus upon her. Merry ceased struggling, staring at her in amazement.

"You don't know where it is!" Merry whispered, astounded. "You can't. She wouldn't have told you. She thought you were pathetic."

"She didn't tell me. I discovered it by myself."

"You're lying." This from Callum.

"Do you want to take that chance? *Can* you take that chance?" Kate asked.

"All right. Where is it?"

"Not until Merry leaves the room."

He snorted derisively.

"Listen to me, Mr. Lamont. What do I stand to gain by lying to you? I know you will insist I go with you; you'd be a fool not to take me. I know that if you discover I have lied to you, you will kill me. Would I be willing to trade my life for hers—a murderess and liar—if I wasn't absolutely certain where the treasure was?"

He was silent, studying her intently.

"Maybe she does know," Merry breathed. She started laughing suddenly, a choked sound of hysteria. "You canny little black-haired cat! All the while you knew. Is it not rich, Callum? Is it not grand?"

"Shut up and let me think."

"Let her go, Mr. Lamont. We'll be off a minute later, and I'll show you where the treasure is. I'll even get you the map if you'd like. You can come with me. Only let her go first."

Whether he'd forgotten his broken heart or decided he could address the problem of Merry later, Kate would never know. He released Merry's hair and slammed his palm into the center of her back, sending her careening across the room. "Get out of here, before I change my mind!"

Merry needed no further encouragement. She stumbled past Kate without looking at her, wrenched the door open, and darted out, slamming it behind her.

She will send help, Kate thought. She will find the butler, and aid will be here in a few minutes.

"She won't send help, you know." He must have read her mind, for he was coming toward her, an expression of pity on his dark visage. "She had Grace Murdoch killed, and you know it, and she doesn't want anyone else finding out. So right now she's hiding in her room, hoping against hope that as soon as I have the treasure, I'll kill you, and no one will ever know what she did."

The sick thrill settling in her belly told Kate he spoke the truth. There would be no aid from Merry Benny. "And will you?" she asked.

"Not if I see that gold."

She swallowed. Callum had moved between her and the door. She didn't have a single possible weapon within reach. There was no escape through another door. Even if someone heard her shout, they could not stop Lamont from killing her before they arrived.

The situation was hopeless.

She turned away from him and closed her eyes. How much time did she have left to live? A few minutes? She thought of Kit, of the last sight she'd had of him astride Doran, his long legs in their scarred leather boots, the wind whipping his plaid from his broad shoulders, his hair gleaming red-gold beneath the morning sun. She thought of the last words they'd spoken, of her pride, of asking him to find a reason she shouldn't stay with the marquis.

The door crashed open behind her, and she wheeled around.

He looked terrible, a human sacrifice that had walked off the altar, battered and broken but still somehow alive. Blood drenched the left side of his face and stained the collar of the ragged jacket that was all he wore over his naked chest. A dirty strip of cloth bound the fingers of his right hand together, but in his left he held the heavy claymore.

"I've thought of a reason," Kit MacNeill said.

# TWENTY-SIX

⬔⬔⬔

# SOME SITUATIONS IN WHICH BRUTE FORCE HAS MERIT

RELIEF SWEPT THROUGH KIT like pure, cold water. She wasn't hurt and now she wouldn't be.

"MacNeill." Callum snorted in disbelief. "By God, man, I don't know whether you're more dead or alive."

"Shall we find out?" Kit asked. The damn blade was too heavy; the tip kept dropping on him. His head spun, the floor bucked, and it occurred to him that he might die. Yet even as the thought formed, a smile took it, for he'd thought he'd been dead a hundred times in his short life. Death didn't frighten him. "Go, Kate."

He didn't look at her, just moved past her into the center of the room, eyeing Lamont. He wasn't a man to underestimate his foe, and Lamont had been taught by a master, Ramsey Munro.

Kit didn't have any great arts as a fencer. His

weapon had always been the heavy claymore, his style, to meet resistance with strength, not finesse. The image of Ramsey Munro came alive in his memory, elegant and thin and moving like black silk at midnight. Aye. Ram knew the rapier. But this was no time to indulge in memories. He shook his head, trying to clear his thoughts and focus.

" 'Kate,' is it?" The rapier slid from Callum's belt. "Well, I'm afraid Kate has to stay. She knows where the treasure is, or so she says.

"So you'll stay, *Kate*. Because I might just leave your lover here alive enough so that you might staunch his wounds and save the rest of him. But if you go, I promise I'll have sliced him open in so many places, he'll bleed to death in ten minutes."

Kit saw her hesitation. "He knows that if you stay, my attention will be divided."

"And if you leave, he'll die for certain."

"Kate, he wouldn't let you tend me," he said desperately. "He'd make you watch until you told him where the damned treasure was. I'd die anyway, and afterward he'd kill you, too."

"I don't *know* where it is."

"What?" roared Callum, spinning to face her, and Kit realized in horror and grim admiration that she'd deliberately provoked him in order to give Kit a second's advantage.

He took it.

Gathering the last of his strength, he lunged forward, swinging the heavy claymore like an ax. But blood loss and pain slowed him. The claymore felt like an anvil, unwieldy and thick. Callum ducked, avoiding the blade and lunging forward, the flashing tip of the blade stabbing at Kit's face, going for his eyes.

Reflexively, Kit backed away, and Callum pressed forward. A step, two, a third in quick succession, and they were past Kate. Kit's back hit the damned door, and he held his blade up like a shield, desperately parrying the thin needle that pierced and pricked with so little effort.

Callum was no Ramsey Munro, but he knew the strengths of his weapon and he knew how to use it. Kit prayed he did not know its weaknesses. Callum slashed and dropped back, delighted by the thin red line he left on Kit's belly, his lips curled in an excited smile. Another feint, another slice, and another gash opened on Kit's forearm.

His vision sparkled at the edges and his ribs screamed in agony with each twist that took him just out of the lethal distance of Callum's flickering rapier. His shoulders felt unhinged, acid eating at the joints, his wrists rubbery. The claymore rose, each second heavier, unsteadily meeting the flurry of blows and feints Callum delivered.

He staggered beneath the onslaught, barely cognizant of the bite of steel each time it tasted his flesh, knowing it was only a matter of time. All he wanted now was to win free of the door so that Kate could flee. But he could barely mount a defense, let alone carry the battle to the other side of the room.

How many minutes since he'd entered? Three? Four? So. "Run. For my sake, run now, Kate!"

Suddenly a vase came hurtling from the side of the room, catching Callum between shoulder and neck, staggering him sideways but not felling him. Kit leapt forward, but Callum had already caught Kate's arm as she reached for the vase's twin. He whirled around, viciously jerking her against him, pinning her arms and using her body as a shield. He dragged her forward as he advanced, the rapier's point in front.

There was nothing Kit could do. He could only wait—

*"What the hell are you waiting for, Kit?"* Ramsey *laughed scornfully, his rapier making delicate figure-eights in the air.* The image came from out of nowhere, crystal clear and acid brilliant. Blood loss was making him see things. *Ram's elegant eyebrow rose sardonically as he whispered, "Are you going to just stand there and wait for me to impale you?"*

And suddenly Kit knew what he had to do. Slowly, he let the tip of his blade fall toward the floor, held his other hand open and down at his side in a universal gesture of defeat.

"No!" Kate cried.

Callum put his lips very close to her ear. "All these tears for a filthy Scottish soldier. I doubt he's worth it, m'dear."

"At least there'll be tears for me," Kit said, waiting and watching his words penetrate the haze of victory Callum was tasting. "Which is more than Merry will give you. Was that her and Watters I saw as I—"

With a roar of pain, Callum shoved Kate aside and jumped forward, plunging straight ahead. Kit stepped directly into the rapier's path. The tip sank into his shoulder, and with a savage sound, Kit drove forward.

And now Callum understood. Desperately he clutched the embedded sword's hilt, trying to yank it free of its human sheath. He could not, not before Kit grabbed his neckcloth, jerking his throat down hard against the claymore's sharp edge.

"Wait!" Lamont sputtered, terror filling his face. "I saved your life!"

"And I already spared yours once," Kit answered, his voice cold. "We're even."

"If you kill me, you'll never know who betrayed—"

A pistol report exploded by Kit's ear, and Callum's chest bloomed red around a gaping red hole. He crumpled to the ground, his deadweight pulling the rapier free of Kit's shoulder. In the doorway, Merry Benny dropped the still-smoking pistol and fled, having made certain Callum Lamont wouldn't be seeking revenge.

Kit staggered and fell. Kate dropped to her knees beside him and cupped his face, frantic to read life in his eyes. But he couldn't see; he could barely feel.

"Kit! You stay with me! You promised you would do anything I asked. Anything!" She was sobbing and he could feel her body shaking and he hurt, but dear God, it was glorious to hurt, because pain meant life and life meant Kate.

"Please, Lord . . ." Her voice broke and she dragged in a ragged, angry breath, glaring at him. "You have to stay with me, Christian MacNeill! Do you hear me!? *Promise me!*"

She needed his word and he would give it. "Aye, ma'am. As you will."

She stumbled to her feet and fled for help.

Twenty miles north of Clyth, a few hours later on the same day that Christian MacNeill fought for his life, a capricious wind snickered along a desolate shoreline and swung behind a monolithic boulder that shielded a tiny crest of beach. There it plucked anxiously at the sleeve of a sodden gown. Its owner was beyond caring, her pretty face perpetually arrested in an expression of surprise. A few tresses of pale hair drifted in the swirling water. In only a matter of minutes, she would be submerged.

On a shelf of rock projecting above the beach, Captain Watters quieted his anxious steed as he stared down at the forlorn scene below. With a small, disgruntled sigh he removed the white wig from his head and was Captain Watters no more.

He had failed. MacNeill lived. Kate Blackburn, whose father had saved everyone from that hellish place, was alive, and the scene he had so carefully, so artfully arranged to destroy them both had fallen apart.

It would be so much easier if he could just bring himself to murder them one by one. A chance meeting in an alleyway, a bit of poison in their ale. But the same fissure that split them, saved them. They were scattered like the chaff before the wind. He reached into his pocket and idly withdrew a slender penknife, thumbing the mechanism's trigger until the blade sprang free. He regarded the shiny blade thoughtfully.

If one died, how soon could he locate the next? Before that next victim had heard of his erstwhile companion's death and became suspicious and put himself on guard?

The man astride the horse knew there was yet some connection between them. If one died, the others would hear about it. He couldn't safely reside in England, in London amongst the ton where he belonged, until they were all dead. They were the only ones who could reveal his treachery and ruin the culmination of long years of plotting and planning.

He turned his hand over and looked down at his bare palm, scored over with a thousand little scars. Years ago, he had learned that pain helped a man focus. He set the tip of the penknife against his thumb and pressed, feeling the bright stab of pain as the blade severed delicate nerve endings. At once he felt his anxiety loosen.

There would be other opportunities. Though he would have to be more careful now. Pure hubris had led him into the melodramatic episode with the rat at the old castle ruin. Still, it had been worth it to see the anguish of frustration and rage on MacNeill's face as he forced himself to flee to St. Bride's with the girl.

He should feel no undue alarm. He *felt* no undue

alarm. Why, he doubted whether they would ever realize that he had been the one that had bribed Katherine Blackburn's maid into abandoning her. As for the rose that had found its way to MacNeill's hand and sent him on his precipitous flight to Scotland, when they discovered that neither of Kate Blackburn's sisters had sent it, who would they suspect?

It would be unwise to target MacNeill again so soon. He would be on guard. No. He must turn his attention to the others. One by one, everyone who knew, or suspected, his true identity must be eliminated. He had no doubt he would succeed. The blood dripped from his thumb onto the rock below. With a start he realized that the tip was still implanted in his flesh. Idly, he withdrew it and wiped his thumb on his saddle blanket. Then he returned his attention to the dead girl on the beach.

Already the surf washed over her knees and lifted one limp arm, buoying it gently, so that she seemed to be beckoning playfully to some unseen companion. Waves licked at her ears and bathed her face and finally swept over her chest, picking Merry Benny up in watery arms and carrying her gently out to sea.

High above, the man piously sketched the sign of the cross before turning his horse's head south.

✕✕✕✕

# TWENTY-SEVEN

# SECURING A PLEASANT SITUATION

Kɪᴛ ʟɪᴠᴇᴅ. Aɢᴀɪɴsᴛ ᴛʜᴇ gravest reservations and direst forecasts, he mended. True, for two days and two nights, he soaked in his own sweat, railing against unseen foes and exhorting phantom companions, but on the third day the bandages came away unmarked by blood, and they knew he would survive.

To the Murdochs' great discomfiture, Kate insisted that Kit be brought into the small dressing room attached to her bedchamber so that she could hear him should he call out in the night. She would not leave his side.

The marquis came twice, the first time to see if Kate might require any assistance and the second to see her tending MacNeill and thus force himself to recognize that she was not his nor ever would be. It took but a few minutes. A third visit was never made.

Truth to tell, those at the castle soon forgot their misgivings about the nighttime proximity of the dark widow and the lean, grievously injured Highlander. They were occupied with their own concerns.

As Kit had foreseen, Watters had sent the militia, under the command of the soon-to-be-feted Lieutenant MacPheil, to rout Lamont's gang at the croft and, from there, raid the inn at Clyth. Hidden beneath the bales of hay in the inn's stables, they found crates filled with goods from wrecked ships.

In the days to come, it would be revealed that Captain Greene had been waylaid and killed by Lamont's mysterious partner, the same man who then donned the identity of the fictitious Captain Watters and who, for a short time, had taken command of the militia. Of Captain Watters no more was ever seen. He disappeared, as did his wife, Merry.

The family honor thus impugned, scandal reared its ugly head. But the Murdochs proved a practical people, pointing out that Merry, though the marquis's legal ward, shared no blood with them. They had tried their best to overcome the propensities of what could, in light of the situation, only be regarded as "suspect lineage." It was hardly their fault if they'd failed.


"Blast your pet seamstress!" Kit declared. "These stitches itch like the devil."

Kate looked away as Kit pulled irritably at the neck of his night shirt, exposing the muscular dark chest beneath the tame linen. He scratched at the sutures with which Peggy had sewn up the worst of his wounds.

"I suppose you would find a huge scar preferable?" she asked. It was the afternoon. Kit had just woken from his sleep to find her at his bedside, her embroidery hoop in hand, Grace's open trunk at the foot of the bed.

She had taken up the pastime while he recuperated, telling him it was one of the few skills from a gentrified upbringing that one did not have to eschew in poverty. Indeed—she was thinking of devoting a chapter in her book to it. But now, she found herself studying each tiny stitch, in an attempt to avoid staring at Kit's muscular chest. "You seem lamentably fond of collecting scars."

He tilted his head, regarding her from beneath his lids. "Only if you find them interesting."

The look in his eyes made Kate blush, and as she felt it would not be wise for him to become overly agitated—not to mention herself—she steered the conversation back to safer ground.

"The one I feel most sorry for in this entire affair is Merry Benny," she said, rummaging in Grace's trunk for a silver scissors.

"Why?" he demanded. "Because she will not be able to live as luxuriously as she'd anticipated? She is a murderess who has gotten away with her lover to live on his ill-gotten gains."

"I am sorry for her," Kate said calmly, clipping a silk thread, "because she is responsible for Grace's murder, and she loved Grace. No, don't look like that. She did. You did not see her when she spoke of how much she missed her. Not all love is decent and unselfish. It can torment and damn as well as ennoble and elevate."

"Indeed." His brow furrowed, and Kate knew he was thinking of his companions and the betrayal they had suffered.

The time had come. She could no longer avoid what needed to be said. She set down her embroidery hoop. "I suppose that as soon as you mend you will be leaving."

He frowned more deeply. "Well, I can hardly stay here, can I?"

"That's not what I meant, and you know it."

"What *did* you mean?"

"Where will you go?"

"Back to the army. I have been thinking of late that I have eschewed my responsibility there too long. I am a good soldier, Kate. I am a good leader. I can . . . make a difference." His skin grew dusky and in amazement Kate realized he was blushing. He also hadn't mentioned seeking the man responsible for their betrayal. Kate's gaze sharpened.

"Besides," he went on gruffly, "with a bit of luck, I might make something of myself."

"I see."

"Kate—" He took a deep breath.

"Yes?"

"Nothing." He jaw clenched tightly for a second. "And you?" he bit out. "What about you?"

"I don't know." She tried to sound nonchalant. She

doubted she succeeded. "Back to York, I expect. Or London."

"What? Why?" he asked, sounding taken aback.

"Well, I haven't much money—though I do hold out great hopes for the publication of my instructional book on how to live respectably while one's fortunes plummet. I believe there is a ready readership—"

"Yes, yes," Kit interrupted. "But what were you saying about going back to York?"

"As I was *saying*—" She eyed him sternly, daring him to interrupt. "I have little money, and while I suppose I could impose upon the marquis, I should hate to do so, as I"—she hesitated, trying to find some way to say this delicately—"as I believe he had certain hopes regarding our relationship that I find myself unable to encourage him in and told him as much."

"You turned him down!?" Kit exploded, surging up against the pillows and wincing. She half rose from where she was seated, hating to see him in pain but he waved her back angrily.

"My God, woman," he said, "you have spent days reciting to me the criteria that forms your idea of the perfect future, and as far as I can tell, the marquis could ensure you of each and every one: Safety. Security. A home. Peace of mind. Wealth. *Are you daft?*"

"I hardly had a choice," she retorted defensively. "I can't marry a man and spend the rest of my life closing my eyes every time he come near me, pretending—" No. She could not be that bold. Even under the most extenuating circumstance.

"Pretending what?" the blackguard asked. It wasn't gentlemanly.

"Nothing."

"No, please. I'm interested." He regarded her like a great tawny lion. "Pretending what?"

She raised her brows, as if amazed she needed to finish the sentence. "Pretending that I . . . wasn't there. What else would I be pretending?"

He didn't hesitate for an instant. "That the marquis was me."

Her mouth fell open and clicked shut. "You certainly give yourself credit."

Kit pushed himself more upright. "I have to. I have to believe that you see something more in me than a man willing to forfeit everything in his quest for vengeance. For three years I've thought that all I wanted was to find out who gave our name to the French—but you have taught me to want something different."

She held her breath, anticipation rising and beating like the wings of a trapped bird in her chest. "What is that?"

"A future," he said, his gaze holding hers. "I always thought there must have been something fundamentally wrong within me that had made me blind to the character of the person who betrayed us. That by refusing to see this bastard for what he was, I had been complicit in our capture and imprisonment.

"But I have come to realize that whatever seeds of betrayal were sown in the past, were not sown by me.

I did not fail. Whether the person I loved was real or not, worthy or not, doesn't seem to be the question. A heart loves where it will. It does not ask permission." He studied her with such an expression in his eyes that made her breath catch.

"You will not seek him anymore?"

His expression turned cold and implacable. "I cannot promise that. He threatened you. Someday he will pay for that, but not now. There is a war on and I am needed. I don't have the time for revenge. I have come to believe there are more important things to fight for." He gazed at her, his heart in his eyes. "Do you see? Do you agree?"

"Yes." She could barely breathe. "Yes, I do."

"Do you?" He looked dissatisfied lying so big and dark against the white linen sheets. So many scars. So many wounds.

"Before you fought Callum," she said, "when you came into that room, you said you'd come because you remembered a reason why I shouldn't marry the marquis. I have wondered what you meant by that."

He looked embarrassed. " 'Twas nothing. Stupid nonsense. I was being heroic."

"I noticed."

He stilled, his mouth curving in a self-deprecating grin that she found well-nigh irresistible.

"The reason I ask," she continued, rising and moving slowly to his bedside, "is because an instant before you crashed through the door, I was thinking of you, recalling your face and trying to remember the last words you'd said to me."

At that his gaze shot up to hers. "Why would you be thinking of me at a time like that?"

"Because I love you."

In answer, he reached out and secured her hand, pulling her down into a crushing embrace against his bandaged chest. "Marry me," he demanded hoarsely, pressing kisses on her eyelids and the corner of her mouth.

"I will be someone someday, Kate. With you by my side, there is nothing I cannot accomplish. *We* cannot accomplish. I know the life I am asking you to lead will not be easy, but I swear I will devote myself to making certain you do not regret marrying me."

He smoothed the hair back from her face, his look intent, his voice passionate. "Besides, if you say no, I'll have to steal you away. You love me, Kate. You said it yourself."

She realized with a little thrill that he meant it. But . . . he wouldn't have to. "Yes," she said. "Yes."

"When?"

"Today. Tomorrow. But where? I can't ask—"

"Nor would I let you. We're two days from St. Bride's. There's a group of monks there that'll find great consolation in thinking you are making an honest man of me."

She laughed and he smiled, his arms tightening around her, and it was then that she noted the small, new stain of blood on his bandage. He was so vital, so stalwart, one forget he was mortal. She pushed away

from him, scrambling back and regarding him in consternation. "I've hurt you."

He looked down, saw the stained linen and
laughed. "This? Don't be ridiculous. Come back." He
held out his hand.

"No. It has only been three days. I will not have
you hurt."

"I love you," he suddenly whispered in such a
bemused voice she smiled but then, abruptly shook
her head.

"No," she said sternly. "No. Lie back. Rest. Be well."

She reached down for the embroidery hoop she'd
dropped into the trunk and her hand caught in the
hastily repaired lining of the lid, pulling the corner
down. She bent to fix it, and as she did she noticed
that the gold embroidered stars were all of a different
size, slight but unmistakable, and that if the material
were folded, as it was now, they aligned . . .

She straightened. Grace had embroidered this lining. Grace who, along with Kate, had shared those long
summer nights with Kate's father before the telescope
and there developed a life long interest in astronomy.
Grace whose belongings had included a telescope.
Grace, who had sworn to Merry that she had sent a map
of the treasure location. And so she had: a star map.

Kate straightened slowly, a smile dawning on her
face. Kit would have his commission. He could have
ten commissions if that is what he wanted and
Charlotte could have her London season and Helena
could leave the employ of that harridan.

There was still a war to fight. Still men who needed her husband's leadership. They would still follow the drum to whatever place His Majesty sent them, because Kit MacNeill was a soldier. And she, the daughter of a solider, the widow of another, who a year ago would never have believed herself capable of committing herself heart and soul to such a man, had already done so and would have him no other way.

"Kate, what is it?" Kit asked. "You look right pleased with yourself. Come here to me, now."

Whatever loot was heaped in whatever cavern or chamber, paled beside this treasure.

She went.

⋈⋈⋈

# TWENTY-EIGHT

# MARRIAGE IN THE
# BEST INTERESTS

*St. Bride's Abbey, January 1802*

THE BRIDE WAS BEAUTIFUL and the groom stern and watchful, his warrior mien only relaxing when his gaze fell unguarded upon his wife. They left St. Bride's small chapel to find their footsteps cushioned on a carpet of dried rose petals, and Brother Fidelis beaming with pleasure. Kate was so touched by this demonstration of affection that she left her husband's side and rose on her tiptoes to kiss the huge monk on his round, smooth cheek.

"The roses are beautiful!" she said.

"There's lavender and mint, too," Brother Martin said, elbowing his way through the little crush of monks congratulating the celebrants.

"Ah! I thought I detected some other wonderful fragrance," Kate said

"I don't suppose you'll be happy until you've kissed me, too!" he said in gruff, disgusted tones.

"No." Kate's eyes sparkled. "I won't."

He resisted, but not much. "Silly, over-affectionate goose eggs, is all young women are today," he blustered but scuttled forward quickly.

"There," she said, bussing him soundly on the cheek.

"Ach," Brother Martin blushed deeply and retreated quickly, his expression an odd mixture of amazement, disapproval, and pleasure. He turned to his fellow monks. "Now there's no need for all of you to indulge this young lady's secular whims. And when Father Abbot is done in the vestiary—"

"Father Abbot is done." The straight-backed abbot of St. Bride's descended the short flight of stairs. His brows rose at the sight of the floral carpet. "How . . . festive. Brother Fidelis, I presume."

"Aye, Father Abbot."

"And me, too, Father Abbot," Brother Martin said.

"Thought it cause to put on a bit of pomp, the young wolf being tamed by the pretty widow," Brother Fidelis explained. All around them the other monks nodded vigorously.

"Young wolf?" Kate whispered in an aside to Kit.

"Tamed?" Kit whispered back and both smiled.

"You were going to say something, Brother Martin?" the abbot said smoothly.

"Only that there wouldn't be any need for any of us to be creeling the groom," Brother Fidelis said piously, referring to the Scottish custom of lading the groom with a sack of rocks, and sending him forth in the village where his friends would add to the sack until the bride cut him free of his burden. Likewise there would be no beddin' the bride as the traditional role called for women to prepare the bride in her chambers.

Kate could not say she was disappointed. She was only happy the banns had finally been read three times and they'd finally been married—though who in this place was likely to object to their marriage, she had indignantly asked the father abbot. He had replied with a stern, implacable silence. These past three weeks had seemed endless. But tomorrow they would be leaving St Bride's as man and wife and tonight . . . She looked shyly up at Kit and the blackguard, as if reading her thoughts, smiled—and yes, it was a wolfish smile and no, it did not look tame. A wash of warmth swept through her upon seeing and interpreting that smile.

"Kate! Kate!" Kate turned around as a pair of horses pulling a closed carriage entered the churchyard. A young woman with gingery hair half protruded from the window, wildly waving a lace kerchief.

"Charlotte!" Kate cried, breaking from her husband's side and running toward the coach.

"For the sake of decorum, come back inside!" she heard Helena say and then the door was opening and Helena was emerging, all calm and grace, her lovely face alight with a warm smile, and from behind her shoved a small dynamo in layers of mink-trimmed gray velvet, her arms already out-stretched to embrace Kate.

Charlotte flung her arms around Kate's neck and

squealed. Helena, ever circumspect, stopped and awaited her turn, looking about at the multitude of brown-robed men, trying to hide her curiosity.

"We've only just arrived!" Charlotte said. "We came all the way from London! The marquis sent his barouche to Helena and a letter relating the most extraordinary tale and bidding us come to Castle Parnell at once.

"So Helena fetched me from the Weltons—we were halfway to Brighton, don't you know, and so put poor Helena out terribly—and to Castle Parnell we came, only once we arrived, we found out you'd come here, to this *abbey*, and were being *wed!*" Charlotte babbled, her eyes wide. "To that *Scotsman!* And not the handsome one either, but to that frightening-looking fellow you—"

"Ahem."

Charlotte whirled around, only to find the "frightening-looking fellow" looking down at her, one brow cocked inquiringly. She gasped. He smiled—charmingly, Kate thought.

"My new little sister," Kit purred. "I am delighted to make your acquaintance again." He sketched a bow, and then his gaze moved beyond the wide-eyed Charlotte to Helena, her composure in no manner disturbed by the odd circumstances in which she found herself.

"Miss Helena, I am delighted."

"Thank you, sir."

"As you can see, regardless of the marquis's 'tale,' whatever that might be, your sister is in perfect health. As you can also see, it is now my honor and privilege to see she remains that way." His gaze held Helena's questioning one for a long instance. "And I shall. Or die doing so."

"Oh, my!" Charlotte breathed waving her hand at her flushed cheeks. "I begin to see why you married him."

"Charlotte!" Helena chided her baby sister. "Some decorum!"

"Why?" she glanced around at the monks, and then whispered, "Would they even know decorous behavior?"

"To some small degree," a smooth voice answered.

They turned as Abbot Tarkin came toward them. "Ah! I see your family has arrived."

How had he known? Kate wondered but then her curiosity was replaced with happiness.

"We have prepared a little celebratory feast for our newlyweds. Perhaps you would like to adjourn to the dining hall?"

"You are too kind!" Kate exclaimed.

"Oh, do let's!" Charlotte enthused. "I am famished." She linked her arm through Kate's, and then Helena's, and they fell into step behind Brother Fidelis, who, still beaming and chattering happily, led them toward the dining hall.

"More women. Why don't we just reassign our charter as a nunnery?" Brother Martin muttered from behind them.

Kate looked around for Kit. He was standing beside the abbot, his head bent near the older man's, his expression concentrated. But upon seeing Kate look back, he smiled and called out, "Entertain your sisters, my love. I will join you shortly."

Kit turned back to the abbot, his genial expression fading. "Where is he?"

"In the chapel," the abbot said quietly. "He saw you wed."

"The hell you say. How did he know?"

"I sent word. A rose. He is the only one to answer. At least as far as I know."

"But why send a rose?" Kit asked, his gaze flickering toward the dark entry to the chapel.

"You said you needed to know who betrayed you. I thought this might provide you with an answer."

"Aye. I thought I did, but past sins don't seem so important anymore. Especially as they're not mine."

"Then perhaps I have made a mistake. By all means, move on. As you pointed out, if he was the one at the ruined castle, and he wanted to kill you, you would be dead. He didn't. *If* he is the one who betrayed you."

"There's only one way to find out."

"Kit."

"Don't worry, Father Abbot. I'd as soon not incur my bride's wrath by spilling another's blood today," Kit said with a grim smile and left, heading into the chapel.

Inside it was cool and dark, the smell of incense still hanging subtle and smoky in the air. It took a second for his eyes to adjust and—

—the point of the épée pressed lightly against the side of his throat.

"And here they'd told me you'd become a soldier," a once familiar voice drawled. "God help the country if this is the best—"

Kit sidestepped, ducking his head and lifting his elbow at the same time, knocking the small sword away as he moved in closer. Within a split second the small sword was back at his throat, but this time his own dagger's point was pressed hard against his antagonist's belly.

"Touché," Ramsey Munro said softly, his brilliant blue eyes glittering.

"You look bad, Ram," Kit said conversationally. "Worn out."

Ramsey shrugged apologetically. "I fear you are right, Kit me lad. But you look blooming with health. Must be the bride's influence. Bonny girl there. My blessings on the union."

"Does that mean you don't intend to try to kill me?"

One of Ram's black wing-shaped brows rose. "Well, now, that would depend on whether you were trying to kill me. It's a miserable life, I confess, but mine own." He smiled with the same urbane suavity he'd possessed even as a lad.

Slowly, Kit withdrew the tip of his dagger from pricking Ram's stomach. Just as slowly, Ram dropped the tip of his épée.

"Tell me, Ram. I won't kill you if you did, for the love I bore you as a lad and for the love I know you once bore me. But I need to know, did you betray us to the French?"

Ram cocked his head. In the shadowed confines of

the chapel his face looked unworldly beautiful, like a weary warrior saint. "No."

"Good." Kit tucked his dagger away.

"I suppose this means that you too are blameless."

Kit snorted. "Hardly, but of that particular sin I am innocent."

"Then that means—"

"Dand."

"Or Toussaint."

Ram nodded thoughtfully.

"Kate and I board a packet out of Portsmouth next week. By month's end I will be on the continent with my new command. I don't have time to go looking further for answers."

"I have the time." Ram smiled. For a long minute the two men met each other's gaze. Whatever they saw there pleased them both.

"If you should ever need me . . ." Kit said gruffly. "You know how to contact me?"

"Aye." Ram smiled suddenly, and his face softened, and he was once more recognizable as the brother of Kit's youth. "I missed you, Kit."

"And I you."

"So much for sentiment. Now, you'd best get back to your bonny bride, Kit MacNeill," Ram said, "before she finds a better man."

Kit grinned. "Luckily all the men at St. Bride's are sworn to a life of celibacy."

"Not *all* the men," Ram said. "Luckily for you I have a penchant for the fair maidens."

"Luckily for *you*," Kit corrected him smoothly.

With a laugh, Ramsey Munro disappeared back into the shadows.

The monks had turned the small shed at the back of the rose garden into a bridal bower. Thin, gauzy curtains of linen hung across the front opening, wafting in the gentle drafts. The interior had been cleared of everything but a soft, down mattress set upon the tiled floor, piled high with plump pillows and fitted with sheets of brilliant sun-bleached linens. A single table stood beside this, set with a pitcher, two goblets, and a platter heaped with wrinkled brown pears brought up from the cellar.

The last rays of the late afternoon sun turned the glass roof overhead into a prism, spangling the greenery around them with myriad colored lights. The scent of living things, green and rich and loamy, mingled with the fragrance of clove, cinnamon, and other exotic spices mulling the warm wine in the silver pitcher.

"No bride has ever been so well fêted," Kate murmured happily. Her sisters had been led to the guests' apartments on the other side of the abbey and she was alone with her husband. Finally alone. After nearly a month. She felt a little thrill of apprehension—but it was not unpleasant.

"I could fete you in more elaborate surroundings," Kit said. "We could afford a castle if you wanted."

The star map had proved authentic. As soon as Kit had mended well enough to ride, they had followed the map miles up the coast to a place where a monolithic rock stood sentry some distance out in the churning surf. There, in a hollowed out watery grotto, they had found the French treasure. Even after turning it over to the marquis—who acted as magistrate for the area—the finder's portion had been a fortune. They were rich.

But then, Kate thought, she had been rich before they'd found the treasure. Behind her, she felt Kit move closer. His hand looped around her waist, and he drew her back against his muscular chest. Aye, she was a veritable queen if riches were counted by the fortunes of the heart.

"I thought this last week would kill me for want of being with you," Kit whispered in her ear. His breath was warm, his voice like honey. "Of wanting you."

Her heart tripped into a faster beat as he nibbled her earlobe. "Not for want of loving me?" she asked, knowing the answer full-well but wanting to hear the words.

With exquisite care he curled his broad hand around her neck, and tipped her chin up with his thumb, tilting her head back against his shoulder. He looking deeply down into her eyes. The look in his own silvery green eyes took her breath away. She could hardly concentrate; his gaze was so avid, his feelings for her so naked.

"Do you want words? Or will you let me show you?" he whispered urgently, pulling her slowly around, his lips seeking hers.

"Both," she answered breathlessly.

"As you wish, ma'am." And he obliged.

And obliged.